Sunkissed

COLORADO

SUNKISSED COLORADO (Hart County Series Book 4)

Ebook Cover Photography: Jane Ashley Converse Photography

Cover Design (Ebook and Print): Angela Haddon

Produced by Diana Road Books

HART COUNTY BOOK 4

HANNAH SHIELD

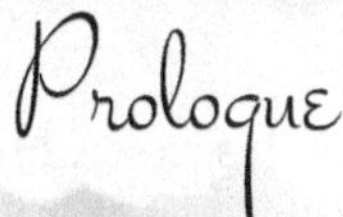

Prologue

Zandra
Sixteen Years Ago

Music blared in my headphones as I walked down the hall, dodging couples making out against lockers, cheerleaders hanging all over football players, stoners casting paranoid glances.

I hate high school.

Only about eight months left of this. Graduation couldn't possibly come fast enough.

I steered into the classroom for Ms. Washington's third period English, taking off my headphones. My grin appeared as I slid into the seat beside my best friend, Jessa Mackenzie.

Jessa leaned in. "So. I may have secured us an invite to the bonfire tonight."

I sighed. There went my smile. "Jessa..."

"*Please.*" She clasped her hands under her chin. "You have to go with me. I need you."

"Are you finally going to share the identity of this guy you're into? Who is supposedly on the football team and *not* a douche?"

"He's not—"

"Not like Callum and the rest of them," I finished, because she'd said it so many times. "I find that hard to believe."

Right on cue, my least favorite person strutted into the classroom. Mr. Football Captain and Homecoming King. Ruler of Silver Ridge High, or so the conformist sheep in our class would have us believe.

Callum O'Neal.

It was Friday, so he wore his jersey. He'd paired his red and black school colors with ripped jeans and a backward ball cap, though both were expressly forbidden by the dress code. If someone called him on it, he'd probably flash an innocent expression. *Who, me?*

Look, I thought the dress code was stupid too. I doubted short-shorts on girls were going to cause a riot. So sexist.

What irked me was the way Callum could simply get away with it. He was the type of golden boy who got away with *everything*.

Even worse, he sat down at my and Jessa's table beside his friend, fellow footballer Tommy Pickering. Ms. Washington had assigned us all to the same table group.

"Bro!" The two boys slapped palms and did a stupid dancing shimmy like they were going clubbing, instead of settling in for a boring lecture on unreliable narrators.

Callum winked as a cheerleader sauntered by. She trailed her red nails over his shoulder, biting her lip. Not his girlfriend, because Callum O'Neal never had girlfriends. But they were still lining up in the hopes of being the first to tie him down.

"Vomit," I muttered.

His gaze shot to me. "Hey, Z."

"Don't call me Z. We've been over this."

"*I* call you Z," Jessa whispered.

I flipped my long braid over my shoulder. "Because you're my friend. He's not."

Callum stuck his lower lip out. "Z, you wound me. Why are you so mean?"

"Because you and Tommy slack off and make Jessa and me do all the work."

"That was *one time*."

"Here's how much I care." When I brandished both my middle fingers, making sure our teacher wasn't looking, Callum laughed. But there was a glint of *something* in his eyes.

Callum was hot, and he knew it. He looked more like twenty-five than eighteen. Tall, leanly muscled, wavy brown hair. A big dumb grin that drew teen girls like purple coneflowers attract honey bees. *He's, like, the sweetest*, they cooed.

Blegh. Good thing I was immune to him.

The bell rang, and Ms. Washington started class. I focused on her lecture for a while. Until inevitably it was time for group work. Tommy and Callum started talking about the party tonight and who would be there, while Jessa kicked my foot under the table.

Please come tonight, she mouthed at me.

Tommy's shrewd eyes glanced over. "You coming to the party, Zandra?" he asked. "You should. First one of the year. Don't you think she should *come*, Cal?"

Like I didn't catch that unsubtle innuendo. Callum crossed his arms over his meaty chest with a frown, tilting his head to study his friend, then me.

The bonfire party after every football game was a Silver Ridge High tradition. The football players held it on private land, somebody's daddy's ranch, and it was technically invite-only. Those invites were coveted. Most of the time, you wouldn't catch me dead at their dumbass wannabe-frat party.

I didn't mix with football players like Callum and Tommy. This was no surprise to anyone. I was more of an outsider with big ambitions for my future. Picked my friends carefully, biding my time until Jessa and I could finally get our asses out of this small mountain town.

But Jessa was dying to go tonight because of this secret boy she liked. Didn't she deserve that rite of passage, no matter how ridiculous?

I loved her like a sister. I'd already been rude to Callum today, so it was time to lay off. I couldn't mess this up for her. Otherwise, what kind of best friend would I be?

My shoulder shrugged up and down. "Jessa got an invite for us. So I guess I'll be there."

Jessa's face lit up.

Only to free-fall when Callum opened his big mouth. "I don't think so." He looked at Tommy. "Z doesn't want to go to the party."

"I just said I do."

"You hate being around guys like me so much. Wouldn't want to make you uncomfortable."

Jessa laughed nervously. "Callum, Z was just kidding around earlier."

Smirking, Tommy punched Callum's upper arm. "Relax, man. Don't take it personal."

"I'm not," Callum said matter-of-factly. Not a trace of animosity. "But Zandra's not invited." He shrugged and smiled.

One point to O'Neal. For being so much more devious and petty than anyone had expected, including me.

The rest of the class had suddenly gone quiet, because of course they'd all been eavesdropping. "*Damn*," someone whispered. It was the sound of my senior social status crashing and burning. Like I cared.

Until I saw the look of devastation on my best friend's face.

"I'm sorry," I said again. "You could've gone without me. He didn't disinvite you, just me."

"Whatever. It's fine." Jessa skipped a rock into the creek. "I didn't want to go that much anyway."

Geez, I really was the worst.

I still thought Callum was obnoxious, but I'd probably gone too far. *Why are you so mean?* he'd whined. I didn't know. I would never win the title of Miss Social Butterfly. But Callum O'Neal did not bring out the best in me.

People just *loved* him, no matter what he did, and it wasn't fair.

"I'm a terrible best friend. Epically bad. Please accept this offering?" Unzipping my backpack, I pulled out the Hearthstone tall-boy cans I'd brought from my parents' fridge. "Trust me, it's only the start of my groveling."

Jessa snickered, accepting a can and popping the tab. "You're lucky your grandpa runs a brewery and your house is always overflowing with so much beer they don't keep track of it."

"Seriously. Callum is so short-sighted. I could've hooked up his *bros* for their parties all semester."

She arched a brow. "Would you?"

"Hell, no."

Her mouth opened on a belly-laugh. "That's what I thought. It's really okay. I promise. I don't wanna hang out with people who don't like my best friend." Jessa slurped foam from her can.

I dug the toe of my Chuck Taylor into the soft dirt. "That's sweet of you."

"Plus Leo's going to the bonfire, and he's mad at me."

"Why?"

"Just...stupid sibling stuff. Trust me, you don't want to know the gory details."

Leo was a year younger than us and far more popular. I knew that bothered Jessa. How her brother was having the wild and crazy high school experiences she didn't. He wasn't a football player, but he had the cheerleader girlfriend and that cocky swagger. She loved him, though. Jessa and Leo had always been close. I was surprised they'd fought at all, but they'd probably make up in no time.

"What about your super-secret guy?" I prompted. "Didn't you want to meet up with him?"

Her smile turned smug. "We still might."

"Wait, what?"

She chewed her lip. "He said he'd text me later. He's at the bonfire right now because his friends expect it. But he knows we're at the creek, and he said he'd come hang out. He really wants to see me."

"Won't you just tell me who your crush is? He's not Tommy Pickering, right? Because ew. We shouldn't have secrets from each other."

Jessa's expression did something complicated. "I don't want to keep secrets from you, Z, but some secrets aren't mine to tell."

Wait, were we still talking about her crush?

I laid my head on her shoulder. "Pleeeease tell me his name? This mystery is killing me. I'll be your best friend," I sing-songed.

Jessa laughed, seeming to shake off whatever had been bothering her. "You're already my BFF. But I just don't want to jinx this yet. I don't want you to tell me you hate him."

"*Me* hate someone?" I asked innocently.

She elbowed me. "He's not the love of my life or anything. I just don't want to go to college a virgin next year."

"So what? I'm a virgin."

"By choice. You're so gorgeous, Z. Your long, straight hair and your eyes. Guys are always into you, but they're just too intimidated to do anything about it."

"Shut up. You're way prettier than me. I want blond curls and an angel face like you."

"*You* shut up."

We cackled. "Fine, we're both gorgeous supermodels," I said, "and we'll be breaking hearts left and right in Denver next year." Because we'd be heading off to college in the city. We didn't know yet where we'd get accepted, but we'd applied only to Denver schools so we'd be together. Jessa would become a kindergarten teacher, while I was going for a business major.

That was all that mattered to me. Jessa and I would escape this small-town prison. She was the only thing about Silver Ridge that I truly cared about, aside from my family and all.

Jessa made a worried face. "It's going to be so different in college."

I held up my beer like I was making a toast. "Let's promise to always be friends. We'll always find a way to be in each other's lives, no matter what."

Jessa tapped her beer against mine. "Friends forever."

"Friends forever."

We sipped and relaxed for a while. Talked more about next year. The beer went straight through me, creating a pleasant buzz in my head. Even though my stomach was less happy about it. I'd been having a lot of stomach aches lately.

"I'll be right back, okay?" I said. "Need to pee."

"Fine." Jessa wandered over to the bank of the creek. She'd already finished her beer and taken off her shoes. Moonlight sparkled on the rushing water. She dipped her toes in as she checked her phone yet again, wobbling like she might lose her balance.

"Hey, don't get too close to the water. Especially while I'm gone."

"Go on and empty your bladder, worrywart. I'll be right here."

"And stop checking your phone. Surprised you can even get reception."

"I've got one bar."

I shook my head. "If he's smart, he'll text. Mystery man would be lucky to get a girl like you."

"Thanks, Z." It was hard to see Jessa's expression, but from the tilt of her head, it seemed like she was pleased.

I wandered off into the trees, zipping up my jacket to my throat. The night was dark and cold, especially in the woods, but at least the moon was half full.

Too bad I didn't have a phone with a fancy flashlight. Didn't have a phone at all. My parents never inventoried their beer, but they were super strict about devices and social media and stuff.

Freedom was going to look so good on me next year.

Finding a clear spot, I crouched down. "Come on," I muttered to myself. "Hurry up and go. It's creepy out here."

After doing my business, I pulled up my jeans and headed back, following the rushing sound of the creek. But I must've gotten turned around because I came out in the wrong spot. Jessa wasn't here, and this clearly wasn't where we'd been standing earlier.

Thick bushes blocked me from just following the bank, so I retreated and tried to retrace my steps in the darkness.

A voice came from up ahead, talking loudly. Thank goodness. That was Jessa. Maybe she was on her phone.

But she sounded upset.

Then I heard a second voice, which made me pause in surprise. It wasn't coming from a speaker. This voice was low, distorted by the rushing of the creek as the sound reached my ears.

Jessa wasn't alone. Had her guy shown up? Was something wrong?

There was a scream and a splash.

"Jessa?" I started running. At first, I didn't see her. Or anyone else.

Something in the creek caught my eye.

Jessa was lying facedown in the water, the shape of her body curved against a rock. My heart lurched. "No!" Splashing into the water, my hand reached out to grab her as the current tried to pull me down. "No, no, no. Jessa, I'm here, okay? Can you hear me?"

Somehow, I managed to get her onto the bank. Turned her onto her back.

Dark red poured from a gash on her forehead.

"Jessa?" She wasn't responding. My shaking hands felt around for her phone in her pockets, but it wasn't there. And I didn't have a damn phone of my own to call 9-1-1.

"Help!" I screamed. "Anybody, please!"

But we were out in the woods. If anybody was nearby, they didn't answer.

Jessa wasn't breathing. CPR. My brain searched for what I'd learned in that first-aid class. *One, two, three, four...*

It wasn't working. I struggled to lift my best friend into my arms. My knees banged the ground as I slipped. Could I get her to the car? That was what I had to do. Had to get her to the hospital. Her skin was so pale.

But deep down, I knew there was no way I'd make it in time.

Tears streamed down my cheeks, hot in the chilly night air. "Please don't leave me, Jessa. *Please.*"

Don't go.

ONE
Zandra

Present Day

The moment I crossed over into Hart County, I felt it in my gut. It wasn't just the sign proclaiming "Welcome to the Hart of Colorado," though that was certainly a major clue.

With every mile that took me closer to my hometown, it felt like layers of skin were peeling away. Years from my past stripped bare.

Sixteen. It had been sixteen years since the last time I'd called Silver Ridge, Colorado, home.

Of course, I'd visited here and there over the years for holidays, but never more than two or three nights at a time. I hadn't brought Ian here much, though we were together for six years. That probably said more about our relationship than anything else.

The last time I had called Silver Ridge home, my best friend had still been alive.

A disgruntled meow came from the backseat, as if Chloe had sensed the morbid turn of my thoughts. Or maybe she just wanted to get free of her cat carrier. I couldn't blame her.

"We're almost there, Coco. I promise. Just a little further."

We were both grumpy after an endless day of driving. At least mid-July in Hart County was just as beautiful as I'd remembered. The meadows and hillsides were vibrant green, dotted with colorful grasses and wildflowers. Fireweed, columbines, yarrow. I smiled, surprised I still recalled those names from my childhood.

A slow drive down Main Street brought more familiar sights. The coffee shop, which was now called Silver Linings and owned by Piper Landry, or so I'd heard. Except her last name was different now, wasn't it? Auntie Rosie had mentioned Piper getting married and then divorced. I was really behind the times.

I'd heard about Piper's older brother Teller dating a pop star, too. Silver Ridge had been in the media a lot lately, which had been surreal. Ian had joked about it. *Hey, isn't that your town they're talking about?*

But Silver Ridge hadn't been my town for a long, long time.

There was Main Street Market, where I'd run through the aisles as a kid after school, getting into mischief because Auntie Rosie let me get away with it.

And of course, Hearthstone Brewing, the origin of the Alvarez family business empire. My heart twisted as I thought of Grandpa Manny's booming laugh as he welcomed customers. Nana Julia's warm smile and open arms.

Memories of my past running headlong into my present.

And then I caught sight of the creek, sunlight glinting on the water down below the bridge as I drove across. My stomach roiled.

Nope. I couldn't let my mind go there. My memories of that night were strictly off-limits.

My phone rang, and the caller ID displayed Ian's name. For safety's sake, I pulled off to the shoulder, letting the engine idle. "Hello?"

"Zan," he said in a syrupy tone. "How are you?"

At the start of our relationship, I would've fallen for that tone instantly. But I was smarter now. The fact I'd answered him at all just showed how much I wanted to get my mind on something else. Even my obnoxious ex.

"What do you want, Ian?"

A beleaguered sigh came through the phone speaker. "Business-like, as usual. Not even going to pretend we can be friends?"

"No, because we can't. We were nothing but roommates for the last few months, and now we're not even that."

I'd been fooled by his shiny shoes, impeccable haircut, and old-money pedigree. Such a contrast to my background in small-town Colorado. I'd made the mistake of believing in Ian's aura of success. When really, it was just his trust fund.

He dropped the act.

"I'm looking for my tie with the houndstooth pattern," Ian said. "Have you seen it? You didn't accidentally take it with you, did you?"

Un-fucking-believable.

"No, I didn't take anything of yours with me. You were standing over my shoulder while I packed, remember? I don't know where you put your shit. I'm not your secretary."

He scoffed. "Believe me, I know. My secretary would never have stocked my pantry and freezer with this gluten-free, vegan crap."

"Then throw it away! Buy your own groceries!"

"I really wish you would do something about your anger issues, Zandra. More than anything, that's what came between us."

"*Really*?"

I'd put years of my life into launching a startup with him. I'd been all-in. Then I found out Ian had been lying to me *and* to our investors. Because of Ian, my credibility had been destroyed when the startup went south.

But *I* was the bad guy. *I* was the bitch with anger issues.

"Ian, don't call me ever again." I hit End, tossing my phone onto the passenger seat. Chloe meowed.

"I agree. What a dipshit. What did I ever see in him?"

My eyes closed as I rested my forehead against the top of the steering wheel, trying not to cry. Chloe meowed sympathetically.

I'd known for months that I had to start over. I'd been stuck living in Ian's guestroom in Chicago because I couldn't afford to move out. No job despite searching, and no prospects. My former friends had lost interest in me once I didn't have money to go out anymore. Ian was in debt too. But unlike him, I didn't have a trust-fund cushion.

I'd been a good roommate, though. I'd cleaned and paid for groceries, not that Ian seemed to appreciate it.

Then I'd gotten word. My grandpa Manny had fallen in the storage room at Hearthstone, shattering his hip and fracturing his femur. A week later, he was still at Hart County General, and I was home to offer my help.

But I was also here to make a fresh start.

Unfortunately, that meant facing my parents. The very reason I hadn't run home to Silver Ridge before now.

"Give me strength, Coco," I said. "We're gonna need it."

I pulled back onto the road and steered toward my parents' house. I hadn't told them I was coming. Between Ian and packing up my life in Chicago, I just hadn't been able to deal with Mom and Dad too.

Now, there was no more delaying. Time to rip off this bandage, possibly reopening the old wounds hidden beneath.

Or maybe I was just being dramatic, as Ian had often accused me of being.

My tires crunched over the driveway. It was half a mile long, twisting through pine trees. A huge clearing opened at the end with a sprawling house of red stone, manicured planting beds, and a carefully trimmed lawn. A slice of upscale suburbia in the middle of the mountains.

While our family's business empire had started with Nana and Grandpa's brewery, my parents had taken it to the next level. Mom and Dad had started their company Elevated Adventures when I was a kid. An outdoor excursion company for the elite set. After a few years, they'd expanded their operations all over the region. Their success had really taken off after I graduated and moved away.

Now, Javier and Eliza Alvarez were enjoying their retirement in luxurious style, leaving the day-to-day operations of their business to their employees. For Mom, that meant an active social life among the higher reaches of the Silver Ridge community. Dad had traded his former love of the outdoors for an obsession with playing the stock market.

My parents had never wanted me to move away from Silver Ridge. Even while I was in business school pursuing my dreams, they'd bugged me about coming home. Until I'd introduced them to Ian. Since then, Mom had been salivating for a wedding to plan. Or at least an IPO to brag about to her friends at the Hart County Golf Club.

But now, after all these years pursuing my fortune in Chicago, I was slinking home with *nothing*.

I knocked on the door. The housekeeper, Gladys, answered. Her eyes widened.

"Gladys, tell them we're not interested in whatever they're selling," Mom's voice called from somewhere inside. "Javi must've left the gate open again."

My face heated. "It's me," I called out. Then lowered my voice. "Hey, Gladys. Sorry. They weren't expecting me. It's good to see you."

Gladys squeezed my arm affectionately. "You too. Please come in, come in."

As I crossed the threshold, Mom's heels clicked rapidly across the hardwood floors. Then she appeared, practically shoving Gladys aside.

"Zandra! What on earth?" Mom's face was smoother than the last time I'd seen her, especially for a woman in her sixties. But her dark eyes were the same, sharp and assessing. Judging.

"Hey, Mom."

She looked over my shoulder toward the driveway. "Why didn't you tell us you were on your way? Where's Ian?"

Before I could answer, she was bustling me into the living room, where Dad sat in his leather chair, scrolling through a tablet that probably contained the latest market reports. He'd gotten softer around the middle over the years, but he was still handsome with his silver-streaked hair and a neatly trimmed goatee.

"Zan!" Dad jumped up to give me a hug. "Where's Ian?"

"Well, he's—"

"Is that cat hair?" Mom eyed my blouse. "You know your father's allergic. Come wash your hands. Gladys, get the lint roller! She's covered in dander."

"Good to see you guys too," I muttered.

While Gladys lint-rolled me, Mom launched into an update about the chaos since Grandpa's injury. "We just got back a little while ago from visiting hours at the hospital. Thank goodness Manny's in a better mood."

"That's partly why I'm here," I said. "To see Grandpa. But also, the thing is—"

Mom went on like I hadn't spoken. "I was just about to head off to bingo. At the club, not that rec-center bingo Dixie Haines frequents. They serve corn dogs there." She shuddered. "You can come along with me this afternoon. The ladies will be thrilled to see you and hear about Chicago."

"But Mom—"

"When is Ian getting here?" Dad asked eagerly. "I've got some stocks I'm eyeing that I'd love to get his thoughts on."

"Yes, Ian," Mom gushed. "We can't wait to see him."

"Would you both *please* let me speak?" I shouted.

And of course, they looked at me like I was a zoo animal who'd just thundered into their home.

I took a deep breath. "Ian and I broke up. Months ago, in fact. Our company failed."

The silence that followed was deafening. Mom's too-smooth

face was hard to read, but her disapproval oozed from her pores. Dad just looked confused.

"What do you mean, failed?" he asked. Like it wasn't possible.

"I mean, we lost everything." I didn't mention that Ian had lied to me, and I'd been too trusting to see it.

The concept behind our company had been my idea. I'd made a personal pitch to every investor. When it all blew up, my reputation blew up with it.

"Well," Mom said after a long pause. *Very* long. "These things happen in business. But breaking up with Ian? Zandra, you can't just throw away six years because of one setback."

"It wasn't just the business, Mom. We were wrong for each other. It's over, okay? All of it. I packed up Chloe and my stuff, and we came home. I'll need to find a new job and a new place to live. It's going to be hard, but I can do it. You don't need to worry."

More uncomfortable silence.

Mom nodded slowly. "Maybe a few days away will be just what you two need. I'm sure you and Ian can work this out."

"Did you not hear a single thing I said?"

"Gladys will get you set up in the guestroom," she continued. "Though you'll have to board your cat at a kennel."

"That won't be necessary," I said firmly. "We're not staying here."

"Then where will you stay?"

"I was thinking a hotel for a few nights until I figure out something else. First thing I have to do is see Grandpa. Then I'll look for work. Somebody's got to be hiring, right? I can flip a burger if I have to."

"Don't be absurd," Mom said. "You'll stay here. And I'll have a list of appropriate positions for you on Monday. I could've had it ready before now if you'd given me notice."

"That's not what I want, Mom. I'm doing this myself."

Dad perked up. "We could put you in the Elevated Adventures main office."

"Yes, Javi. That's perfect. Fire that new receptionist. She's useless—"

"Absolutely not!" I stood up. "Mom, you're not firing someone because of me. I'm going to handle this myself, and I'll find my own place too."

Mom's gaze went cold. "Then I don't even see why you stopped by, Zandra. You didn't bother to tell us about Ian or warn us you were on your way. You've made it clear you don't need us. You never do."

The familiar guilt trip hit right where it was supposed to. But I was too tired and emotionally raw to play this game today.

"I guess I'll see you both later."

Chloe meowed as I got back in the car. "Well, that went about as expected," I told her, starting the engine.

Right now, what I really needed was a drink.

TWO
Callum

"THAT'S IT. I can't take Manny's micro-managing anymore. I quit."

Russ Wheaton had just stormed over to the bar, where I was unloading the glass washer. I smirked and continued stacking clean pint glasses on the shelf. "No, you don't. You love your job."

"But I'm tempted, O'Neal. Swear to God, Manny has got me down to my last nerve. That old man needs to be put out of his misery."

"Hey. Come on, now." I bit back a smirk. "Let's not wish ill on anyone. Especially our boss who's already injured."

"I'm not talking about him kicking the bucket. I'm not a monster. I just mean retiring. Even before the broken bones, it was way overdue."

I shrugged, but I couldn't disagree.

Things had been a little extra hectic around here since Manny's accident. He'd been texting and video-calling us to check up on things. Like, every five to ten minutes. It was a lot.

He never should've been up on that ladder in the storage room anyway. But was I going to say that to an eighty-year-old guy who ruled the brewery like a dictator? Fuck no. I valued my own life.

At least I'd found him quickly after he fell. Kept him stable and had the paramedics there in no time flat. Fall like that could've killed him.

Manny Alvarez had been the owner and operator of Hearthstone for the last three decades. It had started as just a small tasting room before Manny expanded it into the thriving restaurant and bar it was today. We'd been getting accolades for the brews that Russ, as brewmaster, created. He'd been taking Manny's recipes and updating them to the latest trends.

This place was Manny's entire life. So I couldn't blame him for a case of separation anxiety.

I'd been here for the last four years, rising from bartender to manager of our entire bar business. It had been 50% hard work, 50% people skills, and a healthy dash of old-fashioned charm.

Good thing I had all three, in spades.

"Look, I'll take care of Manny," I told Russ. "When I visited him in the hospital a couple days ago, he told me he's starting the hiring process. Once he has his replacement, he'll retire. He's really doing it this time."

"You don't think he'll change his mind and show up here on one of those scooter things, zooming around and shouting orders and hitting us with his cane?"

"Nah. Manny knows it's time. I promise I'll bear the brunt of his crazy until we can get things sorted out and replace him."

Russ's shoulders relaxed, and he exhaled a heavy breath. Then a new worry seemed to take over his expression. "Yeah, but that'll mean a brand-new general manager. I like the way things are. The culture of this place might change."

As I wiped down the bar, a wild idea popped into my head. Not an uncommon occurrence, because my mind was a wild place sometimes. "Maybe I'll apply for it."

"You?" Russ laughed.

And laughed some more.

My towel paused on its cleaning duties, my hip cocking as I frowned. "It's not that funny. I'm already bar manager."

"But running the entire Hearthstone operation? That's a lot of logistics and contracts and spreadsheets. Budgets. You weren't any better at math than I was in school."

"Fuck you. I did okay."

"If it was your sister, maybe, but you..."

"Grace already does the books for this place. She's not looking for another job."

"No kidding. She's shacked up with a rich dude. Why would she?"

My jaw tightened. "Enough about Grace. I was talking about me. Why couldn't I handle being general manager?"

"I didn't say you can't. It's just a lot of numbers in that job, you know. You're more of a front of the house guy. That's a compliment. Besides," Russ added with a grin, "you'd have to act all professional if you were the top boss. Couldn't hook up with customers. Your status as Silver Ridge's biggest man-whore would be in jeopardy."

"Okay, I get it." I tossed the bar towel at his face. "Don't you have some hops to sniff or yeast to babysit?"

Before Russ could respond, my other bartender working tonight hurried over, looking frazzled. "You okay, Winnie?" I asked.

"I'm so sorry, but I just got a call. My niece Ally's got a stomach bug. Apocalyptic level barfing, apparently. My sister's babysitter just scooted, and there's nobody to cover for her."

I held back a wince. "Say no more. Go help your sister. I've got things covered here."

"Thank you." She clasped her hands together. "You're a saint, O'Neal. Seriously."

"Saint might be pushing it," Russ muttered. I almost flipped him the bird, but I was being *professional*.

Before she could leave, I asked, "Hey Win, do you think I could handle being general manager?"

"Of Hearthstone?"

"No, of the Denver Broncos." I winked. "Yeah, I mean Hearthstone."

She paused. "I mean...maybe? You're awesome. But that would be a big jump, you know?"

Russ snorted. "There's a vote of confidence, right there."

Seriously? Did nobody believe in me?

That kinda hurt.

Winnie hurried home, and Russ did whatever brewmasters do at night. Debate the merits of west coast versus east coast hops, probably.

But despite my persistent smile and continuous banter as I served our customers, I contemplated the future. *My* future. The possibility that I might want to be general manager, an idea that hadn't even occurred to me before tonight.

But why the hell not? If somebody had to fill Manny's shoes, why not me?

I was a Hart County boy. A native who, despite playing football for the high school team and then a stint in the military, had never wanted to live anywhere else. I loved Silver Ridge, and I loved Hearthstone. But that didn't mean I lacked ambition.

My older brother Ashford was married and settled. My baby sister Grace was madly in love. Our friend Teller had fallen so hard he upended his entire life to be with his lady.

My point was, I was in my mid-thirties now. Why not try for something bigger?

Not a relationship, of course. I wasn't built for one-and-onlys. Even if I was great at spotting love matches for *other* people. It was a gift of mine.

But more responsibility could be ideal. More money. The more I thought about it, the more it made sense. I loved getting to know people, and pretty much *all* people loved me. When combined with my work ethic, wouldn't that make me a good head manager?

The real question: would Manny agree?

Russ had a point about my hookup habits. I was always clear

about not wanting anything serious, but plenty of women hoped for another ride on this pony. *Who could blame them?* That's why I only hooked up with tourists. They were already in the mood for something fun and temporary.

What better place to pick up vacationing hotties than this very bar, where I spent nearly every night?

But in the name of professionalism, that would have to change. No more hooking up with women I met while at work. I could handle that. Piece of cake.

Next, I would just have to convince Manny I was the guy for the job.

Maybe I could start my no-hooking-up resolution tomorrow.

The most gorgeous woman I'd seen in a while had just walked in the door. Straight dark-brown hair fell down her back to her waist. Her jeans hugged her curves like my truck on a mountain road. And when she settled on a barstool, her eyes landed on me and widened. She glanced away, biting her lip hesitantly.

How was I supposed to resist that?

My smile grew with every step I took closer to her. "Hi, there. What can I get you?"

"I don't know yet." There was something in her tone I liked. A mix of challenge and breathlessness, like I'd made her heart rate increase, but she hadn't decided if that was a good thing.

"Hungry? Thirsty?"

"Just thirsty."

I passed over a menu. "We've got plenty to choose from. Take your time. When you're ready, just wave and I'll hurry back." After adding a wink, simply because I couldn't resist, I gave her some space.

But I kept her in my peripheral view. Her eyes were huge and dark, and her lips were full. The kind that begged to be kissed. She was the type of stunning that took a guy's breath away.

And she kept looking over at me, like she was assessing me too. Something I was well familiar with, but it never got old.

Anticipation rose in my stomach like sparks rising from a campfire.

Had I mentioned I *really* loved sex?

In particular, I loved showing a woman a fantastic time. Making her feel beautiful. Making her moan leading up to that moment when she lost control. But the opening chase, that seductive will-we-or-won't-we dance, was almost as fun. The next morning, if we felt like a second round, it was like a victory lap before parting ways. Happy memories all around, no drama, no repeats.

Already, my endorphins elevated. I could always swear off meeting women at work tomorrow. If this one was interested, there was no way I'd turn her down.

But first, I had to reel her in.

I made my way back over. "Any decisions yet? If you'd like suggestions, I'm partial to the kolsch."

"Then I'll have a vodka soda."

My grin spread. "You got it." She was staking her own ground. I could work with that. I took her menu, turning my smile all the way up. "I'm Callum, by the way."

"I know."

That response caught me off guard. "You do?"

"Callum O'Neal." My name sounded sharp in her mouth. Like she was going to use it against me.

Kinky.

"Have we met?" I asked.

Her dark eyes glittered. "You don't remember me, do you?"

My smile slipped.

Oh, shit. Had I already slept with her before?

Or maybe I'd hooked up with her best friend or sister or something, and she didn't approve. Whatever the answer, I truly didn't recognize her, though I racked my brain for some trace of her in my memory.

There wasn't much I could do except take the blame and shrug it off. Something I had no problem doing. When I screwed up, I was man enough to admit it.

"I guess I don't," I said apologetically. "Which I find shocking. Wouldn't think I could forget someone like you."

"You think you're charming, don't you?"

"I try to be. Some people think I am."

"They must be easy to impress."

Oof. We had a live one here.

"I take it you're not?" I asked.

"Not so much."

Tapping the menu on my palm, I backed away a few steps before turning away.

While I helped other customers and made her drink, I was thinking. Pondering. Trying to figure out where I might have met this woman.

She was in her early thirties or so. Sexy. Smart, at least from what I could tell so far. Playing hard to get, a favorite game of mine.

Obviously not a local. Otherwise I'd have seen her around.

After a few minutes, I returned and set her drink in front of her. "Okay, I must know you from somewhere, but it's not coming to me. Any hints?"

"Nope."

I groaned. "This mystery is going to bug me."

She leaned forward, elbows on the bar top. "Bet you a hundred bucks you can't guess it."

"A hundred? Steep. But you're on." I rubbed my jaw, which was rough from my five o'clock shadow. "Are you a friend of my sister? Grace?"

The brunette shook her head, that little smirk firmly in place.

"Did I meet you outside Hart County?"

"No, it was here in Silver Ridge."

"What year?"

"I'm not just going to hand you the answer." She sipped her vodka soda. "You're never going to get it."

My jaw clenched. This was going to drive me crazy. I had to know.

After several more rounds of guessing, I came back around to the obvious. Tugging off my ball cap, I brushed back my hair and fit the cap back into place. "Did we, uh..." I gestured between us. "Did we hook up at some point?"

If we really had slept together and I'd forgotten her, it would be embarrassing.

But her reaction was even worse. She barked a laugh, making a few other heads at the bar turn. I couldn't help but detect a hint of mockery in her expression. Maybe more than a hint.

"Absolutely not. I've never slept with you, O'Neal, nor would I."

"Okay. Sheesh."

"Ever."

"I get the point. I've never seen you naked." My eyes flicked over her. "Too bad," I muttered. "I'll bet you another hundred bucks we would've had fun."

Her mouth pursed. "You really get around so much you don't remember who you've slept with?"

My palm pressed to my heart. "That's harsh. You saying I'm easy?"

She lifted her hands. "Wasn't judging. I don't slut shame."

"Now you've called me easy *and* a slut. Those might be the same, but you're sure covering all your bases."

"I was being rude. I'm sorry." She didn't seem that sorry.

But I'd never been one to have a problem laughing at myself. "I thought it was kinda funny, actually. You're feisty."

"Ugh." Her eyes rolled. "I hate being called feisty."

"I'm guessing it happens a lot?"

"As much as you're probably called obnoxious."

"That does happen a lot. I'm also called fun. Happy-go-lucky." I shrugged. "Amazing in the sack."

"Don't forget humble."

I barked a laugh, and was gratified that her smirk turned to a real smile. *There we go*, I thought.

Told you I was good.

"Hey!" someone down the bar said. "Can I get a drink or what?"

"Duty calls," I murmured to my brunette.

My brunette. But I was pretty sure she liked me, despite our rocky start. I was turning this ship around. Whatever her issue with me, winning this woman over would be extra satisfying. For the both of us, if ya know what I mean.

Every few minutes, I kept circling back to her with more guesses, each more outlandish. *You're a loan shark I borrowed money from. You're a CIA operative here to recruit me.* My antics coaxed even more sarcastic responses from her lips.

And a few reluctant smiles.

The funny thing was, I didn't want this to be over too soon. Didn't even want to go back to her hotel room or rental condo tonight, simply because I wanted to keep bantering with her tomorrow. How long would she be in Silver Ridge?

Other customers pulled me away again, since it was just me working the bar tonight. But when the rush finally died down, I made my way back to her.

"Okay. I give up. I owe you a hundred bucks."

"Pay up."

"I'm good for it." I leaned against the bar, making sure she got a good view of the muscles and tattoos on my forearm as I braced myself. It was shameless, but it usually worked. "How about I take you out tomorrow with your earnings. Or I guess you'd be taking *me* out. Either way, we can spend some more time together while you're in town."

She studied me for a long moment. "Spend some time together. Are you seriously trying to get me into bed, O'Neal?"

"If I'm lucky." I wasn't a subtle guy. No point in denying it.

"After what I said earlier?"

"I'm an optimist."

She leaned forward, and for a second I thought she was in, at least for getting together tomorrow. That she was just as intrigued by the possibilities as I was.

"I promise you, Callum, I would sooner chug a gallon of generic light beer than *ever* sleep with you. I'd rather eat glass shards."

"*Okay*," I grated out.

"I'd rather spend a month listening nonstop to my mother's unsolicited advice."

"I've got the picture."

"Forget the money you owe me. I don't need it."

With that, she pulled a ten from her purse, tossed the money on the bar, and walked away. I stood there, stunned, watching her leave.

Well, that was a first.

THREE
Zandra

I STORMED BACK to my motel room, fumbling with the key before finally getting the door unlocked.

"Callum O'Neal was there," I announced after slamming and locking the door. "Right behind the bar. Can you believe that?"

Chloe wandered out from her hiding place under the bed, probably as thrilled with these accommodations as I was. The Pine Cone Motor Lodge was about as awful as motels got, reeking of stale cigarettes and onions. Give or take a whiff of cheap perfume.

But with my bank account so low and my credit card balances already inching up, a resort hotel on a mountain top had been out of my price range. Just a tad.

Would've been smarter to take the hundred bucks Callum owed me from our bet. But it was the principle of the thing.

I headed to the mini fridge to pull out dinner for both of us. "He's just as arrogant as he was in high school, strutting around like a peacock who expects every woman in the vicinity to start drooling on command. Well, not me."

When I'd first walked into the brewery, he'd looked instantly familiar. He still had that same shaggy hair, medium brown with just enough curl to make it perpetually tousled. Those thick-lashed eyes that had probably gotten him out of trouble countless times. Backward baseball cap snug on his head. In high school, it had been the Broncos. Tonight, his cap had read SRFD. Silver Ridge...Fire Department?

Not that I'd been memorizing details or anything.

"I don't even care that he didn't recognize me," I continued, ripping open my pouch of tuna to mix in mayo and some pre-chopped veggies I'd picked up at the store. "I've changed a lot since high school. I mean, I should hope so, considering how long ago it was."

If I was being honest, Callum had changed in ways too. Like the tattoos down one arm. His square jaw sported more stubble than it had when he was a teenager. He'd gotten even more muscular, his biceps straining against his T-shirt. Round glutes that filled out his jeans to an obscene degree.

Nnrgh. Okay, his ass was on point. He'd gained bulk in all the right places, and fine, it did look good on him. In an obvious, unoriginal way.

"The man is a walking advertisement for testosterone. Didn't think he could get cockier than he was in high school, but he managed it."

Chloe wasn't paying me much attention, focused entirely on her dinner. I dug into my tuna and munched on a bag of baby carrots.

Maybe it had been a little bit fun, playing that guessing game with him. Trying to get him to figure out who I was. He'd almost made me laugh a couple of times. Plus, an easy hundred bucks to earn, even if I hadn't taken it in the end.

"But then he just expected me to want to sleep with him, Coco." She flicked her tail. "You would not believe this guy's confidence. It's remarkable, actually. Scientists should study him. He's fascinating."

To science, obviously. Not fascinating to me. I wanted nothing to do with the man.

He was the kind of guy who did whatever he wanted, regardless of consequences. Grinning happily the whole time.

Hopefully Callum didn't work many bartending shifts at Hearthstone, because I had every intention of avoiding him.

Of course, I'd been dunking on Callum for being essentially the same person as in high school, but what did I have to show for all my supposed growth? A room in a questionable motel. A business wardrobe with no job to wear it to.

At least I had the freedom to eat whatever I wanted now. Ian had always thrown a fit if I opened a can of tuna fish within a five-mile radius of him.

The smell, Zandra. How can you stand that?

Guess what, Ian? Tuna was an affordable source of lean protein and healthy fats. Though it did have a tendency to smell up a room. Maybe he'd had a point about that particular complaint.

"Be right back, okay?" I told Chloe as I gathered up our trash to take it to the dumpster.

Outside, an old streetlight cast a weak urine-colored glow on the concrete. Ah, small-town charm.

I walked to the dumpster and tossed my small bag of trash inside. The lid clattered as I dropped it, and a few scraps of paper blew past, picked up by the breeze.

It wasn't just the Pine Cone parking lot dampening my mood. My heart felt...desolate. Haunted by old memories that I couldn't let rise to the surface.

Basically, life sucked for me at the moment.

Then I heard a scuff, like boots against concrete. My pulse accelerated.

"Hello?" I asked. No response.

I peered around the corner of the building. Nobody was there. Shit, I was imagining things.

Beyond the wan glow from the streetlight, the darkness was absolute in a way I'd forgotten, having spent so many years in the city. Out here, when the sun went down, it *really* went down.

A thick, suffocating blackness seemed to press against me. A creeping feeling scraped along my spine. Like someone was watching me from the shadows.

My entire body went cold, then hot.

"Nothing to see here," I called out to the darkness. "Just a single lady well on her way into spinsterhood whose only friend is a cat."

The joke fell flat in the oppressive quiet. The feeling of being watched intensified, and suddenly I wasn't in the mood for self-deprecating humor anymore.

I thought of the creek on the night Jessa died. Moonlight glinting over rushing water.

My pulse thrummed against my throat as a thick lump gathered there.

"Hey!" I yelled into the dark. "Whoever's out there can fuck off!"

My voice echoed back at me, but there was no other response. Still, every instinct I had was screaming at me to get back inside.

I rushed back to my room, slamming the door and turning every lock the cheap hardware offered. My hands were shaking as I checked the windows, making sure they were secure.

Then I sank to the carpet, my back to the door. Chloe dashed over and crawled into my lap, bumping her head against my stomach. My fingers smoothed over her soft fur, taking the comfort she knew I needed.

"We have to figure something out, Chloe," I said, scooping her up and holding her close. "Because this is really not working for me."

I didn't know if I just meant the Pine Cone Motor Lodge, or Silver Ridge altogether.

FOUR
Zandra

"Baby Z!" Rosie opened her arms. "Get in here! I need some sugar from my favorite niece."

"Your only niece," I reminded her as she smothered me with a tight hug. My eyes closed as I soaked in the love. A welcome contrast to the otherwise sterile hospital corridor where we were standing.

"Doesn't matter. You're still the best." Rosie patted my cheek. "And gorgeous and smart and a fantastic dresser. This blazer. So chic."

"Thank you, Auntie." I'd worn dark jeans, boots, a silk blouse, and my favorite jacket. I might not have a job, but I had the wardrobe, so I might as well make the most of it.

Rosie studied me. "Did you sleep okay?"

"Uh, yeah. No complaints."

I'd tossed and turned all last night at the motel, hearing creaky sounds and not knowing if they were real or imaginary. Probably just the ancient building settling. But after feeling watched when I'd thrown my trash out, plus the drama of seeing Callum, my nerves had been shot.

I'd woken this morning with a splitting headache, not helped by the fact that Chloe had been draped over the top of my head like a furry hat.

I'd texted my aunt yesterday that I was in town, and again first thing this morning, asking if she could meet me at the county hospital for visiting hours. If I didn't have a good night's sleep on my side before seeing Grandpa, at least I could have Rosie's cheerful face.

"Have you had breakfast?" she asked. "Coffee? Need anything?"

"Not right now."

One corner of her smile slipped down. "I heard about the breakup with Ian. I'm sorry."

Wow. That news had traveled fast. Thanks Mom and Dad. "I'm really okay. What's new with you? Must be something. You look great."

Rosie swatted my arm coyly. "That's just love, honey. Making me young again." She did a little spin. Her bright patterned sundress flared out, and her magenta curls bounced. "Jimmy moved in with me."

"Exciting! Congrats."

"Never thought it would happen. Jimmy and I tend to fight like cats and dogs, but it's just the passion between us, I guess. Since he moved in, it's been like a honeymoon." Then she grabbed my arm. "Listen to me, bragging about my love life when you're hurting."

"Not hurting over Ian. I promise. Already over him."

"You'll find the right one for you. I've never been so happy." She leaned in. "Or this sexed up. Jimmy's a tiger. Wakes me up at all hours."

I cringed. "Really didn't need to know that."

"Don't tell me my niece is a prude. With that body?" She flashed me an exaggerated wink. "Even if you don't have a partner, there's nothing wrong with self love. That's what I always say."

"Oh, I remember."

My Auntie Rosie, ladies and gentleman.

She held onto my arm as we walked down the hall. "Now, where are you staying, Baby Z? With Javi and your mom?" Her mouth tightened. "Can't imagine they're being too nice about Chloe."

"Chloe and I are staying at the Pine Cone for now."

Her lipsticked mouth dropped open. "That old motel out on the highway? That's not good enough for you. Come stay with me and Jimmy, Z. You have to."

"No, I can't interrupt the honeymoon."

"You can wear earplugs. We'll use a system, so you know if it's not safe to come into the living room."

I prayed Rosie would stop talking before I had to bleach my ears or my brain. "I'll be out of the Pine Cone in no time. Just getting my feet back under me." I pointed down the hospital corridor. "Let's go see grandpa."

Rosie huffed. "Warning you. He's been ornery."

I laughed. "When is he not?"

As we neared his open doorway, Grandpa's voice carried. "You're trying to poison me!"

Rosie and I shared a glance.

Here we go, I thought, just as we stepped into the fray.

"Mr. Alvarez, there's no need to raise your voice," the nurse said.

"There's no flavor in these eggs. A person could die from lack of stimulation to his taste buds. You're literally boring me to death."

"Not medically possible, Mr. Alvarez."

My grandpa had celebrated his eightieth birthday last year. His pompadour was pure white now instead of glossy black. But he still had one of the most booming voices I'd ever heard. Growing up, when my grandpa entered a room, everybody knew. Even lying in a hospital bed, dressed in a thin cotton gown, he had a formidable presence.

Then he saw me, his gaze narrowing. "If it isn't my granddaughter. An objective observer. Zandra, try these eggs and tell me they aren't some soy protein monstrosity. Because I guarantee, these didn't come from a natural chicken."

"Hi, Grandpa." I bent to kiss his cheek. Then I gave his nurse an apologetic smile. "Sorry about him."

"I'm used to it," she deadpanned. "He's in quite a mood today. Good luck."

"Don't patronize me. Just get this slop you call food out of my sight. Now, where's my phone? I need to make sure Hearthstone hasn't burned to the ground without me yet."

Oh, yeah. Definitely in a mood.

The nurse left the room, and Rosie and I took up places on either side of Grandpa's bed. Opening my purse, I tugged out the bag I'd brought with me. The stiff paper crinkled as I pulled the box of chicken nuggets from inside.

"I swung by the drive-through on my way here this morning," I said. "In case you're still hungry."

A genuine smile dawned on Grandpa's face. "My granddaughter's the smartest person in our family. Isn't that what I always say, Rosie?"

My aunt grinned fondly at me. "You do. And she is."

Grandpa dug in to his nuggets. He usually turned up his nose at fast food, but these were his guilty pleasure.

Maybe I'd screwed up my life in Chicago, but I still knew how to tame Manny Alvarez when he was being a terror.

I sat gently on the edge of the bed. "How've you been feeling, Grandpa?"

"Like I got cut open and stuffed full of metal pins to hold me together." He wiped his fingers on a paper napkin. "Let's talk about you. Your mother and father already stopped by this morning. They're very concerned about what's going on between you and Ian."

I sighed. I'd assumed my parents had been talking about me, since Rosie had known about Ian too, but I'd hoped to avoid any more lectures about my failings. At least until after the nuggets were gone.

"Promise me one thing." Grandpa turned his intense focus on me. "No matter what nonsense my son and his wife spout, promise you won't take Ian back. Even if he comes groveling, and he will."

A smile played on my lips. "I doubt that. But I promise, Grandpa. Ian and I are done."

"Never liked him anyway. No cojones. Maybe they were there anatomically, but they're tiny and shriveled. You would know better than me."

I sputtered a laugh. "*Grandpa*."

"He's right though, Z," Rosie said. "I never liked Ian either. He seemed all wrong for you."

"Ian was the wrong guy," I admitted. "I was chasing a lot of the wrong things and wasted years of my life without seeing it. But I'm here now, and I want to help however I can."

"Too bad it took this old body nearly cracking in two to drag you home."

I winced. "Sorry, Grandpa."

"No, that's not fair," Rosie countered. "Zandra's done her best, as have we all."

Grandpa grumbled. "Well, at least you're here. Missed you."

"Missed you too."

After he polished off the last nugget, Rosie helped clear away the trash. Grandpa sat up straighter against his pillows like he was about to call a business meeting. "Now, we should get to practical matters. I hear you're looking for a job."

Groan. Mom and Dad had spilled everything, hadn't they?

"That's on my agenda," I said with my jaw clenched. "But right now, I'm here to visit with you. You don't need to worry about my employment situation."

"What I *need* is a time machine to take years off my life and make me buy a new ladder instead of that shoddy piece of crap I fell from."

"But that's not happening, is it, Pa?" Rosie patted his hand.

"You're not going back to work. You're eighty years old and your hip is shattered."

Grandpa made a wry face in my direction. "See how supportive my children are? My best qualities skipped a generation."

"Oh shush." Rosie waved him off. "You've already agreed with Javi and me that it's time for you to retire." She turned to me. "And this works out for Zandra too, doesn't it? *You* can take over as general manager for Hearthstone. It's like it was meant to be."

I blinked. "Wait. Hearthstone? *Me*?"

Grandpa angled his head. "I suppose my daughter does have some good ideas."

"I've never run a restaurant or a brewery," I pointed out.

"But you've always accomplished whatever you set your mind to," Rosie said with the kind of unwavering confidence that made my chest tight.

"Mistakes involving Ian notwithstanding," Grandpa added. "Why else did you go to that fancy business school except to run a business?"

Protests rose to the tip of my tongue. Because I didn't have the best track record recently, did I?

But I'd gotten my MBA. I'd learned a lot in the years since, much of it the hard way. Maybe I could do this.

"I'm…interested," I heard myself say.

"I haven't hired you yet, mind you," Grandpa warned, though his eyes were twinkling. "I'll need a résumé."

I couldn't help smiling. "Yes, Grandpa."

"And I need to see what other candidates are interested. Have to be fair about this. I've got some loyal employees who've worked their way up. Like Callum."

My smile faltered. "Callum *O'Neal*?" I asked, as casually as I could manage. The shrewd look Rosie gave me suggested I hadn't managed all that well. "Didn't expect him to be in the running."

Grandpa nodded. "He's bar manager. One of my best employees. Good kid."

"He's the one who found your grandpa after he fell," Rosie added. "Practically saved his life."

"Are you sure we're referring to the same guy? Jock, unruly brown hair, backwards baseball cap?" My heart rate increased as I thought of his over-the-top handsome features. That smirk and the way he puffed out his chest like he expected to be admired.

Then a new voice chimed in.

"Talking about me?"

I spun around to see the man himself standing in the doorway, and my heart did this annoying skip.

Unfortunately, he was even better looking than he'd been last night. No ball cap today, his messy waves out in full force. He had a touch more stubble on his jaw, and his chocolaty brown eyes were warm and inviting, creasing lightly at the sides.

Then in slow motion, he seemed to register that it was *me*, the woman from the bar last night. And his easy confidence drained away as horror dawned on his face.

Was I awful for feeling just a little smug?

Grandpa gestured for him to come in. "Callum, this is my granddaughter, Zandra."

"We've met," I said coolly.

He cleared his throat, hands diving into his jeans pockets as a flush climbed up his neck. "We, uh, went to high school together."

My lips pressed into a thin line. "We did."

Rosie's eyes bounced from Callum to me.

Just then, the nurse poked her head in. "I'm sorry, folks, but we can only have two visitors at a time."

"I'll step out," Rosie volunteered cheerfully.

"No, wait." Callum pushed back his hair from his forehead. "I actually need to have a quick word with Zandra. If that's okay."

I crossed my arms. "I don't see why. I don't see what we would have to say to each other."

He smiled, though it looked strained. "Silver Ridge High alumni stuff. It'll just take a minute."

"No, I don't think—"

"Just go talk to the kid!" Grandpa interrupted. "I want the nurse to change my catheter bag."

I got up and followed Callum out into the hall.

Once we were out of earshot of Grandpa's room, Callum spun on his heavy boot heel. "Look, about last night—"

"It doesn't matter," I cut him off. "Mystery solved. You know who I am now."

"If I offended you, I'm sorry."

I scoffed. "You didn't offend me."

"You don't look like you did back in high school. I mean..." He let out a low whistle, then quickly forced his eyes up to meet mine. "Shit. Ignore me. I can be an idiot."

"Oh trust me, I'm well aware."

His lips slid into that angle he clearly thought was disarming. "But we're good, right? You're not pissed?"

"Why would I be pissed?" I asked, though I could hear the edge in my own voice. "We barely know each other. We're basically strangers."

"I was coming on pretty strong last night. I wouldn't have done that if I'd known you were the boss's granddaughter."

"But otherwise you're fine making moves on women you meet while you're on the clock? Noted."

"You make it sound bad."

I arched an eyebrow.

"Are you going to say something to Manny about it?" he asked quietly.

I didn't actually want to cause problems for Callum with his job. But he didn't know that, and I didn't mind making him sweat a little. "I haven't decided yet."

"Would you at least warn me? Please? This job is important to me."

Something in his voice made me feel a twinge of guilt. So I relented. “I wouldn’t actually say anything.”

He cursed under his breath, exhaling with visible relief. “Thank you.”

“Don’t take it as a favor.”

But that cocky grin was already sliding back into place. “I’ll probably be seeing you around the brewery a lot, now that you’re back in town. We should catch up.”

“I don’t think so.”

“But you said you weren’t mad.”

“About last night? Not really.”

I remembered watching him get hit on the football field in high school. He’d always been so quick to bounce back up, brush off the dirt, and get back in the game. Nothing could keep Callum low for long.

And that just made my bitter side rear up again. Because after Jessa died senior year, Callum had kicked me when I was down. Just because he could.

He might’ve seemed like the cheerful golden boy on the outside, but the real Callum was ice cold.

“But we are not friends, Callum,” I finished. “We never were, and we never will be.”

I turned on my heel and stormed back into the hospital room, determined to focus on why I was really back in this town. My grandfather. My chance to start over.

Not smirky, infuriatingly sexy himbos like Callum O’Neal.

FIVE
Callum

I SKULKED around the hospital hallways for a while to give Rosie and Zandra a chance to visit with Manny. The fluorescent lights buzzed overhead, and the antiseptic smell made my stomach churn.

Or maybe that was just a rare case of anxiety getting to me.

My flirtatious nature had caused me trouble on occasion, but I'd always managed to skate through without too much drama. Hitting on my boss's beloved granddaughter, though? That had been a mistake of epic proportions. Everybody at Hearthstone knew how much Manny adored Zandra.

The only thing that could've been worse? If I'd actually slept with her, and Manny had found out about it.

Why didn't he have any current photos of Z in his office? As it was, she looked a *lot* more grown-up than she had back in high school.

Back then, she'd always worn her hair in a thick braid, and despite her constant scowling and growling at me in class, there had been something...innocent about her.

Any time she'd been around, my eyes had drifted her way, my brain puzzling over her like she was a complex football play I couldn't figure out. I hadn't been able to understand why she didn't like me.

Didn't make any more sense to me now.

In fact, I was amazed Zandra would care enough about me to hold on to a grudge, considering everything she'd accomplished since graduation. Neither of us was in the same place we'd been back then.

But that same old feeling crept up my spine. Frustration over the fact that Zandra couldn't stand me.

After visiting the cafeteria for a terrible cup of coffee, I poked my head into Manny's room. He was propped up in bed, watching something on the TV.

The coast was clear.

"Ah, there you are, Callum," he grunted. "Was hoping you'd come back. Though you must have better things to do with your day than visit a decrepit old guy like me."

"Please. You can't pull off the humble routine any better than I can, Manny."

He chuckled. "We have that much in common."

"We do. Besides, I had to come see you because I can't resist a pity case." I settled into the chair beside his bed. "Gotta get that good karma."

He laughed, this time deep from his belly. "Anyone else, and I'd assume they're just brown-nosing the boss."

"Good thing you know me better than that." I pulled out my travel backgammon set and placed it on his bed table. "Ready for me to wipe the floor with you?"

"Big talk considering that's never happened yet."

"How do you know I haven't been hustling you?" I asked. "I'm playing the long game."

He snorted. "At this rate, I'll croak before you reveal your skills."

We'd started our routine of playing backgammon last year. Sometimes Manny got worked up about vendors screwing up our orders or budgets not lining up. The many stresses of owning a business, I guessed. When he got like that, I could usually turn around his mood with a game.

Probably didn't hurt that I sucked at this, and he always won. But I was determined to get better at it.

I'd never been close to my own grandparents. Growing up, Mom had done her best to take care of the four of us, no thanks to our dad. After she died, us kids had taken care of ourselves, along with Teller and Piper Landry across the street.

So it was nice to see how much Manny loved his granddaughter, even if a part of me was a little envious too. She had her grandpa, her aunt, *and* two parents.

Only child, though. I wondered what that was like.

Manny and I played in comfortable silence for a while, the familiar rhythm of the dice and the click of the pieces soothing my edges. Finally, I worked up the courage to broach the very subject that had been weighing on me.

"I was surprised to see Zandra back in town."

Manny's face softened with unmistakable pride. "It's good to have her around again, though I wish the circumstances were different. She's had a hard time lately."

My brow wrinkled. "She has?"

"Some drama with a boyfriend. Good riddance, if you ask me. But now she's back home. Maybe I should be grateful her ex is an idiot."

My mouth ticked up with a smile, but the thought of Zandra struggling put a damper on that. I hadn't even thought about other reasons Z might be in town. I'd just assumed she'd left her fabulous life in whatever big city she was conquering to help out the family. The idea that she might be running from something, some asshole guy, didn't sit right.

"She doesn't like me much," I said, trying to keep my tone neutral.

"Don't worry about it. Zandra takes after me. She's crotchety beyond her years."

I laughed. "Not going to argue with you there."

"She doesn't like most folks, and neither do I. But she'll probably warm up to you. I did. You have a tendency to grow on people."

"Like athlete's foot?"

"You read my mind."

Inside, I could only hope Zandra would give me a break. At least it seemed like she hadn't badmouthed me to her grandfather. Yet. She'd said she wouldn't, but she'd always been unpredictable. I was relieved she hadn't done anything overt to screw me over out of spite.

There was more I wanted to talk about with Manny, though. I'd genuinely come to spend time with him. But yeah, I had an agenda. And I had to think he'd understand.

Since I'd started at Hearthstone, Manny had become a mentor. Never went too easy on me and didn't insult my intelligence either. When I'd asked for more responsibility in the past, he'd given me a chance. He'd always been accepting of my volunteer firefighter duties too.

I had to believe that, if I told him I wanted the general manager position, he'd give me a fair shot.

"You haven't changed your mind about hiring someone to replace you at Hearthstone?" I asked.

He made a show of grumbling about it, muttering something about being put out to pasture, but eventually nodded. "It's time."

"I was thinking about applying."

"Bar manager not enough for you?"

"I think I've done a great job, and I'm ready for a bigger challenge. I know Hearthstone inside and out." I launched into the argument I'd rehearsed. "As bar manager, I've gotten to know the brewery side of things by working closely with Russ. I know the restaurant too. And I've been filling in for you here and there while you've been gone. Working with suppliers. Handling employee issues."

"With my active supervision," he noted.

"Yes. But I've been picking things up fast."

He folded his hands on his stomach, his expression turning thoughtful. "You do pay attention. More than most. You're a good kid."

"I'm thirty-four. Hardly a kid."

"When you're my age, everybody seems like a kid. But that wasn't a criticism. I like you, and I trust you. Do I think you're ready to run Hearthstone? I don't know. That's a tall order."

"If you're worried about my firefighting duties—"

"If anything, that proves your resilience. Same with your military service. Numbers and spreadsheets don't come naturally to you, but you're a strong leader to the other employees. I've also never once seen you give up on anything, no matter how difficult. That's a rare quality."

"Thank you, sir."

He sighed, scratching his head. "But the issue is my granddaughter."

Oh, *hell*. Maybe she'd said something to him after all.

But then Manny continued. "With Zandra back in town, she could potentially take over operations herself. Step into my shoes."

And now I truly felt like an idiot. How had I not seen this coming?

Zandra had a business degree. She was family. How could I ever compete with that?

"No worries. I totally get it. Family comes first." I hadn't even considered applying for the job a few days ago, but dammit, the disappointment stung.

"Now, don't give me that hangdog face. I'm not saying you have no shot."

My eyes lifted.

"You really want this, Callum? It's not just an increase in salary. It's a heck of a lot of work."

Before I could respond, there was a soft knock. Zandra appeared in the doorway, but when she saw me sitting there, she took a step back. "Sorry. Rosie and I finished lunch, and I thought I'd say goodbye before I drove back to Silver Ridge, but I can come back later."

"Nonsense," Manny called out. "It's ideal timing you're here. I need to talk to you and Callum both. I've got a proposition for you."

"Uh oh," I muttered. "Is that good or bad?"

"No jokes right now, Callum," my boss grumped. "Zandra, don't make me wait. Come sit down."

She came in, her eyes darting between her grandfather and me. I just shrugged and subtly shook my head. I didn't know what Manny was going to say either.

Yet a touch of warmth flared in my belly, just from having her closer.

"It seems you're both interested in replacing me as the head of Hearthstone Brewing. And I believe you're both excellent candidates."

Zandra's gaze flew to me again. "Callum too? You're sure?"

I gave her a sardonic stare. "I'm the only other person in here."

"Callum, you've been a loyal employee for years. You've proven yourself time and again. But you don't have broader business experience. You also have a tendency toward being too friendly and familiar. In other words, you need to learn to keep your dick in your pants with the customers."

Zandra snorted, then tried to cover it with a cough.

"Yes, sir." My face burned, though everything he'd said was true.

His granddaughter looked like she was loving every second.

Then Manny turned to her. "Zandra, you have the smarts and the degree, as well as business experience. Of course, the results of your last venture were..." He paused. "Less than stellar. More like a dumpster fire, from what I've read about your company's demise online."

That satisfied expression slid off her face, and I felt a stab of sympathy. So she'd had a bad breakup *and* a career setback? Maybe that explained why she'd been so extra pissy.

"I can always trust you not to hold back, Grandpa."

"And why would I? You're both tough. You can take the truth."

I stood and crossed my arms, shifting on my feet. "Then tell me straight, Manny. Would you honestly hire me over your granddaughter?"

"I would. I don't believe in nepotism. But you'd have to earn it, Callum. So would she." There was something devious in his smile.

"How?"

"Exactly," Zandra chimed in. "What is it you have in mind?"

"A two-month trial period. You'll work together. Callum, I want you to help Zandra get to know Hearthstone as it operates today. Show her the ropes. She knows plenty, but she's never worked for a restaurant or brewery before, much less been in charge of *this* one."

"Okay," I said. "I can do that."

"And Zandra, you'll help get Callum up to speed on the business, logistics, and management side. With plenty of input from me, of course, because I need to make sure neither of you messes this up. Hearthstone is special. I'm sure we can all agree on that."

We both nodded.

Meanwhile, my brain was working. Could I really manage this?

"But what if Callum and I don't work well together?" Zandra asked, her voice tight.

"Then you'll figure it out. That's what good managers do. At the end of the two months, I'll hire the best person for the job, whether or not they're related to me."

I felt the muscle in my jaw pulsing. "Are you sure about this, Manny? Can't you just let us interview, and you decide now?"

Z nodded along, for once agreeing with me.

But he studied us shrewdly. "That wouldn't be any fun. Also

a lot less effective. A trial period means the winner will take over with all the knowledge they need. The loser still has a job at Hearthstone regardless. But only *one* of you will be the boss."

Shit. Sounded like we had no choice.

"Not afraid of a little friendly competition, are you?" Manny asked.

"No, Grandpa," Zandra murmured. "I can handle it." Her eyes locked on mine like she was sighting me through a scope and ready to pull the trigger.

I put my hands on my hips. "Same here. Bring it on." Though inside, I didn't feel nearly as confident as my voice sounded.

Zandra had already made it clear how she felt about me, and now I was supposed to work closely with her, train her, and somehow come out ahead in this competition?

I was pretty much fucked.

But, hey. That had never stopped me before.

SIX
Callum

RUSS LEANED against the bar counter, watching me inventory our liquor bottles. "Dude, you're so fucked."

I snorted and shook my head. "I don't need you to remind me."

Manny had started a group text with Zandra and me last night, listing in minute detail everything he wanted us to do on our first day of the two-month trial period.

Which would be *today*.

I'd woken bright and early, hitting the gym to clear my head. After my shower, I'd opted for nicer jeans and an athletic polo and skipped the ball cap, trying to dress up more than usual. Then grabbed some breakfast and got here early to finish my inventory, all so I'd be ready when she arrived.

But I wasn't feeling nearly as down as I had at the hospital yesterday. Last night, while I'd been staring at my ceiling and trying to get to sleep, I'd faced up to some hard truths.

Was Zandra most likely going to win this competition? Yes.

Was I going to give up because of that? Nope.

"But she's his granddaughter," Russ said. "Of course he's going to hire her over you."

I moved on from the tequila bottles to the whiskey, checking where we were low so I could submit an order later today. "That's likely. The bigger issue is that she hates me. She's hated me since high school."

"Why?"

"Damned if I know."

Russ suddenly glanced around in a mild panic, eyes wide. "When's she getting here?"

"Manny's text said nine."

I wanted the general manager job. Wanted to run this place for real. But even if I didn't get the position, I would still develop new skills through this process. Maybe I'd take those skills to another restaurant in Silver Ridge or a nearby town. There were new ones opening all the time, like up at the ski resort my sister's man Dane owned.

It was time for me to take a step up in my career. Prove to Russ and Winnie and Zandra that I wasn't an irresponsible kid anymore, and I hadn't been for a very long time. This dick could and would stay in my pants, thanks very much.

Really, I didn't have a single thing to lose. I just had to deal with little miss grouchy, Zandra Alvarez, for a couple months.

How hard could that be?

I swiped a towel over the bar while Russ checked his watch. "Wait, nine o'clock? That's five minutes from now. I don't want her to see me talking to you as her first impression. She'll assume I've chosen your side."

"My side?"

"There's always sides in these grudge-match situations. Sorry, Callum. I have to be Team Zandra. When she's the boss, I'd like to keep my job."

I rolled my eyes. Nice to know I had such loyal work friends. "You could, you know, actually get some work done. That might also safeguard your job."

"Good idea." With a pat on my shoulder, Russ scurried back to the fermentation tanks in the other wing of the building.

Meanwhile, I dashed off to Manny's office to finish my bar order before Zandra arrived.

Russ wasn't the only one thinking about good impressions.

Let the competition begin.

It was only a minute or two past nine when I strolled into the bar again, a tablet tucked under my arm. Zandra was waiting there, facing away from me.

She looked just as gorgeous as yesterday. Same dark jeans, ankle boots. A different blazer, this one khaki, that accentuated the slim set of her shoulders and the flare of her hips.

And her trademark long braid was back. I imagined twirling it in my fingers. Or wrapping it in my fist while we...

Back up. No. I wasn't supposed to be having any more dirty thoughts about her. Or *any* women while I was at work. Manny had already brought it up once, and that was enough.

Too bad it would take rewiring my brain to keep my dirty mind fully at bay.

"Morning," I said. "Have you had coffee yet?"

"You're late."

I glanced at my watch. "It's 9:03."

"Yes. That's late. I wasn't sure if I should start without you."

"So sorry I kept you waiting. I guess you forgot we're slightly less uptight here in the mountains."

"I'm not uptight. But I have some standards. Also, my grandpa keeps texting for updates. He's—"

"Impossible? Trust me, I know. He'll get his update later. For now, coffee. I brought danishes too. Unless people with business degrees don't need caffeine and sugar. Can you just read a few pages of a management book and it charges you up like a battery?"

She made a sound that was part scoff, part laugh. "I'll take the first option. I'm mostly still human."

"Glad to hear it."

"So, where do you want me?"

Anywhere and everywhere, my brain shot back. Because my brain was very badly behaved. Bad dog.

She sighed. "You're reading something dirty into what I just said, aren't you?"

"I swear, I'm trying to be on good behavior."

"You could try harder."

I tilted my head noncommittally. "I could."

Gesturing for her to follow me, I led the way into the kitchen. The coffee was already brewing, and a few kitchen staff members were here to prep for lunch.

I introduced Zandra, then poured us each a mug. "Cream?" I asked.

"Just sugar. Unless there's any oat or almond milk around."

I shook my head. "We don't usually carry those." People didn't request them too often, and there was Silver Linings just down the street with every possible coffee drink known to the galaxy. "But I could grab some for you next time. Danish? I brought cream cheese and raspberry."

"No, thanks."

"They're good. Not poisoned either. I promise." Holding up the cream cheese danish, I wiggled it at her, making it dance.

"I don't want one," she said tightly. "Stop peer pressuring me."

"Your loss." I shoved half the danish into my mouth, washing it down with coffee.

Zandra stirred hers, then took a tentative sip. "So you're really on board with this plan? This two-month competition thing my grandpa dreamed up?"

I glanced at the kitchen staff, but they seemed to be busy and not listening to us. "Sure. I'm going to give it my best shot. May the best candidate win and all that. What about you?"

"Guess I have to be."

Her lack of enthusiasm irked me. Did she not think this job was worth the effort? "A brewpub probably seems small compared to whatever you were doing before now. Rocking the Chicago business world."

"You heard what my grandpa said. Things weren't going so well for me in Chicago. Any rocking was just me hitting rock bottom."

"Ouch. What happened?"

She glared. The silence stretched.

"Never mind," I said. "So, where are you staying? Your parents' place?"

"We don't have to do this, Callum."

"Do what?"

"The small talk."

"I'm not even allowed to know where you're staying? Is it a secret? Just wondered if you had far to drive."

"The drive is fine." Her pretty lips twisted. "I'm staying at the Pine Cone Motor Lodge."

"*That* place? Sketchy truckers stay there. If there's a motel serial killers would give five stars, it would be that one."

"Well, that's what I can afford right now," she snapped.

"Couldn't stay at Mommy and Daddy's mansion?"

Her expression froze. Then she pivoted and started back toward the doorway to the dining room.

Shit. "Wait." I grabbed her wrist. "I have a big mouth sometimes."

"You always have."

"If you're not staying with your parents, I'm sure you have reasons."

"Which aren't your business." She shook off my grip. "Can we just get started, please? Or do you have more comments to make about my personal life?"

"I'm done with the small talk segment. For now."

She gritted her teeth. "You're so obnoxious."

I grinned. Because, guilty as charged.

We were already in the kitchen, so I gave Zandra an overview. "Alice is our head chef. She'll be in later. She changes the menu every season, and when she does, we all taste the new dishes at our weekly team meeting. Same with any seasonal brews, which are Russ's domain. Not sure if you're familiar with our menu, but—"

"I took a look. It's actually not that different from when my nana was running the kitchen. I grew up hanging around here, and used to hostess in high school."

"Right." My friends and I hadn't been regulars at Hearthstone as teenagers. The food had been too expensive, and the only time we'd indulged in Hearthstone beer had been if somebody's older sibling bought it for us.

Yet another advantage she'd had over me. Not that I was counting.

Zandra played with the end of her braid as her gaze moved over the kitchen, and I wondered if she was picturing how it looked years ago.

I felt like I should say something. "Was it fun? Working here in high school?"

"I didn't always feel it at the time, but it was."

"The computer system's a bit more updated now. A lot of other things are probably the same."

"I assume this old building still has its quirks."

"Like the sticky lock in the back storage room. Gets stuck when you slam the door."

"*That* I remember." Her lips started to curve before she glanced at me, and she remembered herself.

After we finished in the kitchen, I took her to meet Russ. He shook her hand, his mouth open in a big shit-eating grin. "Great to see you, Zandra. It's been forever. We both went to—"

"Silver Ridge High," she finished for him. "There's a lot of us around here."

"I was a year below you and Callum."

For a moment, Zandra had looked amused. But now a crease appeared between her brows. "Same year as Leo Mackenzie, right?"

"Yeah. Terrible what happened to his family. I remember

when that's all anybody talked about." Then Russ stammered, "Fuck. I forgot you and Jessa were such good friends before she died. I shouldn't have brought it up."

Zandra wrapped her arms around her middle, and I felt the urge to reach out and steady her. Make sure she was okay. Because she looked so fragile right now, and that just called to my protective side.

But the hint of vulnerability disappeared as quickly as it had surfaced. "Can you show me around the brewery side of things, Russ?" she asked. "We should probably keep this tour moving."

"Yeah," Russ said on an exhale, clearly relieved at the change of subject. "You got it."

While Russ talked Z through the basics of Hearthstone's brewing operation, I stepped away to deal with some other tasks. About an hour later, Zandra found me in the bar again. The brewpub had opened for the day, but only a few diners had turned up so far. Things were quiet.

"Finished with Russ?" I asked.

"Yep. What's next?"

"I can give you a quick walkthrough around the bar. My domain." I opened my arms like I was showing off the narrow space we were in.

"Fits that you're the bar guy. You're one of the most extroverted people I've ever met. Everyone always liked you."

"Did you just pay me a compliment?"

"I was stating a fact." But coming from Zandra, it had sounded almost friendly.

I leaned my hip against the counter. After making sure nobody else was in earshot, I said, "Hey, I hope Russ didn't upset you earlier. When he mentioned Jessa Mackenzie."

She dropped her gaze to the tile floor. "Why would that make me upset?"

"Obvious reasons." I knew how formative memories, especially traumatic ones, could take hold and refuse to let go. "You *seemed* upset when Russ mentioned it."

"Well I wasn't."

"Jessa was your best friend. I just thought—"

"*Don't*," Zandra spit out. "Don't you dare talk about her."

Geez. She'd wielded that sentence like a knife, and I hadn't even known we were back to fighting.

"Okay. Forget I said anything." Time to get back to safer subjects, like work. "So, I made up a schedule for the next couple weeks. You can take turns shadowing me, then Russ, and then our back- and front-of-house managers." I pulled up my notes on my tablet. "For this afternoon, I was thinking—"

"I'm going to tackle Manny's computer files. I'll be in his office the rest of the day."

"But he said he wants us to work together," I said firmly. "Look, I'll be totally up front here. There's a lot I can learn from you."

"No kidding."

"But the opposite is also true. I understand you didn't like me in high school, and maybe I deserved that by generally being a cocky shit. A typical teenage football player. But that was forever ago, Zandra. I need to know you aren't going to punish me for it."

"*Punish* you? You think I'm going to sabotage your chances at getting the job?"

"That crossed my mind."

Zandra stepped closer, her lips plush and eyes furious. "You're such a hypocrite," she hissed. "I'm not cruel. I would never use my position of power to hurt someone else. Unlike *you*."

"What is that supposed to mean?" Because I was lost. "Is this... Are you talking about the bonfire party senior year?"

Her stare got even more murderous. "No, Callum. What I mean is, you need to stay away from me. You steer clear of me, and I'll steer clear of you." Zandra stalked away from me.

A minute later, I heard the door to Manny's office slam hard enough to rattle the frame.

"Great first day," I muttered to myself. "Two more months to go."

SEVEN
Zandra

Growing up, Hearthstone Brewing had been my favorite place in the world. I remembered one afternoon when I was around eleven years old. I'd fallen from my bike and scraped my knee. But I didn't think of going to Mom or Dad. No, it was Nana Julia I'd wanted.

As soon as I'd appeared in the Hearthstone kitchen, Nana left her staff to their own devices. She sat me down in Grandpa's office and cleaned up my knee. Wiped my tears. Then taught me to properly chop vegetables in the kitchen.

Somehow, she'd known that putting me to work was the way to make me feel valued. *Loved*.

Grandpa Manny had never been great with displays of emotion, but later that same day, he'd put my bike in his pickup and took me home, stopping at the local drive-through for fries on the way. Mom got mad at me for being gone all afternoon and spoiling my dinner, but it had been the best day.

Walking into Hearthstone now, a week after I'd started my "two-month trial" with Callum, I didn't feel any of those warm and fuzzies. More like a mix of dread and anticipation over seeing my nemesis.

Why did Callum O'Neal have to work here and ruin my one comfort zone in Silver Ridge?

"Afternoon." I nodded hello to Alice, the head chef, as I passed through the kitchen. I'd parked with the other employees in the rear lot, coming in through the back door.

"Hey, Zandra. I emailed you and Callum my thoughts for the specials next week. Manny told me to go through both of you, but *also* check everything with him. No offense, but three bosses is a lot."

I laughed. "I was just visiting Grandpa at the hospital this morning. I'll keep working on him. They should be releasing him to recover at home soon." The nurses had him up each day using his walker, but he'd also had some complications.

"Maybe that'll make him less of a pill."

"One can dream."

Over the past week, I'd been doing my best to get to know everyone here. I'd been soaking up as much knowledge as I could from shadowing the other managers. Callum had set up a good schedule for me, I had to admit. There was so much to learn.

Just so long as I didn't have to learn it from *him*.

A slender blond in a mini skirt and a pink tank top was already behind the bar when I approached. She squealed when she saw me, almost spilling the pint she'd been pouring from the tap.

"Zandra, is that really you?"

"It's me. Hey, Winnie."

"You remember me?" She finished the beer and set it in front of a customer.

"Of course. Also, I saw your name on the schedule, so..."

Winnie pointed at me. "Always the smart one. Get over here. I need a hug."

Winnie Peyton had been a couple years younger than Jessa and me in school. A cheerleader, not the usual person I would've spent time with outside of class. We hadn't been part of the same circles, and I doubted the cheer squad would've wanted to hang with me either.

But Winnie had dated Leo, Jessa's little brother. She'd been one of the few bright spots in my life after Jessa died. As in, she would actually talk to me without judgment and accusations in her eyes.

This was the hard thing about working at Hearthstone. This place was a minefield of memories, and some of them hurt so much more than the others.

Winnie pulled back from the hug, holding my arms. "I've been hearing for days about how you came back to town, but I didn't really believe it until I could see it for myself. You look so good!"

"So do you."

"Hardly. I look like a lady who got barfed on for three days straight and barely slept a wink the whole time. That's why I've had to keep calling in. My niece Ally was sick and my sister had nobody to watch her. She's already struggling to pay the bills so she couldn't take off work, you know? A lot of bosses would've told me tough luck because Ally's not my daughter, but not Callum."

My brow wrinkled. "I'm so sorry. Is Ally better? If you needed to take more time—"

"No, she's all set now. Ally's with her dad, my sister's asshole ex. He wouldn't lift a finger while Ally was throwing up, but at least he's good for watching her some of the time. He's sweet to her when it's convenient."

"I know a thing or two about asshole exes."

She nudged my arm sympathetically. "Even the big city girl has love trouble?"

"Former big city girl. Lost my job and my guy. I could write a country song about all the ways my life imploded."

"Then screw 'em, right? It's you and me working the bar tonight. We're going to have a blast."

I laughed. "Oh, I'm here for it. I've been getting an overview of Hearthstone's operations, but I haven't worked any shifts at the bar yet." Because I'd been avoiding anything that would mean dealing with Callum. He wasn't working tonight, though, so that meant I should be safe from his muscles and smirks and those expressive eyes.

Winnie's gaze moved over me, scrutinizing. "You've got comfy shoes. Good. That button-down won't work though. It gets hot as Hades back here when we're really moving. Tonight's trivia night, so it'll be packed."

"I have a camisole underneath." I started unbuttoning my shirt, and Winnie whistled.

"Take it off, girl! Tips will be better this way too."

Another laugh bubbled out of me. "Perfect. You just tell me what to do."

We dove straight into serving customers. I already had the beer, cocktail, and food menus memorized and was getting familiar with our computer system for ordering. But I paid close attention to every bit of info Winnie had for me.

I wouldn't regularly be tending bar as Hearthstone's general manager. But a good boss had to understand as many aspects of their business as possible. Also, I knew Grandpa was going to be quizzing me about anything and everything later. He didn't think any detail was too small.

When it came to the bar business, that was Callum's domain. The man had a major advantage. I had to make sure I knew just as much as he did.

"So, you and Callum, huh?"

"What?" I sputtered, turning to Winnie. "There is no me and Callum."

"I mean this competition thing Manny has going. Everybody's been talking about it. It's kinda wild. He's making his own granddaughter jump through all these hoops? Most people would want to keep a business like this in the family."

"Yeah. But that's my grandpa. Throwing challenges at us is his love language."

I wasn't even mad about this competition Grandpa had set up. I hadn't come to Silver Ridge expecting handouts. And I hadn't even realized how much I wanted this job until it was dangled in front of me, just out of reach.

Hearthstone wasn't some consolation prize after losing my way in Chicago. This place was home. I was going to earn it. Didn't matter who else was up against me.

Just…why did it have to be *him*?

I'd resisted letting Grandpa know about our feud. Instead, every time Manny asked how Callum and I were doing, I said all was fine. If and when I earned this job, it would be fair and square. Not by talking crap about Callum behind his back.

However. I could still gossip a little with Winnie. That wasn't crossing too many lines.

When there was a lull, I grabbed some limes and a cutting board to refill our fruit bin. "What's Callum like to work for?" I asked. "He's been bar manager for a while now, right?"

"Looking for the scoop on your competition?"

I wasn't going to deny it. "Do you blame me?"

She laughed. "Wish I had dirt to spill, but I don't. He's a good boss. Understanding. Responsible and keeps his end of things running smoothly. He's the best."

My knife paused. "*Really*?"

"Speaking of." Winnie elbowed me. "Look who's here on his night off."

My head swiveled until my eyes landed on a broad set of shoulders, narrow hips, and a backward ball cap.

Dammit. What was Callum doing here? I'd thought I was free from him tonight.

He was dragging a few tables together, making a bigger seating space. Like he expected a bunch of friends to join him. A couple minutes later, a big guy with a grumpy expression and dirty-blond hair joined him.

Winnie hummed knowingly. "I get it. That's Teller Landry."

"I remember him and his sister Piper."

"Yep. The Lonely Harts club must be getting together for trivia tonight."

"The *what* club?"

"Hon, you are so behind. I gotta catch you up."

Winnie explained that Callum, his siblings, and their friends and significant others often got together at Hearthstone. They called themselves the Lonely Harts club, whatever that meant.

"But the most exciting part," Winnie continued, blue eyes shining, "is that if Teller Landry's here, Ayla Maxwell must be in town too. There was all kinds of drama going on with her not long ago. She fell in love with Teller, who was the police chief until he quit to be with her. It's only the biggest news that's hit Silver Ridge since...*ever*."

"I heard about Ayla Maxwell and Teller Landry." Also something about a stalker attacking her, though everything had turned out all right. "But I didn't know *Callum* was friends with a mega-famous pop star," I said, pouring a beer for a customer while keeping an eye on my nemesis in my periphery. "I guess more has changed around here than I realized."

"Yes and no." Winnie hunched over, resting her arms casually on the counter. "Sometimes it feels like we're all still stuck in high school, you know?"

I huffed a laugh. "Trust me, I know."

"Callum is one of those guys who grew up a lot. He was in the Army for a while, like his older brothers, but then he came back home. Volunteers for the fire department. Helps out with his niece. Never dates anyone seriously. But he's always been someone I could count on."

Isn't that nice, I thought bitterly. It wasn't just my grandfather who Callum had charmed. My high school enemy was an upstanding citizen who made everyone's day brighter.

How was I supposed to square that with how awful he'd been to me after Jessa died?

Winnie leaned in conspiratorially. "Then you've got your washed-up types. The guys who've never gotten over the fact that their glory days are behind them. Like Tommy Pickering."

I followed her gaze to a table in a dark corner. "That's Tommy Pickering?"

Tommy had thought he ruled our campus back in the day, along with Callum. The two of them had sat across from Jessa and me in English class.

Now, his hair was thinning, with the few remaining strands combed over in a failed attempt to hide it. Tommy's skin was sallow. Heavy pouches lay below his eyes, and his shoulders slumped as he nursed a pint.

"Works at his dad's used-car dealership," Winnie murmured. "But from what I hear, Tommy hasn't made a sale in months. Married with a couple kids at home too. He spends more time in local bars than anywhere else."

"That's too bad." I'd never liked the guy, but I didn't wish his family ill.

Tommy seemed to sense our eyes on him, because his gaze flicked to us at the bar. He squinted and frowned before returning his attention to his half-empty beer.

Of course, seeing Tommy and Callum in the same room just reminded me of Jessa and the day she died.

"Do you ever talk to Leo Mackenzie?" I asked, my voice carefully casual.

Winnie looked surprised that I'd brought him up. "Leo and I dated a few more years after high school ended, but he was already so distant. After Jessa's death, he was—" She cut off, grimacing. "Sorry. I wasn't sure if you'd want to talk about Jessa. Losing her hit you really hard too back then."

A week ago, the last thing I'd wanted to do was talk about my best friend's death. I'd frozen up when Russ mentioned her on my first day at Hearthstone. And got pissed at Callum when he did the same.

But of all people, Winnie might understand how I felt. Even if she'd never been as close to Jessa as I had.

Trivia hadn't started yet, and business was just picking up. The glass washer had finished a load, so Winnie and I started to empty it during a lull in customers. “It’s hard to talk about Jessa,” I said, picking up the conversation. “But it’s also hard *not* to. You know what I mean?”

“Sort of. You must miss her.”

“I do.” So many times, I’d wondered where Jessa would be now. If we’d still be friends the way we’d promised one another.

I liked to think so.

“Leo was really torn up about his sister,” Winnie said. “Wouldn’t talk to anyone about it, even me. By the time we reached graduation a couple years later, all he wanted to do was leave town.”

All of that sounded painfully familiar.

“I would’ve gone with him, but...” Winnie lifted and lowered one bony shoulder. “He didn’t want that.”

I reached out to rub her arm. “I’m sorry. Must’ve hurt.”

“I haven’t seen Leo in...geez, years.” She sighed, glancing away, sadness written across her features. “We weren’t meant to be.”

Glasses clinked as I set them on the shelf. “I still think about their mom. I would stop by and visit Mrs. Mackenzie after Jessa died, but it was so awkward. For both of us. After I left Silver Ridge, I tried writing to her for a while, but I got distracted. Lost touch. That was shitty of me.”

“Anybody would’ve done the same. You had your new life, you know? I try to visit her when I can, but it’s tough. I can’t imagine what Ms. Mackenzie went through. Losing Jessa and then pretty much losing Leo too.”

My hand went still, poised halfway to the shelf. “Some things are impossible to get over,” I said softly.

The past had a way of reaching out and pulling us back, no matter how much time had gone by. No matter how much we tried to let it go.

For some reason, my eyes sought out Callum again.

Well, maybe I *did* know the reason. Because I hadn’t forgotten what Callum did to me back then, and I had no plans to forgive.

EIGHT
Callum

TRIVIA NIGHT at Hearthstone was always a good time. Especially on those rare occasions when the entire Lonely Harts club was present and accounted for.

I had every reason to be having a fantastic night.

My only problem? The gorgeous brunette behind the bar who kept glaring daggers at me.

"What's with the frown?" My brother Ashford plopped into the seat beside me. "Something to do with your coworker hating on you?"

"Who told you that?"

"Teller."

I shrugged. Couldn't believe Teller had narced on me. See if I had a heart-to-heart with the man again. "You know how it is," I said, taking a long pull from my beer. At least Teller had ordered a pitcher. "Some people just can't appreciate true charm and devastating good looks."

"What did you do to her?"

"*Nothing*."

My brother eyed me skeptically.

Aside from Zandra's frequent glares from the bar, we'd had a great night so far. I'd already had a chance to catch up with Teller, who I hadn't seen in at least a month and a half. The bastard was living the good life as the significant other of Ayla Maxwell, chart-topping singer extraordinaire. I'd jokingly called him Mr. Maxwell, and you should've seen the smug smile on the man's face.

Their bodyguard hovered nearby, making sure nobody uninvited got too close, but the other guests of Hearthstone had been well-behaved tonight. Just like me.

I'd stayed close to our table, relaxing with a few pints. Our team had dominated at trivia before Dane and Grace went over to the pool tables to face off against Emma and Piper. Ayla and her man were whispering lovingly into each other's ears.

Which left Ashford to harass me. Leave it to my big brother to pick at exactly what was bothering me.

"Zandra was in my high school class," I said, "and she hated me. You'd think she would've gotten over it in the last sixteen years, but no. The feelings are still fresh, apparently."

"And you're sure you didn't do anything to deserve it?"

"I...don't think so." Though God knew I'd tried to figure out what her problem was with me.

I'd racked my brain for the last week, going over every interaction we'd ever had. What I could remember, anyway. Sure, there was that time I'd stopped her from going to the first bonfire party our senior year. Same night Jessa Mackenzie died. I'd felt plenty guilty about that afterward.

But I'd already mentioned the bonfire party to Z, and she'd said that wasn't the issue. What else could I have done?

My brother leaned back in his chair, scrubbing a hand over his beard. "You can be pretty insufferable." This, from one of the grumpiest men in Hart County.

"Thanks for taking my side."

"You can't keep your mouth shut. Can't mind your own business either."

"I feel so supported, big brother. Really feeling the love."

"Like you need me to coddle you. Most people end up liking

you, anyway, even if I've never understood it. Do you really care that much if this woman doesn't?"

"*Yes.*" I slumped further into my chair. "The bigger issue is that we work together now, and she could take the general manager job right out from under me. She's Manny's granddaughter. She has a business degree and experience from living in Chicago."

"Easy solution." Ashford blew out a breath. "You just have to get rid of her."

Beer shot up into my nose, and I started coughing. "The hell, bro? Get rid of her?"

"I mean, just make sure she doesn't want to stick around in Silver Ridge. Remind her of all the reasons that this town sucks. She should go back to Chicago."

I sat back and laughed. "This town sucks? You love Silver Ridge so much, I remember the time you nearly decked some tourist for saying Vail has better skiing. Which it does, by the way."

Ashford scowled. "I take pride in my hometown. But there are plenty of reasons it can be miserable sometimes. You know it as well as I do."

"Such as?"

He held up his fingers to count the ways. "The small-town gossip mill is a pain in the ass. Cell reception is terrible, and the internet is so unreliable you might as well be living in the stone age. You can't get decent gelato to save your life."

"Gelato," I muttered, shaking my head as I took another sip of beer. "What do you know about gelato?"

"They've got a place now in Hartley. Tried it when we went to see Emma's family." Ashford chewed his lip. "No wait, *bingo night*. Make the city girl call bingo numbers at the community center for an hour and she'll run screaming. Or just stick her in a room with Dixie Haines."

Ashford's wife Emma appeared at our table, looking concerned. "What are you two saying about Dixie?"

"Ideas for how Cal can get rid of his work competition. City girl is gunning for the same manager position he wants."

Emma bent to peck her husband on the lips. "Reminds me of how you tried to get rid of *me* when I first moved here."

"Not like I tried very hard."

"I'm so glad you lacked commitment." She tugged on his arm to get him to stand. "Enough alcohol. We're going home now before you give Callum any more brilliant ideas."

"Good," my brother said in a low tone. "I have some brilliant ideas about you in our bed." Ashford kissed her again, more thoroughly this time. I glanced away, smiling at their happiness. I'd been rooting for my brother to wind up with Emma from minute one.

But his advice for me was terrible. I preferred to take a more direct approach.

Exactly what, I didn't know.

But somehow, someway, I was going to win that woman over. Even if it killed me. 'Cause she very well might.

A few hours later, the brewery had mostly cleared out. My baby sister Grace and her man had already taken off, and Teller and Ayla were saying their goodbyes to everyone. They'd been in their own little love bubble all night.

"See you soon, man," Teller said, pulling me into a hug.

"I can't keep up with where in the world you're jetting off to next."

"Just a quick trip to Nashville, then LA, then we're back here for at least a month."

"I'll believe it when I see it, Mr. Maxwell."

After they left, all my friends had scattered except for Piper, Teller's younger sister. The only other Lonely Hart who was committed to singlehood like me.

"Just you and me, kid," I said to her.

"Not for long." Piper grabbed her jacket from the back of her chair. "Ollie will be up at the crack of dawn wanting pancakes. Almost makes me look forward to him being a teenager. At least then he'll sleep in."

"Come on, one more drink."

"Nope." She gave me a quick kiss goodbye, purely platonic. Piper and I had never felt anything for each other romantically, but we were tight. "Besides, looks like you've got your hands full with that brunette you've been trading glares with all night."

With a groan, I glanced toward the bar where Zandra was drying glasses with more force than necessary. "Yeah, those aren't the good kind of looks."

"Maybe not, but there's definitely something there. Night, Cal."

After Piper left, I sat there nursing my beer and brooding. I could head home. Put my drama with Zandra behind me for the night. There were plenty of other bars in this county, filled with pretty tourists looking for a fun night.

Yet I didn't leave my seat.

What the hell was Zandra's problem with me, really?

Since the day she'd started, she'd been avoiding me and making no secret about it. When I walked into a room, she suddenly realized she had other places to be. She'd refused altogether to shadow me for a shift at the bar, acting like any knowledge I could offer was beneath her.

Instead, she'd been holed up in Manny's office studying his contracts and vendor lists without including me.

It was pissing me off.

Zandra claimed she wouldn't sabotage my application for the manager job. I wasn't so sure I believed her. But even if she changed her mind and went back to Chicago, she could leave a poison pill behind by telling her grandfather what a tool she thought I was.

But the more I thought about it, the more I wondered *why* it bothered me that much that she didn't like me. Was it really just about the job?

No, it felt like more than that.

When she avoided me, it made me feel...*crazy*.

What had she meant the other day about me being cruel? I could be insensitive without meaning to, but cruel just wasn't me. The whole situation was itching at me from the inside out. Like some kind of mental poison ivy I couldn't stop scratching.

Enough was enough.

I waited until after closing. "I thought you weren't working tonight," one of the expos said as he perched chairs upside down on the tables. Nearby, another staff member swept up.

"Can't pull myself away." I helped with closing tasks, pretty sure Zandra hadn't noticed I was still here.

A little while later, I heard Winnie call out, "Night, Zandra," as she grabbed her purse from behind the bar. "See you tomorrow."

"Have a good night," Zandra replied from the kitchen, her voice carrying that warm tone she used with everyone but me.

Then Winnie's footsteps faded and the back door clicked shut. I said goodbye to the last stragglers in the kitchen.

It was just me and Zandra left now.

Showtime.

I found her in the back storage room. Which couldn't have been more perfect. An idea popped into my head. I stepped inside, swiped the key ring from its hook on the wall, and slammed the door shut behind me.

Zandra jumped and looked up from the clipboard she was holding.

"We need to talk," I said.

The storage room was cramped, filled with bathroom supplies and stuff we had no other place for. Even in the harsh overhead light, my brain stuttered for a brief moment over how ridiculously gorgeous she was. The eyes and that long hair...

She set the clipboard on a shelf. "Talk about *what*, Callum?"

"About why you don't like me. Real truth this time."

"I just don't. Can I get by, please? I'm finishing up."

She tried to go past me, but I blocked her way. "Everyone likes me. Unless they have a specific reason not to."

"Maybe I have a specific reason."

"Such as?"

"If you don't have the self-awareness to figure that out, I can't help you."

Great. She was doing that thing where women get mad at a guy because he doesn't know why she's mad, which made my head hurt thinking about it. "Just *tell me*. Please."

"It really bothers you, doesn't it? That I don't find you charming. Or attractive."

I pretended nonchalance, but my defensiveness was rising. "I already apologized for hitting on you. But let's be honest. These genetics can't be denied. I'm just working with what God gave me here."

"You are so arrogant," she seethed.

"You have your moments, believe me."

"And you act so entitled."

"*Me*? You've always had everything." I said this in a mild tone, because I wasn't criticizing, though my blood was definitely up. "Your two rich parents and your fancy business degree. I'm a lot of things, but entitled ain't it."

"Says the guy who was part of a famous singer's entourage tonight."

"I've worked my ass off for—"

"So have I!" she protested. "You don't know a thing about my life."

"Maybe not, but you can't claim to know anything about mine."

Zandra tried to get around me again, and this time she squeezed past me to the door. But when she jiggled the handle, nothing happened. "You idiot. You locked us in!"

I shrugged, because yeah, I'd locked us in. She wasn't getting out of this conversation. Not this time.

Zandra's scowl when she turned around said she knew it too. "We talked about the sticky lock in this storage room the other day. What the hell? Why did you do that?"

"To force you to talk to me. It's been days, and I'm sick of you avoiding me."

"So you locked me in a storage closet with you?" Her eyes went wide with disbelief, and she grabbed a toilet plunger from the shelf, holding it out like she was brandishing a sword.

The sight was so ridiculous I had to bite back a laugh.

"Feel free to call 9-1-1," I said.

"My phone's in my purse. In the office."

"Then use mine. We can both explain our sides of the story to the dispatcher. But while we're waiting for an officer to show up, we'll have at least five or ten minutes to talk. That's all I want. Just tell me what you think I did."

She dropped the plunger. "Why do you care so much? I already told you I'm not going to talk shit about you to my grandfather. I'm going to be fair."

"It's because I care what you think."

"Since *when*?" She paced the room like a caged tiger, though she could only take about two steps in each direction before hitting a wall or a shelf.

"I've always cared what you think. Even back in high school. You were..." I trailed off, thinking about how she'd been the smartest girl I knew in our class. Not just book smart. She could think on her feet, and she was funny. Sometimes damn near mesmerizing.

"You weren't like anyone else in our class," I finished. "You were *more*."

Zandra stopped, the anger draining away and leaving pure confusion in its wake.

Then suddenly, she looked so sad that I had to force down the urge to pull her into my arms to somehow make this better.

But she didn't stay frozen in place for long. She advanced, poking my chest with her finger. "You want to know my problem with you, O'Neal?"

My back hit the shelving unit. "That's what I've been asking."

"Then I'll tell you." Her eyes shone with sudden renewed fury. "You made my life hell after Jessa died."

"Hold on, I did *what*?"

"You spread rumors that her death was *my fault*. You already didn't like me, so you did the most hurtful thing possible. Just because you could. You were the golden boy, so everyone listened like it was gospel. And because of that..." She swallowed. "Because of *you*, people at our school were awful to me."

Zandra's body heaved, as if it had taken real effort to get all those words out. Yet confusion didn't begin to cover what I was feeling.

"But I didn't do anything like that. I have no idea what you're talking about."

"Tommy Pickering told me it was you who'd spread the rumors. He taunted me about it."

"*Tommy*?" Rage flared in my chest so hot and sudden I saw red for a second. Tommy had never been my favorite person, not even in our high school days when we'd technically been friends. But if he'd done something like this and pinned it on me...

I mean, what the hell? Why?

"Now you're Mr. Volunteer Firefighter. Everybody's favorite bartender. But I know the truth. You want to act like the past didn't happen, but it *did*."

"Zandra, listen to me. Tommy was lying. I have no idea why he would do that, but I swear to you, that's what happened."

"Right. Of course you'd say that."

"I swear on my mom's grave that I would never have spread rumors about you, especially not involving Jessa. *Never*."

Zandra took a step back, as if she was finally hearing me.

"Yes, I disinvited you from the bonfire party that one time. It was stupid and immature." I couldn't explain my reasons without sounding like even more of an ass. "I got up in my feelings. But we all knew how Jessa's death tore you up after that. I would never have done anything on purpose to make things worse for you. *Ever.*"

Something in my tone must have convinced her, because her shoulders sagged and she slumped against the closed door, looking exhausted and heartbroken.

A tear slipped free down her cheek.

Fucking hell.

The fight went out of me completely. I almost pulled her close to comfort her, but that would probably get me a knee to the balls. Instead, I pulled the key from my pocket and unlocked the door.

Then she seemed to process what had just happened, and her eyes flashed with renewed indignation. "Wait. You had the key? This *whole time*?"

"It usually hangs on the wall." I pointed at the empty hook. "Right there. In case people accidentally close the door too hard."

"You asshole."

"Come on. You've locked me out of Manny's office plenty of times in the last few days."

"I'm going home," she said, pushing past me into the hallway. "Before you can come up with any new, creative ways to torture me."

"Zandra—"

"Please, Callum." She sniffled, wiping her face. "Just let me go." Her voice was so small and sad. So I stood there and watched her leave, feeling like shit.

Maybe I hadn't done what she thought I did in high school. But tonight, I definitely felt like the bad guy.

NINE
Zandra

THE DOORS of Main Street Market slid open with a gentle whoosh, releasing the comforting scent of fresh bread and the faint hum of refrigeration units.

Inside, the store was a picture of perfectly imperfect charm. A bulletin board by the entrance was crammed with everything from babysitting ads to lost cat flyers, and the overstuffed aisles were just barely wide enough for two carts to fit past.

The familiarity of it all was just the balm I needed this morning.

Spotting Rosie behind the customer service desk, I made a beeline there. "Hey, Auntie."

"Baby Z!" Rosie's magenta curls bounced as she reached out to hug me, and she waved me around to join her behind the desk. A sheet of wax paper lay by the computer with a slice of gooey coffee cake. "Want to share some breakfast? Oh, hold on." She bit her lip. "The gluten. Wait here. I can go grab you something else."

I touched her arm to stop her. "Not that hungry, but thank you for remembering. I need a different favor today, actually. A bigger one."

Her eyes lit up. "Anything for you. What do you need?"

"Any chance you have space for me and Chloe at your house?"

Once again, I hadn't slept well at the Pine Cone Motor Lodge. I'd had that feeling again of being watched after getting home so late from the brewery last night. And then people were shouting in the parking lot at four in the morning. I was *done* with that place.

I'd even moved a piece of furniture in front of the motel room door to block it, which was probably not the safest idea if there'd been a fire or something. That whole place looked like it was made of popsicle sticks.

But the other small issue that hadn't helped me sleep? My disastrous conversation with Callum in the storage room.

I didn't know where to begin with what he'd said last night. Rewriting sixteen years of what I'd believed to be true. My mind was spinning in circles trying to make sense of it. Of Callum not being the sadistic asshole I'd believed.

So, naturally, I was focusing my efforts on something else instead.

"Only for a few days until I find something more permanent," I added. "I just can't take the Pine Cone anymore."

I'd left my car parked down the block with Chloe in her cat carrier and all the windows cracked. My trunk held the sum of my belongings, since I'd checked out of the motel this morning with absolutely no intention of going back.

Thankfully it was a perfect sixty-eight degrees outside today. Not a trace of humidity, unlike sweaty summer months in Chicago. I'd missed summer in the mountains.

"Of course, Z! Jimmy and I would love to have you." Then Rosie paused, her expression shifting just slightly. "Keep in mind, Jimmy's a night owl."

"Yeah?"

Rosie lowered her voice conspiratorially. "Well, he keeps me up. That's all I'm saying. But then he's up at five-thirty for his tai chi routine in the living room."

Stay optimistic, I told myself. *They're doing you a favor.* "Tai chi sounds nice. Maybe I'll join. Stress relief would be good for me."

"Jimmy would love that. Usually he does it naked, but I'll ask him to put on a robe or something."

I felt my face scrunch up involuntarily, though I tried to keep my voice pleasant. "That would be good."

"And then he does his chanting."

"Chanting?"

"Kind of a medieval monk thing, I guess? It's very relaxing and melodic."

"That's...unique." Wouldn't have expected it of Jimmy Perkins, either. From what I remembered, he seemed more like the grizzled hermit type. But if he made Rosie happy...

I glanced out the window and saw Callum walking by, of all people. *Gah.* He stopped in his tracks, backing up to stare at me through the window.

I looked away quickly.

"And after that, when Jimmy's all loose and feeling the good vibes, well, you'd probably be off to the brewery by then, right?"

Oh lord. "I'll make it work. I won't be in your way. I can pay rent."

"The guestroom used to be a closet. Couldn't in good conscience charge you money for it."

This just kept getting better and better.

But if Rosie was willing to take me and Chloe, then I couldn't exactly complain. It was only temporary anyway. Grandpa was paying me right now for the hours I put in, so I'd be able to afford a cheap apartment lease soon. Especially if I found a roommate.

Once I had the general manager salary, I'd have far more flexibility. I *had* to get that job.

I glanced at the window, exhaling when Callum was gone. Thank you. I couldn't deal with him again so soon.

"Here's a spare key so you can move your things over," Rosie said, digging around in her purse and producing a key ring shaped like a miniature shopping cart. "Just make yourself at home."

"Thanks, Auntie. I'll pick up a few things to help stock your fridge while I'm here."

"How sweet of you." She kissed my cheek. "Grab whatever you need, and the next time I do a shop myself, I'll be sure to get lots of gluten and dairy free."

"That would be great. I really appreciate it."

Grabbing a cart, I wheeled to the produce section. This was going to be good. And if the Jimmy-and-Rosie dynamic was a little...intense, I could manage anything for a few days, right?

A bag of pre-washed greens went into my cart. A couple apples. Then I looked up and found Callum O'Neal perusing the veggies across from me.

"What are you doing here?" I asked before I could tell my mouth to hold back the words.

He smirked. "Building a nuclear reactor." He tossed a Granny Smith in the air and caught it. "You?"

Nope. *Do not engage.*

At some point, I'd have to deal with him again, but not right now. Not after crying in front of him last night.

Yet I couldn't stop my eyes from checking what he was doing as we both meandered through the produce section. Callum held up a butternut squash with an exaggerated questioning expression, as if asking for my opinion.

When I pointedly looked away, he moved on to a bundle of asparagus, examining it like it held the secrets of the universe. Next was a couple of limes, which he rolled around in his palm while raising his eyebrows at me expectantly.

Oh. My. God.

I kept my face carefully neutral, though I could feel the corners of my mouth threatening to betray me.

And damn it, even when he was being completely ridiculous, he still managed to look hot. His dark hair peeked messily from under his backward cap, and those gray joggers showed off the exact slope of his glutes. And the bulge in front...

Making a choked sound in my throat, I escaped to the cereal

aisle. Time to study the gluten-free options and try to pretend my pulse hadn't quickened from ogling him.

Yet when I turned around, there Callum was again, just a few feet away with his handcart hanging from his fingers. Nothing was in it.

"You're following me," I said.

"I'm doing some shopping."

"Can you pick a new aisle?"

"Nope. This one's got what I need." He grabbed something randomly from the shelf.

"You need Bran Bites?"

"Yep, my fave."

"A lot of people would find this creepy. Especially after you locked me in a storage closet with you last night. At our workplace."

"But you *don't* find it creepy?" he asked hopefully.

My mouth opened, words failing me.

If he were any other guy, he would've been throwing off so many red flags I'd be worried about a bull stampede. But somehow, no matter how obnoxious he was, Callum never came across as threatening.

It was kind of like being stalked by a mischievous golden retriever.

I just sighed and went to the next aisle. Callum followed, picking up a jar of pasta sauce and holding it up. "What do you think of this brand?"

I didn't look. "Not a fan."

"Good to know." He put it back on the shelf, then picked up a bag of pasta. "Regular or whole wheat? Yay or nay?"

"Are you seriously going to ask my opinion on every item in the store?"

"Only the important ones." He grinned, and I felt that traitorous smile tugging at my lips again.

"I don't eat pasta," I heard myself saying. "Unless it's gluten free."

"Ah. The picture is becoming clearer."

"Is it?"

"Do you have celiac?"

"No. But I do have an allergy."

When I turned a corner and continued walking, he made a sound of protest. "You skipped the milk and the cheese back there. We need that aisle."

"Do what you like. *We* are not shopping together."

Then he actually grabbed onto my cart and wheeled it where he wanted.

"Callum!"

I found him loading up on Greek yogurt, with his cart in hand and mine beside him. "I skipped this aisle because I'm allergic to dairy," I protested. "I sometimes do almond milk, but I wasn't planning on it until I see how much room is in Rosie's fridge."

He picked up a carton of something to examine the label. "Coconut yogurt? What about that?"

"I don't like it."

"So is this why you hardly eat anything at the brewery when we're working? The dairy thing? And the gluten?"

I nodded. "I'm also allergic to raw mango, kiwi, and cucumbers."

"Damn. That sucks. Did you talk to Alice about it? I'm sure our head chef can make stuff that works for you."

"I just don't like making a whole issue of it."

Callum looked down into his basket with a suddenly serious expression, studying the labels on everything he'd collected. "Don't move. I'll be right back. Need to put some things away."

"Why?"

He loped off without answering, returning after a minute or two. And for some reason, I was standing there waiting for him.

Because we really were shopping together now. I had no idea how this had happened.

When he returned, he asked, "You're staying with your aunt now? You're out of the serial killer motel?"

Right. I'd just mentioned my aunt's fridge. I regretted giving him those details. "*Yes*, I'm staying with Rosie now."

He nodded thoughtfully. "Been thinking about what you told me last night."

I groaned. "I'm not ready to talk about that yet."

But of course, Callum forged ahead. He turned to face me, his bulk blocking my exit from dairy land. "I understand now why you hated me. You thought I was the worst kind of asshole bully, and I get that now. But just so we're clear, next time I see Tommy Pickering, I'm going to find out why he said the shit he did. If he was bullying you in high school, that's not okay."

I sighed. "I don't want you to."

"Why?"

"I just want to put it all behind me. Like I should've done a while ago. What happened back then doesn't matter."

Ha. I was so full of it. Those wounds ran a lot deeper than anything Callum might've caused. But I didn't want to share the rest of what happened our senior year.

"You do believe me, though?" he asked. "I didn't do what you thought."

"Yeah, I believe you." I'd spent all these years thinking that Callum was one of the villains. The whole thing was confusing. But to my surprise, I didn't have a doubt that he'd told me the truth.

Other doubts, sure. But not about this.

"Good." He seemed genuinely relieved. "So you'll stop avoiding me at Hearthstone? We can work together? Or I can keep following you around and bugging you..."

"Callum," I groaned.

"*Zandra*. I'm not going to let up."

Maybe there was a reason everyone else in Silver Ridge seemed to like this man.

Either way, there was no use fighting him. On top of everything else, I didn't have the energy for it.

"I'll work with you. Sorry I was so difficult."

He grinned. "Difficult? *You*? I hadn't noticed."

I chuckled, the stress of everything lifting another few degrees.

We continued around the store, and he asked, "So what do you actually eat? Besides quinoa and broccoli and shit?"

I rolled my eyes, though his grin said he'd been kidding. "I like the usual things. I just have to worry about cross-contamination. So eating out at restaurants can be hard unless I trust the kitchen."

"Why didn't you mention your food allergies before, though? Especially when I shoved danishes in your face. My bad for that. A lot of people have food issues these days, and at the brewery, we've been talking about modernizing the kitchen for a while."

"Because I was diagnosed in college, and my parents never wanted to be bothered with it. Same with my ex." Even though our business had been built around modernizing systems to help people with food allergies. Only the money had mattered to him. "I'm used to people not caring."

"Then your parents are jerks. And your ex is a dick."

A giggle snuck into my throat. "You might just be right."

We reached the checkout counter. Callum unloaded his basket. Bran Bites, some gluten-free pancake mix, and a carton of coconut yogurt.

"That's all you're getting?" I asked. "Really needed to shop, huh?" I was unloading my items on the belt, along with the reusable bags I'd brought.

"Yep, I was all out of pancake mix."

"More like you wanted to harass me."

He grinned. "Worked, didn't it?"

The checkout girl, who couldn't have been older than twenty-one, practically purred when she saw Callum approach. "Find everything you needed today?" She batted her eyelashes so hard I was surprised she didn't create a small breeze.

He up-nodded. "Sure did."

"Ex-girlfriend?" I whispered.

"Don't really have any of those."

"A hookup?"

"She's a bit young for me." He winked. "But a lady never tells."

After we'd both paid, Callum hefted all our bags before I could protest. When we were finally outside, he said, "Rosie's place is just around the corner, I believe?"

"Yes. So you can give me my stuff. I'll see you later at Hearthstone."

"Nope, I'll carry this for you now."

"I can carry my own groceries."

"But that would deprive you of my company."

I made a sound somewhere between a growl and a sigh, hurrying to catch up with his longer stride. Chloe was still waiting in my car, but I'd parked her close to Rosie's place anyway.

"So you're really staying with Rosie and Jimmy." His eyebrows lifted. "That's adventurous of you."

"My options are limited at the moment."

"My roommates and I live in a big house. Rent's affordable when we split it up. We've got an extra room open, if you're looking."

"My cat won't like you."

"Your cat? Is that a euphemism?"

"Big word for you."

"Are you impressed yet?"

"Nope." But I wasn't feeling nearly as annoyed as before.

Heaven help me, but for the first time since I'd arrived in Silver Ridge, I was actually having fun.

TEN

Callum

HOLDING OUR BAGS OF GROCERIES, I waited on the porch while Zandra knocked loudly on the door. "Jimmy? Hello? Anyone home?"

The house was a cheerful yellow craftsman with white trim and a wraparound porch. Cute. Even the mailbox had hand-painted daisies on it. I shifted the bags to one arm and braced them against my hip.

"I guess Jimmy isn't home." Zandra took out a key and unlocked the door. Then cracked it open and peered slowly inside like the bogeyman might jump out.

"Everything okay?" I asked with a grin. She was being pretty adorable.

"Just checking. I didn't know if he was doing naked tai chi or something."

"He's doing *what*?"

"Never mind." Zandra opened the door wider. "Any chance you could take the groceries inside while I go get Chloe? I parked close, and she's in her cat carrier with all the windows open, but..."

"No worries. Do your thing. I've got this."

Zandra looked at me skeptically, like she wasn't sure she could trust me yet. But then she nodded gratefully. "Thanks, Callum. I'll be right back. I, um, I appreciate it."

She dashed off, and I felt a surge of satisfaction.

Ha. *See, Ashford?* I thought. No need to get rid of her. I'd won her over, and I'd done it in style. It was clear Zandra didn't let people in easily, which just made me want to open her up all the more. All puns intended.

Yeah, there was the fact that I was attracted to her and couldn't help flirting shamelessly, but it wasn't just about that. Wasn't just about our two-month trial period either.

Zandra was complicated, and I liked that about her. Plus she clearly had some unresolved issues about our high school days, and I found myself wanting to smooth those rough edges.

Maybe it was the firefighter side of me. When I saw someone hurting, it was impossible not to charge in.

I headed inside the house, pausing immediately in the entryway.

Ceramic gnomes were perched on every available surface. Fishing gnomes on the mantelpiece, gardening gnomes clustered around potted indoor plants, reading gnomes propped against books on shelves. I blinked hard, wondering if I was having some kind of hallucination.

Nope. Still there. A hundred of them, grinning their creepy ceramic grins.

Shaking off my shock, I headed in and found the kitchen. More gnomes. Rosie was really committed to the theme. A few of them did look like Jimmy, though. Might explain some things.

I opened the fridge and started unloading the groceries from the bags, doing a bit of rearranging to get things to fit.

Zandra returned a couple minutes later. "Hey, could you give me a hand?"

I jogged to the front door and fount her rolling two suitcases with one hand and carrying a cat carrier in the other. She looked like she was about to fall over. "I'll take the luggage." Reaching forward, I snagged the two suitcases and hauled them inside.

Zandra knelt on the tiled entryway and opened the carrier door. A blur of orange fur shot out like a fuzzy missile, disappearing around the corner in a desperate bid for freedom.

"I'm sorry, baby girl," Zandra cooed in a soft, sing-song voice that was completely different from her usual tone. "You're safe now, sweet Chloe. Mama's gonna get you all settled in your new place."

My grin just kept growing. "So there really is a cat."

Zandra stood, giving me a wry look. "She's mad right now, but she'll come around later."

"That sounds familiar. Does that kind of sweet talk work with you too?"

Zandra actually laughed, and the sound sent warmth shooting through my chest. "Don't try it," she warned.

I just shrugged, committing all this to my memory for later.

Zandra looked around like she was just noticing the decorating theme in the living room. "Is it just me, or are there about a million eyes on us right now?"

"This is what happens when you do all your decorating at Ye Olde Gift Shoppe on Main Street. One day you're buying a cute lawn ornament, and the next thing you know, you're living in Santa's workshop."

She glanced into the kitchen next. "Thanks for putting the groceries away. It all fit?"

"It did. After a little organizing. I am a man of many talents." I leaned casually against the kitchen counter and watched as Zandra walked around, peering into different doorways. Like many houses in Silver Ridge, especially historic ones near Main Street, the place wasn't that big.

"I guess this is the guestroom. Rosie did say it was small."

I followed close behind, looking over her shoulder through the doorway. "Yikes. Looks like one of those rooms where a serial killer keeps his victims."

She glanced back at me. "What is the deal with you and serial killers?"

"I like true crime stuff. The darker, the better."

"Should I be worried?"

I was standing less than an inch behind her, close enough that I got a whiff of her powdery scent. My pulse kicked up a notch. "I'd be more worried about those gnomes watching you while you sleep all night."

She shuddered. "Don't even start with that."

"Okay, we'll talk about something else instead. Come on. Follow me."

"Where are you going?" Zandra asked.

"You'll see." I headed back into the kitchen, opening the freezer and taking out the pint of oat milk ice cream Zandra had bought at the grocery store.

"You're stealing my dessert? I was saving that for later, when I'm all depressed and hiding out in my serial killer room."

I barked a laugh. "It's a taste test. Introduce me to the world of dairy-free dessert. We might want to carry it at Hearthstone. Besides, we'll need a snack to share while we talk." I searched around in the kitchen drawers until I found two spoons.

"We talked enough."

"Nope. We didn't."

"Have I told you I hate you? I really do."

"Not anymore. You like me now."

"I can't tell if we're hanging out," she muttered, "or if this is a hostage situation. What is even happening?"

"Just go with it."

Zandra followed me outside onto the back deck. Probably because I linked my pinky around hers and tugged her through the doorway. But she let me. That was key.

I sat on the top of the picnic table, resting my feet on the bench, and pulled Zandra up to sit beside me. Tugging the lid off the ice cream, I handed Zandra a spoon, then dug mine in.

The salted caramel was rich and creamy, with just enough salt to balance the sweetness. "Not bad. Really good, actually. I thought it was going to taste like oatmeal or something. I mean, I like oatmeal, but it's not exactly indulgent."

Zandra scooped some of the dessert onto her spoon and took a bite. I watched her pink tongue flick out to catch a drop that clung to the spoon, and heat pooled low in my stomach.

I dug my spoon in again. "Sounds like senior year was really rough for you after Jessa died."

"*Callum*," she whispered. "Please, can we not."

This time, I didn't push. Didn't say a word. Just took another bite of ice cream and waited.

A good two minutes later, Zandra started talking.

"She was my best friend. I can't describe how awful it was when she died. Then people started talking." Zandra blinked, looking away.

"The rumors?"

"People said I'd gotten into a fight with Jessa over a guy, and she was trying to get away from me, and I pushed her into the creek. None of that was true."

"Shit." I'd heard some of that, contradictory stuff about Zandra and Jessa being careless or inviting guys to meet them at the creek, but I hadn't put much stock in it either way. It was just a tragic accident. "And you thought I was behind the rumors. Because of what Tommy said."

She nodded. "Maybe that was naive of me. The rumors could've come from anywhere."

"Could've been Tommy himself. He was enough of an ass that I'd believe it. I was an idiot for ever being friends with him."

Zandra had said she wanted to let it go because it was in the past. But the next time I saw Tommy, he was going to have some questions to answer. It made me furious to think that anyone would try to hurt her intentionally. Especially after what she'd already gone through.

Maybe I should've been more cynical by now about how much people sucked. But they always found new ways to disappoint me.

"The thing was, Jessa really had planned to meet a boy she liked at the creek that night. Someone from the Silver Ridge football team."

"Huh. You didn't know who?"

She shook her head. "Jessa wouldn't tell me. At the creek, I was away from her for a few minutes, and I heard someone else's voice." Z's gaze moved to the distance. "*Thought* I did. But the police said I was wrong. There was no evidence anyone else had been there. No football players suspiciously missing from the bonfire party. That anyone admitted, anyway."

I did remember the police asking around about the party and who was there. "Do *you* think you were wrong?"

"I don't know. But regardless of those stupid rumors, it really did feel like my fault. I'd brought the beer. I'd left Jessa alone by the creek." Z stuck her spoon vigorously into the pint while I held it steady. "When people started talking about me, saying I pushed her or something, it just made it all worse."

"It wasn't your fault."

After Jessa had died, I'd felt guilty already for keeping Zandra from the bonfire that night. Because if she and Jessa had come to that party, things might've turned out differently. They wouldn't have been at the creek.

But there'd been a lot of stuff going on for me as well. My home life as a kid had never been easy. But I wasn't going to bring that up and make this conversation about me. Wasn't going to make excuses for myself either.

"I noticed how you withdrew from everyone," I added. "I should've said something." Even if I'd been an idiot teenager myself and hadn't known how to handle my own experiences with grief, much less Zandra's. Even now, I still wasn't all that great with the heavy stuff.

"It's okay, Callum. You and I weren't friends."

"That doesn't matter. I should've tried to help. Made sure you were okay."

"There was no way I could've been okay after losing her." She smiled ruefully, then announced, "I need more ice cream."

"Rest is yours." I handed her the carton, which had about a quarter left.

"So generous of you. Considering it was mine in the first place."

My grin was dazzling. "I'm just that kind of guy."

She took a huge bite, then winced. "Ouch," she said, mouth full. "Shouldn't have done that."

"Ice cream headache?"

"Oh yeah."

"My mom had a trick for that when I was a kid." I gently massaged the top of her head with my fingers. Zandra tensed, and I pulled back. "Sorry. Should've asked first."

She was still holding herself tightly, but her shoulders lowered a bit. "It's okay. Go ahead. It was...nice."

My fingers trailed down to her neck to work into the tightness there. Zandra moaned softly, and the sound shot straight through me to my dick.

I imagined my hands exploring other places, finding all the spots that would make her moan again. All the pleasure I could give her. With my mouth. My cock.

"He had a thing for you," I blurted.

"What? What are you talking about?"

"Tommy Pickering. That's why he wanted you to come to the bonfire that night. Why he brought it up in our English class. He was into you. Tommy didn't deserve you. That's why I put a stop to it."

"You stopped me from becoming Mrs. Pickering? I'll never forgive you."

I snickered. "Look at you, making jokes."

"I make plenty of jokes." Her arm brushed against me as she shifted. "Besides, if Tommy had tried anything back then, I would've kicked his genitals so hard he'd be coughing them up."

"*Ouch*. Vivid image."

"I didn't need you to defend my honor."

"Trust me, my reasons would've been more selfish than that." I still had my hand on the back of her neck. Something possessive and ugly twisted in my chest, which was weird. I'd never been jealous over another girl. Nobody but Z. "I might've had a little crush on you."

She gaped at me. "Liar," she scoffed. "You had cheerleaders and popular girls falling all over you."

"The one has nothing to do with the other."

"You barely ever said anything nice to me."

"I said hi to you all the time."

"In a smarmy, borderline harassment kind of way."

"Come on, now. I was being cute and flirty! I'm never smarmy. I'm adorable."

Zandra laughed. "You're ridiculous is what you are."

"Look, you were one of the prettiest girls in our class. One of the smartest too. It was only natural I'd respond to that. And I do plenty of stupid things, but I don't lie."

Her dark eyes studied me, and then she swallowed. "I get that. Um, I'm better now."

"Better?"

"The ice cream headache. Thanks."

"Ah." I lowered my hand, resting it on the table behind her and angling my body toward her. "What about you? Were you into me in high school?"

She snorted. "Absolutely not."

"Who's the liar now?"

"I wasn't into you," she insisted.

"Then how do you explain all the tension between us every day in English class?"

We'd been leaning closer as we talked, and in the sunlight, the details of her stood out. The way her dark lashes cast shadows on her cheeks, the tiny freckle beside her lips.

We were just centimeters apart. All I had to do was inch forward slightly, and I could taste her. My heart hammered against my ribs as I imagined how soft her lips would be. How she might sigh against my mouth.

"Callum," she whispered, eyes wide. "What are you doing?"

Shit. Just like that, the moment was over, and I sat back.

It would've been foolish to kiss her, and not just because she didn't want me to. We were competing for the same manager position. We were supposed to work closely together for the next couple months.

Worse yet, it could get back to her grandfather if we messed around and it didn't end well. Bad idea.

But sometimes the bad ideas were the most fun...

I stood up, brushing off my sweats. "Guess I should take off. Thanks for the ice cream. Gotta get home and change before my shift at the bar. See you at Hearthstone in a bit?"

"Yeah. I'm ready for you to teach me everything you know."

"Only if you teach me all the numbers shit."

"Yep. Numbers shit. My favorite course in business school."

Grinning, I headed back inside, putting our dirty spoons in the sink and the carton in the trash, and then went for the door.

"Don't forget your groceries."

When I turned around, Zandra was holding out the bag with my cereal, the weird yogurt, and the pancake mix.

"Right. My super important groceries that I was very eager to get." I took them from her.

Her dark lashes fluttered, and she tugged her lower lip with her fingers. Damn, she was pretty. "See you later, Callum."

"Bye, Z. See you later."

I'd called her Z. And she didn't even complain about it.

ELEVEN
Callum

Piper looked up from behind the counter, her blond hair escaping from its messy bun. "So you *do* still live in Hart County. I was starting to wonder."

"Ha. Very funny."

"Haven't seen you since trivia night when the Lonely Harts club was all together. Where've you been hiding?"

"Just busy with work." I rested my hands on the counter, perusing the chalkboard menu over Piper's head.

Silver Linings Coffee occupied a cozy corner spot on Main Street, its large windows letting in streams of morning sunlight. The early rush had died down, leaving contented, busy customers scattered at tables with their laptops and books.

One side of the shop was lined with floor-to-ceiling shelves packed with well-loved paperbacks, their spines creating a rainbow of faded colors. And on an opposite wall, a handmade quilt hung above overstuffed chairs, making the place even more cozy.

"Did Hearthstone's coffeemaker finally give up the ghost?" Piper asked. "Is that why you're here? Desperation?"

"*No*. I was longing to see you because I've missed you so much."

Piper snorted, wiping down the steam wand. "Okay." She drew the word out. "What's the real reason? You hardly ever come in here for your caffeine fix."

"I just wanted something different this morning."

"Alright, lay it on me. What can I get you?"

I glanced at the menu again. "Your pistachio latte is totally dairy free, right?"

Piper narrowed her eyes at me. "Yes. I make the pistachio milk in-house."

"How do you milk a pistachio?"

"Are you trolling me, Cal? April Fool's was months ago."

"This is serious business. I'll take a pistachio latte. Medium." I studied the pastry case next. "And these gluten-free cinnamon-sugar muffins. Is your kitchen allergy friendly? No cross-contamination?"

Piper laughed, the sound echoing off the exposed brick walls. A few curious customers looked up. "You have new food allergies I've never heard about in the thirty-ish years I've known you?"

"Hey, you don't know everything about me, Piper. I've got layers. Always something new to discover."

"Layers," she repeated, shaking her head with a grin. "Right. Well, Mr. Mysterious, your gluten-free needs are covered. I run a tight ship here." She started pulling shots for the latte, the machine's rhythmic grinding adding to the quiet hum of conversation in the space.

Today, each of the small wooden tables was decorated with a jar holding a wild sunflower. And for some reason, that reminded me of Zandra. Maybe the way those flowers grew in tangles along all the highways, resilient and impossible to keep down.

Over the last couple weeks, since we'd shared that pint of ice cream, Zandra and I had been getting into a groove. Working together at the brewpub had been a process of give and take, both of us learning the ins and outs of the general manager position while sharing responsibilities.

We'd had hiccups with a few suppliers, inventory to double

check, accounts to balance, orders to submit. Also fielding Manny's nonstop texts asking for updates.

But it wasn't just about understanding Hearthstone's operations anymore. Zandra and I were getting to know each other, figuring out each other's strengths and working styles.

Some days we clicked so well it felt effortless. Other days we butted heads over just about everything. Yet even our disagreements felt productive, like we were building something together. I liked to think so, anyway.

Once I got the general manager position, that solid foundation would only take me higher. Hopefully with Zandra sticking around, no hard feelings when I was her boss.

I was all about the optimism.

Last week, I'd brought almond and oat milk to add to the employee fridge at Hearthstone, and Zandra had been using it in her coffee. But I thought she'd like a fancy latte, and I'd noticed that Zandra was being super careful about spending money. So I figured I would treat her today.

But Piper was right that I hadn't seen my family and friends much lately. Zandra and Hearthstone had been taking up not just my time, but my headspace.

"How's Ollie doing with his summer league?" I asked.

"He's killing it. Three home runs last week alone." Pride radiated from her as she steamed the pistachio milk.

"Damn. Future in the major leagues."

"He missed you at his last game. Next one's Thursday evening."

"And I'll be there. Had a firefighter training at the same time as the last one, and work's been crazy, but I'll be there Thursday. Wouldn't miss it."

Piper was perpetually single and liked it that way, just like me. Though I blamed her terrible ex-husband for some of her cynicism about relationships, since she hadn't been anti-love before. But Piper had plenty on her plate between running Silver Linings and raising nine-year-old Ollie.

"I really am sorry I missed his game," I added. "Ollie's my guy."

She smiled, rolling her eyes a little. "You don't have to be everything for everyone, Callum. I was just giving you a hard time earlier. Anything else?"

"Just a large black coffee. Those tongs didn't touch the gluten stuff, did they?"

She was grabbing the muffins I'd ordered and placing them in paper bags. "Relax. I know what I'm doing."

"Just making sure."

Piper rang me up at the register. Then she asked casually, "So, how are things going with you and Zandra Alvarez? That's who the pistachio latte is for, right?"

"What makes you think that?"

Piper sighed, leaning against the counter. "Because you think you're subtle, Callum, but you're really not."

I scratched the stubble at my jaw, not really sure what she was implying. "Zandra's doing great, actually."

"She doesn't hate you anymore?"

I glanced around to make sure nobody else was listening, because Manny's spies were everywhere. He was barely mobile, but that didn't matter with access to a phone and the internet.

"I'm deep in the process of winning her over." I pointed at the latte and muffin. "As you can see. Practically got her wrapped around my finger."

"Riiight. So this is all part of your plan to get the job?"

"Exactly." I tapped my forehead. "It's all tactics and strategies in here, Piper. I could've been a chess master."

"Just don't forget, while you're working hard to charm her, that you're in competition with this woman."

"How could I possibly forget that?"

"Because you're a people pleaser, Cal. Classic middle child."

I scoffed. "That's ridiculous. Layers, Piper. You might not know me as well as you think you do."

"Okay. Sure. You're an enigma of masculinity, and I couldn't possibly understand all the complex things happening in that brain of yours."

"Thank you for acknowledging that."

"Aww, do you feel better?"

"Yeah, I do."

She emptied the espresso grounds from the machine. "So you're really serious about the general manager job."

"Yep. Haven't even picked up any women lately. This is what professionalism looks like."

Piper's eyes went wide. "Wait, you haven't hooked up? With tourists at Hearthstone, or with *anyone*?"

I shrugged. "Anyone, I guess."

"In how long?"

"Like...a week or two."

I realized it was longer than that. I hadn't hooked up with a single person since Zandra arrived back in town.

I hadn't even *looked* at any of the tourists coming to the brewery. Which was weird.

"Two weeks?" Piper stared at me like I'd just announced I was joining a monastery. "You feeling okay? Should I check you for a fever?"

"It's not a big deal."

"Whatever you say."

"I *do* say." I tapped my payment card, grabbed the to-go bag and the coffees, and set off toward work.

People pleaser. Hardly. Just because people loved me didn't mean I was always bending over backward to please them.

And I hadn't forgotten for one second that Zandra and I were competing for the same job. Yes, I'd been doing nice things for her. For strategic reasons. Seeing her rare smiles was only a bonus.

Though I *did* like the idea of Zandra and me being friends. We could have both, right? Only one of us could get the general manager spot, but we should still be able to come out of it getting along.

Last week, when we'd spent that morning together at the

market, Zandra's vulnerability had been crystal clear. No wonder she'd stayed away from Silver Ridge so long when this place brought up only terrible memories. Didn't sound like her parents had helped there.

At least she had her aunt Rosie, and even Manny, who was gruff on the surface but a softy underneath. A personality type I was well familiar with.

Yet I still felt like there was more that Zandra was holding back from me. Like there was more to what had happened back in high school than she'd shared. It had been weighing on my mind, even as I'd been focused on work.

And the lack of hookups... That was just my new resolution to act like the boss. I had to prove to everyone at Hearthstone that I was top management material. Not a slavering sex fiend, desperate to mount anything that moved. My right hand could help me deal with temporary celibacy.

Of course, any time I'd taken myself in hand lately for a stroke session, only one face had appeared in my mind.

Full rose-colored lips, long hair, angry dark eyes...

Just the thought of Zandra made my blood rush and my cock twitch with interest. Even if that particular hookup was *never* going to happen. It was still an energy rush every day that I got to see her.

This pistachio latte was going to earn me another smile. Today was going to be a great day. I could feel it in my bones—

Until I saw the crowd of people and the flashing lights of a police car down the block.

Right in front of Hearthstone.

I started jogging, trying not to spill the coffees. The closer I got, the clearer the scene became.

Bits of glass were strewn over the sidewalk, and one of our front windows was a web of cracks with a gaping hole in the middle. A uniformed officer was taking notes while gesturing at the damage.

I spotted Russ near the entrance and grabbed his arm. "What the hell happened?"

"Someone threw a brick through the window." His words came fast, like he was hopped up on adrenaline. "I was here early around six. Was checking the fermentation tanks. Heard the glass breaking."

"Did you see who did it?"

"Nah. By the time I made it outside, whoever did it was gone. But when Zandra got here, she flipped. Took off."

"What do you mean, took off? *Where is she*?"

TWELVE
Zandra

"I CANNOT BELIEVE you just asked me that." I pressed my back against the rough brick of Hearthstone's exterior, my phone clutched to my ear. The parking lot behind the brewery was quiet, despite the police activity going on out front.

Of all the days for Ian to call with a guilt trip, why did it have to be today?

And why had I even picked up? It was like this man could sniff out my most vulnerable moments.

"Your parents are loaded, Zan," Ian whined. "I just need a short-term loan to cover things until my next payout from my trust fund. You know I can't touch the principal."

"What about your new job? The one your fancy contacts got you, even though I couldn't get a single employer in Chicago to take my calls?"

"It fell through."

"Wow." I gripped the bridge of my nose. How had I ever been so foolish as to believe any of this man's lies?

"Don't forget, I let you keep living at my place rent free. Even after you stopped sharing my bed."

"That's why I paid for the groceries and cleaned like I was your maid, all while still trying my damnedest to fix things with our investors." Meanwhile, Ian had continued to spend money on things like his obscenely expensive car. I'd known he had some debt, like me, but I'd had no clue it was this bad.

"I put years into our relationship and our company, Zan. You still owe me."

I rubbed my chest, feeling the familiar knot of anxiety tighten there. "You and I are over. I owe you *nothing*."

He changed tactics. "These people I borrowed money from... They don't play around. Please. If you ever loved me—"

"I have to go." I hung up before he could finish, immediately switching my phone to silent.

My hands were trembling as I shoved it into my back pocket.

The sight of the spider-webbed hole in the window, the shards of tempered glass littering the concrete, appeared in my memory. Only becoming more vivid when I closed my eyes.

It was a coincidence. A random act of vandalism that had nothing to do with me. *Or* Jessa.

But it was yet another reminder that I still wasn't over the things that had happened years ago. I'd been back in Silver Ridge for *weeks*, and I still hadn't worked up the courage to visit Jessa's mother.

Why couldn't I just put all the heartache behind me?

"Get it together," I murmured to myself. "Someone's going to see you like this."

Of course, the universe had a sick sense of humor. Because, as I pulled the door open, I walked straight into a solid wall of muscle and woodsy cologne. The guy who'd already seen me sad and pathetic more times than I ever would've wanted.

Callum's warm hands came up to steady me. "There you are. I just got here. Russ said you were upset."

"I'm fine," I insisted.

He seemed to get a better look at me. And it must've been obvious I was very much *not* fine. "Nope. Back outside."

"Callum, I—"

But he was already nudging me out the back door, shoving it

closed again with his foot. "What's going on? Was it the broken window? Or the phone call you were just having?"

Embarrassment soured my stomach. "You heard."

"A little. Didn't mean to eavesdrop, but it sounded unpleasant."

"Just my ex being his usual self."

"Your ex, the dick?"

"That's the one." I sighed.

My head fell back against the brick wall for another moment as I tried to collect myself. The rough texture bit into my shoulders through my top, pulling me toward the present.

But the memories still had a hold on me.

Jessa. Not just her death, but everything that happened after. That broken window...

Callum was waiting, and I had to tell him *something*.

"I only got here about a half hour ago. After Russ saw the broken glass, he called the police and my grandpa, and then Grandpa called me."

"And?" Callum prompted.

And then, when I got here and saw the glass, I might've... crashed out. Just a little. But I wasn't going to confess that bit of truth aloud.

"It's upsetting to see someone throw a brick through Hearthstone's window," I finished saying. "This place means a lot to my family."

Callum's dark eyes were studying me way too closely. "But you're all right?"

"Yep."

"Good. Next time, I'd appreciate a call when things go wrong. It's still the trial period, and we're supposed to be in this together. I was down the street at Silver Linings with no clue what was happening here."

I groaned. "Crap, I meant to call you. I told Russ I would, but then..." I gestured vaguely at my phone, feeling heat creep up my neck.

"The ex called?"

"Yes. Ian. I'm sorry. I didn't leave you out on purpose, I swear."

"All forgiven," Callum said easily.

"Really? That fast?"

He winked. "People do accuse me of being fast."

And we were back to the flirting. The baseline Callum always seemed to return to.

Over the last couple of weeks, things had been pretty good between us. We'd worked together most days with hardly any arguing. Well, only *necessary* arguing. Because Callum loved to poke at me, and when he did, I couldn't hold my tongue.

Winnie had also caught me checking out Callum at work. I'd denied it, but yeah, I'd been obvious. The man had an ass made for ogling. So sue me.

The truth was, I liked Callum. A *lot*. Just like everyone else in town did, and it was disconcerting. I felt like I was in one of those old sci-fi movies where an alien slug takes over someone's brain. *You're one of us now.*

But at the moment, his ridiculousness was just what I needed for a reset.

Okay. My freakout was over. Ready for business.

"We should go talk to the police," I said. "Then call a handyman about putting plywood over the window."

"On it." Callum opened the back door and steered me inside. "But first, breakfast. I assume you haven't had your coffee yet?"

"Coffee. That is exactly what I need."

His long fingers ghosted over the small of my back.

In the kitchen, the staff was getting started on prep work after the unexpected drama of the broken window. Instead of going for the coffeemaker, Callum grabbed a couple of to-go cups marked with the Silver Linings logo.

"Pistachio latte for you," he said, looking pleased with himself. "And a cinnamon-sugar muffin. All confirmed to be allergy free."

"You are..."

"Jaw-dropping? Gorgeous?"

"I was going to go with...awesome." Because the guy did deserve some credit. He was turning my bad day around fast.

He beamed. "I'll take awesome."

Chuckling, I took a sip of the latte. Then closed my eyes as the warm, nutty flavor hit my tongue. For the first time all morning, something felt right. "Oh, that's really yummy."

"Piper knows her coffee."

"Thank her for me. Also, thanks to you too. This was really nice."

"My pleasure." He stuck a hand in his pocket, the other lifting his coffee to his lips. "I do owe you a hundred bucks. It's just my start to paying it back."

I snorted, coughing on a mouthful of my drink. That first night I'd seen him at the bar felt like a lifetime ago. "I forgot about the hundred bucks."

"I didn't." He flashed his grin. "Now we're caffeinated. Let's go talk to the police."

The Silver Ridge PD officer had already taken a statement from Russ, and he promised to check around with our neighboring businesses to see if they had camera footage.

"No cameras here?" the officer asked, glancing at the eaves of the building.

"Manny was against it," Callum said. "He claimed he's, quote, *morally opposed to the modern surveillance state.*"

Totally sounded like something Grandpa would say. "We'll get a security system and cameras installed soon," I added, glancing at Callum, who nodded. "Was there a note attached to the brick or anything?"

My stomach twisted as I asked the question.

But the officer just shook his head, eyes on his notepad. "Nope. There was a music festival over in Pine Creek. Drew in more than the usual crowd of out-of-towners. Hart County Sheriff has been dealing with issues all week. Probably just more of that. Doesn't seem like the culprit tried to get inside, so I doubt they were even interested in stealing beer."

I nodded, my anxiety fading. It had been random, and I'd been upset over nothing more than a minor case of vandalism. Which made perfect sense.

It had nothing to do with me.

Within a couple hours, we had plywood over the window and the mess cleaned up. Everything was back to normal, the dining room ready for another day of serving customers. In the kitchen, the familiar sounds of chopping and sizzling filled the air.

Callum and I headed to the office to deal with some other tasks, but soon he was stretching his arms over his head. "Lunch? Cobb salad again, hold the cheese?"

"Uh, yeah." But before he could put in our lunch request with the kitchen, I said, "Hey, Callum. Can I ask a favor?"

I'd been thinking about this all morning after the pistachio latte. If I didn't ask him now, I was going to lose my nerve.

The thing was, Callum had been great lately. Like bringing me breakfast today. Also, starting up a conversation with Manny and the head chef about updating their cross-contamination procedures. Now I had several tasty options for meals here, like the Cobb salad sans blue cheese and croutons. I always got extra avocado. *Yum.*

And he'd been so reassuring after the broken window and that awful phone call with Ian.

Either Callum was genuinely a sweetheart, or he was trying to lull me into a false sense of security before an evil about-face. But I didn't think so.

Callum stood, readjusting his cap over his waves. "Sure. Ask, and it shall be done, my liege."

His goofiness gave me the last bit of courage I needed. "I've been meaning to go see Mrs. Mackenzie. Jessa's mom. Winnie said she's not doing well, and I felt like I should go spend some time with her. It's the right thing to do, but I'm honestly kind of dreading it. Which probably makes me a terrible person."

I was rambling. But Callum smiled softly. "Pretty sure it just makes you human."

I forged ahead. "So I was wondering..."

"Yeah?"

"If you might come with me."

He shrugged, as if this was a simple request and not a subject that had been plaguing me for weeks. "Yeah. Yeah, of course. I should've gone to see Mrs. Mackenzie a long time ago too."

"You weren't close with Jessa or her family. No one would've expected you to."

"But as you said, it's the right thing to do. Name the date and time, and I'm there."

I exhaled. "Thanks, Callum. This really means a lot."

"You got it." He plopped back down in his seat. "But you have to order lunch. And serve it to me and call me Mr. Charming, as in *Prince* Charming, because I really fucking am."

"No."

He leaned back in the chair. "That's the deal."

I made a frustrated noise. "But you realize 'Prince' is the title, right? So it should just be *Prince Charming*, no mister."

"I don't think so. Prince is his first name in those old movies."

I blinked at Callum. He was serious.

This. Man.

There really was no use fighting it. "Fine. What can I get you for lunch, *Mr. Charming*?"

"Don't say it like that. Sounds like in your head, you're calling me Mr. Asshat or something."

A smirk teased my lips. "Gee, I wonder why."

"You know you love me."

My cheeks heated as blood rushed to my face. Love was seriously overstating it. But I was quite possibly in *like* with him.

So help me, I really was.

THIRTEEN
Zandra

CALLUM GAVE me a once-over as I climbed into his truck. "I thought your entire wardrobe was business casual and designer jeans."

"It's my day off." I was wearing my favorite worn-in cut-off jean shorts and an oversized sweatshirt that fell off one shoulder.

The interior of Callum's truck was surprisingly tidy. Clean dashboard, no random papers or fast-food wrappers cluttering the console. The seats were worn leather, comfortable beneath me as I climbed into the passenger seat, holding a potted plant in my lap.

"You may notice, I mixed it up too." He pointed at his hat. "Wearing my ball cap facing forward."

"Almost didn't recognize you," I deadpanned. "Mr. Charming."

He grinned. "And there it is."

Over the last few days, we'd kept up a low level of flirtation while working together. Essentially, Callum making ridiculous little requests and me protesting before giving in. But our ongoing banter, silly as it was, had made this trip to see Mrs. Mackenzie feel less intimidating.

"You got the address?" Callum asked.

It hadn't been hard to track down Mrs. Makenzie's number

through the Silver Ridge grapevine. When I called, she'd told me Monday, *today*, would be good to stop by. Which was perfect, since Callum and I had the day off.

I read the street address off my phone, and Callum put it in his GPS. "Thanks for doing this with me," I said. "I mean it."

"I know. Joking aside, it's no problem at all."

Funny how I didn't mind Callum's teasing about "owing him" for doing me this favor. While Ian's claim that I owed him made me want to punch my ex through the phone. Probably because I trusted Callum would never really be that petty.

Once, I'd thought otherwise. But these days, Callum was one of the people I trusted most. How was that for a turnaround.

We talked about work stuff during the fifteen-minute drive. Then Callum put his truck in park in front of a run-down house that desperately needed a paint job. He eyed the street. "Didn't realize Mrs. Mackenzie had moved out here."

"Must've been at some point after Jessa died."

This place was far more depressing than the house I'd spent so much time at in high school. I'd remembered a bungalow with flower boxes and a white fence. Not this lonely road that dead-ended into a gravel pit.

"Ready?" Callum asked.

"No, but I'm going anyway." I pushed open the door and got out. More of a jump, since Callum's truck was a good distance from the concrete.

Really, if I wasn't such a coward, I would've faced this by myself.

But instead, I was showing up here with an indoor plant as a gift and the town's favorite golden retriever bartender to act as a buffer. Since everybody loved Callum around here, Mrs. Mackenzie would be no different, right?

Today, he'd worn a snug T-shirt in a dark green, along with jeans that didn't have a single rip or tear. But Callum looked effortlessly sexy in anything. Just throwing off masculine pheromones like it was his side hustle.

I had to get a grip.

Without a doubt, seeing Jessa's mom would sober me up.

I hesitated in the overgrown yard. "We could do this another day," Callum offered.

Get moving, I told myself. *You're a grown woma*n. As much as I wanted to slink off and hide like Chloe, I couldn't.

"No. I'm good." Callum was here beside me, and I was so dang grateful for that.

On the porch, I shifted the potted plant to one arm and rang the bell. The door cracked open, and a thin woman with wiry hair peered out. "Hello?"

"Hi, Mrs. Mackenzie. I called you a little while ago?" I lifted up the plant, because I didn't know what else to do.

"Oh. Of course. I remember you, Zandra."

Nothing could've prepared me for how much Mrs. Mackenzie had changed. She had to be in her mid-fifties, but she looked at least a decade older. Her once-full cheeks had sunken in, leaving sharp angles where there used to be soft curves.

Yet seeing her face brought everything rushing back. Jessa's funeral, where I'd stood frozen beside the casket, unable to find words that could possibly comfort this woman who'd lost her daughter. The candlelight vigil, where Jessa's mom couldn't even speak for crying.

Now, sixteen years later, the guilt crashed over me like a tidal wave. My throat tightened, and my chest felt heavy with the weight of all the things I should have said, should have done.

I should have stayed in touch.

I should have saved her daughter.

While I stood there numbly, Callum stepped in beside me, making the porch groan. "Hello, Mrs. Mackenzie. I'm Callum. Zandra and I work together at the brewery now, so I thought I'd join her."

"The O'Neal boy from Jessa's year." She opened the door a bit wider. "I don't have many visitors these days. But you can come in."

We stepped inside the narrow shotgun-style house. The front door opened directly into the living room, which flowed into a small kitchen.

Aside from a pile of mail on a table by the door, everything was tidy. A worn couch faced an old television, and in the corner sat a small desk with a laptop computer and landline phone. But there was an overwhelming sense of loneliness here, as if most of the room was rarely touched.

I held out the potted plant. "I brought this for you."

That's when I noticed the collection of planters by the sliding patio door, all of them holding the brown, withered remains of what had once been houseplants. My heart sank a little more. But Mrs. Mackenzie took the gift anyway, setting it on the nearby kitchen counter. Her expression still hadn't changed since she'd opened the door.

"Won't you sit down?" She gestured haltingly at the couch. "I got out a soda for you. It's on the coffee table. A Coke. I remembered that's what you liked, Zandra. Just like my Jessa."

I took a seat on the lumpy couch and reached for the soda. "This is perfect. Thank you."

"Son, I didn't know you were coming. Did you want a drink?"

"That would be great, ma'am. I can get it myself."

"You can just call me Paula."

He covered the distance to the kitchen in two long strides, grabbing a can from the collection on the counter. Callum sat beside me, while Paula took a narrow, straight-backed chair from a corner. She glanced around like she was searching for something to say.

"I just got back to Silver Ridge a few weeks ago," I started. I told her how I'd come to help out after my grandpa's accident, which it seemed she hadn't heard about.

But every word from my mouth was as stilted as Jessa's mom was acting. Who could blame her? This woman had spent the last sixteen years without her daughter. Without Jessa's laugh, without her bright smile, without all the grandchildren she might have had someday.

And I couldn't shake the feeling that if I'd been faster, smarter, *braver* that night, Paula wouldn't be sitting here alone in this sad little house.

Callum jumped in like he could sense how close I was to falling apart. "That construction up the road must be a headache for you, Paula."

"Oh, yes. They've been making a racket."

Thank you, Callum, I thought. Now there was a perennial topic of conversation in any town. The endless indignities of road construction.

I got up from my seat to look at the framed pictures on the walls. Beside the TV was a display of old photos of the Mackenzie family from when Jessa and her brother Leo were kids. The siblings had shared the same pale blond curls and round faces.

In one picture they were kicking a soccer ball around. In another, Leo was by himself holding up a fish he'd caught.

Leo's cocky smirk made me think of Callum. Two confident boys who'd swaggered down the high school hallways, though Leo was younger. Yet there had been something harder about Leo too. Something...angry. Which must've just gotten worse after Jessa died.

And then there was a selfie of me and Jessa as teenagers, our arms around each other with the creek behind us. Her pale complexion was flushed pink from laughter. I stood beside her with my long braid draped over one shoulder, my skin golden and hers pale.

We looked so young, so full of hope and possibility. So alive.

I startled when Paula spoke from right behind me. "Jessa's beautiful, isn't she?"

I didn't trust myself to speak. All I could do was nod, my eyes stinging and heart thumping painfully in my chest. Paula had talked about Jessa that way at the funeral, too. In the present tense. Like she simply couldn't believe her daughter was gone.

But then I felt the warmth of Callum's hand on my arm. "Jessa was a great girl. I remember how kind she was. Could make anyone smile. Even Zandra."

I was surprised Callum could recall that much about my friend. But then again, he'd apparently noticed plenty about me back then too. The Callum I thought I knew wasn't the real him.

And he'd just reminded me what Paula really needed. To hear about how much her daughter had meant to me.

I cleared my throat. "Jessa was the most loyal person I ever knew. She stood by me no matter what. Made me laugh all the time. Just...brought sunshine to my day."

Paula's face softened for the first time since we'd arrived. "And to mine."

"She'd show up at my house with some ridiculous story about something that happened on Main Street after school, or she'd drag me down to the creek just to sit and talk about our dreams for college."

Paula reached out to touch a photo of Leo. "After he left Silver Ridge, Leo took a job on a fishing trawler up in Alaska. It's been a long while since I last heard from him. No clue where he is." Something in her tone made me pause, though I couldn't pinpoint why.

"Losing Jessa was really hard for him," I replied, remembering what Winnie had said.

Paula nodded, eyes still on the photo. "Especially because he and his sister fought a few days before that awful night." Her gaze suddenly darted to mine. "He never would tell me what they argued about."

Jessa had said something about sibling drama. I'd forgotten until now. "I'm sorry. I don't know what they fought about either."

Her composure slipped, her small form swaying, and she reached out to brace herself on my arm. Her fingers tightened painfully on my wrist. "I miss my girl."

My heart was breaking for her. "Can I give you a hug?"

"Alright."

As I wrapped my arms around her, my eyes locked with Callum's. He nodded and gave me a closed-mouth, sympathetic smile.

I breathed easier once we were back outside and out of the stale air of Paula's home. We got in Callum's truck, and he turned on the engine, but he didn't drive away.

"There was a Mother's Day card on that table by the door," he said quietly. "It was sitting on top of an envelope. Already open. Did you notice that?"

"What? A card?" I was half listening, while the rest of me was still stuck in that house.

My responsible, adult side knew I should go back and see Mrs. Mackenzie again soon. She was lonely. Yet I couldn't stomach the thought of returning to that oppressive space, surrounded by all those memories and nothing else. Like breathing in pure sorrow.

That had to make me a bad person, didn't it?

I'm the worst, Jessa, I thought. *I miss you. Please tell me to shut up and not be so hard on myself, because that's what I need to hear.*

"A Mother's Day card," Callum repeated. "I think it was from Leo. Which is odd, right? Didn't she say she hadn't heard from him? Doesn't know where he is?"

"Maybe it was from last year," I said, though even as the words left my mouth, I knew how weak they sounded. "Or maybe someone else sent it."

Callum's brow furrowed. "Who else would've sent it but her son?"

I understood what he meant. But why would Paula have lied to us?

FOURTEEN
Callum

"YOU LOOK like you could use a distraction," I said.

"Hmm?" Zandra turned to face me, a few strands of hair falling over her cheek, and I fought the urge to brush them back.

Since we'd left Paula's house, Z had been staring off into space. Clearly deep in thought.

There'd been something...off about Mrs. Mackenzie. I'd felt an odd tension during that entire visit, as if there was something wrong in that house. Not that I wanted to judge a poor woman who'd lost her daughter.

And her son, though in a different way.

I remembered Leo from high school. He'd been a year or so younger, but the type of guy you noticed in the halls, talking a big game and catching people's attention. Not always in a good way. But a lot of us were stupid in high school.

Leo had all but disappeared inside himself after his sister died. From what I'd heard—mostly from Winnie Peyton—he hadn't been back to Silver Ridge after he left. Which matched more or less with what Paula had said.

As for that Mother's Day card, maybe I was blowing it out of proportion. Maybe I shouldn't have said anything to Zandra about it at all. She'd already been wound up after the visit.

Either way, I didn't like the thought of driving her back to Rosie's house and abandoning her after that.

"What would you say to a field trip?" I asked.

"Now?"

"Yeah. Unless you have plans the rest of the day."

Zandra wiggled around in her seat. "Is this field trip work-related?"

"Does it need to be?"

"Boundaries are a good thing, Callum."

"But we're friends," I reasoned.

"Barely."

Don't forget, while you're working hard to charm her, that you're in competition with this woman. So Piper had said. But today was our day off. Hearthstone was closed on Mondays.

And that visit with Paula Mackenzie had left Z unbalanced, I could tell. It wasn't even about charming her. This was about following my instincts, and my gut told me not to let Z out of my sight too soon.

Because this woman had taken over my head, and I didn't mind that one damn bit.

Then Zandra asked, "What kind of field trip?" And I knew I had her hooked.

"Just say yes. You won't regret this, I promise."

Her brow arched.

"Don't you trust me?" I asked, sticking out my lower lip.

"Define trust."

"Fine, it's work-related. Cross my heart." I traced my finger in an X over my chest, and Zandra's lips twitched.

"Why am I not reassured?" she muttered.

"Is that a yes?"

She crossed her golden legs. They looked so good in those shorts. "Yes."

"See, that wasn't so hard."

"I need to make sure Chloe's settled without me, though. I wasn't planning to be gone all day."

"And I need to pick up a few things. How about I drop you at Rosie's, then come back in about an hour?"

❀

The hour went by a little too fast. I wound up having to rush.

But when I pulled up in front of Rosie's, I still had a minute to spare. After a brisk knock, Zandra pulled the door open. "Come in. I'm almost ready." She dashed off toward the kitchen, and I closed the door and followed.

"I told you an hour. You're not late, are you Z?"

"Shush. I'm doing my best."

When we reached the kitchen, Zandra picked up a can of cat food and a can opener. Movement on my periphery caught my eye, and Jimmy Perkins walked in cradling a mass of orange fur in his arms.

Jimmy was wearing a short, floral robe. *Very* short. As in, I'd never needed to know exactly where the tan-line ended on Jimmy's hairy legs. But now I did. He'd tied his hair in its usual low ponytail, his beard as scraggly as ever.

"Hey, Callum," he rumbled in his gravelly voice. "Would you like to pet our little queen here? She's a grumpy puss today."

"Zandra? I'll pet her anytime she wants. Wait, were you talking about Chloe?" I smirked, proud of myself.

Z gave me a look, half amusement and all exasperation, as she forked cat food into a bowl.

"Chloe's grumpy," Jimmy cooed, nuzzling the cat's head. "Aren't you, precious? Yes, you are. She's as mad as I am about what this town is coming to."

Uh oh. Jimmy clearly had a rant coming on.

While he went on about whatever "they" were doing to the town, something about ugly new streetlights, I went over to give Chloe some chin rubs. She might've looked grumpy, but that smooshed-face scowl was also pretty cute.

Maybe I should've known grumpy cats were my jam from how often they showed up on my social feeds. Damn that algorithm.

"Chloe doesn't need any more spoiling than I give her already," Zandra complained.

"I'd be happy to spoil you too, if you're jealous," I said over my shoulder.

With an eye roll, Zandra set the food bowl on the floor, then grabbed a messenger bag she hadn't been carrying earlier. "You can refill the fountain if she needs, right?"

Jimmy grunted affirmatively. "'Course. I wouldn't want to drink water from a bowl that's been sitting out all day."

"Chloe would agree. She's way too fussy for that. Bye, Jimmy. Thanks for taking care of her. I'll be back later."

"After dinner," I added. "Don't wait up." Once we were outside, I said, "Does he always wear that tiny robe around the house?"

"It's Rosie's. And believe me, the robe is better than the alternative."

"Should I be worried about you?" I asked, mildly concerned even though Jimmy had never come across as that kind of creepy. An old coot who Rosie somehow put up with, sure, but nothing worse.

"He's fine. Honestly, I'm just grateful Rosie and Jimmy haven't kicked me out yet. I meant to find my own apartment over a week ago, but it's hard to find a cheap place with normal roommates."

I opened the passenger door of the truck for her. "I did offer you the spare room at my place."

"Exactly my point. I said *normal* roommates."

I chuckled as I rounded the truck and got into the driver's seat.

"I could've gotten the door for myself," Zandra grumbled as soon as I was inside the cabin.

"I thought you wanted someone to spoil you."

"I didn't say that. Or think it."

"We'll see." I reached over, took the seatbelt from her hand, and buckled it for her. Then booped her chin affectionately with my finger.

"I thought you said I wouldn't regret this."

"Okay, okay." I held up my hands. "I'll behave myself. Starting...now." Fuck, I had fun with her. "What's in the bag?"

Her brow wrinkled. "The what?"

As my truck pulled away from the curb, I nodded my head at the big messenger bag she clutched on her lap like it held the secret Hearthstone beer recipes.

"Uh. So," she stammered. "I brought you something. A gift."

"You did?" I glanced between her and the road. "You brought me a present? For real?"

"A thank you gift for going to Mrs. Mackenzie's with me earlier." Opening the flap and dipping inside, Zandra pulled out a lump in tissue paper. "I would've wrapped it better, but Jimmy didn't know where Rosie keeps the wrapping paper. And she's busy at the market today."

My grin was impossible to suppress as I drove, waiting until a stop sign with no other traffic around to pluck the gift from her hands.

"You could wait until we're not in a moving vehicle."

"My foot is on the brake. And *no*, I can't wait. I need to see what you got me." Ripping open the tissue, I blinked at the small figurine lying inside.

Holy shit. This was epic.

"You got me a *gnome* dressed as a football player?" My voice was steeped in excitement like a little kid's.

Z bit her lower lip. "I noticed Rosie had two of them. It made me think of you. Seemed funnier when I was alone with Chloe in my room." She tried to take it from my hand. "Never mind, it's dumb."

I held it out of her reach. "Are you kidding? I love this. A gnome of my own! I'll put him in my room and think of you whenever he's staring at me."

She relaxed into her seat, fighting a smile. "I just wanted to do something to show my appreciation. For earlier. I'll get our coffees tomorrow from Silver Linings, too."

"Thank you." My gaze stayed glued to her. Until a honk came from behind us. Oops. I was blocking the way.

With an apologetic wave at the driver behind me, I set my gnome in the cup holder and started driving again.

"So where are we going?" she asked.

"You can't take the suspense?"

"You're the one who couldn't wait another moment to open his present."

"This is different. *This* is a surprise. Are you the type who turns to the end of the book because she has to find out how it ends?"

"Do you even read books?"

"Oh, harsh." I grinned. "If you really need a hint, you can look in the backseat."

She reached into the back, digging around inside the grocery bags I'd left there. During our brief separation this afternoon, I'd paid a visit to Main Street Market to pick up everything we'd need.

"What is all this for?"

"I said I'd give you a hint, not spill all the beans."

She kept digging in the grocery bags. "Are there beans here too?"

"Your jokes need work, Z."

"You started it."

While I drove, I kept glancing over at her, feeling the wide grin on my face. She was just...freaking cute. But beautiful too, and I kept noticing new details about her, even though you would've thought I'd had the woman's face memorized over the last few weeks. Like the way the skin just past her mouth creased when she was trying not to smile.

"Here we are," I said, putting the truck in Park in front of a sprawling, ranch-style house.

"And where is that?"

I took a breath, surveying the property where I'd lived happily for several years now. And somehow, it felt important that Zandra see it. Not only that, but *like* it.

"Welcome to my place."

"You told me this was work-related."

I unbuckled her seatbelt. "It is. Ye of little faith."

The day was warm and sunny as we got out. I waved to a kid riding past on a bicycle, then got the groceries from the backseat, tucking my gnome into one of the bags.

"I can carry something," she offered.

"Nah, you just keep looking pretty. There you go. Just like that."

"I'm not doing anything."

"You sure?" My eyes took a trip down her body and back up again. Those shorts were killing me. The hint of shoulder every time her sweatshirt drifted down. Fuck. She was doing all kinds of things to me.

"Stop that," she said.

"Stop what?"

"You know exactly what you're doing. You're staring."

"Like the way you stare at my butt when I'm turned around? Hearthstone does have mirrors."

Her mouth dropped open. But she didn't deny it. "This is work-related," she repeated. "So behave."

"I will if you do."

Inside the house, it was cooler, and the sound of the TV came from the living room. "Cal?" a deep voice called out. "That you? Did you bring food?"

I tilted my head at Zandra and lifted my eyebrows. "Roommates," I whispered, then raised my voice. "Yes, I brought food. No, it's not for you."

My roommate Connor rounded the corner, stopping short when he saw who else was here. "Oh. Hey. You're Zandra Alvarez."

"I am."

"I remember you from way back. Silver Ridge High, right? I'm Connor." He was in athletic shorts and a tee with the sleeves cut off. Ran a hand through his shoulder-length hair, and I swore he fucking flexed.

Really?

Darius came out of his room next, striding over and holding out his hand. At least I could count on him for being a gentleman. "Hi, I'm Darius."

"Hey. Zandra. I work with Callum."

"We know," both Connor and Darius said.

They walked into the living room, while I carried the grocery bags over to the kitchen.

"Cal talks about you all the time," Connor said.

"Does he now?" Zandra glanced over at me.

"Oh yeah," Darius added. "Zandra this, Zandra that."

Traitors.

Peering into one of the bags, I took out the football gnome and set him on the kitchen island with a smile. I doubted I'd ever received a better gift than this weird little figurine with its pointy helmet. Just because Zandra had given it to me.

Because she'd been *thinking of me.*

"What are you and Cal up to today?" Connor asked in the living room, sidling closer to her.

"He won't tell me. Supposedly it's work-related."

"He's working on his day off, now?" Sarcasm was thick in Connor's tone. "That's not usually what Callum gets up to in his free time."

Okay. Enough with the friendly introductions.

I went back to the living room and hooked Zandra's waist. "We're going to get started now."

Darius stood with his arms crossed, looking amused, while Connor was studying Zandra with way too much interest. "Can I help?" Connor asked.

"No," I growled. "Stay out of the kitchen."

FIFTEEN
Zandra

Once we were in the kitchen, Callum announced, "We're cooking."

I looked around at what he'd spread out on the counter. On the way here, I'd seen a lot of this stuff in his grocery bags. Carrots, onions, canned pumpkin, gluten-free flour. Plus cocoa powder and chicken breasts.

"And this has something to do with work?" I asked skeptically.

"We're going to test out allergy-conscious menu items. I think Hearthstone needs more options."

My first reaction was that Callum was being ridiculously thoughtful, yet again. But something held me back from just going with it. "Isn't that Alice's job? As the head chef?"

"This is background work. We're gathering intel. Doing recon."

"Recon?"

Connor wandered in, grabbing a spoon from a drawer and the jar of almond butter from the counter. "Every once in a while, Cal drops into military speak."

"Hey!" Callum picked up a wooden spoon and poked his friend with it. "I told you to stay out of here." He snatched the almond butter away. Connor looked bewildered. But Callum plucked a container of yogurt from the fridge and shoved it at Connor, who shrugged and wandered away.

I was pressing my lips together, but my smile snuck in at the corners.

"Where were we?" Callum asked.

I barked a laugh. "Cooking. Apparently. But I have no idea how to cook."

"I can show you. It's easy." He was bustling around, organizing ingredients and grabbing mixing bowls.

"No, I mean it. I'm legitimately a terrible cook. Everything I make comes out tasting awful at best, food poisoning at worst. My nana learned when I was a kid that chopping veggies was the extent of my abilities."

"Then you're in luck. I'm a fantastic cook, and I'm going to teach you. While we both learn, together, how to do the gluten and dairy-free cooking thing."

"Do I have a choice about this?" I asked.

Connor peered in through the pass-through, shoveling yogurt into his mouth. "You do not," he said with his mouth full.

"We're ignoring you," Callum said, and I gave Connor an apologetic smile.

Okay. Callum O'Neal was going to teach me to cook gluten and dairy free. Because he wanted to do something sweet for me after the rough morning I'd had.

A more sensible woman would probably be thrilled at this prospect, but there was this weird pressure in my chest. A fizzy, unsettled feeling, like I didn't know what I might do. Like cry. Or throw my arms around him.

My professors used to comment on how poised I was during class presentations. I'd used those same skills in my pitch meetings with investors. Yet Callum had me all shaken up like a can of beer that was about to foam over.

Callum stopped right beside me. "Don't worry," he said, voice low. "We'll just go step by step."

A languid sensation caressed my spine. "I guess I can follow your lead. It's happened before."

"And you're always in good hands."

The thought appeared in my head. *I wouldn't mind your hands on me.*

Oh, no. There was no way I could have a crush on Callum O'Neal, so I was going to ignore it and act normal.

A foolproof plan.

It turned out we were making chicken pot pie with a gluten-free biscuit crust and brownies for dessert, which did sound pretty delicious. Callum set me to work chopping vegetables. That much I could handle, based on the knife skills Nana had taught me years ago.

"So," I said as I diced carrots, "do you like having roommates?"

"Are you asking why I'm thirty-four and don't have a place of my own?"

"I'm not one to talk."

He was smiling. "I happen to like having roommates. I'd hate living alone. We're all volunteers for Silver Ridge Fire. Dare's a mechanic, Connor's a personal trainer, and our other roommate Niko...he's the baby. Out with his girlfriend right now."

"I'm guessing you're the oldest of the group?" I teased.

Callum made an exaggeratedly shocked face. "Dare and Connor are barely younger than me. We all played football together in high school. And if I'm old, so are you," he added.

"Maybe." I sliced into an onion, knowing my eyes would start stinging any minute from the fumes. "I didn't expect to be single, broke, and starting over back in Silver Ridge in my mid-thirties."

"Who says your life has to follow some pre-planned track record?"

"My parents," I said without thinking.

"You care about their opinions?"

My knife paused. "I don't want to care. But it's hard not to."

After Callum finished dicing the chicken breasts and I had a bowl of chopped veggies, we started the pot pie filling. "Don't turn the burner up too high," he said. "Once the vegetables are sweating, we'll add the chicken."

"Veggies sweat?"

"When you treat them right."

I shook my head, because Callum could turn just about any topic into something that sounded sexual.

While I stirred the contents of the skillet and Callum scooped flour into another bowl, I said, "Connor mentioned military speak. You were in the Army, right?"

"Yeah, in my twenties. Like my brothers."

"Hard to imagine you marching around all serious and following every order. Sir, yes sir."

He aimed his lopsided grin my way. "There was a *little* more to it than that. But you're partly right. Loved the people I served with, didn't love following arbitrary orders and being shuffled around with no control."

"And then you started at Hearthstone after you left active duty?"

"You got it. Started as a bartender. Didn't have much experience with that, but I talked Manny's ear off and convinced him to give me a shot."

"I can imagine."

"What about you? What were you doing in Chicago before you came back?"

Ugh. My mood instantly wobbled. This wasn't a fun topic.

Yet I found myself talking.

"I had an idea to help food manufacturers track their ingredients more effectively, all the way from sourcing to production to delivery. To make it even easier to prevent cross-contamination."

"For people with food allergies like you?" He came over to dump the chicken into the skillet.

I nodded. "My ex Ian had all these contacts in the business world. He said he'd landed a huge client for us. A major food manufacturer." I grimaced. "We touted that client to investors to get them to back our company. But Ian didn't tell me when the big client pulled out."

"That sounds bad."

"Very bad. He lied to me, and I had no idea I was giving false information to our investors." I focused on stirring, not wanting to see pity in his eyes. "Long story short, once the truth came out, our investors panicked. Everything fell apart. We worked out a settlement, and I walked away with nothing. My savings and reputation were destroyed. Had to keep living with Ian for months because I couldn't find a new job and had no money for my own place. I guess I'm lucky he didn't kick me out, but I was the one paying for groceries and keeping the place clean."

"Damn."

"Yeah. Damn is right. So...now I'm here. You know the rest."

We worked in comfortable silence for a while. I had to admit, there was something soothing about the rhythm of cooking together. Callum would give me advice or show me a technique, then watch patiently as I tried to copy him. Before long, we had the pot-pie filling off the heat. It already smelled incredible, and was thick and creamy from the non-dairy creamer we'd used.

Then Callum instructed me on the biscuit dough. "Not that bad, right?" he asked as we scooped and mixed.

"Just wait. Even my nana couldn't teach me to cook. Something usually goes wrong with me involved. Salt will get switched with sugar, or the oven will break."

"Don't jinx it." He knocked on the butcher-block counter. "We've got this. I believe in us."

"You cook for people a lot?" I dropped big spoonfuls of the dough onto the top of the pot-pie filling.

"For my family, mostly. We try to get together every week or two, if possible. At least once a month. I don't like going too long without seeing them."

He sounded much closer to his family than I was to mine.

"This is my first time giving a cooking lesson, though," he added. "It's fun, right?"

"It is."

A warm, achy feeling spread through me. Like with just a soft look and some kind words, Callum had opened me up and all the things I kept hidden were about to spill out.

I had to get myself together. I was tougher than this.

Once the pot pie was baking in the hot oven, we started on the brownies.

"The usual key to good brownies," he said seriously, "is not to over mix. I don't know if it's the same for gluten free. But usually, you want to fold in the flour gently, like you're tucking a baby into bed."

"You've had practice with babies?"

"Not *exactly*. I didn't see my niece much when she was a baby. But I figure it's the same. A delicate process, Zandra. You gotta respect the batter. I'm not kidding around."

I laughed. "Sir, yes sir."

Once we had the dry and wet ingredients assembled, it was time for folding. "Like this?"

Callum cringed. "If you want the baby to never sleep again, sure. And to have nightmares for the rest of its life."

"But I'm folding!"

"Looked more like stabbing. Here." Callum suddenly shifted so he was behind me. Close. *Really* close. His hand covered mine, both of us now holding the spatula.

"What are you doing?" My voice was tight.

"Just trying to show you. Don't fight it, okay? Twist your wrist. Feel that?"

"Uh, yes. I feel it."

I could hardly breathe as he guided my hand, slowly turning the ingredients over to gently mix them. But I was hardly concentrating on the batter. His scent was everywhere. That woodsy cologne and the herbs from the pot pie, mixing with the sweetness of chocolate and sugar. It shouldn't have worked together, but it did.

I wanted to eat him up.

If I scooted back just a little, we'd be touching. Would I fit right into him, his shoulders creating a perfect curve for my smaller ones? His arms would close around me. He could lay his cheek on top of my head, and I'd be surrounded.

I was getting dizzy.

When he stepped back, I had to reach for the counter with my free hand to brace myself. Wow. No wonder he'd always had so many women passing through his bed. How could anyone resist?

I was just annoyed at myself for being that predictable.

My phone rang, and I pulled it from my pocket, eager to get my mind on something else. Not on Callum's endless charms. But I groaned when I saw the screen.

"Who is it?" Callum asked.

"*Ian*."

"He been calling a lot?"

"Unfortunately. But I'm not going to answer."

Since that call a few days ago, he'd been lighting up my phone way too often. Sending me texts begging, *Zandra please*. Like it was my responsibility to solve his problems when *his* actions had left me bankrupt. The nerve to demand I ask my parents for a loan...

I went to put my phone away. But before I could, Callum grabbed it from my hand.

"What—"

Callum already had the phone up to his ear. "Z's phone," he said calmly. "Callum speaking."

Ugh. Great. I palmed my forehead.

I could hear Ian's confused voice through the speaker. "*Who*? I'm trying to reach Zandra."

"But you got me instead."

"And who the fuck are you?"

"I'm the guy who's with her now. *You* are rudely disrupting our date."

What? I perched my hand on my hip, frowning at him.

Callum shrugged at me.

"Date?" Ian's voice shot up an octave. "Put Zandra on the phone. Now."

"Nah." Callum's tone remained perfectly pleasant. "Here's how it's going to go, Ian. I'm gonna get off the phone so I can focus on Zandra. You interrupted us at a key moment, if ya know what I mean."

Ian sputtered incoherently, while I gaped. *A key moment?* I mouthed. Callum grinned, clearly very proud of himself.

"And you are going to stop calling her. Or we'll have a problem."

"A problem?"

"Is this hard for you to understand? I thought you big-city business types were smart. Zandra's done with you. If you keep bugging her, I'll stop being polite. I'll have to make this awkward. You'll probably cry. In short, a headache for all of us."

"You can't just—"

"Bye, Ian. Have a nice life."

Callum ended the call and held my phone out to me. I snatched it from his hand, torn between wanting to be angry at what he'd just done and wanting to laugh, so I settled on shaking my head. Because he was just too much.

And I kind of adored him for it.

"We're not on a date," I said.

"Obviously we're not. But making dinner together would be a very good date. It feels a *little* like a date."

"We work together. I just got out of a relationship, and you have no interest in being in one. You've never even had a girlfriend, or so you claim."

"It's true. I'm a girlfriend virgin. Just saying it *could* be a date. If it were, it would be going well. I mean..." He gestured around us, like his amazing dating skills couldn't be denied.

My skin was heating up. I didn't even know why I was arguing about this. "But it's not."

His eyes turned devious. "Z, you're protesting an awful lot."

"No I'm not."

"Do you *want* this to be a date?"

"*What*? I—You—" My tongue had twisted itself into a knot.

So I grabbed the spoon from the brownie batter and smeared it down his face. Callum's jaw dropped open.

"That's exactly what a girl on a date would do," he said.

"How would you know?"

He laughed, lunging forward and pinning me against the counter, his body flush with mine.

Shit.

Then he reached behind me, dipped his finger in the brownie bowl, and smeared chocolate across my cheek.

"Oh, you did not just do that." I grabbed another spoonful.

We were both laughing and dodging, getting brownie batter all over ourselves and probably half the kitchen. We wound up with my back against the fridge, him pinning my arms in front of me with a firm grip. His weight pressed into me, and he gazed down at me with a smirk. So close I could see the golden flecks in his brown irises. The faint stubble on his jaw.

His tongue licked batter from his lower lip, and I wondered what his stubble would feel like against my skin if he kissed me.

All the blood and all the common sense were rushing away from my head.

And that's when Darius stormed in, just as the oven timer for the pot pie was going off. "What the hell is going on in here?"

Oops.

Callum stepped back. I looked around at the disaster we'd made of the kitchen. There was brownie batter on the counter and splatters on the floor. Both Callum and I were smeared with it. Our hair. Our clothes.

Darius put his hands on his hips. "Is there any of that left to bake?"

"We made extra," Callum said smoothly, before whipping off his chocolate-stained shirt.

I tried not to stare, but holy hell.

The man was built. Full six pack plus juicy pecs, all golden and smooth. I'd seen the assortment of tattoos on his right forearm and bicep before, but they stretched all the way up to his shoulder. His baseball cap had been knocked to the floor during our batter fight, and his dark wavy hair was as wild as his eyes. My mouth went completely dry.

"We both need to shower," he said. "Z, you can go first if you want. Or if you want to save water—"

I tore my gaze away from Callum's torso, lifting it to his face. And he was smirking like he'd very much noticed his effect on me.

"Do not suggest it," I warned him.

"I was just gonna say I could have Dare hose us off in the yard."

"Keep me out of whatever this is." Darius swiped a dab of batter with his finger and tasted it. "Just let me know when the brownies are ready."

Callum rolled his eyes. "Z, you shower. I can clean up the mess. Even though, I'd like the record to show that *you started it.*"

"But you deserved it." Turning away from him, I asked, "Where's the bathroom?"

It was difficult enough to resist Callum when he was fully clothed.

Shirtless? He should have come with a warning label.

SIXTEEN
Callum

I KNOCKED on the bathroom door, running my fingers through my damp hair.

Zandra cracked it open, and I passed her a small stack of folded fabric. "Fresh clothes for you, as promised."

"Thanks," she said through the crack in the door.

I was trying not to think about the fact that she was in nothing but a towel in there. *My* towel, since she'd used the bath attached to my room.

"Did you get the batter out of your hair?" I asked.

"I think I managed. Did you shower already?"

"Used Darius's bathroom after promising I'd leave it pristine. I put your dirty clothes in the washer. Speed cycle."

"Thank you again."

"Feel free to use any of my toiletries."

"Got it."

There was a pause. I braced my hand against the door frame, looking in at her through the narrow opening, and we stared at each other for a beat too long.

She'd been so gorgeous in the kitchen when we were smearing each other with brownie batter. Who knew a food fight would be that sexy?

The way she'd laughed, completely uninhibited. I wanted to see her like that again, unencumbered by any worries. It was all too easy to imagine us pressed together again, feeling her body respond to me...

She shut the door, and I blew out a breath.

I had to calm down. This wasn't the first time I'd had a woman over. Far from it. So why was I so worked up?

Then again, usually the showers were *after* we'd already seen each other naked, and that wasn't going to happen with Zandra. I'd pissed off her ex on the phone by hinting we would spend this evening horizontal, but she and I both knew all the reasons that was a terrible idea.

So stop thinking about it, I told myself.

I headed out to the kitchen, where the pot pie was cooling and the brownies were in the oven.

"Smells good." Connor was eyeing my and Zandra's dinner.

"Keep your hands to yourself," I warned him. "Or you'll lose them."

Darius poured a glass of water. "Relax, Romeo. We're about to head out to grab burgers at Hearthstone. Some of the other guys are meeting us."

Connor's expression turned calculating. "Save us some corner brownie pieces, and we'll stay away until late. Give you the house to yourself. Niko's at his girl's place, so he won't be back."

I glanced to the side and stuck my hands in the pockets of my sweats, all casual. "It's not like that with Z."

Connor and Darius exchanged a skeptical glance. "You've never brought a woman over and cooked before," Darius observed.

"Sure I have." Not a cooking lesson, but surely I must've made dinner for a girl at some point.

Connor snickered. "No, you haven't. You also haven't bitten my head off just for looking at a woman you brought over before."

Don't look at her, I wanted to bark, which would only be proving his point.

"You're into her," Darius said flatly. "More than the usual. A lot more."

"I can't be into her. We're competing for the same job."

Connor glanced toward the hallway. "Then you won't mind if I ask for her number? Text her tomorrow so I can teach her cooking next? I make a mean omelet. A perfect breakfast after a night of—"

A feral growl rumbled from my chest. "I thought you two were leaving."

They were both laughing as they grabbed their wallets and hustled out the door. I'd do just about anything for those guys, because they were my friends as well as my fellow firefighters. But they were getting on my nerves.

If Zandra was different from any other woman I'd brought home before, it was just because she was an actual friend. Not a hookup. And when you slept with a friend, much less one who was also a coworker, things got complicated fast. Z and I could flirt and have fun together, but we wouldn't be crossing any lines. Regardless of how much I might want to get naked with her.

Fuck. *Really* wanted to get naked with her.

It had been too long since I'd gotten laid. That was my problem. Maybe I'd go out to a bar next weekend. Not Hearthstone. I could meet a tourist, get my fix, and I'd be good to go.

Yet the thought of Zandra doing the same with any other guy made me want to get stabby with my chef's knife.

I busied myself in the kitchen. Cleaning up a few smears of batter I'd missed, checking on the brownies in the oven. Starting to set the table for our dinner.

Then a couple minutes later, Zandra emerged from the bathroom. And she looked so good, she was already testing my resolve.

Her long hair was damp and falling down her back, leaving wet spots on my T-shirt. She kept hitching up the shorts I'd given her, which sat low on her hips. My breath caught in my throat.

Seeing her in my clothes... *Nngh.* It just made me want to rip them off her and cover her with my body instead.

I cleared my throat. "Comfy?"

"I look ridiculous," she said, tugging at the gaping collar of my shirt. She glanced around the kitchen. "Where are Connor and Darius?"

A wave of her scent rolled over me. Oh, hell. She'd used my body spray. Why was that so hot? It should not have been that hot.

Maybe it was a bad idea that Connor and Darius had left after all.

Ignoring the bolt of lust tightening my boxers, I went to grab us some drinks. "They bailed. It's just the two of us. That's okay, right?"

"Sure." She sounded quieter than usual.

"Want a glass of wine?" The words left my mouth before I could reconsider. Did I really need alcohol in my bloodstream with Zandra looking and smelling like that?

"You have wine? I would've thought a bunch of firefighters would have nothing but beer and whiskey in here."

"We're full of surprises." I pulled out a bottle of Pinot Grigio. "Besides, Niko's girlfriend left this here a couple days ago."

She smiled. "In that case, yes."

I poured the wine, then finished setting the table. "Let's eat before it gets cold."

We sat down at the small dining table, and the intimacy of the moment hit me. It wasn't just that we were both dressed in my worn-in clothes with wet hair. Something about the soft lighting, the home-cooked meal, the wine glasses catching the light, made this feel...significant.

I'd been giving her shit about this being a date earlier, but now the thought wouldn't leave my head. Especially after what Darius and Connor had been saying.

Did *I* actually want this to be a date?

I managed to shut up my overactive brain while we ate. The

pot pie was spot-on. Rich and savory filling, tender and buttery biscuits. Even if it was vegan butter.

Zandra took a bite and moaned. Which didn't help the interest my dick was already showing in her. "This is amazing. Seriously, Callum, this might be the best thing I've ever tasted. How'd you think of pot pie? I haven't had anything like this in forever."

"My mom used to make it when we were kids."

Her expression softened. "She passed away, right? You mentioned that."

"When I was in middle school." I dipped my spoon into the creamy chicken mixture.

"I'm sorry," she said gently. "And there were four of you. That must've been a lot for your dad."

"It would've been, if he'd stuck around." I kept my tone nonchalant, but I saw her eyes widen.

"He left?"

"About six months after Mom died. He hadn't been around that much before, but after, he was definitely finished with us."

"I'm so sorry. I had no idea."

I smiled, wanting to ease the concern in her eyes. "It's all right. That's why I'm so close with Ashford and Grace. Same with Teller Landry and his sister Piper. They lived across the street from us."

"What about your oldest brother?"

I felt my jaw tighten involuntarily at her mention of Grayden. "That's a really long story, and not as fun."

She kept her eyes on her food, but her next words were full of understanding. "We don't have to only talk about fun things. You've listened to me about Jessa and my parents. All my failures in Chicago."

"True." But there were some things about my history with Grayden that even Ashford and Grace didn't know. I didn't want to get into it with Z. Not because I didn't trust her, but because dwelling on bad shit wasn't my style. What was the point? "I assume being an only child means you have less sibling drama."

She laughed, but it sounded hollow. "My parents make up for it. They always wanted me to work for their company, but on their terms, not mine. Maybe that's why I wanted to be a business major. To make them proud. Prove I could do it on my own. I guess that backfired in several ways, because it turned out they liked Ian a lot more than they've ever liked me." She took a sip of wine.

"Good thing you've got Aunt Rosie, and she's worth ten of anyone else."

That brought a real smile to her lips. "Living with her and Jimmy isn't as bad as I thought it would be. Though I feel like I'm imposing."

"We do have that spare room," I said before I could stop myself. The thought of having her sleeping right next door to me was so tempting it was dangerous.

"I couldn't handle living with you."

We held gazes across the table, the air between us charged in a way that had nothing to do with the wine. The moment stretched until the laundry machine buzzed.

"Time for the dryer." I started to get up, but Zandra was already on her feet.

"I can do it," she insisted.

"You don't need me to push the buttons?"

She pressed her lips together. "Somehow I'll figure it out."

I pointed toward the hallway. "Laundry room's that way." But when she got up, I caught her by the wrist, my thumb pressing to her pulse point, feeling how rapidly it was thrumming. "For what it's worth, your parents and Ian are idiots for not seeing what was right in front of them. You're brilliant."

"You don't have to say that."

"I'm just stating what's obvious to me. Even back in high school, I could see it. You're somebody special."

Her gaze dropped. "So are you," she murmured. Zandra was

so tough all the time that when she let up, damn, it did things to me.

Once she was down the hall, I exhaled, glancing at the ceiling.

"*Fuuuck*," I whispered.

While she was gone, I put the dishes in the sink. Cut pieces of brownie and scooped oat milk ice cream from the carton I'd bought. All the while lecturing myself about what was *not* going to happen. If I kissed her, it could screw a lot of things up.

But it could still be worth it, a very dumb part of me said. The devil in my pants.

"Ice cream too?" she asked, joining me in the kitchen. "I'm going to gain a million pounds around you. Especially if any of this ends up on the Hearthstone menu."

"I'm sure it'll look great on you. Like everything else does."

"Stop flirting, Callum." But her words lacked their usual bite.

I picked up our bowls. "Dining table? Or living room?"

With her eyes averted, she said, "Living room. I like to curl up on the couch while I'm having dessert."

"Like a cat?"

"Shut up." Again, zero bite. "Are you watching any shows on Netflix?"

Totally a date, my rebellious side cheered. "I could put on a movie."

"Okay. I'll grab the wine."

"Perfect." My heart took off like I was running a 5K. And my cock was imagining Zandra and me cozying up, which was *not* supposed to happen. She was my competition. I had to be selfish.

But keeping my distance wasn't the particular way I wanted to be selfish right now.

I carried the bowls of dessert to the living room, while Zandra brought over our wine glasses. We settled onto the couch. I grabbed the Netflix remote and switched it on. "Rom com?" I asked. "Or action?"

"I'm good with anything." But when I clicked on something,

she made a cute sound of protest. "Not *that.* A serial killer documentary? No."

"I can comfort you if it's scary."

"But there's good scared and bad scared, and your creepy killer show is the latter for me."

I nudged her with my arm. "Pick something then. You're so fussy."

After a couple more minutes of arguing, we settled on an action romantic comedy. The dialogue was awful from minute one, but I wasn't paying that much attention. We finished our dessert—delicious—and then sipped wine while things exploded and the movie leads traded quips.

Zandra folded up her legs, bringing them closer to me. I widened my knees, wishing I wasn't wearing long sweatpants so our skin would touch.

But after a few more scenes in the movie, she was pressed in close enough that her arm draped over mine. Her laughter went to my head far more than the wine.

Whatever was happening right now, I didn't want it to end.

Unfortunately, I'd picked a short movie. Those ninety minutes had gone way too fast. "Another one?" I asked. "I think there's a sequel."

"If there is, I can't take it. Thanks, though. For the whole evening. This has been fun."

"If it had been a date, it would've been fucking amazing. Admit it."

"Fine. I admit it. It would've been a really good date."

I pretended to glance around the living room. "I don't even have an audience to witness this. My first real, official date, and I aced it."

"Not a date."

"Yeah, yeah. That's for the best anyway. Because if this really were a date, then the next thing I would do is kiss you."

She opened her mouth again, like she was about to tell me all the ways I was an arrogant prick. Our usual banter, which was pretty enjoyable in itself.

But instead of all the protests and indignation I expected, she started leaning in. Then stopped so close I could feel her exhale on my skin.

You're playing with fire, I told myself. But fuck it. I was trained for that, wasn't I?

"Zandra," I whispered. "Do you *want* me to kiss you?"

"No."

"Okay."

Her gaze flicked down to my lips. "I don't."

But she didn't back away. Didn't get up. Didn't put one single centimeter between her body and mine. Instead, she seemed to vibrate with wanting.

Or maybe that was me.

In that moment, I didn't care about Hearthstone. Didn't give a damn about bad ideas or two-month trials. This was complicated and messy and exactly what I'd said I wouldn't do.

But if Zandra wanted it, I didn't care about any of that. I would've given just about anything to taste that mouth.

Then she was the one who closed the last inch. And suddenly, her soft lips were on mine.

Fuck. Yes.

I stroked into her mouth with my tongue, and Zandra melted into me like warm sugar. When I tugged her closer, she came willingly, her hands fisting my shirt.

The kiss was everything. Slow and deep. Hot and desperate. Nothing tentative or testing about it. No, we kissed like we'd been building toward exactly this for a long damn time.

To my surprise, she pushed me onto my back. I bounced against the couch cushions. My mouth opened to make some teasing comment about how she didn't need to get rough with me. She could have anything she wanted.

But Zandra was already crawling over me, fusing our lips again.

After a while, my arms circled her waist, and I flipped us so I was on top. Hadn't even broken the kiss. She moaned and arched into me, her thigh brushing the thickening length in my sweats, and I thought I might lose my mind.

I wanted her naked. Writhing beneath me. My cock pumping inside her, driving us both wild in every position until we couldn't take anymore.

Then just as suddenly, she was pushing me back, forcing enough space between us that she could slip off the couch and scramble away.

"Z?"

"I need to go," she said, breathless and panicked.

I sat up. "Zandra, wait."

"I can't do this." She was already on her feet, heading for the front door.

"Okay, that's...fine." A shake of my head brought me back to reality. "We don't have to do anything. But—"

"I'm sorry. I just need to go."

"Then I'll drive you home." If I could just get a handle on this raging tent in my sweatpants first.

"I can walk."

The hell? "Come on, Z. Just wait for me." But she shoved her feet into her shoes, grabbed her bag, and was out the door. Still wearing my clothes and practically running down the driveway.

Fuck. *Fuck.*

Not even bothering with shoes, I palmed my keys and followed. Her silhouette was visible partway down the block. She hadn't gotten far.

Jumping into my truck, I drove slowly down the street and buzzed my window down when I reached her. "Get in."

"I'm fine walking."

"It's dark out, and your aunt's place is a mile away. Get in."

She must have heard something in my voice, because she stopped and climbed into the passenger seat.

"Look, Z, I'm sorry if I—"

She shook her head sharply. "We're not talking about it."

"Are you serious?"

"Deadly."

Oh-kay. *Play with fire, and you might get burned*. But my mouth wouldn't stay shut. "It's okay that you changed your mind. Alright? I'm not mad. Just to be clear."

"I know that."

"It was a great kiss too, for what it's worth."

"Callum."

"Also, you kissed me, if you recall. You started it, not me. Like the food fight."

"And it's never happening again," she said firmly. "Can you drive now please?"

I pulled away from the curb. "I mean, it *could* happen. Only if you want it to."

Silence.

When we reached Rosie's house, Zandra jumped out before I'd even put the truck in park. "Never mention this," she said through the open door.

"Zandra, come on—"

She slammed the truck door and hurried up the walkway. I waited until she was safely inside, the porch light casting a warm glow as she disappeared through the front door.

I sat there for a long moment, trying to figure out what the hell had just happened.

SEVENTEEN

Zandra

I WOKE to a warm lump trying to smother me.

"Chloe," I tried to say, though of course the word came out muffled. When I attempted to move, Chloe meowed indignantly about being disturbed from her beauty sleep. "Get off me, you menace."

She shifted and I sat up, greeting the same view I'd faced every morning for the last couple of weeks. The tiny guestroom in my auntie Rosie's house, with sunlight streaming through the gingham curtains and a bed narrow enough to make me feel like I was back in my college dorm.

Then everything about last night rushed back to me. Proof that nothing was the same, because I had done something unforgivably stupid.

I'd kissed Callum.

I had pushed Callum onto the couch and practically mauled his face.

"Oh geez. Why did I do that?"

Well, perhaps the answer to that was obvious. I'd wanted him. Callum had been so sweet and sexy and *lickable* last night that I'd lost all reason.

My body heated and my heart raced as my mind replayed the

memory. In the past, I would have expected Callum to be pushy and careless with a woman, rushing through the kisses and caresses in the hopes of just getting off.

But he hadn't been that way at all.

He'd kissed me like he wanted to memorize my taste. Like if my kiss was the entire meal and nothing more was on the menu, he would've been completely satisfied. I'd felt his erection, of course, but he hadn't seemed to be in any hurry.

If anything, *I* was the one who'd been pushy.

His touch had been firm but deliberate, holding me close. The way his tongue had teased my mouth, and his lips had nibbled mine...

"Why did it have to be so good, Chloe?"

She jumped down from the bed and trotted toward the door, clearly ready for breakfast. I was about to kick off the covers and follow when I realized I was still wearing Callum's clothes.

I smoothed my hands down the cotton of the T-shirt, then fingered the thin athletic fabric of the shorts.

Oh, this was so bad.

I jumped up, quickly getting undressed.

At least the gnomes from Rosie's collection on the nearby shelf were all turned around to face the wall. I couldn't take those ceramic eyes staring at me, which was why I'd repositioned them my second day here.

Which reminded me of the gnome dressed like a football player that I'd given him. How genuinely happy he'd been about that silly gift. Like it really mattered to him.

I was so confused.

Callum was a man I'd hated for most of my life. Of course, I didn't hate him now. I liked him way too much. I'd had an amazing time with him last night. Better than any date I'd been on before, and it hadn't been a date at all.

But that didn't change the fact that this was the worst possible idea. I couldn't fool around with Callum O'Neal. Certainly couldn't have *feelings* for him.

The only solution was denial. I just had to pretend last night never happened. As I'd said to Callum just as I'd leaped from his truck like a spy escaping an enemy airplane. *Never mention this.*

He would do as I asked, right?

Ugh, I was screwed.

After throwing on a different T-shirt and my own pair of shorts, I ventured out of my room with Chloe leading the way.

Breakfast was a quick affair. I was still full from the pot pie and brownie sundae, so I just had a piece of gluten-free toast smeared with apricot jam.

Rosie and Jimmy's voices carried from the main bedroom, but they didn't emerge, and I was grateful. Didn't want them asking about what Callum and I did last night. What if I slipped up and told the truth?

We cooked one of the best meals I've ever had, snuggled up on the couch, then I crawled all over him and tried to eat his face. Why? What did you do?

Rosie would've loved hearing those details. Then probably would share too many details of *her* sex life. And then I'd be scarred forever.

"Sorry, Coco," I said quietly. "I'm getting out of here. You're on your own." Not that she cared after I'd set out her food and topped up her water. Besides, she adored Jimmy.

I was quick with my morning routine in the bathroom. No need for another shower since I'd had one last night at Callum's place. Along with using his body spray, which I could still smell on me, and it smelled so yummy. *Gah.*

As I dressed in work clothes for the day, I told myself not to think about how ridiculously attractive Callum had looked in those sinfully snug sweatpants. I started moving faster, like that would somehow help me outrun the images in my brain. Or the remembered sensation of Callum's thick erection when I'd bumped against it. His lips. His tongue. His hands.

But after I grabbed my purse and keys and ran out the front door, I stopped in my tracks.

Callum sat on the porch steps, wearing his ripped jeans and an SRFD shirt.

He glanced up and grinned. "Hi. Brought you a pistachio latte." Standing up, he held two paper coffee cups in his hands and extended one toward me.

"Thanks," I said carefully, taking the drink. Because there was no way I was turning it down. Pistachio milk was a glorious invention. "I'll get the coffees next time."

"No worries. How'd you sleep?" he asked. As if it was perfectly normal for him to show up at Rosie's and make small talk at eight in the morning.

"Um, okay. What are you doing here? Aside from delivering coffee, apparently."

"Just wanted to see you. Figured I'd walk you into work."

"Why?"

"Because I want to." Callum's smile was softer at the edges than usual. *Knowing*.

Like he was thinking about the kiss.

A cascade of flutters erupted in my stomach.

"Alright." It wasn't a very long walk to Hearthstone. Rosie's house was practically on his route anyway. This didn't have to be weird.

Except for the fact that he would've driven to Main Street, gone to Silver Linings, and then backtracked to walk here and meet me.

Oh, and the part where *you kissed him last night. And then ran away.*

But I was not acknowledging that.

"Also, I thought we should talk about last night," Callum said.

Dammit. "No, thanks."

"I realize you told me not to mention it. But what was that intelligent phrase we used to say on the playground? Ah, right. You're not the boss of me. *Yet*, anyway."

Ha. If he wanted to be cute about this, I could too. "What did you want to talk about? The brownies?"

His smile grew as he sipped his coffee. "I was thinking more about the part that happened after."

"Can't recall. Oh, the movie?"

"Play it that way if you want, Z, but we're going to talk about it eventually. I'll wear you down."

"Stop calling me Z."

He tipped his head back and laughed. "It's way too late for you to object. I've been calling you Z for weeks."

I decided the silent treatment was in order, because he was infuriating. And also correct. Him calling me Z wasn't such a big deal, but it was a symptom of my larger problem. Clearly I hadn't been thinking straight around him for a long while now.

We turned onto Main Street. Callum seemed to know half the people we passed and said hello, slapping backs and shaking hands like a future politician. I sipped my latte.

But we were only halfway down the block when he said, "You're seriously going to pretend that kiss didn't happen?"

"What kiss?" I was all-in on this denial thing. I smiled and nodded at someone walking by with a Jack Russell on a leash.

"Our epic, hot-as-fuck make-out session—"

"Lower your voice," I hissed.

"Which definitely happened. Ring any bells?"

"Nope."

Callum glanced over at me, his cheerful expression hardening.

Then he tugged me into a narrow gap between two brick buildings. "I'm going to make you talk."

"You can't."

"I've proven before that I can." He took the coffee cup from my hand, setting it and his own on the concrete.

"Hey! I was drinking that."

"You can finish it later. After you admit the fact that you kissed me." The smirk made a reappearance as he blocked my way out, one arm reaching to brace against the wall. "And you liked it."

I sputtered, backed up against the brick wall. Both a real one and a metaphorical one.

"Zandra, you kissed me. You practically crawled on top of me, forced me back on the couch, and had your way with me."

I glanced to the side, mortified at the idea of someone walking by and overhearing this. Which anyone could at any moment. "Fine. I kissed you, okay?"

He leaned closer, placing both hands against the brick on either side of me. "And you liked it."

"Good lord. You're incorrigible."

"Nothing else has to happen between us. Unless you want it. But I just need to hear you admit you liked kissing me."

"What is wrong with you?"

"Just need to hear you say it. *Callum, I liked...*"

"We are not doing this." I slipped under his arm, escaping the narrow space between the buildings.

And then I ran for Hearthstone. Like the coward that I was.

Work was normal. The cooks moved around the kitchen, Russ did brewing things. Customers ate. Or so I assumed. It was impossible for me to concentrate.

Instead, I paced around in Grandpa's office.

This wasn't me. I didn't flip out this way, especially not about a guy. When Ian had first asked me to dinner after our Business Analytics class, I'd actually drafted a pro-and-con list before accepting.

For most of my life, I'd been steady and responsible. With a sassy attitude, sure. Did I get testy at times with people who disrespected me? Yes. Like any strong, opinionated woman, I'd been called difficult. I owned it.

But nobody, *no one*, had ever turned me inside out and upside down like Callum O'Neal.

I managed to get some work done. By late afternoon, it was time to head home. Callum had been behind the bar all day, so thankfully I'd hardly seen him at all.

Opening the office door, I peeked out. Chef Alice gave me an odd look as she wandered by. "Are you okay, Zandra?"

"Yep. I'm peachy." Closing up the office behind me, I walked toward the back door. I would slip out and walk home to Rosie's.

"Z," an all-too-familiar voice said behind me.

My eyes closed as I sighed. "Callum."

"Can I talk to you for a sec?"

"I was just about to head out."

"It won't take long." His fingertips touched the small of my back, guiding me toward the storage room near the back of the building. The one with the sticky lock.

We went inside. I spun to face him. And just like before, he shut the door behind us.

"This again?" I asked.

"I didn't close the door very hard. Even if it stuck, the key's right there." He pointed to it hanging on the wall. "You can leave if you really want to. I'll let you go. But I think it's wiser if we finish this conversation. Otherwise, we'll have this unresolved tension hanging over our heads. Making it impossible to concentrate."

"There's no tension."

"No?" He stepped closer.

My body felt like a live wire. "None whatsoever."

He brought his lips within inches of my ear. "At some point, you're going to have to admit you like me."

"I do. As a *friend*." My voice shook on the word.

"That's not what I mean. You can't fake sparks like the ones we had last night. I'm a firefighter. I know sparks." Another step closer. His breath ghosted over the skin of my neck, covering me with shivers. "I've been half hard ever since. Considered taking care of that when I woke up this morning, but I'm not against a little edging."

"*Callum.*" I pressed my palm to his chest with every intention of shoving him away and getting out of here.

Big mistake.

Instead, I became all too aware of how firm his chest was. How it had felt against me last night, after he'd flipped our positions on the couch and held me down with his weight. How I'd craved so much more.

A moan slipped from my throat.

Callum's eyes traced down to my lips. "See, I've been thinking about it. Could hardly sleep from the way my mind kept turning over what happened. You know what I figured out?"

"That it's a terrible idea?"

"It is a pretty bad idea. Yeah."

His words caught me off guard because he was agreeing with me. "And we should never do it ever again, right?"

"At first, that's what I was thinking too. Just forget about it and focus on work. But we could make this beneficial for both of us. We're together all the time. Why not take advantage of that?"

"Did they not show you the hostile work environment video? I have to think there was a training at some point."

"*You* kissed *me*." Callum's mouth curved in a wicked smirk, and I followed the movement, remembering how he'd tasted. Heat was rising to my skin, burning me from the inside out.

"We're not doing this. We can't."

"We can do whatever we want. If we're careful." He inhaled, nostrils flaring. "You still smell like me."

"I slept in your clothes," I heard myself saying.

"Fuck, that's hot. Tell me you don't want me."

"I don't." *Liar.*

"Tell me you don't want to kiss me again right fucking now." He used his lower lip to bump mine. I whimpered like a desperate, needy thing.

"I don't." *Pants on fire.*

And then, the same bizarre trance overcame me as last night. Like something had completely possessed me. Taking over my brain.

I grabbed Callum's face and pressed my lips to his.

He grunted, his hand going to my chin to hold me there as he took control of the kiss. Callum tilted his head and his tongue licked against mine, sending shudders of arousal down my spine and between my legs.

There were Hearthstone employees in the kitchen. Someone could come this way and hear us. Or they might need toilet paper, head to this storage room and find us here.

But right now, I didn't care. There was only Callum standing between me and the rest of the world, his mouth dueling with mine. His solid strength under my hands as I tentatively touched him.

Oh, I wanted to touch him.

Sneaking beneath the bottom of his T-shirt, my fingers met hot, smooth skin over hard muscle. Callum kept dominating my mouth with his kisses while I caressed the ridges of his abs. My thumbs found his nipples, my hands squeezing the thickness of his pecs. He groaned, lips breaking from mine.

"You like getting your hands on me?" he rasped.

"You're so hot."

"So are you, beautiful. You drive me fucking wild."

His hands, so much bigger than mine, suddenly gripped my butt cheeks through my jeans and hoisted me up. Spun me so my back was to the door. I crashed against it, the vibrations sending a few rolls of paper towels and random boxes of supplies careening to the ground.

Then Callum bucked his hips against me. The swollen ridge of his cock pressed between my legs through our clothes, and I jolted with another fierce bolt of arousal.

"That feel good?"

My moan was wanton. He lifted my legs more, wrapping them around his waist as he thrust, his crotch rubbing on mine.

Nothing had ever felt so good. So dirty and forbidden and perfect.

Like we were two teenagers stealing a moment together, giving in to our irresistible need, heedless of the consequences.

What was this man doing to me?

"Open your eyes. Look at me."

I did, meeting the lust-filled gaze of Callum's brown-and-gold irises. His breaths came shallow and quick, like mine. Like this was affecting him as much as it was me.

"You want me to make you come, Sunflower?"

"Yes," I whispered. "Make me come."

He grasped my chin. "Say it louder. Say you want me." Another thrust. "You want my cock."

My throat worked as I swallowed. Even with the haze in my brain, I was still aware of the rest of Hearthstone outside this door. The risk we were taking. "I want it."

"I can't hear you."

"I want you, Callum," I gritted out.

His smirk could've been cruel or mocking. But it wasn't. It was more like the sun rising, lighting up everything in this dim, crowded space. "I want you too, Z. I've always wanted you."

His mouth dove onto mine, tongue sliding past my lips as he rocked his erection over my clit through our clothes. His hands squeezed, holding me up. It was rough and urgent. Almost too much sensation. But exactly what I needed.

The orgasm came on me fast. Flooding my body with overwhelming pleasure. I cried out, but the sound was thankfully muffled by Callum's tongue. Then I realized he was shaking too. The flat of his palm slapped against the wooden door by my head as he groaned through his own climax.

He'd just come in his pants. In the back storage room at Hearthstone.

What the heck were we thinking?

Callum rested his forehead against mine, breathing hard.

Then slowly eased me down so my feet touched the concrete floor. "Don't freak out," he murmured.

Too late.

"What if they heard us?" I hissed.

"They probably didn't."

"Probably?" I put my ear to the door, listening.

Callum was adjusting his clothes. "But if they did, we'll deal with it. It's going to be fine."

Panic clawed at me. Same thing I'd felt last night at his house, but so much worse. I needed this job. What if I embarrassed my grandfather? My parents' disappointment was bad enough, but Grandpa too...

"I need to go." I picked up my purse from where I'd dropped it.

Callum sighed, lifting the key from its hook. But I tried the knob and found it unlocked. He'd been right. He hadn't closed the door hard enough to make the lock stick. Someone could've walked in on us.

Sliding out, I didn't see anyone. Thank God.

"I'll call you later, okay?" he said.

"Please don't."

"Z—"

I turned to him, pleading with my eyes. "I...I liked what we just did. Even if that was the most reckless thing I've ever done. But we got that out of our system, and it's finished now."

His mouth opened like he might disagree, but nothing came out. Because he knew I was right.

We were still competing for the general manager position. This had been a one-time indiscretion. And his reputation spoke for itself. Neither of us wanted anything...more.

I couldn't afford to.

EIGHTEEN

Zandra

OPERATION *STAY AWAY from Callum* was well underway.

Callum and I had gone back to carrying out our Hearthstone duties separately. But this time, there was no animosity behind our enforced separation. More like self-preservation.

If I was calling vendors, he was working on the schedule and handling employee issues. If I was going over menu changes with Alice, then Callum was troubleshooting the brewing operation with Russ. We were polite and professional, but nothing more.

Anything to avoid being alone with him. Or, heaven forbid, talking about what had happened.

Because part of me *did* want to do it again. I couldn't stop thinking about how good he'd felt. How he'd made me shameless, and it had been more satisfying than any sexual experience I'd ever had. No wonder he'd had an endless parade of women through his bed even in high school.

Callum was...*ugh*. Dangerous.

Hard to say which scenario would be worse. That we'd keep hooking up and then Grandpa—and the rest of Silver Ridge—would find out.

Or that Callum would lose interest, and I'd be the stupid girl panting after the town's most notorious man-whore. *Such an offensive term, I know*. But it was true.

I couldn't trust myself around him.

At least we were a month into the trial period. Halfway through. I could make it through another month of this, right? Another month of keeping my distance. Not sharing jokes and morning lattes and cooking lessons. Four more weeks of pretending I didn't miss spending time with him.

After one of us got the job, then that person would be the boss. And this ridiculous pull I felt toward Callum would have to end.

The following Sunday after the storage room *encounter*, I pulled into a familiar gravel driveway. My tires crunched over the small stones that led to Grandpa's modest ranch house.

The place wasn't fancy by any means, but it sat on nearly ten acres of pine-dotted land that stretched back into the foothills. The nearest neighbor was a quarter mile away, hidden behind a stand of aspen trees. Grandpa had always valued his privacy.

He'd gone home from the hospital weeks ago and was now terrorizing his in-home nurse instead of the hospital ones. He'd even made a couple of visits to Hearthstone, putting the team through a surprise inspection, though it had exhausted him.

I was here today for our standing Sunday visit, which was also a convenient way to avoid Sunday dinners with my parents. *Win*.

I usually brought chicken nuggets, sometimes bringing Rosie along with me. But today it was just me, and I'd brought something different for him to try.

The door was unlocked as usual, so I went ahead inside. "Grandpa? I'm here."

I heard his voice coming from the living room. "Zandra! Finally, someone I *want* to see."

His nurse streaked past me, heading for the kitchen. She gave me a long-suffering look. *Sorry*, I mouthed on my way to the living room.

"How are you feeling today?" I set my purse down and walked over to kiss his forehead.

"Like hell. I've been thinking about hiring someone to come redo my walls so I can watch the paint dry. It would be better than the crap they put on TV anymore."

I hummed understandingly. As I always did when he made this same exact speech. "Sounds rough."

"They've got me shuffling around on that infernal walker when I'd rather take a nap. Can't go by myself to the toilet to move my bowels in privacy. What'd you bring me? Nuggets?"

I held up the container with a grin. "Brownies."

His face fell. "Brownies? Where are my nuggets? You know Sunday means nuggets."

"Enough about the nuggets. I made these yesterday. Dark chocolate."

"As long as they're not health food," he grumbled, but he was already reaching for the container. Of course, he nodded appreciatively after he took a bite. "Not bad. You made these?"

I decided not to reveal they were gluten free. "Don't sound so surprised."

"What inspired the baking? Was it Rosie's idea?"

Callum's smile appeared in my mind. The way we'd both laughed while splattering each other with brownie batter. How he'd stood behind me, holding my hand to show me how to fold the ingredients...

"I felt like trying something new," I said, my heart squeezing.

So stupid.

For about five minutes there, Callum and I had actually been friends. And *I* was the one who ruined it by kissing him. Twice. Callum had been an active participant in us fooling around, but I doubted he would've crossed the line if not for me crossing it first.

Talk about a shocker. I had corrupted *him*.

The craziest part was how much I missed him.

Grandpa took another bite. Chocolate crumbs gathered in his

whiskers. "It's been a month now. Halfway through your and Callum's trial period."

I brushed lint off my pants. "Yep. I've had my eye on the calendar."

"Well, time for your unvarnished opinion. Off the record and confidential. What do you really think of Callum's performance? What are his weaknesses? Go ahead, rip him to shreds." Grandpa waved his hand impatiently, like he hadn't just asked the impossible.

The muscle in my chest squeezed painfully again.

I chose my words carefully. "He's very capable. Good with the employees and customers, and he's quickly getting to know the business inside and out. He's still less comfortable with the numbers part, but he's learning."

Grandpa's eyes narrowed. "And that's exactly the vague kind of drivel he said about you. How is that supposed to help me make my decision on which of you to hire?"

I sighed. "I don't know, Grandpa."

"Where's your competitive fire? Where's the passion?"

Where Callum was concerned, *passion* was exactly what I needed to avoid.

Grandpa kept muttering about young people these days, but I managed to change the subject and talk about Russ's next batch of beers. Then Grandpa got to ranting about his hatred for hop water, and the conversation was on far safer ground.

As I left my grandfather's house, a text buzzed my phone. My breath caught when I saw it was from Callum.

Z, could you cover for me behind the bar tonight? Emergency came up and I can't be there for bar manager duties

Of course. Hope everything's okay

Thx!

I stood outside my car, tapping my phone on my palm and

wondering if I should write something more. Should I ask if Callum needed anything else? Was the emergency about his family?

But I stopped myself. *Professional distance.* That's what I needed.

At Hearthstone, Winnie was on the schedule tonight. She nodded to me when I arrived, heading straight for me after she finished serving a customer. "So you heard about the fire?"

"*Fire*?" My stomach swooped. "What fire?"

"That's why you're here, right? To fill in for Callum?"

Russ appeared, joining our huddle. "Any updates?"

"I don't even know what's going on," I said loudly, my anxiety rising. I felt Russ and Winnie staring, plus some regulars at the bar.

But I wasn't feeling calm and collected at the moment.

As I got a rundown of the fire up on Copper Road on the west side of town, my dread only grew. "Started as a grass fire earlier this afternoon," Winnie said.

Russ cursed. "Red flag warning today."

She nodded, flipping her blond locks over her shoulder. "Yeah, high winds. It's not threatening homes yet, but the situation could change fast if they don't get it contained. That's where Callum is."

The volunteer firefighters had gotten called to the fire. He was *in danger*.

"I didn't get any notifications on my phone," I said, pulling it out to check. Nausea swirled in my gut. I couldn't believe all this had been going on, and I didn't know.

Why hadn't Callum told me the emergency was a *fire* and he was heading toward it?

Because was a fighter. A warrior. A flipping hero, and that was just what he did.

"There's an app you can download," Winnie said. "I'll show you. But a lot of the updates are on group texts with my neighbors, you know? The Silver Ridge gossip grapevine."

As the evening wore on, there was no real news. Not what I wanted to hear, anyway. That all the firefighters were completely safe and everything would be fine.

"Hey Zandra, you sure you're okay to finish up without me?" Winnie asked after closing, grabbing her purse. She'd already told me she had a date tonight.

"Yeah, go. I'll be fine," I assured her, though my voice sounded steadier than I felt.

I went through the familiar routine of wiping down the bar, running the dishwasher, counting the till. The tasks helped keep my mind occupied, but every few minutes I found myself checking my phone for updates about the fire.

In the kitchen, the last staff members finished up their work and said goodnight, one by one.

Finally, I locked the doors and headed for the back parking lot. It was a cool summer night, and without the warmth and high energy of the brewpub around me, I shivered in my short-sleeved top.

Main Street and the surrounding neighborhood were quiet. Calm. A couple of bright lights shone over the parking lot, so there was no reason for me to feel nervous.

Maybe it was knowing Callum was risking his life right now. It made everything feel more fragile, more uncertain. I knew what it was like to lose someone who mattered to me.

Oh. The realization dawned. *Oh, wow.*

Callum mattered to me a lot. He wasn't my best friend like Jessa had been, yet the thought of anything happening to him was enough to steal my breath from my lungs.

Somehow, I had to see him tonight. Had to make sure he was okay.

I was halfway to my car when I saw movement near the far end of the lot. Smelled tobacco smoke. There was someone standing beside a dark sedan, just lurking there in the shadows. The end of a cigarette glowed red.

My steps slowed.

The figure turned, and I recognized him. Thinning hair, sunken eyes. A harsh smirk. His athlete's build had gotten softer over the years, but he was still tall and broad.

Tommy Pickering.

"Hey, Zandra. Heard you were back in Silver Ridge." The words were harsh. Sarcastic. "Seen you working the bar." He flicked his cigarette butt to the ground.

I crossed my arms over my chest, gripping my keys in my hand. "What're you still doing here, Tommy?" I tried to keep my voice light, casual. "We closed a while ago."

He shrugged, not moving away from the car. "Didn't have anyplace better to go."

"Are you safe to drive?" The question slipped out before I could stop it, though I hadn't even seen him drinking at Hearthstone tonight.

"You offering to take me with you? We could go somewhere if you want." Tommy's gaze wandered down to my shoes and up again. His smirk slid into a knowing leer. "The creek?"

I inhaled sharply, taking a step back. "You need to leave. Right now."

"Still an ice-cold little princess, huh? You were even more of a prude than Jessa was."

"*Leave,*" I shouted. "Get off my grandfather's property before I report you for trespassing."

My whole body was shaking. I couldn't breathe all the way until he finally got into his car and drove away, his taillights disappearing around the corner.

Tommy had brought up Jessa and the creek to provoke a reaction from me. I knew that. But he'd still gotten to me. Just like he had with his lies back in high school.

Lies I still didn't understand.

I took an unsteady breath, walking quickly toward my own car. I'd come here straight after leaving Grandpa's, so I hadn't walked from Rosie's.

As I approached, I noticed something tucked under my windshield wiper. A piece of paper. Probably an ad for a local service, or a notice about some upcoming festival. I almost crumpled the paper in my fist.

But something made me unfold it.

What I saw there made my blood turn to ice, terrible memories flooding my mind from every direction.

Someone had scrawled in blood red: *Murderer*.

NINETEEN
Callum

My body ached, and I was covered in dried sweat and soot. What a hell of an afternoon. And evening.

Fuck, what time was it anyway?

We'd gotten the alert around midday, calling any available volunteers to a fire off Copper Road. The initial attack was always a rush, working in tandem to anchor the fire and establish control lines.

By the time most of us were released, close to midnight last I checked, I was beat. We'd spent the last several hours mopping up and cold-trailing. Checking for hotspots. A crew had stayed behind to monitor the site overnight.

A job well done, and that felt good. Now, I just couldn't wait to crawl into bed. I was too tired to even think about Z.

Okay, maybe not *that* tired.

Darius drove with me in his passenger seat. Niko was a few minutes behind us. Connor hadn't responded to the fire, apparently busy with something else tonight.

As Darius pulled onto our street, all was quiet. Yet immediately, something seemed off.

A car I recognized was parked in front of our house, but it wasn't one I'd expected to ever see here. Not after what happened on her last visit. And in the storage room at Hearthstone the day after.

"Hey, isn't that Zandra?" Darius asked.

Fresh worries churned in my stomach. I'd checked my phone already, letting my siblings know I was safe. I hadn't seen a single message from Zandra after the few we'd exchanged about her taking my shift.

She'd been avoiding me the last several days. Upset about our mutual orgasms in the storage room. Which was frustrating, though I didn't know what to do about our situation either. I didn't date. Wasn't a relationship guy, and that hadn't changed. I didn't even know *how* to do relationships.

All I knew was that I still wanted her.

And the thought that something bad had happened set off a chain reaction inside me, my adrenaline racing like I was back at the fire again. If it was that douchewad Ian...

"Stop here," I said. "Let me out."

"We're almost to the driveway."

"*Right now.*"

Darius cursed, braking hard. "Let me know if I can help."

"I've got it." My friend was being a solid guy, but the instinct that leaped to my throat was, *Keep your distance. She's mine.*

Not really true. Not helpful either, but damn, that was what my gut told me.

Z's mine.

I jumped out and headed for Zandra's car. If she needed me right now, then nothing else mattered.

She was slumped in the front seat with a thin blanket wrapped around her. I panicked for a moment, tugging on the locked handle, but as soon as I knocked on the window, she startled and sat up. Hurried to unlock the door. I had to back up for her to push it open.

And then she lunged for me, wrapping her arms around my middle.

"You're okay," she said.

"Yeah, I am. Are *you* okay?" I held her close, breathing in the familiar scent of her hair. This was unexpected. But felt so fucking right. "What happened, Z?"

"Everyone was talking about the fire. I downloaded an app. It finally said the fire was contained, but that was after… And I didn't know…"

"Hey, slow down. I'm just fine. Okay?" I stroked her hair. "I'm fine."

"Your roommates? And the other firefighters?"

I nodded toward Darius, who'd pulled into the driveway. "Dare is over there. Niko is heading home, and Connor was elsewhere. No injuries. It all went well."

She nodded, still clinging to me. "I know I'm being ridiculous. I'm sorry to show up like this."

"I don't mind. We should go inside, though. I'm getting dirt all over you."

"I know I've been avoiding you. But when I heard you were in danger…" Her fingers lifted to trace my jaw, clearly unconcerned about how dirty I was, and my heart did some kind of dance inside my rib cage.

I had never seen Zandra like this before. Made me wonder if something *else* happened, beyond just worrying about me.

"Don't stress about it. Come on. Let's just go inside, and we can talk."

Z glanced at her car. "Maybe I should…"

I held her chin, gently turning her head to face me again. "Don't even think about leaving here. If you do, I'm just gonna chase you."

She blinked, making a sharp sound with a quick intake of breath. I felt the movement of her chest against my torso. The *aliveness* of her, like something soft and beautiful in my hands.

"I'm so confused. I have no idea what I'm doing."

That honesty slayed me. "Baby," I murmured, lips brushing her hairline. She shivered.

"You shouldn't call me that." But there was zero conviction in her voice.

"Just come inside, and I'll make everything better. If you let me."

"Okay," she whispered.

"Good."

Whatever this was, whatever was happening between us, we'd figure it out. But I was *not* going to let her go.

With that settled, I picked up her purse from the center console and the keys from her hand. When I twined our fingers together, she came willingly, that thin blanket still draped around her shoulders.

Inside, I led her straight to the kitchen. Darius had already beaten us there. "I was putting on some coffee. Figured you might need it."

"Thanks, man." I tugged Z closer, arm going around her waist. "You can jump in the shower, Dare. First round of hot water is yours."

In other words, give us some privacy, I said with my eyes. But my friend didn't get it.

"You sure?" He glanced between us. "Zandra looks pretty shaken up."

Her head dipped, hair falling in front of her face.

"We'll be fine," I insisted.

As soon as he'd walked off, leaving us alone in the soft glow of the kitchen lights and the gurgling of the coffeemaker, I turned Zandra to face me. Grabbing the edges of the blanket she was wearing, I tucked it tighter around her. The fleece was well worn, with a cartoon pattern of paw prints along the border.

"Is this Chloe's?"

"I keep it in my car for her when I take her to the vet," Zandra said quietly. "I didn't have a jacket, and it's a cold night."

"It is. You came here straight from Hearthstone?"

"Yeah."

The thought of her sitting outside in the cold, worried about me, twisted in my chest. I hated that she'd been scared, but a part of me liked it too. Suggested she might've been thinking about me the past few days as much as I'd been obsessing about her.

And I just wanted to wrap her up all warm and snug, tuck her into my bed with me, and never ever let her leave. Was that wrong?

"You sit right here, and I'll make us coffee." Moving her to a barstool by the island, I nudged her to take a seat, still making sure the blanket was draped around her.

I would've preferred that *I* was draped around her, but I needed a couple more sets of arms.

Also, I was still pretty grimy, so my first stop was to the kitchen sink for a perfunctory scrub of my face and arms. After that, I opened the fridge to take out the carton of oat milk. The coffeemaker beeped right on cue.

"I'm surprised you have non-dairy milk," she said, watching me pour.

"Bought it at the market a couple days ago." I handed her the mug across the island. "Just in case you came back."

"But I was avoiding you."

"I'm an optimist," I replied, settling onto the stool beside her with a mug of my own. I watched her sip the coffee, noting how her hands still trembled slightly around the warm mug. "Z, is anything else bothering you?"

"How can you tell?"

"I might be just a little obsessed with you." I held up my thumb and forefinger, holding them slightly apart.

The beginnings of a smile curved her lips. I wanted to kiss her to feel the shape of it.

Then she pulled a crumpled paper from her pocket. "This was under my windshield at Hearthstone tonight when I left."

I unfolded the paper, and red tinted my vision. Not just because of the garish ink.

"What the *hell* is this?"

The most prominent thing about the sheet of paper was the

word "murderer" scrawled across it in red marker. But that wasn't all. Still visible beneath that accusatory word was a printed notice for a candlelight vigil, dated sixteen years ago.

A vigil for Jessa Mackenzie.

I hardly knew where to begin. "Who would still have a copy of this?"

"Anyone could. The flyer for the vigil is still online. Someone printed it out."

"You don't have a theory about who would do that?"

She shook her head, dark eyes downcast. "Not really. But just before I found the note, I saw Tommy Pickering hanging around the parking lot. He...said some things."

My gaze narrowed. "Like *what*?"

"I'd rather not repeat most of it."

"Z."

"Him being a creep doesn't matter."

"Yes, it does. Matters if I need to beat his ass. Which, it sounds like I do." I hadn't even confronted Tommy about that nonsense he'd said to Zandra about me in high school. And now he was skulking around her in the parking lot at night?

"Tommy mentioned Jessa to me tonight. I just want to know if he left the note on my car. And if he did, why."

I tossed the note on the counter. "We have cameras around Hearthstone now." We'd installed them after the broken window. "Maybe they show if it was Tommy or someone else."

Zandra took another sip of coffee. "I checked. The camera's view didn't reach that part of the parking lot. It's focused on the perimeter of the building, windows and doors."

"Then we need more cameras."

"This is small-town Colorado, not New York City, Callum. Cameras are expensive, which is why we didn't get a million of them in the first place to cover every inch of the Hearthstone property. You know I'm right."

"Maybe. Still don't like it." I tugged her stool closer to mine, my legs bracketing hers. "Pisses me off that you were scared tonight, dealing with Pickering and that note, and I wasn't there."

"You were fighting a fire. I'm just your coworker."

"Z, you have never been just that to me." I reached up, tucking a strand of her hair behind her ear. "Maybe you were right, and we shouldn't fool around again."

"Probably." The look she gave me was pained. Yet it made me hope, so I kept going.

"But what we did in the storage room? That was hotter than anything I've ever done. And I wasn't even inside you."

If anything, feeling her give in once had only ignited my need instead of extinguishing it.

"You're nowhere near out of my system," I said. "It's like all other women have ceased to exist. As far as sexual attraction goes, anyway. You're the only one I want."

Her eyes searched mine. "I want you too. But this, *us*...I don't know what this is."

"I don't either." I stroked my thumb across her cheekbone. "I just know it feels really fucking good to have you close to me. It's nearly impossible not to kiss you."

"Then do it."

I leaned in and tasted her, slow and deliberate. Eased my tongue between her lips. This wasn't like any of our desperate kisses before. This was deeper, more significant, though I couldn't put a name to what it meant.

She'd just gotten out of a bad relationship, and I'd never even had one. Then there was the whole *competing over a job* thing, where I was far more likely to get burned if this went wrong.

But the thought of *not* kissing her was like thinking of not breathing. Why choose to suffer when the oxygen, the very thing I needed, was right there?

Then the sounds of shuffling feet and a throat clearing made us both look up.

Connor was smirking, while Niko just looked exhausted and bewildered. They must've gotten home at the same time.

"Darius made coffee if either of you want some." I grabbed Z's hand, tugging her to stand beside me.

"That's Zandra, by the way," Darius said.

Niko's eyes widened. "Oooh. I get it now. Hi, Zandra. Nice to finally meet you. Niko."

She waved. "Hey. Glad you're all safe after the fire."

Darius shrugged. "It wasn't a bad one."

"We were just heading to bed." I pulled Z toward my room. She gave me a skeptical look, and I smiled sweetly at her. "You didn't think you were leaving tonight, did you?"

Zandra had been to my room once before, on her last visit here. I brought her inside and flipped on the light. Shut the door.

Opening a drawer in my dresser, I handed her a soft T-shirt and a pair of sweats. "Change into these. I need to shower."

"I don't know if..."

I leaned in to kiss her forehead. "We're just going to sleep. We can talk more in the morning."

She exhaled, taking the clothes from my hand. "Okay."

Then I headed for the bathroom, ready to wash away the grime and smoke of the day. And even more ready to get into bed with Z. This was about to be a cuddle fest.

After the quickest shower possible, given how dirty I was, I stepped back into my bedroom wrapped in a towel. "You can brush your teeth with my toothbrush." I dug into my dresser drawer.

"I am *not* using your toothbrush."

"Alright, if you want to be wasteful, I guess you can use the new toothbrush I set out on the counter." With a flick of my wrist, my towel fell to the rug.

Zandra made a small, choked sound. And when I glanced over my shoulder at her, I was gratified to find her gaze glued to my bare ass. As my grin spread, I wiggled my hips.

"Like what you see?"

"I've stared at your butt plenty of times before. You know that. This is just a clearer view."

"Shocking, Z. Sounds like workplace harassment to me."

"Please. You'd pay a hundred bucks for me to harass you. On top of the hundred you already owe me."

"Truth."

"I'll add it to your tab." Her gaze moved down again, and her tongue darted over her lips.

Warmth spread through me, briefly chasing away the exhaustion as my cock swelled. But I really was too worn down to get fully hard.

Felt good to be admired, though. And *so* good to hear that sexy sarcasm back in her voice.

I pulled on a pair of pajama pants, going commando, and crossed toward her. "You tired?" I asked, thinking I could get her off, if she wanted. Lay back and let her ride my tongue. I could just imagine her breasts swaying under that T-shirt. It was obvious she'd taken off her bra in preparation for bed. She'd braided her long hair too.

But she responded with a nod and a yawn. "Caffeine didn't even make a dent. I'm wiped."

Maybe tomorrow then.

After we'd both brushed our teeth, we crawled under the covers. I pulled her close. She fit perfectly against my side, her head on my chest, one hand resting over my heart.

"Love when you wear my clothes," I murmured. Sometimes women tried to steal my T-shirts or hoodies, and I'd let it slide, even though it had annoyed me. Not with Z, though. I wanted her to shop from my closet.

Wondered how she'd look in my underwear. Probably hot. *Definitely* hot.

"I like it too. It's weird." She rubbed her face against me. "I like you," she added, quieter.

"I know, Sunflower. I like you too." I kissed the top of her head, savoring the sweetness of the moment. There was no way I could've predicted any of this. But I loved it.

Reaching toward my nightstand, I flicked off the lamp. Snuggled into her. "Thank you for making me stay, Callum," she whispered into the darkness. "I'm glad you're safe."

I tightened my arms around her. "We both are. And we'll both stay that way. I'll make sure of it. Now go to sleep." My eyelids were heavy. But I stayed awake long after she drifted off, marveling at how *right* it felt to have her here.

Honestly, I couldn't remember a woman sleeping in my bed unless she was naked, and we'd just had sex. Z and I had barely done more than kiss tonight. But this, with Zandra, it was...

Better. So much better than anyone had ever felt in my arms.

I didn't know what this woman was doing to me. Yet I already knew I'd give just about anything to keep this feeling going.

TWENTY

Zandra

I WOKE to warm yellow light shining onto white walls. The murmur of voices from somewhere nearby. I was in a nest of thick blankets up to my neck, and I wasn't alone. A large arm draped over me, absently caressing my belly through my sleep shirt.

Even if I'd somehow lost all memory of last night, I'd be able to tell it was Callum in bed with me. Not just from the combined scent of cologne and masculinity. But the electricity I felt from his touch.

I'd felt it all last night too. I couldn't even explain the relief I'd experienced after seeing him safe and sound. The loved ones of first responders and soldiers had to get used to it, right? The helplessness.

I was hardly his *loved one*. We were just getting to be friends.

But in my heart, I knew the world would be a much darker place without Callum's irreplaceable light in it. And my world was already so dark sometimes.

It was terrifying how much I craved having his light shine on me.

"You awake?" Callum's voice was rough from sleep. His lips pressed soft kisses against my neck, chin scratchy with stubble. "I think you're awake."

"Need the bathroom," I murmured.

When I tried to scoot from him, though, he clamped his arm down. "Nope."

"Callum, I'm serious."

"Same." Another kiss. "You know how long I've been wanting you in my bed? Not letting you escape."

I huffed a laugh. "I'll come right back."

"Promise?"

Turning my head, I locked eyes with him. "I'll hurry back."

"'Cause you like it here, huh? My bed is the best place ever. Ten out of ten." He pulled me even closer and burrowed his face in my neck.

"Let me go!" But I was full-on laughing.

He released me, and I scrambled to the bathroom, shutting the door and locking it. Because who knew what shenanigans Callum might come up with. I did my business quickly, then brushed my teeth and washed my face. My hair had come partly out of its braid, but at least my eyes weren't as bloodshot as last night.

That awful note, on top of the fire and what Tommy had said... I swallowed down a lump, but it sat at the back of my throat. Still there.

Was it foolish to be here with Callum? Probably. But it was hard to care. I was happier around him. After Jessa's death, I'd gotten used to a base level of unhappiness. That was probably why I'd put up with Ian for so long.

I liked how I felt when Callum was around me.

Emerging from the bathroom, I found Callum leaning against the wall right outside. His rumpled bedhead only made him sexier. The way his pajama pants hung low enough to reveal the base of his happy trail? Sinful.

"Here to escort me back to bed?" I asked.

"In a sec. I need the bathroom too. But keep in mind, I hid your car keys."

"Callum, I wasn't going to leave."

"Just making sure. On foot, I can definitely chase you down." With a grin, he vanished behind the bathroom door.

The clang of dishes and scents of bacon and coffee came from the kitchen. Which meant Callum's roommates were up. I wasn't hungry though, and I wasn't interested in socializing. I really *didn't* want to leave this room.

While Callum was in the bathroom, I took the opportunity to glance around. I'd seen it the night we cooked together, after I'd showered off the brownie batter. I'd been surprised at how tidy the place was.

Walking over to his desk, I touched the framed photos there. His brother Ashford, sister Grace. A little girl I assumed was Callum's niece, Maisie. There were lots of candid poses of family and friends.

Callum was always surrounded by people. That had annoyed me when we were younger. But had I just been jealous? Of him for effortlessly having so many friends. Or maybe jealous of everyone else, because they got to have Callum's happiness shine on them.

My teenage self would've denied such longings to her last breath. Also she would've had an opinion or two about my sanity.

I was still studying his photos when the bathroom door opened. Half a second later, Callum's arms had closed around me, my feet had left the ground, and he was carrying me back to the bed.

"Hey!"

He knee-walked us both across the mattress, lying me down and stretching out over me. "If you want your car keys back, you'll have to earn them."

"*Excuse* me?"

His mouth dropped to nibble my neck. "Kidding. But I think you should spend the day with me. It's Monday. No work."

"Spend all day in your bed?"

"Doesn't sound so bad."

"I should text Rosie."

"I already did last night. I let her know you're safe."

"Without asking me?"

"Z," he said softly. "You don't need to fight me on everything." He lifted his hand, brushing his thumb down my lower lip. I shivered as threads of pleasure worked their way through my body, forcing me to relax.

"Since I got here last night, I've been very agreeable, I'll have you know."

"Yes, but your first instinct is to push back. To grump at me and tell me to fuck off. No matter what I'm asking."

My mouth opened, but I didn't really have a response to that. Because he was right. I knew it, and I wanted to be easier. To not have the word *No* be my first thought at all times.

At least, not with him.

I wanted everything Callum could give me.

The gold in his irises glittered. "Say yes to me. For one whole day, just say yes unless we hit something that's a hard limit. Bet you a hundred bucks you'll enjoy it."

I found myself nodding, not quite trusting my voice. This was not comfortable for me. Yet at the same time, I craved it. The power to let go and let Callum make me feel good.

Make everything better, like he'd said last night.

A slow grin spread his lips wide. "Let's start with an easy one. Can I kiss you?"

"Yes," I whispered.

His lips slanted over mine. Kissing gently at first before deepening the connection. At the same time, he took my wrists in his hands and brought them over my head, placing my hands beneath the pillow where my head rested.

"Now I'm going to kiss and touch the rest of you." It had been a statement, yet his eyes held an implicit question. Another test.

I nodded, my body vibrating with nerves and from how much I wanted this.

He scooted down until his jaw was level with my belly button. My borrowed shirt had already ridden up, exposing my stomach, and I gasped as his lips made contact with my skin. His fingers rucked the shirt up higher. *His* shirt.

"So pretty, baby." His breaths were hot. "So sexy."

As he kissed a line up my torso, he kept moving the shirt too. Until the cotton tugged over my breasts, creating friction against my nipples just as they met the open air.

"Fuck, Zandra." His gaze hungrily traced my curves. "You're—"

The rest of his sentence was lost when he twirled his tongue around my nipple. I moaned, clapping a hand over my mouth when I realized how loud I'd been. His roommates were out in the kitchen and living room, having breakfast.

But Callum didn't seem to have the slightest concern about that. He moved to the other nipple and sucked until I was biting my lip to stay quiet. While he lavished attention on my breasts, his thumbs hooked the waistband of my borrowed sweats and worked them down past my hips.

Then his mouth kissed downward again. He nosed at the skin just above my panties, which had tugged down slightly. Someone laughed in the living room.

"Lift your hips," he urged, lowering my panties when I did. He quickly tossed the clothing somewhere on the floor, kneeling over me and eating me alive with his fierce gaze. His erection tented the flannel of his pants.

I'd never felt so exposed. Shirt up over my breasts, naked everywhere else. And this was *Callum O'Neal*. The boy I'd despised in high school. Who I maybe, secretly, had wanted.

He stroked the length of his shaft through the fabric. "Z. You don't disappoint. I could almost come just from looking at you."

"Hope you'll do more than that."

"Oh believe me, I plan to." Scooting down further, he suddenly grasped my thighs and pushed them apart. "I'm gonna kiss your pussy now," he growled.

"Yes. Yes, yes," I rambled.

"Good girl."

When he pressed his face between my legs, I almost levitated off the mattress. This was an out of body experience. Yet I'd never felt more physical either. Never felt more *desired*.

His tongue delved inside me. Licked and flicked my clit. Callum's eyes closed and he moaned, and I saw his hand reach inside his pajama pants to grip his cock. Everything about Callum was so overtly sexual, unapologetic, and I was wild for it.

Suddenly he sat up, shoving his pants down to free his erection. He roughly groped for his nightstand, drawer flying open as he rummaged around. He came back with a condom. The gold foil caught the light as he lifted it up.

I nodded vigorously. "Please." I needed this. Couldn't wait another second to feel him.

With a few practiced movements, Callum got himself ready. I felt his tip press to my opening. His eyes were fixed on mine, but I was glad that he didn't ask for permission now.

Instead he held my hips and slid every inch of his cock inside me, his chest rumbling with a groan. No hesitation.

It was like he just *knew*. Right now, I needed to be taken.

He rested more of his weight against me as he started to move. One hand braced on the mattress by my head, the other hooking below my knee to bend it wider for him.

I reached for him and dug my fingers into his messy hair. My hips lifted with every thrust, meeting his. The headboard banged against the wall, and I flinched. But he just bent down to kiss me.

"Focus on me," he murmured. "Nothing matters but us. Forget everything else."

Slowly, I relaxed. Let Callum hypnotize me with his sexy expressions and the sweet, dirty praise he whispered in my ear. *You're doing so well for me. Love how wet you are.*

When he pulled out of me and rolled me onto my side, arranging me so he was spooned behind me, I just let him position me. His cock slid easily between my legs, entering me again, and I whimpered at how his shaft felt inside me, stretching me.

"Here, let me fix this," he said, gathering up my hair, which had come out of the braid and was all over the place. He carefully laid my locks over the pillow, then nuzzled his nose against my temple. "Better?"

"Mmhmm."

Callum pulled me tight against his big body. Like he was cherishing me and filling me up at the same time. Like he could surround me and swallow me up if he wanted to. I was half drunk on this man. He did things to my brain that were inexplicable.

But also…we weren't moving.

"What's happening right now?" I asked dreamily. "We're just lying here."

"It's snuggle sex." He ran his hand down my side. "I don't want this over too fast."

"Snuggle sex?"

"Yep." His fingers trailed down to squeeze my butt cheek. "This way, I can keep you on my cock for as long as possible. I think this will work well for us."

"Callum," I grumbled.

His fingers danced over my inner thighs next. Teased between. "What is it? You need something?" His fingertip glanced over my clit, and I shook with how good it felt.

Especially when he shifted slightly, and the sensation of his thick cock inside me lit up every one of my nerve endings. "Do that again," I moaned.

"Only if you beg me."

I'd like to say I stayed strong. But I didn't.

After several more minutes, I barely knew what I was saying. "I want it, Callum, want you so bad, I—oh, yes, *please*."

"Don't you worry. I've got you." His panting was loud in my

ear. Our hips slapped together as he pulled me onto his cock again and again.

Suddenly he changed our position. Sprawled me out, flat on my back, while he went to his knees, towering over me. "Just look at you." He licked his lips. "Never seen anything like you, Z."

"I'm enjoying the view myself." All that smooth skin over muscle, the tattoos. And that sexy smirk. Ugh, it did me in.

"Grab the bottom of the headboard."

I reached up and slotted my hands under the headboard to hold on. Callum spread my legs and pulled me back onto his cock. My head tipped back, my lips closing to muffle a desperate moan.

If the younger me had any idea Callum would be this hot in bed, maybe I would've overcome my hate for him sooner.

He pushed my knees up, and I felt him so deep. The mattress shook with every thrust. Sweat beaded between his pecs. "You close, Sunflower? Gonna come for me like you're mine?"

"Yes. *Yours.*" The curl of tension inside me ignited. A fuse lighting and starting to burn. My hands grabbed at the headboard. Then my back arched and my legs cinched around his waist as rolling waves of pure pleasure took me over.

Nothing existed but us. My body singing while the hottest man in the world took me over the edge and kept me right there, quaking and chanting his name.

"*Z.* That's perfect. You're gonna make me—" The pulse of his orgasm inside me gave me another jolt of pleasure. And the look on his handsome face just heightened the sensation. Almost always, Callum looked happy, but right now he seemed struck by awe. Like he was just as overwhelmed by this moment as I was.

I couldn't believe how much I wanted that. To give him as much as he was giving me.

Callum lowered himself to the mattress and pulled out, moving down slightly so he could kiss me. I got lost in the caress of his lips, his warm body rubbing against me like he couldn't bear for us to be separated, even though the sex was over.

A dose of clarity hit me.

Oh, this was so, so bad.

Yet the wave of comfort that flowed through me as he held me in the afterglow, gently kissing my hairline, was even worse. Because I already knew one time with Callum wouldn't be enough. Why did I have to like him so much?

This was probably going to hurt when it was over.

TWENTY-ONE
Callum

"CALLUM, why did you call me Sunflower?"

"What, baby?"

She gave me a patented grouchy Zandra look. "You've called me Sunflower a few times now. Why? What is that, something you call women when you're getting frisky?"

"Aw, you jealous? Thinking about me with other girls?"

I could see the shape of the "no" on her lips. But her scowl said everything she was really thinking.

So fucking cute.

After the hottest sex of my life this morning, both of our stomachs had been growling. About an hour ago, I'd made myself just presentable enough to venture out to the kitchen. Darius, Connor, and Niko had all been up, eating breakfast on the back patio. They'd whistled and smirked at me through the screen door as I made a plate of bacon and eggs for us to share. Darius had helpfully left extras on the stovetop.

No, they didn't hear us at all, I'd told Zandra when I got back.

They'd totally heard us.

Now, we were cuddled up beneath a pile of blankets with our bellies full. Zandra had been lying on top of me, naked of course, while I drew pictures on her back with my fingertips. A bluesy playlist from my phone added to the atmosphere.

I hummed, pretending to think about her question. "Sunflower. Let me see... No, don't think I've ever called anyone else that before. Just you."

She crawled up my body so she could cross her arms on my chest. "Are you going to tell me what it means? Or do I have to guess?"

"I do love your guessing games."

"Come on, Callum."

I'd gotten enough of her adorably grumpy reactions to satisfy me for the moment. "It's because sunflowers remind me of you. The wild, small ones that grow everywhere around here. They're beautiful, but they're tough. Nobody can keep them down."

For several long seconds, she stared at me. Then she dropped her head, hiding it against her arms on my chest.

"You don't like it?" I asked softly.

"I do. Just don't know if I deserve it."

"Sure you do." Zandra had to know how amazing she was. Even with her setbacks in Chicago, she'd charged back into Silver Ridge with that same old fire. She didn't put up with bullshit. Including mine, and I liked her all the more for it.

I felt her fingers on my arm, tracing the patterns of my tattoos. "I didn't feel resilient after Jessa died. It was so hard, Callum. Every day, going to that school and feeling so alone."

My heart clenched painfully at the reminder that she'd been struggling back then, and I hadn't done anything to stop it.

"But there was more," she went on. "Things happened that I haven't told you."

"I'm listening." I rubbed her back.

"There was..." She swallowed. "Someone was harassing me."

My hand went still. "What do you mean?"

"I told you about the rumors going around that it was my fault Jessa died. That we were arguing and I pushed her."

"You thought I had something to do with spreading that around." Because of Pickering.

She nodded. "Jessa's vigil was just a few days after she died. But then weeks later, I started getting copies of the leaflet. Stuck in my locker, in my backpack when I wasn't looking. Under my car's windshield wiper. I didn't get it. Why someone would do that. Like, were they trying to make me feel bad? Make some other point? But then the person started writing words in red marker on the leaflets. 'Liar.' '*Murderer.*'"

"Shit," I murmured. "That's horrible."

"I didn't think *you* did it. Not exactly. I thought...I guess I figured people believed the rumors, and somebody decided to punish me for what they thought I did to Jessa. Then there was the time I went out to my car after school and found the driver's side window broken."

I gently tipped her to the side so she was lying on the mattress, and I could see her face. "Z, why didn't you tell me about that? After the broken window at Hearthstone a couple weeks ago?"

Her eyes shone. "I thought it was random. Nothing to do with me. But after the note last night..."

"You think it's the same person doing these things. Tommy?"

I was trying to stay cool and calm because I didn't want to upset her even more. But if Pickering was behind this, they weren't going to find his fucking body when I was done with him.

"I don't know. I don't see why he would do it. He didn't care about Jessa."

I didn't understand it either, but the whole thing had me on edge. "You shouldn't be going anywhere alone."

"A little harassment isn't going to kill me."

"I really don't like that choice of words."

She twisted a strand of her dark hair around her finger. "Whoever was doing it in high school never said anything to my face or threatened me. They just wanted to make me miserable. Clearly they want the same thing now. When I was at the motel..."

I sat up. "The serial killer motel?" I asked incredulously. "Something happened there?"

That strand of hair kept winding tighter and tighter around her finger. "I might've thought someone was watching me a couple times at night."

"Fucking hell, Z. You should've shared all this before."

"I didn't connect it all until last night. And I didn't want to talk about it when you got here. You'd had a long day, and I just wanted..."

"To be cozy with me?"

"Yeah," she whispered.

My arm hooked around her, tugging her into my side. Where she belonged.

If Teller Landry had still been chief of police, I would've called him up right now. We had to find out who was harassing her and vandalizing Hearthstone.

Now that Chief Susan Nichols was in charge, I was sure she'd do a good job as well. But I just didn't know the new chief as well as my friend. I wasn't entirely confident in Chief Nichols keeping this quiet, and I had the feeling Z didn't want to be a renewed subject of Silver Ridge gossip.

Teller was still a part-time member of Silver Ridge PD, though. I could ask for his advice. Earlier this year, when Ayla had a stalker, Teller had used some less official means of investigation.

I'd have to look into that later.

"Even better reason for me to keep you here," I said. "We have cameras and an alarm system. Installed them when my sister lived here and there was a break-in. It's perfect."

"I am *not* moving in with you."

"You're supposed to be saying yes to everything today."

"Not if it's unreasonable."

"You know I'd treat you right. It would be like a sexy B&B. Meals included. Booty calls on demand."

She laughed. "And I know you're not serious."

"I am. Why wouldn't I be?" I pulled her on top of me,

nudging her to straddle me high enough that I could kiss her breasts. They overflowed my hands when I cupped them. So sexy. I could feast on these all day.

"Because we're—I don't know what we are."

"Do we need a label?" I licked her nipple and then sucked it into my mouth. She moaned before batting me away.

"We have another month of working together, and then one of us will be the boss."

"So, we have a month of enjoying this. That's what I'm hearing."

"You'd...really want that? To keep hooking up until we have to stop?"

"Sure. Coworkers with benefits." I'd never had an ongoing benefits arrangement with anyone before, but it sounded ideal for me and Zandra. "And an extra benefit," I added, hands roving down to squeeze the fullness of her hips, "is that you and Chloe can stay in the spare room here, with a security system and four firefighters standing guard for you. Making sure you get to work and back okay and keeping an eye out for this fucker who's harassing you to make a mistake."

Once that happened, we would nail him.

She tilted her head, hair spilling around her shoulders. "Four firefighters is a plus."

"But there's only one you share special benefits with," I growled.

"I dunno," she teased. "Your roommates seem pretty nice too."

She'd *better* have been teasing.

Possessiveness ran hot through my bloodstream and down to my cock. Another new experience, because I normally wasn't remotely a possessive guy. No woman had ever made me want to lock her down. Until now.

Her gaze dipped, eyelashes splaying. "Callum, I don't want anyone but you."

"Good. Same here." And it made my blood run all the hotter

that she admitted she wanted me. *Only* me. My shaft swelled against my thigh. "C'mere, Sunflower. Give me what's mine."

Zandra leaned forward to kiss me, hair falling all around me in a sweet-smelling curtain. She started rocking back and forth on top of me.

When I brought my hand between her legs, I felt how wet she was. "You want to ride me this time, baby? You look so pretty sitting on me."

She nodded, biting the corner of her lower lip.

I loved that she was already naked. We both knew what to do. After being inside her once already, I had a sense of what Zandra liked. How to touch her and how to hold back in the exact ways to drive her wild. And now that I thought about it, wasn't that a big benefit to repeats? Hooking up with the same person meant my knowledge could be put to ideal use.

I'd just never felt the urge before her. I'd actually wondered if something was connected differently in my brain, because I'd never wanted *more* with anyone. Not like my siblings had with their partners.

After growing up watching my father's shitty treatment of my mom, I'd thought I was the lucky one. No love, no marriage, no chance of making a heartbreaking mistake.

But with Zandra, I could imagine more. The strangest thing was, it didn't *feel* strange at all.

Just felt damn good.

I scooted Zandra down until I felt that wetness sliding over my cock. "Rub yourself on me, Sunflower. Just like that." A groan rumbled in my throat from the sensations on my sensitive tip.

Nngh. I wanted her mouth all over me, mine all over her. So many different filthy images were floating through my head already. And we had a month to try everything I dreamed up.

Zandra reached over to my nightstand to grab a condom from the drawer. Alright, I liked my girl impatient. Ready to take matters into her own hands.

Less than a minute later, I was deep inside her with Zandra

bouncing on top of me, and this was a sight I intended *never* to forget. So many lush curves I didn't know where to look. Finally, I settled on her gorgeous face.

Her eyes were hooded. Pink lips parted. A vision made of sex.

Z's palms rested on my pecs as she braced herself, me holding on to her hips. I bucked into her, loving every slick slide of my cock in and out of her. "You're tight, Z. Hell. Even my fist doesn't grip me like you do."

She made a needy sound, blinking those long lashes at me. "I love how you feel in me."

"Yeah? Tell me more." I bit back a smile as she hesitated. "What? That smart mouth of yours can give me a tongue-lashing when you're mad, but you can't talk dirty to me?"

"Your...cock is so...big."

My grin went wide. "What else?"

"You're the sexiest man I've ever been with." Her mouth opened on a moan. "I've never come as hard as I do with you."

"Mmm." I'd heard filthier things, but nothing had ever been as satisfying. "Love making you come. Just me. This sweet body isn't for anyone else."

"*Just you*," she moaned.

Yet while she was riding me and we were taking pleasure from each other, there was something beautiful about the way we were connecting too. The way Zandra had already become someone important to me, trusting me with so much.

With the rhythmic way our bodies kept meeting, I felt my orgasm already barreling toward me. But I didn't want to slow her down. Watching Z like this, just letting go, was hypnotic.

The moment her channel tightened and she cried out, I was coming too. I held her hips, fingers digging in, as we rocked together and drew out every last pulse of pleasure. But even then, I didn't want to stop.

Just a few tastes, and I was addicted to her.

My Sunflower.

TWENTY-TWO
Zandra

I STARED at the words on my screen, as if they would magically shift into something less horrifying.

> MOM
>
> We've been waiting long enough, Zandra. You're coming to Sunday dinner tomorrow. No excuses.

While I contemplated what to do about this impending disaster, the door to Grandpa's office opened and closed. I didn't have to look up to know who it was.

Strong arms closed around me, and a kiss pressed to the back of my neck. "Hey," he said quietly. "Miss me?"

"We're at work, Callum. I was doing some filing." I stuck my phone back in my pocket and shut the filing cabinet, where I'd been organizing vendor contracts.

"Yeah, and work lasts hours. I need a fix. Just a small one. I trust you not to jump me and do anything too inappropriate."

"Maybe you shouldn't. Remember the storage room?"

He snickered and rubbed his nose against my hair. "But I do enjoy taking the risk. Win-win either way."

I turned my head so I could see him. "Maybe just a few kisses."

Who was I kidding? I was an absolute sucker for this man.

I'd woken in his bed this morning, but I still couldn't get enough.

I'd moved my things to Callum's place on Tuesday, and today was Saturday. Living with Callum and his roommates had been... not what I'd expected. While I'd envisioned something like a party house of overgrown frat bros, Callum's roommates were mostly quiet and polite. The most raucous we'd gotten in the last few days had been a Mario Kart tournament on their big screen TV.

Rosie and Jimmy hadn't minded my absence much. Especially when I brought over a batch of brownies after Callum and I made them again. Rosie had saved my butt by letting me live there for those weeks, and I was beyond grateful for it.

Even Chloe was settling in to her new surroundings. I'd set up her fountain in the kitchen and her litter box in a quiet corner of the laundry room, and she hadn't hesitated to explore the rest of the house. Last night, I'd found her curled up on the lap of Niko's girlfriend while the guys were making dinner.

And somehow, even though I had my own room at their place —a much larger one than my former closet at Rosie's—I'd spent every night so far in Callum's. Naked.

There was the fact that his room had an en suite bathroom, and mine didn't. But also, I had zero self-control when it came to this man.

Exactly why it was so dangerous to start a make-out session at work.

Nobody at Hearthstone could know about this *thing* we had going on. *Coworkers with benefits.* Callum had agreed. We couldn't let word get back to my grandfather, and we didn't want to make things awkward with anyone else at work.

Yet when Callum started rocking his bulge against me while we kissed, what I wanted most was to hike up my skirt and see how quick and quiet we could be.

Then I remembered Mom's text, and that was as good as an ice-cold shower.

"What is it?" Callum asked. "You tensed up." His hands went to my shoulders to knead the muscles there. "Did something happen?"

"Nothing like that."

I knew he was thinking of the creepy note on my windshield. But I'd had someone with me whenever I went into Hearthstone or left at night. Usually, it was Callum, but Darius and Connor had made appearances too. No one else aside from Callum's roommates knew about my harasser, and I wanted to keep it that way.

Tommy Pickering hadn't been seen at the brewpub or anywhere else in my vicinity either. Whoever had been harassing me, I just hoped they were done. Hopefully scared off by my new twenty-four-seven bodyguard patrol.

The worst was thinking about Hearthstone being vandalized because of me. If anything happened to this place, I couldn't bear it.

I turned around and sat on the edge of the desk, lifting my phone. "Just a text from my mom earlier, weaponizing Sunday family dinner."

"Sunday dinner doesn't sound so bad."

"Yet it is. I've been avoiding it since I got back. My parents will use it as an excuse to grill me about all the ways I'm failing. It wouldn't be so bad if Grandpa or Rosie would be there, but they only turn up on special occasions or holidays. This is my mother's show."

Mom usually invited a couple or two from the Hart County Golf Club. I'd heard more than I ever needed to about putters and real estate at these dinners.

Callum sidled closer, putting his hands on my hips. "I'll come with you."

My heart leaped. I told it to stay down. "You don't need to do that. It's going to be miserable."

"Then we can be miserable together. I hear it's not as bad."

"But why?" I sputtered. "We're coworkers with secret benefits. Not..."

The corner of his mouth lifted with a smirk. "Not friends?"

I crossed my arms. Maybe pouting, just a little. "I wasn't going to say that. We're friends."

I didn't even know what I'd been going to say. Just that we weren't the kind of involved where the guy wanted to meet the parents. He hadn't introduced me to any of his family, and that was fine.

We weren't dating. It was all *fine*.

"I should hope we're friends." Callum pinched my chin playfully. "Friends support each other."

"Yes, we're friends," I said with a huff.

"Besides, rich people usually have tasty food."

"The food's good," I admitted.

"Then it's settled. RSVP for me. Is this black tie?"

My snark resurfaced. "What do you think?"

"Shit, white tie? My white tux is at the cleaners."

My lips fought to keep from smiling. "You can wear whatever you want. Do not cater to my parents. Most of the time it backfires."

"Got it. I'll wear my favorite G-string and nothing else."

"Please do. At least I'll be entertained."

He brushed a kiss to my cheek. "I promise, Z, with me around, you will be entertained."

I circled my arms around his waist, wishing I didn't feel anything deeper for him than that.

Callum whistled. "So this is how the other half of Silver Ridge lives. Fancy."

He'd just pulled his truck past my parents' open gate. I'd been stressing since yesterday about Sunday dinner at my parents' place. The anxiety had wound me so tight last night that Callum had given me a massage, which had turned deliciously filthy in the best way. He'd delivered a very happy ending that finally allowed me to sleep. But I still had to face this dinner, so was the relief really worth it in the end? At least I was well-rested for whatever fresh hell awaited me.

"Not too late for you to bail. You could just drop me here and flee. I would." I was tapping nervously at my leg, so Callum reached over to grip my hand.

"I've got this. Parents always love me."

"You're not accounting for the fact that my parents' favorite hobby is being disappointed in me."

"Which makes no sense at all, because you're you. But aside from that, I'm here as your buffer. I can compliment your mom's cooking. Every cook appreciates that."

I scoffed. "You think Eliza Alvarez is going to cook our meal tonight? No. That'll be the housekeeper, Gladys. Mom plans the menu."

Of course, Mom had taken it as a personal offense when I stopped eating the menus she planned after I figured out my allergies. Thank goodness for Gladys. She usually set aside portions for me without flour or cheese or cream added.

Which drove Mom crazy whenever she noticed.

I'd texted ahead that I was bringing a coworker tonight. Mom had just texted back, *Very well*, which was mildly foreboding.

"Then I'll compliment the menu planning," he said. "And I'll make you something afterward if you're still hungry."

He parked next to my dad's massive SUV. At least I'd have eye candy tonight. Callum was wearing a pair of khakis I'd never seen and one of his polos that managed to look put together while hugging his pecs perfectly.

"Come here," he said, tugging my hand. "Let me relax you."

"But my parents will see."

"Nah, I've got tinted windows." He patted his thigh. "Come

here, baby. You're beautiful and brilliant, and just thinking about how awesome you are makes me need to kiss you."

I crawled over into his lap. This man could truly talk me into anything, couldn't he? And I'd go willingly. Like melted chocolate pouring into a bowl to make brownie batter.

Callum kissed me slowly, somehow making me zero in on the present moment like nothing else existed. I'd always meant to get into meditation, but this had to count, right?

"I want you to remember this for the rest of the night. You're perfect." He gave me a few more slow pecks, each one more chaste.

"You're pretty perfect too."

"I know," he said lightly. "Now, we better stop or I won't be presentable. Either that, or I'll have to get you undressed right here, and we'll be late. I know you hate being late."

"But my parents will complain no matter what I do." I went in for another kiss, and he smiled against my lips.

"Naked time later. Let's get this over with, and we'll have something to look forward to. I just need to grab something." He stretched to reach into the back seat, producing a small white box with a silver ribbon around it.

I scooted off his lap. "What's that?"

"A gift for your mom."

My eyebrow raised. "Good luck with that. My mother is impossible to please."

"You need to sit back and let the master work." His grin was far too confident for someone about to meet my parents.

As we approached the entrance, I was straightening my blouse and pencil skirt, trying to smooth away invisible wrinkles. "We're just friends tonight," I reminded him, then felt my face heat. "I mean, obviously we *are* just friends. That's not—I meant—"

"Relax, Z. I knew what you meant." His hand briefly touched my hip. I exhaled.

Get it together, woman.

Before we even reached the door, Gladys was opening it,

looking curious. I made the introductions, trying to act casual and normal. "Gladys keeps this place running and my parents fed."

"Pleasure to meet you," Callum said warmly.

She smiled. "Please come in. They're all on the patio."

As we walked toward the patio doors, I wondered if I already had pit stains on my blouse. I was definitely sweating. "Fair warning," I whispered to Callum, "my parents will have friends here tonight from the golf club."

"Didn't even know we had a golf club," he whispered back.

"The one course in the county. Most of the members have a third or fourth home here in Hart County and have never heard of Hearthstone, much less tried a beer there."

"Got it," Callum replied, completely unfazed.

We reached the patio, and my parents were standing with two other couples dressed in far nicer clothes than you usually saw on Main Street. An actual waiter passed around a tray of appetizers like this was a swanky event at the ski resort. My parents looked polished as always, Mom in her silk blouse and pearls, Dad in his pressed slacks and golf shirt.

All conversation stopped when we walked out.

"Oh, here's Zandra," my mom said smoothly. "And her... friend."

"Coworker," I blurted.

"Callum O'Neal." He strode over to my mom and held out his hand.

"From the brewery. Of course." Mom barely touched his fingers. "Lovely."

I cringed at her obvious dismissal. "Mom, Callum is the one who helped Grandpa after he fell."

"We certainly appreciate that," my dad chimed in. "I think Pop has mentioned you." Dad came over to shake his hand next. Unlike my mother, he usually wasn't overtly rude. His digs were more subtle and came later, once you dared to let your guard down and thought it was safe.

"But Zandra hasn't mentioned you once." Mom glanced slyly at me.

Callum laughed, and it was eerily close to the way my dad and his golf buddies sounded when they were sharing a joke. Damn. He was good. "I was on the football team in high school, and Z just tolerated my antics. But I wouldn't have passed senior English without her." He held out the gift. "Appreciate you having me, Mrs. Alvarez."

Everyone leaned in, watching as Mom pulled open the ribbon and stared skeptically at the contents. "Chocolates?"

"Made here in Hart County," Callum said.

One of the golf club wives came over to peer into the box. "Oh, Eliza, are those from Scarlett's Sweet Shop in Hartley? Those are nearly impossible to get these days. They only make small batches." She was giving Callum an appreciative look that I didn't care for, but at least Mom seemed to warm up to him a few degrees.

He just shrugged. "I know a guy."

While Mom drifted to fuss over the chocolates with her friends, Dad clapped Callum on the shoulder. "What'll you drink? We've got a nice selection."

"Anything with a respectable rating from Wine Spectator," Callum replied seriously.

I almost choked on air, covering it with a cough.

But my father nodded. "I like you, Callum. You're quite a surprise."

While the others gravitated toward the bar area, I whispered to Callum, "Wine Spectator? Really?"

"I did some googling," he said under his breath. "The chocolates are vegan and gluten-free, by the way."

The words slipped out before I could stop them. "Oh my goodness, I love you."

Then I replayed them. *What* had I just said?

"Good to know," he murmured. Callum's eyes danced with amusement, and I felt my face flame.

While I fumbled for something sensible to say, Dad called him over to show him the wine selections.

"Duty calls. I'll be back." He left me standing there, drowning in my own mortification. I was a mess of nerves. Nobody could trust *anything* I said tonight. He had to know it had been a turn of phrase. A colloquialism. Right?

This was going to be a very long night.

TWENTY-THREE

Callum

SUNDAY DINNER at the Alvarez house was a unique experience, at least for me. Dinner with the O'Neal clan had nothing on this.

I really needed to bring Zandra along the next time my siblings and I got together. So she could experience a more low-key family gathering. Because tonight, the key was *very* high. Like, soprano level.

During wine and cocktail hour, we'd moved from the patio to their pristine living room with an actual chandelier. I'd watched Zandra fidget, her shoulders rigid as her mother introduced us to the other guests. Every instinct had screamed for me to put my arm around her.

But that wouldn't have been very *friendly* of me.

Another unfortunate side effect of just being Zandra's coworker: the way her mom's friend Mitsy kept trying to palm my ass when the others weren't looking.

Getting along in mixed company wasn't usually a stretch for me, given the different people I met all the time at Hearthstone. But these people were a tough audience. Basically, I was trying to channel Dane Knightly, my sister's boyfriend. The guy was a billionaire with a filthy rich family even more vicious than Zandra's could be.

"This looks delicious, Eliza," Javi said to his wife as the first course arrived at the dining table.

Zandra's mom nodded. "Beef tartare. Enjoy everyone."

I was sipping on a glass of French red, which was pretty tasty. The dishes and glassware looked expensive, far from anything we'd ever use at Hearthstone. If I broke anything, it would probably cost several months of paychecks to replace it.

A joke about being a bull in a china shop was right on my tongue, but I figured I should hold it in. Maybe I could tell Z when we were alone later.

Probably shouldn't mention we were roommates, either. Too close to the truth about us sharing a bed and her coming on my cock every night.

The waiter set my plate in front of me. My stomach was growling. The first bites were as good as I'd been hoping. Savory beef with capers, minced onion, and a tiny little egg on top. But when I noticed Zandra was actually eating hers, I slowed down.

"Enjoying that?" I asked quietly, elbow bumping hers.

"Gladys knows I love tartare," she whispered back. "I could eat a pound of it. And she always serves the toast points in a separate basket."

"Javi, what's your take on that last jobs report?" This was from Richard, Mitsy's husband. While the rest of the table was distracted by that fascinating topic, I added the rest of my appetizer to Zandra's plate. Just in case the main course wasn't as allergy friendly.

Unfortunately, her mom noticed. "You don't like the beef, Callum?"

"Love it. This is delicious. I just thought Zandra looked extra hungry."

"She always was picky about food," her mother sniffed.

I opened my mouth, but Zandra whispered, "*Don't.*"

So instead of remarking that allergies had nothing to do with pickiness, I just pressed my knee against Zandra's.

When I felt something massaging my leg, I wondered if that was Z.

Until I noticed the way Mitsy was smiling from across the table. The lady was in her sixties with her husband sitting right beside her, and that was only the start of what was wrong with this picture.

Nope. No, thank you. I stuck my feet under my chair.

After the first course, Richard turned to me. "So Callum, I understand you work for that restaurant Javi's father owns on Main Street. What is it that you do?"

"Whatever Manny tells me," I joked.

The waiter returned with the main course. Some kind of chicken with cream sauce. Not Z approved. Good thing I'd given her the rest of my tartare.

"Callum's been the bar manager at Hearthstone for a while," Zandra piped up. "And now we're both in the running for general manager to replace Grandpa."

"Competing against each other?" Mitsy asked. "How juicy. Who's winning?"

I smiled at the beautiful woman beside me. "I think it's Z. She's got experience and business savvy."

"Callum's holding his own."

Our gazes met, probably lingering too long.

A loud huff from the other end of the table made everyone's head turn. "It's shocking that Manny is making Zandra compete to run a family business," her mother said.

"Pop likes to do things his way," Javi countered.

"Character building," Richard added, lifting his wine.

Zandra gulped from her own glass. "I'd rather earn it than have something handed to me."

Her mother's fork hit the plate with a clang. "But I'm not going to sit here and pretend any job at a brewery isn't beneath you, Zandra."

"*Mom.*"

"You and Ian were building something. Not just a company

but a relationship. You should be picking out wedding dresses, not vying with some local blue-collar boy for the privilege of slinging beers for a living."

Zandra threw her napkin on top of her plate of chicken. "Don't talk about Callum that way."

"It's alright," I murmured to her, squeezing her knee under the table. I gave zero fucks what these people thought of me. I'd tried to work my charms on her parents for Zandra's benefit, but if it didn't work, it was no skin off my back.

Besides, *some local blue-collar boy* was a ringing endorsement considering the things they might've called me. I had no shame about who I was or where I'd come from.

Mitsy, Richard, and the other couple were watching all this unfold with varying reactions of enjoyment and disdain.

"I apologize for my wife," Javi said to me. "You're a guest in our home." But then he kept going. "It's just that Zandra had a very promising future, especially after meeting a man like Ian, and it's a shame to see her throw it all away."

Z pushed back her chair. "I'm not listening to any more of this."

"Dinner isn't over," her mother snapped.

"I can't eat this anyway." She stormed out of the dining room, and then her feet pounded on their way up the stairs.

At that very moment, I felt Mitsy's pointy toes working their way up my shin again. Geez. My chair scraped as it scooted back.

I needed to go after Z. But first, there were a few things I had to say.

"Zandra is the smartest woman I've ever met. Whatever she does with her future, it'll be something to be proud of. If you'd open your eyes to that, maybe you'll get to be a part of it."

Her dad frowned at me, while her mom reached for the wine bottle.

I tossed down my napkin, got up, and headed for the stairs.

TWENTY-FOUR

Callum

IT TOOK a little while to find her. This house was massive. There was an actual oil painting of Z and her parents hanging in the hallway, all of them dressed up in formal wear, with her looking stiff and uncomfortable. It was weird.

Growing up, I never would've known we had houses like this in Hart County.

Yeah, I'd gotten to know Dane, and Ayla was super rich too. But neither of them were this stuffy. Javi and Eliza were on another level.

Finally I came to a door at the end of the hallway and heard a faint sound from inside. I pushed the door open and saw Zandra sitting on the bed with her knees pulled up to her chest, hair falling around her shoulders.

I went in and closed the door behind me. "Hey."

"Sorry I took off like that."

"I can't blame you. I would've left with you, but I had to take care of something."

She pulled at a thread on the thick comforter, one of those types that hotels always have. A duvet. "I was standing on the stairs. I heard what you said. Thank you."

"Just told the truth, as I see it."

"I can't believe what my mother said to you. I'm really sorry about that, too."

"I mean, she wasn't wrong."

Zandra sat forward. "Of course she was. Working at Hearthstone is not beneath anyone. Least of all me. It's like she was implying—"

I heard the rest of that sentence. *That you're beneath me too*, she might as well have said.

And I'd really thought her mom liked the chocolates. Not enough to make me appropriate for her daughter, it seemed. Not like that mattered, because Z and I weren't together or anything.

"Well, you did good getting us out of there," I said. "Mitsy was trying to get into my pants via the bottom cuff."

"What? Right in front of her husband?"

"She thought I looked like I was up for it."

"Well..."

"Careful. Your mom didn't hurt my feelings, but you might."

Zandra smirked, and I came over to sit on the edge of the bed. She tipped her head back against the headboard.

"Was this your room? Seems a little bland for you."

I looked around at the space that could have been lifted straight from a corporate hotel catalog. Comfortable enough, with neutral furniture and generic landscape prints. Zero personality, which was the exact opposite of the woman sitting beside me.

"I never lived in this house. My parents bought it after I graduated and their business really took off. But this is the guestroom I always stay in."

"What was your high school bedroom like?"

She got up and walked around the room, gesturing as she went. "There would've been a bookcase about here. Posters on all the walls. My bed had a floral comforter my mom picked out. But she let me pick the sheets. My favorites had hands flipping middle fingers all over them."

I barked a laugh. "I bet your mom loved those."

"Oh, she had feelings, alright."

My grin was irrepressible. "I wish I could've seen these infamous sheets. We should've been friends."

"Like I ever would've let you up to my room to see my sheets. The biggest player at Silver Ridge High? I think not."

"I wasn't that much of a player."

"Yes, you were." She bent down to peer under the bed. "There should still be a box of my old stuff somewhere. Ah, here it is. Mom threatened to throw it away a few years ago, and I stored it here." She pulled it out and took off the lid. "This is like a time capsule."

I got on the floor and poked through the box with her. "Math Bowl?" I asked, pulling out an old T-shirt.

She snatched the shirt away. "It was a math competition, and we won. Not that anybody cared compared to whatever the football team was doing."

"Wait a minute. What is this?" I pulled out a glossy eight-by-ten of a bunch of young men posing and making eyes at the camera. "Is this a signed photo of a *boy band*?"

"Give me that! It's not even mine. It was Jessa's."

"Sure. Did you dance around holding this photo?" I held it up, examining it in the light. "I think there are kiss prints on here."

"Shut up. There are not."

"*Oh, girl...*" I sang.

Zandra pushed my shoulder, laughing.

We kept looking through the box. She got quiet when we found a few snapshots of her and Jessa, but Z told me about each one and smiled sadly at the memories. "I remember looking through this stuff, wondering if there was something to explain what happened the night she died. Some hint I'd missed about who her crush was, or who left those cruel notes and broke my window after. But there was nothing."

"I'm sorry, Sunflower," I said softly.

She dug around a bit more, pulling out a notebook. "I even

still have my diary. If this were a who-done-it movie of the week, there'd be some clue in the margins to explain it all. But real life isn't like that."

"What *did* you write in your diary?"

Her eyes narrowed. "Nothing interesting."

That sounded like a challenge to me. I snatched the book from her hands.

"Callum, put it down! I'm warning you." She tried to grab the small book, but I jumped up, using my height against her.

"*Callum is the sexiest guy in school,*" I pretended to read, "*and I wish he would sneak into my bedroom and rub his hot naked bod all over my sheets—*"

"I never wrote anything of the sort!" Z jumped in a futile attempt to steal her diary back.

I wrapped an arm around her waist, handing her the diary but not letting her go. "I would never actually read it. But there's gotta be something about me in there. Right?"

"Nothing nice."

"If I'd had a diary, you would've been in it for sure."

"If you'd had a diary, it probably would've been nothing but a record of sex dreams."

"Obviously," I grunted. "And, as I said, you would've been in there."

She glanced down, the way she always did when she got shy. A common occurrence when I talked about how much I'd always wanted her.

"I guess I did think about you," she admitted. "I noticed you a lot. And it wasn't all bad."

"Yeah?" I pulled her closer by her waist, my grip loose and playful.

"But even if we'd been friends, I never would've tried anything. I had plenty of attitude, but I was shy when it came to boys."

I bent to kiss her. "Such a good girl, and your parents didn't even appreciate it. I think you should do something bad and rebellious to even the score."

She reached around to squeeze my butt through my khakis. "Such as?"

"Get on your hands and knees on the bed," I rasped.

Z pulled back and stared at me. Clearly trying to decide if I was serious, and if I was, whether she wanted to go along with this.

Several moments ticked by as I held her gaze. Because I was *damn* serious.

Then she rushed over to the door and locked it.

Two seconds later, she was on the duvet on her hands and knees. Eagerly awaiting what I might do next.

Nice.

With the heel of my hand massaging my thickening cock through my pants, I slowly walked toward her.

"We have to hurry," she whispered.

"Shhh." Easing one knee onto the bed behind her, I slowly worked her skirt up her thighs and over her hips. "I need you to stay still and be quiet, okay?"

I wasn't going to rush this for anyone, certainly not her self-centered parents.

"I can't believe we're doing this," she said, wiggling around.

"Stay *still*," I instructed again. I brought my hand to the crotch of her panties, feeling the dampness there. "Getting wet for me? Are you excited about what we're going to do while your parents and their snooty friends are downstairs?"

"Callum," she whimpered. Exactly the tone of voice I wanted. Desperate.

Bringing my mouth to the back of her thigh, I pressed kisses along her smooth skin. Then the other side. My hands joined in, inching upward until they reached her panties.

Soooo slowly, I tugged the damp cotton down until she was exposed to me. "You have no clue how sexy you are, baby."

"Please lick me, Callum. I want your tongue."

Mmmm. Z's request, which was pretty blunt for her, had my cock fully hard and aching.

Okay, maybe I didn't want to drag this out forever.

"You got it, Sunflower. Stay quiet, now. We can't get in trouble."

The first taste of her sweetness on my tongue was even better than I remembered from the other night. Zandra let out a breathy cry. "You make me feel so good," she whispered.

All I wanted was to give her more.

Yanking her panties down to her bent knees, I helped her pull one leg free so she could widen her thighs. Time to dive back in and get her screaming into the mattress.

I licked her sensitive folds. Sucked her clit. Slid my tongue to her opening and thrust it inside her with my hands roughly gripping her hips. Zandra's arms bent, and she hid her face to quiet the sounds of her ecstatic cries.

"Callum," she said, the words muffled, "I'm going to come!"

"Already?"

"*Yes—*"

Two of my fingers pushed inside her while I kept tonguing, and a split second later she was convulsing and crying nonsense words into the duvet. I *loved* the sound of her falling apart for me.

As she came down from the high, I licked her gently with the flat of my tongue and massaged her thighs, savoring, until she collapsed to the side and tugged her panties back into place. "No more. I'm too sensitive."

I wiped my mouth, standing. "Are you happy?"

"So happy." She sprawled flat on the bed, smiling and looking debauched. "I can't believe we did that."

Knee-walking onto the bed, I palmed my straining erection through my khakis. "I can. It was hot. Just need to finish myself off." Pop went my button, and down went my zipper so I could ease my dick free of my pants.

"Wait." She propped herself on one elbow. "I want to suck your cock."

My teeth dug into my lower lip. It drove me crazy when she told me exactly what she wanted, *especially* if it was to do something dirty to me. "Right here in what could've been your high school bedroom? With your mom and dad downstairs?"

Some of the languidness in her expression wore off, and there was that intense Zandra glare we knew and loved.

"Feed it to me," she whispered.

Ungh. I'd never been this turned on.

"Good thing my cock is dairy and gluten free," I quipped, and her little snort of amusement was so worth it.

Crawling over her, I went to my hands and knees, my cockhead hovering right near her mouth. With her naughty gaze locked on mine, her tongue flicked out and tasted my tip. *Shit.* I was the one who needed to stay quiet now, and it wasn't going to be easy.

Then Zandra's eyes fluttered closed as she took me into her mouth and started to suck. I moved my hips, dragging my cock over her tongue, and nothing had ever felt this incredible. I was going to lose my mind.

Zandra moaned around my shaft. The rocking of my hips sped up, feeding her more. I wasn't going to last any longer than she had.

The orgasm hit me with no warning. I had to clench my teeth hard to keep from shouting as I came down her throat.

As soon as my brain could function again, I got up and grabbed a tissue from the box on the nightstand to wipe her watering eyes and the corner of her mouth. "I always knew your mouth was lethal, Z, but I never knew you could do me in like *that.*"

She gave me a smug, satisfied smile.

After I'd tucked myself away and fixed my pants, I helped Zandra get her clothes back in order. Her hair was wild though. I doubt it there was any fixing that.

"Never had to do a walk of shame from my parents' house,"

she said. "Do you think we can sneak out without them noticing?"

I wrapped her in my arms and kissed the top of her head. "Why should we be ashamed? We're grown adults, and that's probably the first decent action this room has ever seen. These walls needed something to talk about."

Just then, a voice shouted up the stairs, echoing against the cavernous vaulted ceiling of the stairwell. Her mother. "Zandra, are you going to pout up there all night, or are you going to come back down here for coffee and brandy like a civilized person?"

I shot Zandra a look, and we both burst out laughing.

TWENTY-FIVE
Callum

As WE STEPPED out of Silver Linings, coffees in hand, I paused on the sidewalk to inhale the crisp morning air. "I love First Fridays," I announced.

Zandra eyed me over her pistachio latte. "Why?"

We started walking toward Hearthstone. "First Friday of the month means new specials at places all over town. Live music in the park. Sidewalk sales. We didn't do much at Hearthstone last First Friday with Manny out, and you and me just starting our trial period. But don't you remember from growing up here?"

"Yes, I remember. But it never seemed like that big a deal."

I scoffed. "Blasphemy. I bet you're one of those grinches who never went to pep rallies or town festivals either."

She strode along casually beside me, sipping her drink. "Sometimes I went with Jessa, but no, really not my scene."

Lengthening my strides, I got ahead of her and spun around to walk backward while facing her. "At the summer festival right after you got back to town, you would've seen me in my full turnout gear. I looked smokin', pun intended."

"Wow, I missed out," she deadpanned.

"Us firefighters will be at the fall festival next month. FYI."

"I'd better hurry up and get it on my calendar." She took another slow sip.

Grinning, I fell back into stride alongside her.

As we went down the block, Zandra gasped. "Why is there a huge line in front of Hearthstone?"

"First Friday, baby. How did you miss that at the last staff meeting? Some general manager candidate you are." Nobody was looking our direction, so I snuck in a pinch of her butt cheek. She glared. Worth it.

I slung my arm around her shoulder, because friends and coworkers did things like that. "Russ is debuting his new beer today."

"The new golden ale? I thought that was tonight."

"We officially add it to the board tonight. But people always show up early to taste the first pours of the new beer on First Fridays."

"Russ mentioned we'd have a crowd for the tasting. I just didn't realize it would be...*this*."

"Impressive, huh?"

Her smile glowed with pride. "Yeah. It is."

Hearthstone was loved by so many people in Hart County. It was an honor to be a part of this place.

And somehow, running the brewpub with Zandra over the last six or so weeks had only made that sense of pride stronger. Working with Z was a blast, I'd learned a ton, and Hearthstone was thriving more than ever.

Even more importantly, since we'd installed a couple additional cameras at Hearthstone and Zandra had moved in with me, there hadn't been any further harassment or vandalism incidents. Tommy Pickering hadn't dared to show his face around either of us, which might've had something to do with that.

We were sailing toward the end of the summer. I was having the best sex of my life with the same gorgeous woman in my bed every night. And it felt like only good things were ahead.

Once we got to Hearthstone, there was a sense of anticipation and excitement in the air. I greeted a bunch of regulars waiting in the line as Zandra and I headed inside.

As soon as Russ tapped the new keg to a chorus of cheers and shouts, I grabbed one of the first tastes. It was a golden-colored brew called Alpine Dawn.

"This is great. Nice job, man."

Russ glanced around. Our servers were busy pouring tasters while the crowd buzzed happily. "Zandra didn't want to taste it?" The poor guy seemed a little hurt.

"She can't."

He cursed. "I forgot about the gluten thing. Damn. Not very fun to work at a brewpub when you can't drink the beer." Then he got a thoughtful look, which was something of a stretch where Russ was concerned. "Hey, there's that new gluten-free brewery over in Pine Creek. Have you heard about it?"

I perked all the way up. "No. Tell me more."

A few minutes later, I'd joined in to help behind the bar as we were mobbed for samples of Alpine Dawn. And I had an idea for how Zandra and I were going to spend our next night off. It was going to be an epic date.

Then I froze, right in the middle of pouring a taster for the next customer in line.

Z and I weren't dating. She'd made that clear, and of course, I wanted things that way too. Coworkers with benefits. I wasn't a dating kind of guy.

Right?

"You okay, Callum?" Winnie asked, blond ponytail swinging as she angled her head.

"Uh, yeah." I handed the taster to the waiting customer with an apologetic grin. "Just some things on my mind."

"I bet. Only two more weeks until Manny makes his decision. You must be sweating!"

Oh, shit. Two weeks.

Of course, I'd known that in theory. But I hadn't been focused on the reality. Only two more weeks of Zandra in my bed. Once one of us was the boss, we weren't supposed to be getting busy anymore.

I mean, was that a hard and fast rule? In the employee handbook anywhere?

"You know," Winnie said when the crowd had died down, "you and Zandra seem to be getting along real well. Nobody saw that coming."

I shrugged, collecting dirty taster glasses. "I knew I'd win her over eventually."

"Yeah, but you *really* won her over," Winnie replied, speaking low with a mischievous glint in her blue eyes. "And under, I'm guessing?"

I grinned. "Winnie, I'm shocked at what you're suggesting." Sounded like Z and I hadn't kept our sex life under wraps as much as we'd thought. "I can neither confirm nor deny."

"Don't worry, I'm not telling Manny. But in a couple weeks, one of you will get the job, and the other will be pissed. Aren't you worried about that?"

"I won't be mad if she gets the job." Those words came out before I'd really thought about them. Yet I didn't have a single doubt. A month and a half ago, I'd wanted general manager more than anything, but now…I could imagine other scenarios working out too.

"But what about if it's *you* who makes general manager? How do you think Zandra will feel about it?"

And there was another hefty dose of reality, courtesy of Winnie Peyton.

I didn't want to think it was possible. But Zandra had already proven she was a woman who could hold a grudge.

What if I won this competition, and Z went back to hating me?

❀

Late in the afternoon, I found Zandra putting cash into the safe in Manny's office.

Well, it wasn't going to be Manny's office anymore in a couple of weeks. It would be one of ours.

Fuck, I didn't want to think about that.

"Hey." I shut the door behind me. Zandra stood up and smiled, meeting me by the door. Her arms went around my neck, and her lips landed on mine.

After a kiss that was just this side of filthy, she pulled back.

"That was quite a hello," I said.

"Didn't see you for a couple hours. I kind of missed you."

"Missed you too." My chest was all weird and tight, and I wasn't sure I liked it.

"How's the tasting going?" She sat on the edge of the desk. "I meant to go check on Russ, but I got caught up in a few things."

I leaned back against the door and crossed my arms. "The fans have spoken, and they love it."

"So Russ is having a great First Friday. What are you up to?"

Making my head hurt with all these questions spinning around, I answered silently. "Wondered what you're doing for dinner."

She frowned, like she suspected this was a trick question. "Same thing as usual. Hope that you or one of the guys will make food, and I'll take care of the dishes. Why?"

"Would you wanna do something different? Just with me?" My hands dug into my pockets.

"Callum, what are you asking me?"

I'd invited her to my place for a cooking lesson, and that had practically been a date. Hell, I'd asked her to move in with me. Sort of. She slept in my bed nearly every night. Why was this so hard?

"Would you want to—"

My phone buzzed, and I pulled it out of my pocket instead of finishing my sentence. Because for the first time in over three decades, I'd decided to get shy around a girl.

"Anything important?" Zandra asked.

Actually, it was. "Text from Teller Landry."

Her eyebrows drew together. "Yeah? He found something?"

Last week, I'd asked my buddy Teller to look into Tommy Pickering, since he was still our main suspect for the note left on Z's windshield. But I'd cleared it with Zandra first. I knew she didn't like the idea of a stranger getting into her business, especially anything related to Jessa, but since it also could involve vandalism at Hearthstone—the broken window—she'd relented.

I read her the text Teller had sent.

TELLER

Finished background on Pickering. One arrest for drunk and disorderly last year, nothing else. Also confirmed he occasionally stays at the Pine Cone Motor Lodge when his wife kicks him out. Couldn't find any other link yet to harassment of Ms. Alvarez.

"So he stays at that motel sometimes," I said. "He could've seen you there." The thought of Pickering watching her made me ill, but we still had no evidence he'd done more than that.

Zandra nodded with a blank expression. She'd gone inside herself, as she sometimes did when she was feeling vulnerable. "Anything else?"

"I also asked Teller to check on Jessa's brother. Find out what Leo's been up to." My eyebrows lifted as I read the next message.

TELLER

On Leo Mackenzie, we've got an arrest earlier this year for felony assault in Fort Collins. Bar fight. But he jumped bail. Known associates haven't seen him since, no credit card use, nothing. Either he's hiding out, or he's dead.

"Maybe that's why Paula said she hadn't heard from Leo,"

Zandra mused. "He's got warrants out for his arrest. She's trying to protect him."

And what better place for a man to go when he was desperate than to his mother?

Yet there hadn't been any sign at Paula's house that more than one person lived there. Also, wouldn't his mom's house be the first place the police looked?

I sent a text thanking Teller for his help, then tucked my phone in my pocket. When I opened my arms, Zandra came right to me, fitting herself against me. "What were you saying about dinner?" she asked.

Before I could answer, there was another phone notification.

"Dang it, now that's mine. Seems we're destined to be interrupted today." Z pulled out her phone, making an annoyed huff when she saw the message. "My mother wrote. She actually apologized and asked if I would come for dinner tonight."

My heart sank a little because dinner with her parents wasn't the evening I'd had in mind. "Happy to come along for moral support."

"No, I can't subject you to that again." She rubbed her face and groaned. "I'll go. If I refuse, then I'm the bad guy who won't forgive. And who knows, maybe things will start being different." She gave me a weak smile.

"Hope so." I *really* hoped so, for her sake.

"Sorry to bail on you for dinner."

"Another time. Let me know when you're ready, and I'll take you home so you can get your car." *Home.* Meaning my place. Would she want to keep living with me and the guys after Manny made his decision?

Was I overthinking this? Probably, and it wasn't like me.

The sun was setting as we pulled up to the house. She didn't bother going inside, just jumping out of my truck. I got out too and walked her to her car.

"Can you feed Chloe for me?"

"Sure. Coco and I have an exciting evening ahead of us. Nail painting, hiding under the couch..."

Z smiled, going onto her toes to give me a soft kiss. Right here on the street where anyone could see. "Save some energy for me? For when I'm home later?"

"I'm planning on it."

As she drove down the street, I stood on the sidewalk, my gaze not leaving her taillights. Felt like my heart was leaving with her.

I didn't know what the hell I was doing, but if Zandra drove away from me for good, I wasn't going to be okay with it. "So do something about it, O'Neal," I murmured to myself, wiping a hand down my face.

Then I heard a scoff.

My eyes zeroed in on the figure hiding between an SUV and a lifted truck. "What the fuck are you doing here?" I grated out. "In front of my house?"

Tommy Pickering stepped more into view, glancing up and down the quiet street. "You own the road? Looks like public property to me. Anybody could walk by and see you pining away for your boss's granddaughter."

Rage flared in my veins, but I kept it down. "Have you been watching Zandra? Leaving notes?"

"I might've seen her when she was staying at the Pine Cone motel. Wasn't *that* a surprise? Little Zandra, all grown up."

Rage made my vision blur. "You've been following her."

"No. But if I was, could you blame me? She's an even sweeter piece of ass than back in high school."

Surging forward, I slammed him against the side of the lifted truck, barring my forearm against his throat. "Did you harass her back then too?"

Tommy's mouth cracked with a knowing smile. His breath smelled like stale garlic and tequila. "Not me. I wasn't the one with a pathetic little crush on her. The only girl at school you couldn't have."

"*Bullshit*. You had your sleazy eye on her."

"Maybe. The bonfire party would've been the perfect chance for me to pop that cherry. You cockblocked me 'cause you worried I'd have her first."

It took all my training and self control not to throttle him where he stood. "So that's why you lied to Zandra about me after Jessa died? You told her I'd spread rumors about her."

"That was me cockblocking you back. I didn't want her drama after Jessa dying and all that shit, but I told her you were to blame for the rumors flying. Just in case you decided to come around trying to comfort her. Seemed like something you'd do."

"Were you harassing her back then? Leaving notes and breaking her car window? Trying to make her life miserable?"

His smirk made my fury rise even more. "Nah, man. She made her life miserable by herself. Snapped at anyone who tried to get close."

"Because she was in pain."

"But why the fuck should I care about any of that?"

"Because you're supposed to be a decent human being." I pressed my forearm against his throat. "A woman like Zandra is worth a million of a bottom feeder like you."

Tommy's face turned bright pink. When he shoved at me, I let up, and he started coughing and spitting onto the concrete. "And you think she'd ever wind up with *you*? You're nothing, O'Neal. You're a bartender. Just a weak little bitch whose mommy died and whose father didn't give a shit about him. You've spent your whole sad life trying to make people love you. You think Zandra doesn't see that?"

My vision clouded. If I didn't get him out of here, I was going to do something I'd regret. There'd be bloodstains on the concrete for me to explain to Zandra when she got home. All around unpleasant. "You're banned from Hearthstone. Find a new bar. Better yet, stop drinking and go to therapy so you can be a decent husband and father to your family."

"I don't need your crap beer anyway."

"Stay the hell away from Zandra."

"My pleasure. But you just better watch out for who *else* is hanging around her." He backed up, still smirking, then got into a car and drove away.

Maybe I should've stopped him, considering the scent of alcohol on his breath. But I didn't. I just wanted him *gone*. Before I did something myself to make that happen.

TWENTY-SIX

Zandra

AT FIRST, I didn't notice the extra car parked beside my dad's SUV when I pulled up. Too many other distractions were taking up space in my head.

The new info from Teller Landry had been anticlimactic. Far more momentous was the dinner thing. Almost like Callum had been asking me on a *real date*.

We'd eaten dinner together plenty of times now. He'd joked about the cooking lesson being a date, just because Callum joked about everything. But he'd never formally asked me *to dinner*.

It had felt...different.

But I was being ridiculous. Just last night, he'd bent me over the edge of his mattress and fucked me like a rough rider subduing a bucking bronco. Then he'd cuddled me and been sweet and funny all day today. His usual. That was just Callum. It was how he'd always charmed women into his bed. But he never held on to them for long. There was no way he'd meant to ask me on an *actual* date.

Yet even the possibility had my heart dancing hopefully.

I had to shut that down right now.

The gravel crunched under my tires as I pulled into the area my parents used for overflow parking. Every window of the house was lit up like they were having a photo shoot. As I marched toward the front entrance, I did a double take, noticing the black Maclaren 720S Spider. A car I unfortunately knew all too well.

What. The. Hell. Was he doing here.

Mom, you didn't.

The front door opened, and Mom stepped out, a huge grin on her face. That was all the confirmation I needed.

I stopped on the bottom step. "He's *here*?"

"Come in, Zandra. Gladys was just setting out some appetizers, and your father uncorked a lovely bottle of red."

I didn't take one step closer. "I know Ian's here."

She rolled her eyes like I was an unreasonable toddler. "Fine, yes. He is. This misunderstanding between you has gone on long enough."

"*Misunderstanding*? He's a liar. He was horrible to me."

"So dramatic. But lovers' quarrels can be that way. Just come in, Zandra. Give the man a chance. He drove all the way here from Chicago."

"In the most absurd car possible." *How can he even afford that thing if he's in so much debt*? I wondered to myself.

Oh, no. Was he here to ask my parents for money? Would they actually give it to him?

"Mom, please—"

She came out farther onto the porch. "Enough. I know we argued last time, and I am sorry about that. I only want what's best for you. Just come in and have dinner. Ian was your partner for six years, and he meant a lot to this family. Even if you decide not to take him back, at least give us all some closure."

Wow. The guilt voyage had already set sail and was heading straight for the iceberg. Mom had dangled exactly what I wanted. The chance to close the book completely on my past with Ian.

If I didn't say yes to this, I would never hear the end of it.

"Fine. I'll come in to talk. But I'm not staying for dinner." I walked up the steps, and Mom swept an arm around me, guiding me through the doorway.

"Of course you're staying. I had Gladys make that complicated food for you."

I kind of hated myself for feeling a surge of gratitude, even though I knew I was being manipulated.

I was going to need backup for this, and as much as I didn't want to bring Callum into the crossfire of my family drama, I didn't know what else to do.

Stopping in the entryway, I took out my phone. My thumbs flew over the screen.

Ian's here. They ambushed me. Please come.

My breath held as I walked into the living room. Dad gave a glass of wine to Mom, nodding his head when he saw me as if this was a normal dinner invite. "Hey, sweetheart," Dad said. "Look who's here."

Bracing myself, I turned to face the other man in the room. "Ian."

"Zan." Ian was dressed in one of his tailored suits, hair slicked back like he was ready for a board meeting. He opened his arms as he came toward me. One hand slid onto my hip, and he leaned in to kiss my cheek.

"Do not touch me," I said through clenched teeth. "Why are you in Silver Ridge?"

"Zandra," Mom scolded. "Be civil."

For a good ten minutes, I swallowed my fury and sipped red wine while my parents and Ian made small talk. All the while, biding my time. *I can do this*, I thought. *I can be the grownup in the room.*

But when Ian touched my hip again, like he owned me, I jolted away.

"*No*. You know what? I'm not going to stand around pretending everything's okay." I stood back, facing them across the living room while smooth jazz played on the sound system. "You said this was about closure. So let me be clear for you, Mom and Dad. Ian and I are *never* getting back together."

Ian sighed, looking into his wine glass. "Can't we discuss that later in private? There are things I'd like to say."

"You don't even want me back. Did you tell them you're really here for money? Did you ask for a loan yet?"

"Zan," he hissed. "I'm here because I care about your well-being."

"My life is not your business."

"I called him." Mom lifted her chin. "But even before that, you were his business. Six years together doesn't just vanish into thin air."

"He forfeited any rights when he lied to me and destroyed our company."

"I can acknowledge I made some mistakes. Okay?"

"How big of you."

Ian turned to my parents. "Javi, Eliza, I'm sorry about this. Please excuse me and Zandra for a moment."

"I have nothing else to say to you."

But he'd grabbed my elbow and was leading me back to the entryway. Ian knew the layout of my parents' house well from his visits over the years.

As he led me into my father's study, I shook him off. "I'm not doing this with you."

"I know you're mad. But I'm just here for a chance. We'll be better this time around. Stronger. What we went through was just bumpy road on the way to our future." He dropped his volume. "Help me with the loan I need, and you can come back to Chicago with me. We'll be a team again."

"And *there* it is. The truth. This is about money. It's always been about money with you."

"Part of the loan could be for an engagement ring. You know how happy that would make your mom."

This man disgusted me. Standing this close to him made my skin crawl. How had I ever been foolish enough to give him my heart? “We are not a team. We have no future. There will be no loan, no ring, nothing that involves us. There is no *us*.”

He sneered. “You think you can do better than me?”

“Yeah, she fucking can.”

Callum stood in the doorway to my father’s study. Neither of us had heard the front door, but I guessed I’d been yelling loud enough that Callum had followed the sound.

How fast had he driven to get here? Had to be some kind of land-speed record.

He was wearing his ripped jeans, a Hearthstone Brewing T-shirt, and his backward cap. Looking more gorgeous than I’d ever seen him, like a low-key avenging angel who did not give one shit what anyone else thought.

Callum walked over to stand beside me, his fingertips resting on my arm with gentle reassurance. But the next words out of his mouth were nowhere near subtle. “We talked on Z’s phone weeks ago, Ian. I told you what would happen if you didn’t leave her alone.”

“You can’t seriously be with this guy, Zan.”

“I’m in his bed every night. I think that speaks for itself.” No matter where things stood between Callum and me, I wasn’t ashamed of anything we’d shared.

“I told you weeks ago, *Ian*,” Callum went on, as if there’d been no interruption, “that I’d have to make you cry.”

Ian’s mouth dropped open.

Callum took a few menacing steps toward Ian, making a low, threatening sound.

“Is he *growling at me*?” My ex’s incredulous eyes focused on me. “This is who you’d pick over me? Some Neanderthal?”

Defensiveness rose to gather in my throat. How dare he talk about Callum that way? “He’s one of the best men I’ve ever known. You don’t even rank.”

Ian held up his hands, a cruel smirk on his face. “Your parents are right. Your judgment is way off. Keep this up, and nobody with any standards is going to want you.”

Callum growled again.

"You might want to run now," I said lightly. "I'm not sure he's had his shots."

Ian flinched. "I won't be treated this way."

"Good," I snapped. "Then get back in your penis car and keep on driving."

Callum grabbed Ian's wrist. Twisted it behind his back. Ian made a small, high-pitched keen as Callum marched him toward the front door and opened it.

With his eyes watering, Ian stormed off, passing my mother in the entryway, who looked shocked and bewildered. I wondered how much of that she'd heard. We hadn't been quiet.

"You're going, Ian?" Mom asked, and he didn't even respond. Just scurried toward his Maclaren, slammed the door, and gunned the oversized engine.

"We're leaving too," I said. Callum was right behind me, his hand resting on my back.

Mom reached for me. "Zandra, please don't go like this. I didn't know—"

I couldn't even look at her. "Mom, I can't right now."

"You can try calling her later, Eliza," Callum said in a soothing yet firm voice. "It's up to Zandra if she decides to answer."

Outside, my fingers shook as I tried to unlock my car. Callum took the keys from my hand. "Ride with me. We can come back for your car later."

My heart was going a thousand miles an hour as we drove away.

A couple miles from my parents' house, Callum pulled onto a quiet dirt road and parked. When he switched the headlights off, the night closed in around us, quiet and comfortable. "Wanted to make sure you're okay."

I was probably supposed to say *yes*. Shrug off what had just happened and make a joke. Callum wasn't my boyfriend. When this benefits thing ended, we'd still have to work together. No matter how wonderful he'd been to me, we didn't have a future as anything more.

But I couldn't hide what I was feeling. I wiped my face roughly as a tear escaped down my cheek.

"Sunflower," he whispered. "I hate to see you cry, baby."

Fuck it. Crawling over his center console, I climbed into Callum's lap and threw my arms around his neck. "Thank you for coming to get me. I should've been able to deal with them myself, but—"

"No, I'm glad you texted me. Anytime you need me, I'm there."

"Because that's what friends do?"

"Yeah," he said softly. "But I think we gave away that we're sleeping together. It could get back to your grandfather."

"Maybe Grandpa wouldn't care that much. He's never been a traditional thinker."

"Wouldn't care that I'm boning his beloved granddaughter? I doubt that very much."

"Well, definitely don't describe it as *boning*."

But he was right. This could hurt Callum's chances to get the job, and I would never want to be the cause of that.

I cared about Hearthstone. But after weeks of doing this job together, it was hard to imagine one of us doing it alone. One of us "winning," and the other "losing."

Callum was nothing like Ian. But money and competition had a tendency to get in the way of friendships.

"I don't care what Ian or my parents think about us. I'm just embarrassed I gave so much to him in the past." I rubbed my eyes again. "I can't believe my mother tricked me into coming over there."

He cupped my face with both hands. "None of them deserve you."

"Why are you so good to me?" The words just slipped out. Couldn't hold them back. But I didn't think I was ready to actually hear the answer.

So I kissed him.

This man who'd come for me exactly when I needed him. Who always stood up for me, at least when I let him get close enough.

The kiss turned heated in seconds. Tongues clashing. Hands roving. "When you walked into the room earlier, I was tempted to jump you right then," I said.

"Would've been a nice show for Ian."

Ugh. "Please don't say his name. I'm done with him."

"Alright. But I wouldn't mind claiming you in front of any other man who wants you. Make sure they know you're mine."

I knew that was just sex talk, like always, not some big declaration. But I still couldn't help the flutters that rushed through my stomach and seemed to brush all over my skin.

"Claim me right now."

He cupped the back of my neck and pulled me forward for more deep, toe-curling kisses. Then said, "Good thing my truck has an extra large cabin."

I tugged at his shirt, and he reached for the back of his collar to yank it off. His hat knocked off in the process.

I grabbed the cap. "Put this back on. You're sexy in it."

"You think so?" With a crooked smirk, he fit it backward over his messy hair again.

He laid back the driver's seat. It took some maneuvering to slither my jeans off. Callum unzipped his and shoved them down along with his boxer briefs. His erection popped free, red at the tip and ridged with veins.

"Hold on." He reached for his wallet, producing a foil packet from inside. An involuntary frown darkened my expression as I suddenly wondered how long he'd had that in his wallet. I mean, of course a guy like Callum carried protection with him at all times, just in case there was an opportunity.

But how often was he needing to replace those?

Just because we had an arrangement didn't mean...

"Hey, don't scowl like that," he said in a teasing tone. "I've only got a rubber in my wallet to use it with you."

"Okay." I sounded calm. As if the thought of him sharing his body with other women didn't make me want to go nuclear. As in tear-her-hair-out, break-all-her-bones feral.

"Sunflower." He brought his hand to my chin to keep me from turning away. "I haven't even looked at another woman since you rejected me that night at the bar. I'd rather have your scowls than the smiles any other woman has to offer."

My lips twisted. "I haven't been with anyone else either. I've told you already I don't want anyone but you." In fact, I was probably giving away too much by saying that.

It was his turn to scowl. "Better not. If I find out some other guy touched you, I'll spit in his beer next time he's at Hearthstone. And then I'll lace it with cyanide."

"That seems extreme."

"Don't test me." The glint in his brown eyes was only half joking. "This sweetness belongs to *me*." I gasped when he shoved the thin cotton of my panties aside and pressed a finger into my slick opening.

"*You*," I moaned.

"Want me to own you?"

I nodded.

"Say it."

"Own me with your cock, Callum. *Please*."

With his eyes locked on me, he tugged his hand free and sucked his finger into his mouth.

After suiting up, he slid my panties out of the way again and pulled me down onto his hard length. I put my hands on his bare, smooth chest and just held on for the ride.

I didn't understand how he could be so perfectly rough with me, filling me just the way I needed, *owning* me, while also touching me so gently at the same time. Brushing my hair from my face. Ghosting his lips over my temple, hot breaths on my skin while he bucked his hips so hard the truck shook.

With Callum, I felt safer and more supported than I'd ever been. But he also knew exactly how to turn me *out*.

When we were together like this, breathless and moving in sync as he brought me to ever-greater pleasure, I could imagine—for a little while—what it might be like to truly be his.

TWENTY-SEVEN
Callum

MANNY

I want you both here Monday morning at 9 for a business meeting. I know there's over a week left in the trial period, but I don't need it. Made my decision. Don't be late. Callum, that's directed at you.

I DECIDED to ignore that dig at me being late. First, I was hardly ever late.

Second, and far more importantly, *what*? Who the hell told Manny he could move the damn deadline like that?

A jolt of sudden panic seized me. It was Friday, and we were home. Zandra and I had been at the brewery that morning, then came back here for some lunch and to take care of household stuff before we returned to the brewery later for the dinner rush.

Also for a midday roll in the sheets, because we couldn't help ourselves. With Zandra around being gorgeous all the time, I needed orgasms with her twice a day if I could get them. And luckily, she seemed to feel the same.

With every day that counted down toward Manny's decision, I'd been getting more restless. Yet I wouldn't have brought that deadline forward for anything. Because that could mean an end to everything Zandra and I had right now. An end to our perfect arrangement—living together, working together, sharing meals, sex, cuddling...

Not cool, Manny. Not cool.

This meant I had to move up my other plans too.

I went into Zandra's room. Her door was cracked open, so I knocked, pushing it without waiting for a response. She was sitting on the bed with Chloe in her lap and her phone in her hand, looking so cozy that I was halfway across her room before I stopped myself.

A soreness started in my chest, and I resisted the urge to rub at it.

"Did you get Manny's text?" I asked.

"Just did." Her expression was unreadable. "He wants to see us Monday."

"Think it's a good sign your grandpa decided early? Or a bad one?"

She scooped up Chloe in her arms and got off the bed, approaching me. "For you or for me?"

Somehow, I found my smile and my cocky attitude. "Obviously for you. I'm not worried."

"Bringing the smack talk late in the game? You're not the one who's been smuggling my grandfather nuggets and treats this whole time."

"But I'm cuter," I said breezily. "That counts for a lot."

"And there's the typical Callum O'Neal overconfidence."

We were joking around like usual, but it seemed forced. Like we were both acting out our roles. Friends who gave each other shit, but didn't want anything deeper. Coworkers whose biggest concern was the end of Manny's trial period.

I couldn't believe that almost two months ago, a promotion was the only thing I was stressing over.

A few days had passed since Ian turned up in Silver Ridge and we'd had that confrontation with him and Z's parents. I knew

Zandra was feeling a lot of ways about all of that, so I'd been trying to keep things light and easy.

Even though this restless, unsettled feeling in me was anything but.

Zandra also knew about my run-in with Tommy, at least the part where Tommy had denied harassing her. Both Zandra and I weren't so quick to believe him. Without some kind of evidence beyond pure suspicion though, we had nothing to prove Tommy had targeted her or vandalized Hearthstone.

If he kept staying away from her, that would be enough for me. So long as I could keep her close.

Now this.

I scratched beneath Chloe's chin, and she rumbled with a purr. "Hey, no matter what happens, you're welcome to stay here. The guys like you. And we're all adoptive dads to Chloe now, so if you move out, you'd have visitation to deal with."

Zandra snickered. "Living here has been a good setup."

"It's a perfect setup. It doesn't have to change."

"Callum." Her dark eyes were sad, aiming at the rug. "How can it not?"

Because I'm going to figure out a way around that, I thought. "Think about it. If you move out, I'll have to stake out your new place to make sure you're safe, and I'll end up being late for work all the time. Which as the boss, of course *I* could get away with, but it's not the best example to set."

She was covering a smirk. "Mmhmm. You've thought this out."

I tapped my forehead. "That's me. This machine is always working."

I wasn't kidding though. And really, that had nothing to do with convenience or concern over her safety.

With every day that I came closer to the possibility of losing her, I was just more convinced that I couldn't let it happen.

Truth was, the shit Pickering had said to me the other night had gotten under my skin. That I'd been trying to convince people to love me my entire life. That I was just a bartender, and everyone including Zandra knew she was too good for me.

Hell, I agreed. She was too good for me.

But that just meant I had to figure out how to be good enough for her too.

She set down Chloe and stretched. "We'll have to get ready for work soon, so if you want to do anything else first..."

Chloe dashed out of the room in search of other entertainment.

"I can think of a few things." I shut the door with my foot, walking Zandra over to her bed. We started kissing, going from lukewarm to surface of the sun hot in moments. We stretched out on the mattress.

But I also had a plan to put into action. And that made me stop kissing her, propping on my elbow to look down at her.

"What is it?" she asked.

"We never got that dinner like we were talking about the other night. Do you remember? We were talking about it before your mom texted, and the whole Ian debacle."

"I definitely remember."

Once again, I had no idea how to read that expression Z was giving me. It was kind of like when Chloe gave me her cat-stare, and I had no idea if she was going to hiss or jump in my lap to cuddle. Nothing to do but forge ahead.

"I was thinking we could try again. I've been wanting to take you to the new gluten-free brewery in Pine Creek," I continued, watching as she seemed to deflate, though I had no idea if it was from relief or some kind of disappointment.

"This would be a work-related dinner?" she asked neutrally. "Scoping out the competition?"

I hadn't thought of it that way, but sure. That could be a side benefit. "It could be relevant to Hearthstone, if we decide to start carrying gluten-free beer. But not entirely work-related." I shifted to lie on my side next to her, playing with her hair. "I was also thinking of inviting my brother and sister and their significant others. I don't think you've met them yet, unless it was back in high school, but Ashford was older and Grace was a lot younger."

"Do you *want* me to meet them?"

"Of course I do. And after the brewery," I added, my voice rougher than I intended, "I want to take you somewhere else special. But it's a surprise."

"I don't like surprises."

"Yes, you do. When they're from me." I leaned down and kissed her nose. "Let me take you out. Promise it'll be fun."

"Okay," she said breathily.

We were staring at each other for a bit too long, the air between us thick with everything we weren't saying. I was fairly certain there was a question in her eyes. The same one that had been bouncing around in my head for days now.

She'd said yes to tomorrow night, and that was just step one of my strategic plan. I already knew we would be incredible together. She knew it too. How could she not? It was obvious that I had to keep this good thing going.

But I wasn't going to mess around with arguments, letting Zandra talk her way out of this with that clever mind of hers.

I was just going to have to show her.

"Now, where were we?" I asked.

"Callum." She laughed as I kept kissing her, rolling her onto her back again. Then she surrendered to the kiss, pulling at my clothes.

In the past, the thought of being someone's boyfriend had been a foreign concept. But it was like I'd just been waiting around for Zandra to get here. If being her boyfriend meant spending time with her every day, her in my bed every night, *and* the rest of the world knowing what she meant to me, then sign me up.

While I had a competitive streak, I'd never been the type to obsess over the outcome of every little game. I still sucked at playing backgammon with Manny. But being victorious wasn't always the point.

When it came to Zandra, though, winning and losing meant *everything*. But it wasn't about competing for the job anymore.

It was about winning *her*.

I spotted Dane's fancy-ass SUV as we drove up to the brewery, which meant my sister was already here. I wanted tonight to go exactly right, and having people arrive on time was a decent start.

I was maybe a *tad* bit nervous. Where was that overconfidence Zandra liked to complain about?

"Are we getting out?" she asked. "Or is this like a drive-in brewery? Can't imagine that's legal."

"Your jokes are almost as cute as your scowls," I said.

"I haven't scowled once today."

I pretended to study her. "I know. It's slightly unnerving."

"I've been making an effort. Don't want to be all grumpy in front of your family, and then they don't like me. I mean, it's probably not that important that they like me, but—"

Fuck, it was adorable when she rambled. Was she nervous too? I loved that.

I reached over and touched her hand. "It's very important. But they *will* like you, I promise. You're extremely likable."

"Have you met me?"

Laughing, I parked the truck.

There'd been something new in our interactions since she'd said yes to this outing yesterday. Like we were both dancing around each other, feeling this sense of anticipation. I wanted tonight to be perfect for her. For *us*.

"So here's the deal about my family," I said, turning to face her. "They do well with grumpiness. Ashford is impossible most of the time, but he means well. His wife Emma softened him up a lot. They'll probably have my niece Maisie with them."

"I can't wait to meet her."

"Maisie's going to love you." A warm feeling spread through my chest. "Ollie too. Piper will be here with him, and Ollie-dude is nine years old and already a fan of any pretty girl. Then there's Grace and Dane. My sister can seem quiet at times, but don't let that fool you. Once you get her going, she won't shut up. Trust me. And Dane—you never know what's going to come out of his mouth. But it's probably going to be something about how incredible Grace is."

"That's sweet."

"Theoretically."

"Never knowing what's going to come out of his mouth." She tapped her chin. "How can you stand that? He's like, your *exact opposite.*"

"Ha, ha. He kind of is. He's a billionaire business owner and I'm...me." I gestured at myself.

She smoothed a hand down my shirt. "Right. Just a guy everyone adores, who volunteers his time to fight fires and who served his country, who does kind things for people without them even asking. And he's also far smarter than he gives himself credit for. As smart as anyone I went to business school with, even without any expensive degrees. Not impressive at all."

I shrugged nonchalantly. "Feel free to talk about me as much as Dane talks about Grace."

She got an odd look on her face. "Do they know about us, though?"

"I haven't told any of them specifically. But is it a bad thing if they know about us?" Without letting her answer, I jumped out of the truck, rounding it to open her door. "Let's go. We need to scope out the beer menu."

But as I stood there, waiting for her to jump out, she glared at me.

"Callum, I told myself I wouldn't make a big deal out of this, because we're meeting with my grandpa on Monday anyway, but now you're talking like this is... And it's starting to freak me out, not knowing..."

"Not knowing what?"

"Is this a date?" she demanded.

I grabbed her hands, gently pulling her out of the truck. "Would I invite my family if this brewery thing was a date?"

"That's not an answer. You said you're surprising me with something later."

My thumb brushed over her lower lip. "Let's worry about that when it happens. *Later*. Right now, I want to take you in there and introduce you to the people I'm closest to. I want them to get to know you. Because you're important to me, Sunflower."

I kissed her then, soft and sweet, then held out my hand. But my Zandra rarely backed down from me. So I should've known she wasn't done.

"I need to know how to act. Are we supposed to be together in front of your family or not?"

"Z, I don't intend to hide from my family. I want them to know about us. But even more than that, I'm trying to show you how great things could be. You're big on data and all that. So I'm giving you more data. Enough to convince you."

"How great it would be if *what*?"

"If you were really mine."

TWENTY-EIGHT

Zandra

If you were really mine.

I couldn't believe Callum had said that to me, then continued to saunter inside the brewery to meet the others like he hadn't just opened up my ribcage. My heart was out of control. Something wild and hopeful unfurled its wings in my stomach.

How was I supposed to act normal around his family when the man had just said a thing like that?

He stopped as he held the door open, looking back at me. "Dane and Grace are here. Come on. I can't wait for you to meet them."

I hurried to follow him.

The brewery was housed in a typical mountain-style building, but the interior had been renovated to be slick and modern. "Wow," I said, glancing around and trying to steady my nerves. "This is impressive."

"It is." Callum's hand found the small of my back as we walked deeper into the space. "But not as great as Hearthstone."

"Definitely nothing compared to Hearthstone."

Dane and Grace were already standing at the counter to order. They turned as we approached, and Grace's face lit up with such genuine warmth that some of the tension in my chest eased.

"Zandra!" she said. "I'm so glad you could come. We've been dying to officially meet you."

"Uh oh. What's Callum been saying about me?"

"Only good things," he murmured in my ear, "since you stopped hating me." Callum was so close behind me that his chest brushed my back, and I felt his hand resting on my hip. And of course, Grace's eyes tracked that immediately, widening slightly.

"He told us you're running Hearthstone together," Dane said, leaning against the counter. "That's got to be interesting, working with this guy."

"It has its moments. Though he's actually not as impossible as he pretends to be."

"Hey," Callum protested before kissing the side of my face.

Okay. So we were diving right into the *together* stuff. He'd said he wasn't hiding this—*us*—from his family, and Callum was being true to his word. He could've given me a bit more warning though.

Dane and Grace exchanged a curious glance. There was a definite sense of awkwardness, like they weren't totally sure if I was *with him* with him. Made sense, since Callum had never even had a girlfriend before. I hardly knew what I was doing with him either. Or where this was going.

Yet I also realized how much I *wanted* them to like me.

Dane pointed at us. "What can I get you two?"

"You're buying?" Callum asked.

"Unless you annoy me too much," Dane shot back, but it was obvious he didn't mean it. Dane handed me a menu. "Have you been here before?"

"No, this is my first time. Haven't been to Pine Creek in years, and I had no idea they'd opened a gluten-free brewery."

"Well then, you need the full experience. Grace and I just ordered a tasting flight."

"That sounds perfect."

While Dane and I chatted and waited for the beers, Callum stepped a couple feet away to murmur with his sister, and that just got my nerves going again. My heart kept thumping as I repeated the words Callum had said.

I'm trying to show you how great things could be.

It meant a lot that he was introducing me to his family. He'd told me plenty of times how important they were in his life. Knowing he wanted *me* to be a part of that made me happier than I could say.

But I'd been part of a group of friends in Chicago too. Until I broke up with Ian, and they all scattered.

"Have you thought about what I texted you the other day?" Grace said under her breath. "He would love to talk. If you're willing."

I glanced briefly over my shoulder and saw Callum's expression change, his easy smile vanishing.

The server behind the counter handed me my tasting flight, and I turned back toward Callum and Grace, trying to look like I hadn't been eavesdropping. I caught the tail end of what Callum was saying.

"I don't know, G. I'll think about it."

"You'll think about what?" I asked.

Callum's smile returned, but it didn't quite reach his eyes. "About getting the next round if Dane can resist talking about Manhattan or Rolexes for a whole ten minutes."

But nobody laughed. Dane gave Callum a skeptical look as he and Grace headed toward a table with their tasting paddle. I could practically feel the weight of the conversation I'd interrupted.

"Seems like that was about more than who should buy the next round of beers," I said quietly.

"I'll tell you later."

"Apparently, *everything's* going to be later."

Callum tilted his head, a silent admission that yeah, I was right. His hand cupped the back of my neck as he kissed my cheek. "Forgive me?"

"Nothing to forgive. I'm not mad." I leaned into his touch.

"But you've been there for me with all my family stuff. I'm here for you too."

"Thank you, baby," he whispered against my temple, and the answering thump of my heart seemed to fill the whole room. I was still anxious about today, but I wanted so much to be here. *With* him.

It was terrifying.

❀

Within a few minutes, Ashford had arrived with his wife Emma and daughter Maisie, followed by Piper and her son Ollie.

There was suddenly a *lot* of energy in the room.

When Emma said she'd brought her dog Stella, everyone jumped up, grabbing pints and tasting paddles, then headed outside to the brewery's patio. There was a grassy area just beyond, with lawn games set up. Maisie and Ollie ran out to play.

At the new table, Callum wrapped his arm around my shoulders again. Like we were just as much a couple as Emma and Ashford or Dane and Grace.

It was obvious he had no idea how much I was *freaking the hell out* inside.

Luckily, Stella and the kids provided something else to focus on. Stella came over, all friendly, wanting to give me a sniff and a greeting. But that didn't last long. She backed away, dashing off to visit Grace instead.

"Sorry," Emma said, leaning her elbow on the table. "I don't know what's gotten into her."

"Stella probably smells my cat on me. Chloe."

Callum planted yet another kiss on me, then said, "Stella will warm up to you in no time. It's impossible for her not to make friends."

"Sounds like someone else we know," Emma said. "You and Stella have a lot in common, Callum."

I snapped my fingers. "Stole the words right out of my mouth."

Emma laughed, but Callum was unruffled. "If either of you ladies think I'm going to take offense at that, you're wrong. Uh oh. Looks like Stella's running off with the cornhole beanbags."

Emma jumped up, but that just made Stella run circles even faster.

"Are you going to rescue them?" I asked. "Seems like a job for a firefighter. Running headlong into the thick of danger." Also, I'd get to admire his butt in his jeans when he bent over.

"Will you survive without me?"

"I'll manage somehow."

Callum aimed his dazzling grin at me and jogged over to rescue a beanbag from Stella's jaws.

I really had to get my heartbeat under control, because this could not be healthy.

A soft chuckle came from across the table. Like me, Ashford was watching the antics. Maisie and Ollie dissolved into giggles as Callum wrestled the bright-red beanbag away from Stella. He tossed it back toward the cornhole boards, then scooped up Maisie and spun her around, making her shriek with laughter.

"Maisie's cute," I said.

Ashford grunted in the affirmative. "Thanks. Growing up faster than I'm ready for."

"I hear kids do that."

He glanced over at me. "She loves her Uncle Callum. My brother's a kid at heart sometimes. Probably explains why he has so little filter when he's talking."

"That aspect of Callum's personality is growing on me. He usually lets me know where I stand. Or more often, *tells* me."

Ashford laughed again, giving me a wry look from the corner of his eye. "You're pretty blunt too, from what I hear. You didn't make any secret of how you didn't like my brother. Believe me, he was obsessing over it."

"That changed once I got to know him."

"Funny how that happens." Ashford looked over at his wife. Then he shifted around in his seat. "Uh, I have a confession."

"Oh?"

"When Callum said he wasn't getting along with you at work, I *may* have told him to get rid of you. Just by reminding you of how small-town life isn't always the idyllic stereotype, that's all," he rushed to add.

"Wow." At least the guy was being honest. Also, it was kind of funny, since I would've loved to get rid of Callum at that point too. "That's cold, O'Neal."

"But clearly I was wrong." Ashford side-eyed me again. "Callum might drive me nuts sometimes, but he's really fucking loyal. In case you had any doubts."

After a while, Ashford got up and went to join the game, and Piper slid back into her seat beside me. "Having a good time?" she asked.

"I am," I said with a sigh. "Mostly."

"Oh, no! What happened? Who do I need to lecture about politeness, and does his name rhyme with *Smashford*?"

"No, the opposite. Ashford was really kind."

"Phew, that's a relief."

I knew Piper already from Silver Linings. My addiction to pistachio lattes had been an easy way to start up a conversation with her on my first few visits to the coffee shop with Callum.

Piper could be intimidating, what with her height and gorgeous looks, but she was one of the most welcoming people I'd ever encountered. Which was a perfect fit for the fact that she owned a cozy coffee shop.

But she still felt like Callum's friend, not mine. He'd told me she was like a sister to him.

She sipped her half-empty glass of beer. "I've been wanting to get to know you better, so I'm thrilled Callum brought you today. But I have to admit, we were all a little surprised at him having a plus one. Well, *I* wasn't that surprised. Because it's so stinking obvious whenever you come into Silver Linings how much Callum likes you." She bumped her shoulder into mine.

I traced the edge of one of my taster glasses. "I like him too."

"Okay, I'm not trying to pry, but I *might* perish of curiosity if it don't find out whether you two are dating."

I wasn't sure if I should talk about this to one of Callum's best friends. A woman he considered family. But at the same time, this was burning to get out of me. If I didn't find someone to talk to about him, I might explode.

Sadly, talking to Jessa inside my head hadn't been doing the trick.

"Well, we...*might*...be dating. We've gotten pretty close after working together."

"*I'll* say," Piper said in a comic voice.

I snickered. "He wants to show me how good we'd be together."

"He really said that? You swooned, right? Please say you swooned."

Ugh, my face was on fire. Thank goodness nobody else was in earshot. I was fairly sure, anyway. "I swooned. But swooning is not all that pleasant in reality. It involves loss of blood to the head. Dizziness. It's seriously concerning."

She was nodding along with that same wide grin. "Uh huh."

"But he's never been in a relationship," I added, feeling the need to point out the painfully obvious. "I just got out of a bad one. And we still have to work together."

"Sounds like those are well-established bullet points. Like you've got a list memorized, and those three are only the top."

"Get out of my head."

"But..." Piper prompted.

"But." I chewed my lower lip. "Being with him is incredible. I don't want this to end."

Things were getting so deep so fast, and I didn't see how this could work out. On Monday, my grandfather was going to announce his decision about whether Callum or I got the general manager position. Callum knew that as well as I did. But he didn't seem the slightest bit worried.

It felt like our competition over the job and our fledgling relationship existed in two different worlds. We couldn't have both, and we'd been ignoring how problematic the whole thing was. As if it would all somehow resolve itself by magic.

But that wasn't real. That was not *my life*.

I wasn't the girl who got the happy ending.

"You're one of his closest friends," I said. "Maybe we shouldn't be talking about this."

"On the contrary. You and I are quickly becoming friends too, and really, who better to talk about Callum behind his back than someone who's known him for her entire life?" She downed the rest of her beer. "But first, we need a little more privacy, and we need more to drink."

Piper took me inside, and we walked up to the sleek brewery counter to wait our turn to order. Everyone else from our group was still outside.

"A month or so ago," Piper murmured, "when you kept scowling at Callum at Hearthstone, the man could not stop looking at you. Every five minutes, he was talking about you. And then a day or two later, when he came in suddenly wanting pistachio lattes and gluten-free muffins? How often do you think Callum comes into my shop, practically giving himself *hives*, over trying to make the perfect order for a woman?"

I suspected I knew the answer, and somehow, it only made me more nervous. "Once a month?"

She snorted. "Try never, babe. I've never seen him like this with anyone. And yes, I know, *that's what they all say*. But I'm one hundred percent for real. He lights up around you."

"There are plenty of ways I could describe Callum, but *lit up* is a constant. He's a walking ball of sunshine."

The bartender approached, and Piper rattled off our order, putting it on Dane's tab. "Sure, we're talking about a relative scale here," she said while the bartender went to fill a pitcher. "Callum is never going to be the dark and broody type. But there's a reason he's always shining brighter when he's around you."

I made a skeptical sound.

"You doubt me? I'm something of a relationship connoisseur. It's all about observing. That's why I'm great at setting people up. For everyone but myself, of course, but that's a different issue."

"I changed my mind. Can we talk about your issue instead?"

"Nope. Focus." Piper grabbed the pitcher the bartender slid toward us, passing over the stack of glasses to me. "Callum might be new to the relationship thing, but if he says he's ready to do this with you, he's in with his whole heart."

"That's exactly what scares me," I whispered, and Piper gave me a sympathetic look.

I *knew* how amazing Callum was. I'd seen the way he made everything better just by being his funny, wicked, unpredictable self. He made me impulsive in the most satisfying ways.

It had been hard breaking up with Ian, even with how toxic our relationship had become. From the start, we'd never been right together. But if I let myself fall for Callum and then lost him? His friendship already meant the world to me. If I was honest, he was my closest friend.

And I knew what it was like to lose my best friend. The person who completed me.

Could I really take the risk of going through that again?

We headed back outside. Callum looked over and waved, giving me a brilliant grin that struck me like an arrow to the heart. And suddenly, it was so painfully clear. The very thing I'd been trying not to acknowledge for days.

I'd come home to Silver Ridge lonely and defeated. But everything had changed. *He'd* changed everything.

Callum, the guy I'd hated for years, was now my best friend. That would've been bad enough. But that wasn't all. Oh, not even close.

Because I was already in love with him.
I'm in love with Callum O'Neal.
And it was the worst possible thing that could have happened.

TWENTY-NINE
Callum

ZANDRA WAS quiet in the seat beside me on the way to our next destination. She'd been subdued ever since leaving the brewery and saying goodbye to my friends and family.

I wasn't worried about that though. Just meant I'd given her a lot to think about. Right? If Zandra wasn't actively glowering at me or grumping, then I figured I was in the clear.

The visit to the brewery couldn't have gone better. Seemed to me like she'd had a great time, especially when she came to join in on playing lawn games and Stella finally warmed up to her.

At one point, Zandra sat on the grass and Stella came right over to lick all over her face. I mean, who could blame Stella? Z's face was pretty irresistible.

I'd also gotten a little status report from Piper, who said things were looking positive on the Zandra front.

I was in a great place. Phase one of my mission was complete, and phase two was a go.

"Not even going to ask where we're going?" I glanced over at her as I drove. We'd just taken a turn away from the route that would've led us back to Silver Ridge.

"Would you tell me if I did?"

"Ah, you're learning."

Zandra punched me in the bicep. "Ow," I complained as I laughed. I had deserved that. I reached for her hand and tangled our fingers together. "Don't stress. You're going to love our first date."

Her fingers tightened on mine. "What about the cooking lesson? Surprised you don't claim *that* was our first date. Retroactively or something."

She was going for a sarcastic tone, but I knew her well enough by now to hear the nerves underneath it. Which just meant I had to do all the more to soothe her and make this perfect.

I brought her hand up to kiss her knuckles. "The cooking lesson would've made a good first date. But *good* isn't enough for me. I'm going for best ever."

"It's wise you don't set your expectations too high for yourself."

"I know. I would hate to be disappointed, but it hasn't happened yet."

The truck bumped along as we drove down a dirt road. The sun was setting, so we would have some ideal colors while I was setting things up.

We were really out in the middle of nowhere now. I pulled onto an even tinier road, past a bunch of no trespassing signs.

"You do have permission to be here, right?" she asked.

"I'm not that reckless. This land is owned by one of the other guys who volunteers for SRFD. I cleared it with him, so we'll have about five acres all to ourselves."

The road wound through grassy fields and stands of aspens overlooking the foothills. When I got to an open space, I pulled my truck to the side and parked.

Zandra looked around, the soft sound of her inhale filling the quiet. "This is... Callum, it's beautiful."

We were in a meadow full of wild sunflowers. Thousands upon thousands of them. Stems and leaves tangled, yellow petals adding splashes of color everywhere we looked.

"I've been here a few times in past summers. You're my Sunflower, so I thought this would be the perfect spot for you."

She looked up at me, those dark eyes so full of emotion that she usually didn't let people see. Sometimes not even me.

Yeah, I was pretty sure she liked it.

"I'll grab our things, and then we can get this party started." I got out of the truck and opened the tailgate, climbing up to grab a plastic container that held most of what I needed. Plus an insulated bag from the backseat.

There was a clearing in the meadow where someone had built a fire pit years ago. Logs surrounded the fire area for seating, weathered but still solid. I carried the plastic container onto the cleared area of dirt and knelt to unpack it. "I thought we'd have a campfire. The full Silver Ridge experience. Supplies for lighting the fire, check. Plus a fire extinguisher and fire blanket in case any issues arise, because..." I pointed to myself.

"Firefighter. Right. Good to know it's safety first around here."

"Always. Then we have our plaid wool blanket in case it gets chilly, check. In our insulated bag, s'mores supplies and a thermos of spiked cocoa. Check."

"You thought of everything."

"Tried to." I stood up, closing the distance between us and holding on to her shoulders. "I wanted to check in with you though. This isn't the same place we held the bonfire party back in high school. But if this brings up anything negative for you, thinking about that night, we can do something else."

I'd known it could be a risk bringing Zandra here if it triggered bad memories, but at the same time, it had just seemed right. Almost like this was something we needed to do.

She put her hands on my chest, smoothing them down my T-shirt. "No, this will be nice. Let's do it."

Zandra and I collected kindling, and I grabbed a few pieces of firewood and got started setting up the pit. Within fifteen minutes or so, we had the start of a decent blaze.

I grabbed the insulated bag and sat with her on one of the logs, draping the plaid blanket around us.

As the sunset filled the sky with pink and orange, the flames rose higher, and the sunflowers danced with an evening breeze.

I poured some spiked cocoa in a single cup, sharing sips between us. The sugar and chocolate went down smooth, and the bourbon added just enough of a burn to keep things interesting. Just like Z.

"It's an excellent first date," she murmured. I had my arm around her beneath the blanket as we both stared out at the landscape.

"I'm still going for best. I'll see what I can do."

S'mores were next. We cleaned off some sticks, then stuck marshmallows on them to roast. We both laughed as I fed her, then licked sticky marshmallow and melting chocolate from my fingers. Which led to us kissing. Sharing that sweet flavor and enjoying the fact that we had nowhere else to be.

It was just us out here for acres and acres. Nothing to intrude on our privacy. We snuggled up again and just watched the fire crackle for a while in comfortable silence.

I wasn't usually the type to stay quiet for long, but with Zandra, I really didn't mind it. It was just peaceful. Nice.

It was Zandra who finally spoke up. "For a long time, I couldn't even think about that night."

I knew exactly which night she meant. I rubbed her back and waited for her to say more.

"The police made me talk about it over and over and over. And then the way people didn't want to be around me after... Looking back, I realize that was more about me pushing people away. But then the rumors started, and Tommy said what he did, and I blamed you. I'm sorry for that."

I shifted to see her better. The firelight caught in her eyes. "Z, you don't have to apologize to me for anything."

"But I was so mean to you when I came back."

"It's all right. Turns out I liked it. Does that make me a masochist or something?"

She snickered. "I don't think so. I think you just like a challenge. And no other woman gave you one before."

"You might be right." Even though my attraction to Zandra went so far beyond anything so simple as being competitive. "I wish I'd been able to know you like this back then."

"If I'd gone to the bonfire party?" She said this lightly, but a sharp pang of guilt hit me in the chest.

So many years ago, and this was still weighing on me.

"Z, there's something I need to say. I wish I could take back everything that happened the day Jessa died, including my part in it. If you'd been at the bonfire party..."

"If Jessa dying wasn't my fault, then it definitely wasn't yours."

"I know. This isn't about me at all. But I just want you to know, if I could go back and take away how much you were hurting afterward, make it even a tiny bit better, I would do fucking anything to make that happen. You are so amazing, and you deserved a lot better."

She sniffed. Wiped roughly at the corner of her eye. "You're going to make me cry."

"If you do, I'll kiss away every one of your tears." I leaned in and kissed her gently, tasting the salt on her lips, and she buried her face against my neck afterward.

"When I left Silver Ridge, I put all those memories in a box. But that meant shutting down the good memories of Jessa too." She took a shaky breath. "It's been coming back since I came home. Like when we were at my parents' house, and I looked through that old box of stuff I'd kept."

"The broken window and that sick note someone left you didn't help."

"No. It didn't."

It still filled me with rage that someone had been actively harassing her after Jessa's death. Someone who still didn't want

Zandra to get over the past, even now. Whether it was Tommy Pickering or whoever, if I got enough proof, that person was going to be very sorry.

She swallowed hard, and when she spoke again, her voice broke. "It's just a few weeks until the anniversary of her death. Another year of her being gone. I want to be able to look back and not hurt. I want to let go of that night, even if I'll never fully understand what happened. And I have to think Jessa would want that too."

"Baby. Of course she would. I'm sure she loved you. Anyone who gets to know you, who sees you for how brilliant and strong you really are, wouldn't be able to help it."

She was holding tight to me, shaking. "My parents don't think so."

"Then fuck them. I'm crazy about everything I see in you. That's why I asked you out and introduced you to my family. Because I'm pretty fucking wild about you."

Her eyes were wide in the firelight. "But this thing between us was supposed to end when one of us got the general manager job. Coworkers with benefits, Callum. That's the deal we made."

"Then I'm negotiating a new one."

"But you can't do that."

I held her chin in my fingers. "Baby, you just watch me."

"What does that mean?"

"It means I'm going to keep treating you so good, doing everything in my power to make you happy, that you can't help giving in." I added my most charming smile. "Because I know you want to."

She huffed a laugh, since we both understood I was kidding. Not like I'd keep pursuing her if she truly wasn't feeling me.

Kind of kidding. But... also serious.

Because no one had ever felt as right in my arms as this woman did. No one had ever made me laugh so much. Made me want to be a better man to deserve her. There was no way in hell I was going to let her go.

My thumb traced her plump lower lip, and the shadows from the fire played across her skin. The wood-smoke scent of the campfire mingled with her flowery one.

"Zandra, if I'm not being clear enough, then let me leave no doubt. I want to be your man. I want your heart. Your snarky attitude. I want this gorgeous body only for me. *Only* for me," I repeated, as a bolt of possessiveness shot through me at the thought of anyone else touching her. The only woman I'd ever gotten jealous over. My hand trailed down to squeeze her waist. "And I plan to keep you."

"Those are big plans." Her voice still sounded hoarser than usual, her shocked expression taking the bite out of her words.

"You could make it much easier for me by saying yes."

Suddenly her arms circled my neck and her mouth pressed into mine. My hands went to grip her sides, my tongue answering hers. I loved the way Zandra kissed me like she couldn't bear not to.

The first time we'd kissed, I'd let Z make the move. Just to know she was sure. I'd let her come to me.

But now, it was time for me to take over. Tonight was *my* show.

I slowed the kiss, turning it more tender. Then I pulled her into my lap and stood all the way up, lifting her in my arms. "I've got a much more comfortable spot for this."

Carrying her over to the truck, I set her on the tailgate and went to grab the stack of blankets I'd stowed in the backseat. I made quick work of spreading them out over the truck bed.

Then I kicked off my boots. Unlaced and took off Zandra's shoes for her too. I kissed her slowly again, but Z was not having that. My girl needed me too much. She popped the button on my jeans, so I went ahead and kicked them off and shucked off my tee. My hat got tossed to the side, and I went to undress her next.

"Cold," she whispered.

"You'll be nice and warm soon."

My fingers moved over her skin. Pushing down her shorts and

sliding her top over her head. Once we were both bare, I arranged her long, dark locks so they'd be out of the way. "I'm crazy about your hair. Have I mentioned that? Just want to bury my face in it."

She laughed as I did just that, rubbing my cheek against that silky soft texture, growling like an animal.

Then I sat back to look at her. Despite it being the peak of summer, the temperatures still dipped at night, and we weren't quite close enough to the fire to catch much warmth against our naked skin. But the way that flickering light hit her—damn. She had never looked more stunning.

Or looked more like *mine*.

I'd come to know Zandra's body in intricate ways. How she loved it when I fluttered my tongue over her nipples, then sucked harder when she really got going. How much attention to pay her less obvious erogenous zones. Like the soft skin of her belly or the delicate inner hinge of her arms.

I could almost sound poetic when it came to her. No woman but Zandra had ever inspired such thoughts in my head.

My lips kissed down along her body while my hands teased and explored. Warming her up. Getting her to relax so those feel-good chemicals would spread.

As for me, heat was scorching my veins from the inside out from how much I craved her. My cock stood up ready for duty. But he wasn't getting any satisfaction just yet.

Well, not directly.

After I'd kissed almost every inch of her, I stretched out and rolled us so she was above me. Her hair flowed over us, tickling my skin, and her breasts pushed into my chest. I reached down to squeeze her soft, ample booty.

"Come up here and straddle me, Sunflower. Sit on my face. I want to eat you and drink you and breathe you in."

See, what did I tell you? Poetic.

Her eyelids went half-mast with arousal, her breaths heavy. "Can't believe how much you turn me on."

"It's a natural gift of mine. But now it's only for you, baby. Get up here."

Within seconds, she was hovering over me, positioning herself. My nostrils flared. Her scent, mingled with the smokiness of the campfire, was becoming an intoxicating mix.

"Hold on to that ledge below the rear window," I said.

My tongue dragged right over her center.

I had no idea how long I lay there, licking and kissing and savoring. Zandra's cries of pleasure echoed against the foothills. Something howled back in the distance, and that just made me more feral for her.

I held onto the backs of her thighs, urging her to rock against me. My tongue found her opening. Slid easily inside as I fucked her with my mouth. It was like everything began and ended with her, like she was everything I wanted and needed. Giving me life with the sweet intoxication of her body.

Then she shouted so loudly it was almost a scream. Her thighs clamped down on me. Her taste covered my tongue, turning me on so damn much a few strokes would've sent me over the edge.

But I waited until she stopped moaning and thrashing before I nudged her onto her back. Grabbed protection. And then my cock was thrusting deep inside her.

"Say you're mine, Sunflower."

"I'm yours," she panted, fingers digging into my hair. "Only yours."

Zandra's hips lifted to meet me. Pleasure lit up my veins, building each time my cock pushed in and her body gripped me so good.

The orgasm slammed into me. Better than any words could describe. More intense than anything I'd ever felt.

Yet that wasn't really true. The way I cared for Zandra was even bigger and bolder. As if we were linked all the way to our souls. Like all these years, even when she'd hated me, we were always supposed to find our way to each other.

THIRTY
Zandra

WE SNUGGLED under Callum's blankets as the fire died down. He probably would've thrown another log onto it if I'd asked, but I didn't want to move from this perfect cocoon of warmth.

I'd never seen a more ideal summer night. Not even back in my childhood days in Silver Ridge. The sky was totally clear, a blanket above us woven with stars. I'd missed those stars in Chicago.

But they'd never looked more breathtaking than right now, with Callum.

Today had been a lot. First getting to know his family and friends better, feeling like I could actually be a part of their circle. And then the field of sunflowers. The fire and feeding each other s'mores and everything we'd talked about.

My heart was still scraped raw about losing Jessa. All these years later, and I hadn't fully healed. But Callum made me think I could. I'd never talked as openly about Jessa as I had with him tonight. I'd opened up to Callum in ways that I never would've been able to imagine with anyone. Certainly not with *him*.

All the things he'd said, and how sincere he had sounded... I wanted to believe all of it. Wanted to trust his confidence that this would all somehow work out.

In the afterglow of spiked cocoa and orgasms, it was easy to be an optimist. To hope that falling in love with him wasn't the huge mistake I'd feared it could be.

Now that I'd realized it, it was so obvious how much I loved him.

"Do you think it would've been like this if we'd gotten together in high school?" To my shock, *I* had asked that question. Clearly I was feeling wistful.

Jessa was gone, and nothing could ever bring her back. Yet would it do any harm to imagine, even for a few minutes, what it would've been like if things were different? If Callum and I had connected back then?

He pulled me closer, rubbing his nose against my hair. I was fitted into his side with my leg draped over his thighs, my head in the divot where his chest met his shoulder. "Would the sex have been that hot when we were eighteen? Obviously, the answer is yes."

I laughed. "You're just naturally that good?"

"Don't expect me to argue." He twirled a lock of my hair around his finger. "But honestly, I wasn't ready for anything like this back then. Not even close."

"Because of your commitment phobia?" I didn't mention the fact that his reluctance to have a relationship had lasted until, let's see, a *day or two ago*. Give or take.

"It's not that," he said in a low voice. "It was my family. Things going on at home."

I lifted my head. "You mean your dad leaving?"

"Yeah. That was rough. But then Grayden and Ashford left for the Army. By senior year, it was just Grace and me, and she was still in middle school. Our brothers were sending money home to us. Mrs. Landry—Teller and Piper's mom—could sign stuff for us if necessary, but she didn't actually care."

"So Grace was your responsibility. I'm sure you did a great job, but I'm so sorry you went through that. None of it's fair."

"It's okay, Sunflower."

He could smile through anything, but it just wrecked my heart to think of how unfair things had been for Callum growing up. He'd said he would do anything to fix what I'd gone through. But the same was true for me.

It hurt so much to think of *him* hurting. And that was love, wasn't it? Ugh, it kinda sucked.

"You don't have to act okay if you're not," I said softly.

Now his hand was on my cheek, thumb caressing. "You're so sweet to me, baby."

"I'm not sweet." No one before Callum had *ever* accused me of being sweet.

"You are. Sweet in the exact way I like. You don't know how addicted I am to you. I could eat you up."

There was a lump blocking my throat. I'd thought I had loved Ian, but it had never felt like this. So consuming. Such a mix of every emotion until everything was just a blur of *him*.

"Will you tell me what you and Grace were talking about earlier? At the brewery?"

He sighed, clearly not wanting to. But he still did. "That was about Grayden. About a year after high school graduation, we got word. He'd been arrested by military police and was going to be court-martialed. The process took a while, but he was convicted of manslaughter and sent to military prison."

He'd said all of that in a monotone. Nothing like his usual vibrant voice.

I sat up all the way, holding the blanket to my chest. "*What*? Callum, that's awful. Clearly you know that, but it's... I don't know what to say."

"You didn't hear about it? I assumed every person in Hart County did."

"I was off at college, and I wasn't exactly close to anyone we'd known in high school. Nobody in my family mentioned it."

He nodded, expression stoic, yet the dark cast of his brown

eyes was telling. "I was already planning to join up myself, but after Grayden destroyed his life, sullied our name, it was like there was a fire under me. I wanted to get out there and help Ashford prove the O'Neals were worth more than a dishonorable discharge."

"And you did."

"Did our best. That's part of why, no matter how much Ashford and I fight, we'll always have each other's backs." He smoothed his hand over my head.

"Did Grayden ever tell you his side of the story?"

"He wouldn't talk to us. Barely even defended himself. Why else would he do that unless he was dead-to-rights guilty? All we knew was he killed someone, whether or not it was intentional, and he was out of our lives. Then Grace got back in touch with him last year. Dane tracked him down for her."

"Wow. That must've been another shock."

"It was. Ashford refuses to hear anything about Grayden. But Grace wants me to talk to him, listen to what he has to say, and I just don't know. Gracie's better than the rest of us, I guess. More forgiving."

I nestled against his chest again, feeling the rapid thump of his heart. That heartbeat betrayed just how deeply this conversation was affecting him. "You're a forgiving person. But you're allowed to feel like he doesn't deserve your forgiveness."

"But *does* he? How do I know that, Sunflower? Not only that, how can I get over the way it ripped me apart when I heard my big brother, the guy who'd been more of a father to me than our real dad, was completely disgraced? Ashford had always seemed fallible. But not Grayden. It was like...like I couldn't count on anybody I looked up to because they would just let me down."

I did my best to wrap my arms around him, holding him as tightly as I could. *I love you*, my heart said. As if love was a balm that could fix everything, though of course it wasn't.

When Callum spoke next, it sounded like the words were

scraping over gravel. "There's something Grace and Ashford don't know."

He took a few more breaths. I glanced up at him again and he was staring at the starry sky.

"When Grayden was released after he'd served his time, he tried to come back to Silver Ridge. This was after I'd left active duty. Somehow he'd figured out where I was living, and he came to me first. Probably because he knew I wouldn't be as angry as Ashford, and he didn't want to upset Grace. He said he was sorry and wanted to explain what really went down with his arrest, and I..."

"What happened, Callum?" I whispered, then pressed a kiss to his jaw.

"I looked my brother in the eye and told him to leave. That we didn't want anything to do with him, and all he would do was hurt us if he stayed. If I'd yelled like Ashford would have, Grayden probably would've waited for things to cool down and tried again. But I was stone fucking cold, Z. So he turned around and went. I think it broke Grace's heart that she never heard from him, and she has no idea that was *my* fault."

"You were trying to protect your family."

"But she'd be so fucking pissed at me if she knew. They're talking again, and it's clear Grayden didn't tell her."

"Maybe he doesn't blame you."

"But do *you*? I didn't do what *you* thought I did, but you accused me of being cruel. I turned my back on my own brother when he came home asking to talk. What's crueler than that?"

My hand stroked his stubbled jaw. "Nothing about you is cruel, baby boy. That's just impossible. You don't have it in you."

Callum's eyes were doing something complicated. I didn't know if it was the dying light from the fire, or the stars overhead. But his eyes went from sad to thoughtful, then seemed to glow from within.

"Z, did you just call me *baby boy*?"

Oh. Shit. I had. "I don't know where that came from. It slipped out." Didn't matter how cold the night air was. My face was burning up.

Callum rolled us so he was on top, smirking down at me. "You did. I'm your baby boy, huh? I just turn you to mush inside from how much you're into me."

"*No.*"

"It's that old boy-band fixation of yours."

"Callum..."

"*Oh, girl, you want me so bad,*" he sang off-key, gyrating his hips. Which, considering we were naked, was getting us both excited.

I laughed, pushing at his chest. "This is not okay. We were having a serious conversation."

He stopped to pepper my face with gentle, affectionate kisses. "We were. I've never told *anyone* the things I just told you. Just know I'd love to be your baby boy, because you're my Sunflower, and if that's wrong I have no interest in being right."

I wasn't sure my heart could survive this. Survive *him*.

So I did the only thing I could think of to shift our focus to safer territory.

Sitting up as much as I could, I reached over to grab his baseball cap and put it backward on my own head. Then propped my elbows behind me to push out my breasts.

Callum's lips formed an O shape. "My eyes are having an orgasm right now."

"Show me again how I'm yours? I think I forgot."

He took me from behind with us both on our knees, my arms braced against the ledge of the truck bed and holding on for dear life while I wore his hat. The whole truck was rocking. The night filled with the scandalous sounds of our bodies meeting, Callum's grunts, my moans. Something in the distance hooted, and something else howled.

I wanted this night to last forever so we'd never have to deal with what was coming next. The job we were competing for, my parents and their judgments, Callum's heartache over his brother. The person still out there, somewhere, who wanted to punish me for Jessa's death.

For tonight, I wanted to pretend none of that would change what Callum and I had. Even though our pasts were still haunting us. And our future was inescapable.

THIRTY-ONE

Callum

We kept that truck rocking until the wee hours. Then slept right there under the stars, curled up in the blankets and around each other. We didn't sleep long though.

Soon the sun was up, shining in our eyes.

"Hey, Sunflower."

"Morning," Zandra murmured, voice rough from sleep. Her hair was wild. We both smelled like sex and each other.

I *loved* it.

Last night had been beyond anything I could've dreamed up. Best date accomplished. It had felt good to finally tell Zandra about everything with Grayden. I still didn't know if it was the right thing to do to turn my brother away. But I regretted not letting Grace make her own decision. I already knew my sister was going to be angry when she found out. I felt like a coward for not admitting it already.

And how was I supposed to read the fact that Grayden hadn't told Grace, either? Like he was somehow trying to save his little brother some face.

I hadn't decided yet about talking to Grayden, but maybe it was time to get things out in the open.

As we drove toward home, I suggested a pit stop at Silver

Linings. Z acted like I'd just proposed we streak naked down Main Street.

"Are you kidding? Piper will take one look at us and know exactly what we were doing all night."

"So?"

She paused. "Right, maybe I don't care if Piper knows. She's cool. But Sunday mornings there are busy. We don't need everyone else knowing our business."

"Can I at least take you out later and hold you and kiss you on Main Street? So word gets out that I'm officially your guy?"

She fidgeted in her seat. "Tomorrow. We have to tell my grandpa first."

I really wasn't worried about Manny. Coworkers dated all the time. A boss and subordinate? That was a bit tougher. But I was confident we could sort it out.

What was Manny going to do, fire me for wanting to take care of his granddaughter and treat her like my personal queen? Nah. Wasn't going to happen.

Zandra was mine. I was way up on cloud ten, and nothing was going to get me down.

The rest was just details.

When we got home, we snuck in, both of us giggling even though we were trying to stay quiet. I let her wear my ball cap over her hair, because I was a gentleman like that.

I started to follow her into the bathroom when she was going to clean up, and she said there was no way she was letting me shower with her. "You'll tempt me into doing dirty things. I'm worn out enough as it is."

"I'll take that as a compliment."

While she was showering, I changed into some clean clothes so I was at least decent, and went out to the kitchen to find coffee and breakfast. After I had the coffeemaker going, Darius came out of his room, yawning and scratching his head.

"It was quiet last night," Darius said, pouring himself a glass of orange juice. "Everybody was out."

"Connor too?" I poured some coffee and handed it to him.

"Yeah. If you hadn't been so obnoxiously obsessed with Zandra lately, you might've noticed Connor's been dating someone new. We're all pairing off."

"Wait a minute, you too?"

"I've got prospects." Darius sipped his coffee, leaning casually against the counter. "How'd things go last night?"

I felt a huge grin spread across my face as I answered. "The mission was a success."

He whistled. "First girlfriend. Look who put on his big-boy pants."

I flipped him off as I laughed. "I was just waiting for the right woman. And Z is it."

"Here's a scary thought though. This could be the end of an era. Zandra was willing to move in here, but now that you're together? She'll want more privacy. Same with Niko's and Connor's girls."

"You think Z and I should get our own place?" I hadn't even been thinking about our roommate situation before. I just knew I didn't want Zandra to move out.

Would she want to get a place with just me? That seemed like a big step.

Darius shrugged. "I'm just saying, things are changing around here. You ready for that?"

The thought didn't scare me. It might scare Zandra, because I'd had to pull her along at every step. First just admitting she didn't hate me, then agreeing to be friends and then more. But I liked having her close. It didn't have to be any more complicated than that.

"I'm not against it," I said. "If I'm with Zandra, that's all I need. I'll miss you guys though if the band splits up. It's been a blast."

Darius patted me on the shoulder. "Guess we all have to grow up sometime."

Zandra and I headed in for work that afternoon. Sundays were always busy at the brewery. A lot of people dreading the start of the work week, getting their drink on one last time before Monday hit.

Today though, I didn't give a damn what day it was. My biggest challenge was not pulling Zandra into a kiss every time I saw her. Because she was *mine*. My girl. My Sunflower.

Kissing at work was probably never going to be appropriate, especially when *she* was the one in charge around here. But at least I wouldn't have to hide what I was feeling about her.

About an hour into our shift, Winnie and Russ pulled me aside while Zandra was in the office.

"Okay, what's going on with you?" Winnie demanded. "You always seem upbeat, but you're acting like somebody shot a glitter bomb up your butt. You're fucking sparkling."

Russ nodded. "We have a bet. I think you got the job."

"You're way off, my friend."

"I *knew* it," Winnie said triumphantly. "You and Zandra finally got together."

She held out her hand, and Russ dejectedly slapped a twenty onto her palm. Ridiculous.

I glanced around to make sure no one else was listening, then leaned in closer. "You guys have to keep this quiet until tomorrow, but yeah. We're dating now. We'll be able to tell everyone officially soon."

"But does Manny know?" Russ asked.

"We're telling him tomorrow. That's the only wrinkle left." I almost laughed, because Manny had his share of wrinkles already, but that would've been rude of me. I basically had him to thank for Zandra and me winding up together.

Winnie lifted her hand for a high five. "Nice."

"Wait, dude, I'm getting secondhand stress from all this," Russ said, running his hands through his hair.

I clapped him on the shoulder. "There's nothing to worry about."

"You don't think this is going to affect the competition for general manager?" Russ asked. "How could it not?"

"Because I've got a plan. I've got this under control."

When we'd started this competition, I'd been afraid I wouldn't have a chance against Manny's granddaughter.

But who needed a job title when what I really wanted was the girl?

Winnie and Russ's third degree had reminded me, though. I had an email to send. A text might've been enough, but this felt like it needed to be more formal. When I next had a break, I found a quiet corner and pulled out my phone.

Dear Manny, I began.

It was getting late when Zandra hooked her pinky around mine and nodded toward the office. "Can we talk?"

"Talk? Is that code for us grabbing a quickie?" I said under my breath. I loved that she couldn't even wait another hour until closing to get with me again. Not that I was complaining.

"That is not what we're doing."

We got into the office, and she shut the door, wearing her most serious expression.

"We need to have a game plan for the meeting with my grandfather tomorrow morning."

I sat on the edge of the desk. "We'll be fine."

"This is not the time for you to be cute or just assume it's all going to work out okay. The minute he tells us his decision about who gets general manager, we tell him we're together and plan to stay that way."

She was pacing around. I watched her fondly, thinking this was adorable.

But I should've told her earlier. So she wouldn't be stressing about logistics all day.

"I think we should lead with the great news about us," I said.

"Before he tells us his decision? But that's asking permission instead of forgiveness. I don't think that's the best strategy."

I got up to hold her hands in mine, stopping her from pacing. "Baby, he won't need to make a decision. Because I emailed Manny this afternoon withdrawing myself. He doesn't need to pick the general manager because it's already you."

"You did *what*?"

I massaged her knuckles with my thumbs. "I took myself out of the running."

"But...why?" she asked incredulously. "You wanted this job. You can't just give it up."

"I already did. For you. I wasn't going to let this come between us. Not after how far we've come."

Should I have told her earlier? Maybe. But this was my choice. I'd done this so we wouldn't argue.

But this was Zandra Alvarez, so *of course* she was arguing.

Her hands slid out of my grip. "So I get the job by default? I wanted to earn this. Not have it handed to me."

"You've already proven yourself. He was probably going to give it to you anyway because you'll be great. But if there was even a slight chance Manny would pick me instead of you, why would I take that? I'm not risking us."

"Why would you think it would come between us? I was going to be fine either way."

"Would you really, Z?" I'd said that lightly. Not as an accusation.

But suddenly it was like all the oxygen had been sucked out of the room with a massive whoosh.

"You think I'd be angry at you if you got the job? That's really what you think of me?" She'd been waving her arms before, but she'd almost whispered those last two sentences.

Like she wasn't mad. She was hurt.

Shit.

I'd expected a few different reactions to my big gesture, but not this one.

"Callum, did you seriously think I would break up with you if you got the job instead of me?"

"I..."

"You did."

"Sunflower." I walked over to her, holding out my hands, but she edged away. "I wasn't trying to—"

"Don't *Sunflower* me. I can't have this conversation with you at work."

"You're the one who started this conversation at work," I said evenly.

"And when would you have bothered to tell me any of this? Two minutes before we walked into the meeting tomorrow morning with my grandfather? *By the way, Z, I'm letting you have the job because I can't trust you to be reasonable if you lose.*"

"That's not what I was thinking."

She headed toward the door. I rushed to follow her, but as I stepped out of the office, she was already halfway to the kitchen.

"*Zandra,*" I called out, far louder than I'd intended.

Heads turned toward me, half a dozen staff members stopping in their tracks to look.

Zandra was glaring murder at me as she turned around. Every bit as furious as when she'd first returned to town. She marched back over to me. "This is exactly why relationships with coworkers are a bad idea," she hissed.

"No, don't do that. Don't make this bigger than it is."

"Because that's what I always do, right? I get it all wrong and then I blow everything up."

From my peripheral vision, I could tell everyone was staring. "We're not finished," I said to her.

"This conversation is. We need to get back to work."

She spun on her heel, and for now, I let her go. Right now, it didn't seem I had any other choice.

THIRTY-TWO

Zandra

"Hey, Zandra. What happened back there?"

I was in the back of the restaurant, supposedly inventorying our stock of condiments, as if our supply of tubs of mayo was life or death.

Really, I was hiding.

Winnie had followed me back here, concern written all over her face. Pretty much everyone in the back of the house had heard Callum shout my name after we came out of the office.

"Did you two have a fight?" she asked gently. "It seemed like something personal."

Which just upset me even more. I clutched the clipboard tighter. "I can't talk about it."

I knew I was doing the same thing I'd done so many times in the past. Shutting down when I was upset instead of talking about it. It was either that, or I would get angry. Which was what Ian had always said, right?

You have anger issues, Zandra. You should see someone about that.

Callum had next to nothing in common with Ian. But it seemed like they could agree on that point. And it hurt more than I wanted to admit.

Callum didn't trust me. How were we supposed to have an actual relationship when he felt like he had to tiptoe around me? When he assumed I'd blow everything up if I didn't get my way?

The heartsick feeling inside me said this was Ian all over again. Callum had gone behind my back. He expected the worst from me.

Logically, I knew that wasn't the full picture. Callum had given up something he'd wanted because he cared about me. But all those same old fears were bubbling to the surface, poisoning everything. What if Callum regretted this? If he decided I wasn't worth the trouble? Or simply realized I wasn't enough for him.

When I'd come back to Silver Ridge, I'd thought I was at my lowest. But now I realized what it would truly mean to lose *everything*. Not just my best friend, not just my reputation and respect among my coworkers.

To lose the man I loved more than anything.

If things went bad with Callum, then I truly could lose it all.

I sleepwalked through the rest of dinner service, ignoring the curious and concerned glances of staff members. And especially Callum, who seemed to be following me everywhere with his eyes, on the verge of saying something though he didn't open his mouth.

If I'd wanted to hurt him, maybe I would've said he had no idea what real relationships were like. But the *last* thing I wanted to do was hurt Callum, and it wasn't even a fair thing to say.

Because what did I know about healthy relationships either? I was a mess.

I was just...scared. So scared of everything that mattered to me being taken away.

Later that evening, I was sitting in the office again, staring at spreadsheets until the numbers blurred. There was a knock, and I knew exactly who it was.

"Come in," I said.

Callum opened the door, shutting it quickly behind him. "It's after closing."

I rubbed my face. "I lost track of time. Sorry. I should've been helping."

"Don't worry about that. Let's just go home."

I hesitated, my body a mess of feelings that seemed to be bleeding out everywhere. An invisible crime scene. "I need to stay here for a while."

A pained look crossed his handsome face. "Just come home with me, Z. We can figure this out tomorrow."

"I need some space to think before the meeting with Manny in the morning."

He looked like he wanted to argue, but finally nodded reluctantly. "Promise me you'll call when you're ready to head home. I'll come pick you up."

"I promise."

Before he left, Callum stopped at the door. "I'm sorry I upset you, but I'm not sorry for taking myself out of the running for general manager. What's done is done. I'm not letting this be the end of us. I won't."

I won't either, I wanted to say.

But the words wouldn't come, and I wasn't even sure I believed them.

Because when in my life had I ever been able to hold on to the things I loved most?

I fell asleep at the desk, my head resting on my arms.

A noise startled me awake. My chair squeaked, my head blurry with confusion as I glanced around. What time was it?

The clock on the wall said 12:30. Everyone else at Hearthstone Brewing would be gone.

So, why had that sounded like a door slamming?

It had to be Callum. Relief spread through me at first. I'd been here stewing for long enough. What I really wanted now was to go home. Just get into bed with him and sleep in his arms.

Maybe his confidence and optimism would somehow seep into me during the night so I could figure out what the heck I was going to say to him tomorrow.

Such as, *I love you*.

I got up and opened the door to the office.

And nearly smacked into Ian.

"What are you *doing* here?" I stammered, my heart immediately racing. "How did you get in?"

Ian's expression was hard. Determined in a way I'd never seen before. "I need you to open the safe."

"I'm sorry, *what*?"

"You heard me." He pushed me back into the office, shutting the door behind us. "The safe, Zandra. Open it."

It had been days since I'd seen Ian at my parents' house. I never would have conceived of him staying in Hart County. Or doing something like this.

"You're *robbing us*? Are you fucking kidding me? Have you lost your mind?"

"It's a loan." Ian picked up my phone from the desk and pocketed it. Not that he would've let me stand here and dial 9-1-1 anyway. But what did he really think was going to happen here?

He didn't have a gun, thank goodness. But this was just *wild*.

I crossed my arms. "No," I spit out.

His fists clenched. "Your boyfriend already threatened me. You stood there while he twisted my arm like he was going to break it. What makes you think I won't do that to you?"

"So you showed up when Callum wasn't here. To push me around and steal from my family."

Sweat beaded at his temples. "The people I owe money to aren't going to be sympathetic if I return to Chicago unable to pay them."

The man had a trust fund, but had still sold his soul for more money, apparently.

"I already asked your parents for a loan," he went on, "but after what happened the other day with you and your Neanderthal boyfriend, your parents want nothing to do with me. I'm going to pay this money back, Zan. I swear. I just need to buy some more time."

I threw my hands up. "The safe has a time lock. It only opens at specified intervals, and otherwise we can just put money *in*. That's how restaurant safes work. You think we just leave thousands of dollars lying around where anyone can get to it?"

Ian's face twisted with frustration. "You have to know a code. Or you have a key." He glanced around the office.

Moving fast, I tried to dart around him toward the door, reaching for the knob. But he grabbed my arm. Twisted. Ian's fingers dug in hard enough to bruise, and I screamed.

"Let go of me!"

"Not until you help me." He pushed me back toward the desk. "I'm not playing around here. These people will *kill me* if I don't pay them back."

Fear shot through me, cold and sharp. This wasn't the Ian I'd known. This person was desperate. Dangerous.

I kicked him hard in the shin and managed to break free, yanking the door open. "Help!" I screamed as I ran toward the back door, though I knew no one else was here.

That's when I smelled it. Smoke.

The smoke detector alarm started blaring, its shrill warning echoing through the empty restaurant. Panic seized my chest as I realized what was happening.

The building was *on fire*.

I could see the orange glow coming from the direction of the back storage room. My lungs burned as I inhaled the acrid air, and I started coughing uncontrollably.

"Ian!" I screamed, my voice hoarse. "Ian, help me! The fire extinguisher!"

I turned to see him stop in his tracks, horror on his face.

Then he turned and *ran*. Saving himself.

Racing toward the kitchen, I grabbed the fire extinguisher from the wall mount, my hands shaking as I pulled the pin.

Near the back of the building, the smoke was getting thicker, making my eyes stream and my chest tighten with each breath. But this wasn't just any building burning. This was *Hearthstone.* My grandfather's pride and joy. The place where he'd built his legacy. Where Callum and I had found our way to each other.

I couldn't let it burn down. I wouldn't.

I aimed the nozzle at the base of the flames. The chemical foam shot out, and for a moment I thought I was making progress. But the smoke was overwhelming now, black and choking.

Please, I thought, coughing as I crouched near the ground. *Please don't take this too.*

THIRTY-THREE
Callum

IT WAS the hardest thing to leave Zandra at Hearthstone and drive away.

But she'd basically told me she needed space, so I had to give it to her. Right? Even if it went against every damn instinct I had to keep her close. Not let her go.

Yet I also couldn't go home *without* Z. That would feel too much like admitting defeat. So I steered my truck onto a road that would lead toward the foothills instead. To my sister's place.

I parked outside Grace's house. It was only about eleven at night, and the lights were still on. I'd thought about texting on the way, but hell, this was an emergency, so Gracie would have to forgive me showing up like this.

There was so much I needed to say to my sister. So much I should have dealt with before, and being with Zandra just opened me up to that truth.

It was either charge back to Hearthstone like a battering ram and demand that Zandra talk to me—which would have been my usual strategy—or sort things out with my sister instead.

And I had a feeling Grace would at least be in the mood to listen.

When I knocked on the door, Dane was the one who

answered. He was dressed in jeans and a button-down shirt, looking like he was unwinding from a day of video calls with international investors. Or whatever the hell it is a billionaire business mogul does.

"Callum?" Dane's brow furrowed immediately. "What's wrong?"

"Everybody's fine," I said quickly.

"Then what..." His voice trailed off as his concern shifted gears. "Something happen with the brewery? With Zandra?"

Grace appeared at the door. "Cal? What are you doing here?"

"There's no emergency. Both of you can chill." I couldn't say there was nothing *wrong*, because there was plenty. But I didn't want to worry my sister either. "I just wanted to talk to you."

Grace stepped back and waved me toward the living room. No further questions asked. "Then come on in."

Dane followed us. "You want a drink? I've got a bottle of Macallan 25 that's been waiting for the right occasion."

I shook my head. "No. Don't feel like it."

Grace stopped in her tracks and stared at me. "My brother just turned down expensive scotch. Now I *am* getting worried." She settled onto the couch and patted the cushion beside her. "Did something happen with Zandra?"

"Yes. And no." I scratched my nose. Grace was several years younger than me. My baby sister, who I'd never hesitated to protect. But right now, I was the inexperienced one.

I wasn't here for relationship advice though. My heart was thumping Zandra's name with every beat, yet I hadn't come here to talk about her.

This was something else that I had to do.

The couch cushion bounced as I sat down heavily. Rested my elbows on my knees. "I've been thinking about what you asked. About Grayden."

Dane hovered nearby, watching us. Grace sighed. "You must have something important to say if you showed up this late."

"I do. We've been waiting a long time to have this conversation. Longer than you think, in fact." I knew I was stalling, so I decided to just come out with it. "Grayden came to Silver Ridge after he was released from prison."

Grace went very still. When Dane came closer, she put up a hand, not taking her eyes off me.

"He wanted to talk, to see us, and he came to me first." There was a faint scratching sound as I rubbed my palm over my jaw. "I told him to leave and not to contact any of us again."

"Cal." Grace's voice was barely a whisper. She stared at me, her face cycling through hurt and confusion. "You never told me."

"No. I didn't."

"Why?" The question came out sharp, wounded. Dane took another step closer to her, but we both ignored him.

"Because I knew you would've wanted to see Grayden. And I thought I was protecting you."

"That wasn't your decision to make."

"I know, G. I *know*." The words felt heavy in my mouth. "I made that decision for all of us, and I'm sorry. I knew you'd get pissed off about me being overprotective. That's why I didn't tell you. Didn't even tell Ashford. He doesn't know either."

She was quiet for a long moment, processing. "When Grayden and I got back in touch a few months ago, he never mentioned coming here. You realize why he would do that?"

I nodded, but Grace still spelled it out.

"He didn't want me to be mad at you. He's still our big brother, Callum. He loves us."

My hands covered my face, my eyes stinging. Fuck, I wanted Zandra here. Just seeing her, feeling her near me, would make this easier.

I inhaled sharply, dropping my hands as I stared at the floor. "Did Grayden tell you what really happened that sent him to prison? Because he's the one who wouldn't defend himself after all that went down."

"I haven't brought it up. He'll talk about that when he's

ready." Grace's voice was firm. "But it *doesn't matter*. Don't you think this has caused us all enough pain?"

"Yeah, but when you've been carrying around something for this long, how do you even begin to figure out how to set it down?"

I wasn't just thinking of Grayden, but of Zandra and everything she'd told me about Jessa's death.

Zandra, my heart thumped with every beat. *Zandra*.

Grace reached over and took my hand. "You just have to focus on the love part, and the rest will sort itself out. Talk to him. Even if you don't want a relationship with our brother, at least you'll be making that decision with your eyes open. Ask me how I know."

What would Zandra say if she were here beside me? Maybe the final call was mine, but I could use that gut check. The way I could just look at her and her expression would tell me if I was on the right track or completely full of shit.

But Z wasn't here right now, and my sister deserved an answer to her question. The one she'd first asked me months ago.

"Okay. I'll talk to him."

Grace's face lit up. "Really?"

"Yeah."

She was already pulling out her phone. "It's a couple hours earlier in Seattle where Gray lives now. It won't be that late."

"Whoa, hold on. I didn't know you meant *now*, now."

"Why wait?"

"Because maybe I need to think about what I'm going to say?"

"You've had ages to think about it. Years."

I couldn't argue with that logic. "Fine. But if this goes badly, Dane, I'll need that bottle of Macallan 25 after all."

He sat on the arm of the couch next to Grace. "You got it."

My sister grinned and hit the call button, then put it on speaker.

It rang four times before going to voicemail. Grace gestured at me when the beep sounded.

I cleared my throat. "Uh, hey. It's me. Your brother." Wow,

nice and awkward. "Callum. Grace is here too. Look, I... I know it's been a while since we talked. Since I told you to leave town, actually. And I'm calling because I think maybe...I was wrong about that. Or at least, I was wrong to make that decision for everyone. So if you want to talk sometime, I'm...I'm open to it. Call me back when you get this. Bye."

When Grace ended the call, she threw her arms around me. "I'm so proud of you. This is the start of something good for us. I know it."

"Hey, Dane?"

"Yup?" He didn't glance away from the sandwich he was making.

"How did you know you were in love with Grace?"

Now, he set down his package of deli turkey, one eyebrow slowly lifting.

We were in the kitchen for a midnight snack. A couple rounds of scotch had indeed been drunk. Grace and Dane hadn't tried to shuffle me off, seeming to get that I wasn't ready to leave yet, and I was grateful for that.

Ever since Grace and Dane had gotten together, I'd rarely spent time with just the two of them. Certainly not with Dane alone, since we'd had our disagreements about Grace in the past.

But Grace had stepped away to put her comfy clothes on, seeming to sense this might be a long night, so this was my chance. I was surprised at myself for wanting Dane's advice. He was Ashford's best friend, not mine. But I was doing it anyway.

He *did* love Grace. Of that, I was sure.

Dane went back to sandwich assembly. Layering meat with cheese. A solid foundation. "I fell in love fast. With your sister, things just clicked into place. I knew we belonged together." He shrugged and let out a short laugh. "Took longer to convince her, but I made it happen."

With a heavy exhale, I grabbed a slice of bread and spread mustard over it. "Zandra is every bit as stubborn as Grace, but with even more attitude. If you've got tips on taming a woman whose love language is sarcasm and scowls..."

Dane pointed his serrated knife at me. "See, there's your problem right there. Thinking you can tame her. You just gotta hang on for the ride. The key is whether you're enjoying it."

"Every damn second of it."

"There you have it." He cut his sandwich diagonally and passed me the knife. "So you think you're in love with Zandra?"

I focused on sandwich building, letting the seconds tick by before I finally answered. Because what the hell did I know about love?

"Every time I think I have her figured out, I screw up again. She's got me doing things I never saw coming. She can make me happier than I ever thought I would be and then wreck me in the same conversation." I slapped the top layer of bread into place. "But the only thing that makes me crazier than being with her is the thought of ever being without her."

"Sounds like love to me," Dane said.

The first bite of my sandwich didn't taste like turkey and havarti.

It tasted like *certainty*.

Because what I really needed wasn't a midnight snack with my future brother-in-law. What I needed was my Sunflower. While I could respect her need for space, it was also my responsibility to give her all the information she didn't have.

I had to tell her I loved her.

"Mind if I take this to go?" I asked, holding up the sandwich.

Dane nodded. "I'll fill in Grace. Go get Zandra."

As I drove back toward Hearthstone Brewing, I tried Zandra's number. She didn't answer. Maybe she wasn't ready to see me yet, but I still had to do this. Had to see her.

If she wasn't up for talking about work or the meeting with Manny tomorrow, then I was going to be okay with that. Just so long as she was *with me*. So long as she knew how I felt.

Whatever it took, I was going to make things okay between us. Better than okay. Because I loved her, and there was no way I'd give up on what we had.

As I pulled into the parking lot for Hearthstone, I slammed on the brakes when a figure darted out in front of me, running from the building. Wait, was that—

Ian?

In an instant, he'd vanished. Running away from the brewery, which was concerning enough. But then I noticed smoke curling from the back entrance of the building.

My heart fucking *stopped*.

I threw the truck into park and ran toward the building. The smoke alarm was screaming, a shrill sound that cut through the night air. As a volunteer firefighter for our small-town department, I knew the procedures. I should wait for a truck to respond. I should assess the situation from a safe distance.

But Zandra could be inside. So I charged in.

The frame of the back door was splintered. Someone had already kicked it in, yet I saw no signs of anyone here. Smoke was thick in the hallway, and I could see the orange glow of flames. The heat hit me like a physical blow.

I dropped low, covering my nose and mouth with my shirt as I moved through the smoke. "Zandra!"

I found her crouched on the ground, coughing violently, an empty fire extinguisher beside her. Her face was streaked with soot, and her breathing was labored. Panic shot through my system.

Quickly as I could, I carried her outside and laid her on the ground in the parking lot just as an engine raced up, sirens wailing. She was struggling to breathe. I tilted her head to help open her airways. "Oxygen!" I screamed as boots hit the concrete somewhere behind me. "She needs fucking oxygen!"

Someone yanked me out of the way, a gloved hand fisting my shirt. "Callum, stand clear. Let us work." It was a familiar voice, but my focus was purely on her. An oxygen mask covered her face.

"You need to get checked out," the guy holding on to my shirt said. It was Jake, one of the few full-time firefighters for the department.

"No, I need to help." All that mattered to me was Zandra, but I also knew how much Hearthstone meant to her. This place was her dream, her future.

I couldn't let it burn down.

Breaking free of Jake's grip, I raced back toward the building. Someone else nearly tackled me, shoving me out of the way. "Don't even think about it, O'Neal!"

"The storage room at the back of the building!" I shouted. "It looked like the fire was coming from there. Back door was forced too. There could be accelerants."

Right now, every second counted. I just hoped that information would make a difference.

This had been no accident, and suspect number one was Ian. If he'd done this, I'd make him pay.

But first, Zandra had to be alright.

My hands shook as I dropped to my knees beside her. "Hey there, Sunflower." I tried to keep my voice calm even though my heart was pounding so hard it could burst. "You'll be okay. We're going to get you to the hospital. Just hang in there."

THIRTY-FOUR
Zandra

"CALLUM," I whispered hoarsely. My throat felt like I'd swallowed razor blades, and my head throbbed. But the man looking down at me was the best thing I could've hoped to see. I reached out for him, and he caught my hand in his.

"Hey." He kissed my forehead. "I'm here."

We were in an ambulance, the world swaying as we moved through the night. My lungs were on fire. Every cough sent sharp spikes of pain through my chest. I was just relieved that Callum was with me.

I kept pushing at the oxygen mask, wanting to speak even though it hurt. "*Callum,*" I whispered again.

"Don't try to talk," an EMT said. He secured the mask back over my nose and mouth.

Callum leaned in again. "I know these guys, okay? They're taking good care of you."

"Shouldn't have you back here at all," the EMT muttered.

"But I'm too much trouble to contain me in the front seat." He smiled down at me. "We're on our way to Hart County General, and the firefighters are getting the fire at the brewery under control. There's going to be some damage, but it looks like they'll save the building, okay? You don't have to worry about that."

Tears started streaming down my cheeks, and I reached out to hold onto him. The memories were coming back in fragments. One minute I was trying to subdue the flames with the fire extinguisher, and the next I couldn't breathe.

Then Callum had appeared like something out of a dream.

He'd saved my life. That thought kept circling through my mind, leaving me completely overwhelmed.

The thought of Hearthstone burning to the ground had been terrifying, but when Callum had suddenly been there wrapping his arms around me, any relief at seeing him had been matched with terror at the thought of him being hurt.

I'm sorry, I tried to say silently with my eyes. *I love you.*

Callum kissed my hand and stroked my hair. "It's going to be okay."

I needed that to be true. But having Callum here did a lot to give me faith.

The hospital was a blur of bright lights and urgent voices. The oxygen mask switched to a tube beneath my nose as I went through examinations and tests. Somehow Callum charmed the nurses into letting him come along with me everywhere I went.

I was worried Callum was hurt and kept nodding at the nurses and pointing at him, wanting him to get checked out too. But he waved that away. "I'm fine, baby. Not a scratch on me. You're the one I'm worried about."

After I was rolled back to my room in a hospital bed, a doctor finally appeared to speak with me.

The doctor glanced at her chart. "Ms. Alvarez, you've suffered smoke inhalation from the fire. Your oxygen levels are stable now, and your airways didn't suffer as much damage as they could have, but you have some inflammation in your lungs and throat. That's why speaking is so difficult and painful right now. You'll need to rest your voice for the next several days. We've started you on some medications to clear those airways, and we'll monitor you overnight to make sure there are no complications. The good news is that with rest and proper care, you should make a full recovery."

"That's very good news," Callum said, squeezing my hand. I nodded.

"The police are here as well, and I know they'd like to speak with you. If you're feeling up for that, and *only* if that's the case, I'm willing to let them come in."

Callum started to protest. "I'll go talk to them. But Zandra needs to rest, not deal with—"

I gripped his arm, nodding. He frowned, but said, "Okay. We'll talk to the police."

The doctor dipped her chin. "I'll send them in to talk with you and your fiancee." She left the room.

Fiancee? I gave Callum a look, and he grinned. "Easier to talk my way into staying by your side if I was your betrothed."

He was so ridiculous, and I loved everything about him. Even if fiancee was *really* skipping ahead. That wasn't the priority right now, though.

With my hand, I made a gesture like I was writing. Callum figured it out and passed me his phone with the notes app open. I typed as quickly as I could.

Ian. He was there. Broke in. Wanted money from safe.

Callum's expression hardened. Yet he didn't look surprised. "He's dead. I'm gonna kill him."

Not worth it.

"You could have died, Z."

I don't think that part was Ian's fault.

As for what had really happened, it was hard to know where

to begin. Just that small amount of typing on the screen was tiring me out and making my head hurt worse.

Callum seemed to notice, putting his hand over mine. "Don't push yourself, okay?"

Police Chief Susan Nichols came in a few minutes later. She was a middle-aged woman with graying hair pulled back in a practical ponytail and a kind demeanor.

"Well, honey, you've had quite a night," she said, settling into a chair beside my bed. "I'm going to turn on my body cam to record our conversation. Ready?"

I nodded.

"Good. Now, can you tell me what happened tonight at Hearthstone Brewing?"

I took Callum's phone again and began typing slowly. It took a while to get the sentences the way I wanted them.

My ex-boyfriend Ian was at Hearthstone wanting money from the safe. I was trying to get away from him, and that's when I realized the building was on fire.

Chief Nichols read the message aloud and frowned. "This Ian. What's his last name?"

Ian Vanderwall.

"The coward left her there to fend for herself." Callum's voice was tight with anger. "I saw him running from the scene as I drove up."

I reached over and took his hand, squeezing it.

"And you don't think Ian set the fire?" Nichols asked.

I wrote my response.

That wouldn't make any sense. He wanted money from the safe. Why would he burn down the building?

"Any idea where this Ian is staying?"

I shook my head but tapped out another note.

My parents might know where he is.

Callum spoke up. "Chief, there's someone else who could be a suspect. Tommy Pickering. He's been bothering Zandra the last few weeks. Showing up at the brewery or outside our place like he might be following her. There was that broken window at the brewery last month."

"You think that could've been him? You didn't report it?"

"He hasn't admitted to anything except seeing Zandra around, and we had nothing to go on but suspicion. But Hearthstone has security cameras. You need to check the recordings. Find out exactly who was there."

She dipped her chin with a nod. "My people are at Hearthstone right now with the fire department, and we'll see about getting the hard drive for the cameras. We're working with the fire marshal to determine the origin and cause of the fire. Could be arson, but it's too early to tell. We'll get to the bottom of it."

When Nichols left, Callum turned to me, his face dark with anger. "I never should have left you alone at the brewery tonight." Then he shook his head. "I mean, you needed space, and I can respect that. But it just...Z, the thought of almost losing you..."

Tears pricked my eyes. I wished I could erase that stupid fight. I typed on the notes app.

I know. Same. I'm so sorry about everything tonight. I said things I didn't mean.

"I'm sorry too. I screwed up by not talking to you before I got in touch with Manny about the job. But we can talk about that later." Callum took the phone from my hands and leaned down to kiss me softly. "All that matters is we're both here and we're safe. You should try to get some sleep."

"You'll stay with me?" I whispered, followed by a fit of coughing.

"If they want me out, they'll have to drag me kicking and screaming." He settled back in the chair beside my bed. "You know what a pain in the ass I can be."

A pain in the ass I'm completely in love with, I thought to myself.

There was so much more I wanted to say to him. But I didn't want to tell Callum how I felt over a notes app. That would have to wait.

I closed my eyes and tried to rest.

Callum and I slept off and on. When morning came, a booming voice pulled me from a doze. "Where is she? Where's my granddaughter?"

"I think Manny's arrived," Callum muttered, sitting up and rubbing his face.

A moment later, Grandpa stormed into the room on his cane, moving surprisingly fast. Rosie came in behind him with a wheelchair. "Pa, you need to sit down. The nurse said—"

"I'm too upset to sit down," he declared.

A nurse popped her head in. "Two visitors only, please."

Thankfully my headache wasn't pounding as much as last night, but this wasn't helping.

Rosie sighed. "I'd better get back to the waiting room and wrangle Eliza and Javi. It's a zoo out there, and I have the feeling Jimmy will instigate something if I leave him alone with your parents much longer."

I looked at Grandpa in surprise. My Mom and Dad were here?

He seemed to read my expression. "Of course they're here," Manny said, finally lowering himself into the chair. "Half of Hearthstone's staff is out there, plus a bunch of other people I barely know, and your parents are near hysterical. At least your mother is. But I insisted on coming in first." He studied my face with sharp eyes. "Hearthstone Brewing has been around for thirty years, and nothing so catastrophic as last night has ever happened."

Crushing guilt hit me all over again, even though I still had no idea how that fire had started.

My ex had tried to rob the place. And that was far from the only suspicious incident that had occurred at the brewery since I came back to town.

"I'm so sorry, Grandpa," I whispered.

"Manny, you're out of line." Callum's brows creased as he reached for my hand. I knew he didn't want me to talk, but I'd had to say that out loud.

Somehow, *I* had brought this on Hearthstone.

"Callum, you can stay out of this. Zandra, I want you to listen to me." Grandpa got up from the chair, wobbling to my bedside. He narrowed his eyes and frowned. "Are you listening?"

I nodded, bracing myself for whatever he was about to say.

"I'd happily see every possession of mine go up in flames before losing you. You hear me? Don't talk again. Just nod."

I did, feeling like I was a kid again, and Grandpa had caught me sneaking sugar cubes from the Hearthstone supply shelves.

"I love you, granddaughter. Your Nana loved you too. If she'd known Hearthstone almost cost your life, she'd never forgive me." His voice cracked when he'd mentioned Nana, and he turned around to sit, but I suspected he was blinking away tears.

Same thing I was doing.

"From what I hear," Grandpa went on, "both you and Callum tried to save the building instead of just worrying about yourselves. Don't know what kind of sense that shows for my general manager candidates."

Then his gaze zeroed in on Callum's hand tangled with mine.

"Unless it's worse than I thought."

Crap. We still hadn't figured out how to have this conversation, and I didn't even have my voice.

Of course, never one to stay quiet, Callum spoke up first.

"Sir, technically, I wasn't able to keep it in my pants like you asked. But I'm crazy about her, so I hope you can overlook it."

I closed my eyes. Wow.

Not how I would've put it, but okay.

Grandpa stared at us. "That might explain a few things. How long has this been going on?"

Before Callum could give any other details my grandfather did *not* need to know, I waved my hands and mimed writing again.

Callum smiled. "Z might have something to add."

You think? I said with my glare. A loving glare, but still.

We've been seeing each other for over a month.

Grandpa read my note, letting the quiet stretch. "When were you two planning on telling me?"

Tomorrow. I'm sorry, Grandpa. It's my fault, not Callum's.

"Z," Callum started.

But I wasn't going to let him take the blame when he'd already tried to give up the general manager position for me.

It's all on me. I kissed him first. I initiated inappropriate conduct in the back storage room.

Grandpa's face was a stony mask as he read my message. Then he did what neither of us expected.

He started to laugh. Long and hard. I didn't think Grandpa had laughed like this since Nana Julia died.

"You're idiots," he said, wheezing. "The both of you."

Callum snickered at that, and I felt myself smiling. "We're

definitely both idiots about how we feel for each other," Callum agreed.

I had more to say, though.

But the general manager job. I want you to still consider Callum for it.

Callum gave me a look. "Baby, no."

Grandpa got up, balancing on his cane. "Work talk will wait. I have phone calls to make about repairs to the building, and I don't want either of you to think about those logistics for a second. I might be retiring, but I'm not keeled over yet. Got that? I will handle this. You just get better."

I nodded, and Callum said, "Yes, Grandpa."

Manny shot him a warning glare, but it was just as full of affection as mine had been. "I'll leave you alone and hold back the rest of the flood who's here to see you. I think you two could use a few minutes to sort yourselves out. And for what it's worth, love matters more than any business ever could."

When Manny left, Callum started talking, and I started typing.

"I need to tell you—"

Callum, I have to

He held up a hand. "Let me go first."

Fine, I mouthed.

"I love you, Z."

Oh.

Even with all the other surprises I'd endured the past several hours, his words stunned me. Then a toasty-warm feeling spread through my body. Gooier than a gluten-free brownie sundae with oat milk ice cream. Better than a field of sunflowers and spiked cocoa around a campfire.

My thumbs tapped as fast as they could on the screen.

I didn't get to say it first.

He grinned. "So competitive. You can write it now, if you want."

But if I had any voice left to me, I had to use it for this. "I love you, Callum," I rasped aloud.

"Fuck, baby. That's what I like to hear." His grin was mile-wide as he kissed me, then rested his forehead on mine. I put my hands on his face, holding him there.

When he pulled back, I typed something else.

I love you, baby boy.

His laugh was so loud the nurse popped her head in to check on us. "Careful or I'll start singing and dancing," he said when she was gone. "I love you, Sunflower."

Love you so much it scares me.

"Good scared or bad scared?" he asked.

Good scared. The kind that makes me want to be braver than I ever thought possible.

"I know exactly how you feel."

THIRTY-FIVE
Callum

I HADN'T JUST CHARMED Zandra. Hadn't just won her over. I'd made her fall in love with me at the same time I fell in love with her.

How badass was that?

"Do you need more water?" I asked, noticing her cup was nearly empty. I gave her a refill to sip through a straw, pulling my chair as close to her bed as I could get.

But while I was fussing over her, trying to enjoy the natural high of knowing she loved me back, there was a dark shadow in the back of my mind.

It was hard for me to think about what happened last night. Running into that building, seeing her on the ground.

I'd never been that scared in my life. Not when I was deployed and getting shot at. Or in other fires, no matter how intense. Nothing had come close to the agony of carrying her out of Hearthstone and feeling her limp in my arms.

So, we were never doing that shit again. It was decided. Zandra would stay out of danger from here on out.

Next time I saw Ian, all I could say was that it wouldn't be pretty. The man's only hope was that the police would find him before I did. Even if the fire was just a freak accident, a random coincidence, Ian had left her there instead of trying to help. After six years of dealing with his version of love, it was a wonder Zandra was willing to try again with me.

I was going to love her the way she deserved.

We heard a faint knock at the door frame, and the door pushed open. Zandra's parents were standing there.

"Oh, Zandra. My poor baby." Her mom rushed forward.

But I stood up, blocking Eliza's path. "Z's been through a lot," I said evenly. "She needs to rest."

"You think I don't know that? She's my daughter. You can't keep us from her."

"Like hell I can't. You'll upset her over my dead body."

Eliza gasped, a hand flying to her mouth, while Javi blanched. Then I felt Zandra tugging at my shirt.

I turned around, and she nodded toward her parents. "I'm okay," she whispered, coughing.

"Are you sure?"

Another nod. She smiled slightly, and her finger stroked down the side of my hand.

"I'll be right here. Give the signal, and they'll be out on their ears."

Not necessary, Z's sardonic expression said.

I kissed her on the forehead, made sure she had my phone for writing notes, then backed away toward the door. Javi and Eliza went past me, standing on either side of the hospital bed.

Her mom's eyes were bloodshot from crying. I had to give her that. "Oh, sweetheart. Look at you. I can't understand how things went so wrong."

Should we start with you inviting Ian to Silver Ridge? I wanted to say. But I didn't. I stayed quiet. Instead, I stood by the door like Zandra's personal bodyguard, watching as she wrote messages to her parents on my phone and they gave quiet replies.

At least they were here, right? That counted for something.

The nurse reappeared. Her mouth opened, and I knew exactly

what she was going to say. "My fiancee really needs me here," I murmured. "Her parents are a stressor. You get it, right?"

I managed to convince her to let me stick around. Some charming smiles may have been thrown in, along with a promise to send over treats from Silver Linings for the nurses' station as a thank you.

Whatever worked.

Meanwhile, I was pretty sure I'd caught the words "I'm sorry" in there somewhere coming from her mom. Something that Z badly needed to hear. It didn't make up for everything, but it mattered.

Finally, Eliza clasped her hands in front of her and turned to me. "Callum, we've invited Zandra to come stay with us for a few days while she's recovering. And we'd..." She pursed her lips like she'd bitten into a particularly mealy piece of fruit. "We'd like to invite you to come along with her. She made it clear she wouldn't come home unless you could join her."

Damn right, I thought. But what I said was, "Wherever Z wants me, I'm there. But what about Chloe?"

"Chloe?" Eliza repeated.

"Zandra's cat. Pets are important while people are healing." I had no idea if that was true, but it sounded right.

Another purse of Eliza's lips. "But Javi is allergic."

Z's dad lifted his hand. "I'll be alright if you keep the cat in the guest wing."

"Perfect. We'll see you there later." I grinned. Maybe it was a little less charming than my usual, because Eliza flinched, and I found that satisfying.

After they left, I gently sat beside Zandra on the mattress. "What do you think? How'd it go?"

"Okay," she whispered, then switched to typing again.

Better than I would've thought. I told them what Ian did, and they feel awful. Have to wait and see, but I think they might actually be listening to me. Finally.

"You sure about going to stay with them?"

She rested back against the pillows, smiling and nodding as she reached for my hand. "Just need you," she whispered, smothering a cough.

And I needed to be with her too. I didn't care what her parents or anyone else thought. The two of us were a package deal.

The funny thing was, we'd been that way almost since the whole ridiculous competition over general manager started. We worked far better together than apart. Just took the both of us a while to figure it out.

Arriving at Eliza and Javi's home that afternoon was a stark contrast to the last time I'd rolled up here. That time, Zandra had texted me to come get her because Ian had ambushed her.

Part of me would have loved to find Ian here again, just to make it nice and convenient for me to rearrange his face and his body parts for what he'd done.

But then again, that would distract me from taking care of my girl, and that was job number one today. Same with all the days in the future if I had my way.

Eliza fluttered around us as I led Zandra inside and toward the stairs. "Are you positive you won't let me set you up in the living room, sweetheart? Then you won't have to manage the stairs."

"We've got it," I said. Zandra and I had already talked this through. Well, I did the talking, she did the typing and speaking through her eyes and expressions.

She did not want her mom eyeballing her every move. Also, she wanted to share a bed with me. So, the guestroom upstairs it was. "I'll take it from here, Eliza."

Zandra's mom jolted like somebody had buzzed her with an

electric shock every time I used her first name. But I was done being formal.

Polite, yes. But was I going to bend over backwards to try to impress them, like the first night I came here for dinner? Nope. They would get the enjoyment of my charm when I was sure they were being fair to Zandra.

We got upstairs, and I picked her up to carry her the rest of the way to the guestroom. I carefully removed her shoes before helping her into bed and pulling the covers up around her. It was clear she was exhausted, and she'd been nodding off in the truck on the drive here. The past day had taken way too much out of her.

I kicked off my own shoes and crawled into bed beside her. After arranging her pillows to make sure she was comfortable and could breathe okay, I spent a few minutes softly kissing her face and stroking her arms.

"I love you," I murmured against her temple.

Her eyes said it back, along with her lips making the shape of the words.

I traced my thumb along her cheek, marveling at how good it felt to have her safe in my arms. "I want you to get some rest, and I'll be downstairs taking care of some things. But I'll be back to check on you."

"Don't go far," she whispered.

"Won't set foot outside this house," I promised, brushing a kiss across her forehead. "Your parents are going to regret inviting me."

I stayed there until she drifted off to sleep, her breathing finally evening out as the tension left her body. Only then did I carefully slip out of bed, making sure not to wake her.

I had some deliveries that would show up soon. And I figured I should be downstairs when they arrived.

I made it to the entryway just in time to hear furious knocking on the front door. A small silhouette stood outside, visible through the frosted glass. "I've got it," I said, throwing a wink at Gladys as she rushed into the entry.

Gladys cast a glance behind her, then whispered, "I heard you saved Zandra's life and you were defending her to her parents, so you go right ahead and make yourself at home."

I was glad to know I had at least one ally here. Luckily, though, I'd already called for reinforcements.

As soon as I opened the front door, my sister shot inside.

Grace went to me for a hug first, already launching into a stream of questions. "How's Zandra doing? Have you heard anything about how the fire started? Oh, Dane has dinner. Point me to the kitchen, and we'll get started setting up."

Dane was right behind her, carrying enough bags of takeout to feed the entire wing of the hospital Zandra had been in. "Put me to work," he said. "You might want to speak up about what you need, otherwise Grace is going to come up with a million things on her own."

I had no doubt of that.

While we'd been waiting for the discharge papers at the hospital, I'd sent out messages on the Lonely Harts Club group thread. I'd already been texting with all of them off-and-on all day to keep them updated.

The O'Neals and the Landrys had a habit of bringing out the big guns when one of us was hurt or in trouble. And thank goodness for that.

Gladys started to point Dane and Grace toward the kitchen, but then Eliza appeared in the archway that led to the living room. "What on *earth* is going on here? Callum, who is in my house?"

"Eliza, this is my sister Grace O'Neal. You've probably seen her around town."

"Yes, but when I invited you here, I didn't expect a crowd."

Grace straightened to her full height, which wasn't all that much. "I'm here for my brother and Zandra. That's what family does. We show up when it matters, and we don't ask permission to take care of the people we love. So if you wouldn't mind, I'd like someone to point me to the kitchen so I can get dinner ready. *Please.*"

Her last word echoed on the vaulted ceiling above us, then fell into silence.

"Very well," Eliza said stiffly. "Right this way."

Dane and I shared a knowing smile. Grace was scary when she wanted to be.

While Gladys showed Grace to the kitchen, helping to carry the takeout bags, Dane introduced himself to Eliza. And wouldn't you know it, when Eliza heard he was *that* Dane Knightly, owner of the Silver Ridge Ski Resort, she got a lot more friendly.

Half an hour later, Piper had arrived, as well as Zandra's aunt Rosie and Jimmy Perkins. Piper's son Ollie was staying with Ashford and Emma today. Ashford had texted that he wanted to come see us, but he and Emma were on kid duty and didn't want to bring Maisie and Ollie if they might disturb Zandra's recovery.

Of course, there were already enough big personalities here to have the noise levels high.

The house was buzzing with activity as everyone pitched in to heat up food, get drinks, set the dining table. Grace had brought a few different kinds of creamy, pureed soups that would be easy on Z's throat. All allergen-free and ready for whenever Z came downstairs.

The doorbell rang. "I'll get it," I said, already heading toward the front of the house. I was pretty sure I knew who this would be.

Connor stood on the porch with a couple of duffel bags. And a cat carrier holding a very grumpy looking Chloe.

I reached out to give him a quick hug and a back slap. "Thanks for this, man. Appreciate it. Was Chloe difficult about getting in the carrier?"

"If leaving a gouge in my forearm is difficult, then yes."

"Shit, sorry."

"It's cool. I'll live. Grabbed all Chloe's stuff I could find."

"Litter? And that fountain thing?"

"Yep. For your bags, I wasn't sure how much to pack, so I mainly grabbed basics."

"And the gnome?"

"The weird gnome too. Let me know if I missed anything else essential."

"I'm sure it's fine." I lowered my voice. "Hoping this will only be a few days."

Connor's smile was half-hearted. "At least it's a fancy place. Is there room service?" He glanced past me into the entry.

"Nah, but plenty of clean towels. You want to come in?"

"I can't. Other plans."

So many people had turned out for me and Zandra today, and my roommates were no exception. I already knew Darius and Niko had been at the scene of the fire last night after the call went out.

Connor was the only one I hadn't heard much from, but here he was, delivering clothes and other essentials he'd packed up from my and Zandra's rooms.

"Darius told me about your new girl. I'm guessing you were out with her last night?"

Connor glanced at his sneakers. "Yeah, she's not from Silver Ridge. Things are...getting more serious. You know?"

"That I do." My last conversation with Darius came to mind. The thought that we might not be living together for much longer. "We should all go out sometime. Me and Zandra, you and your girl."

"Thanks." But Connor's eyes didn't meet mine. "I better go."

"No worries. We'll catch up soon."

He turned around, heading back to his car.

Kneeling, I peered into the cat carrier. Chloe let out an indignant yowl. "Sorry, I know this sucks. But Z misses you. Come on. Let's go see her."

In the guestroom upstairs, Zandra was still asleep. After setting Chloe free and placing the duffel bags on the carpet, I padded over in my socked feet and lay down. Chloe jumped onto the bed. "Don't wake her," I whispered.

She prowled around near Zandra's head, looking for the best spot.

Seeing our families together downstairs, and then Connor at the door, had me feeling all kinds of sentimental. The crew from Hearthstone had been texting all day too, anxious to check on how Zandra was doing. Winnie and Russ had made a brief appearance at the hospital.

We had a lot of people supporting us, and that felt really good.

Before this summer, I'd been satisfied with the life I had. Strong connections with the Lonely Harts club. Uncle time with Maisie and Ollie. A job I liked, volunteer work that mattered, roommates who had my back. Rarely a dull moment.

And yet, I'd been hiding. Refusing to acknowledge the hard truths about Grayden. Never letting any women get close enough to risk actual feelings.

Then Zandra had stepped back into Silver Ridge and into my life, shaking me to my foundations, and nothing had been the same. I liked to call her Sunflower, but she was my light too. Like the sun hadn't truly come up for me until she reappeared.

Now, there was no way I would ever want to go back. Even if it meant some things had to change.

I gently kissed her on the forehead and whispered, "Never knew I could love someone this much, baby." Maybe I hadn't been a forever kind of guy before. But she'd brought that out in me.

I felt proud to be her baby too. Anything the world wanted to throw at us, fine. We could take it.

Zandra was safe now. She was *mine*. And I was going to spend the rest of my life doing everything in my power to keep her that way.

THIRTY-SIX
Zandra

Waking up in my parents' house with Callum in bed beside me was not something I could've predicted at the start of the summer.

First of all, how did he manage to look so sexy after a night of sleep? My skin was always puffy and weird in the morning. Today, add in a headache and a raw throat that probably had me squishing my face up some kind of way.

But Callum looked like he was ready for a photo shoot. He was lying flat on his back, one arm thrown above his head, wearing nothing but tight boxer briefs. I rested my hand on the warm skin of his stomach, feeling it rise and fall.

He'd even placed the ceramic gnome dressed as a football player on the dresser. A little touch of home and a reminder of how far we'd come.

Before now, the only man I'd ever shared a bed with in this house was *Ian*. Ugh. I wanted to erase that man from my memory. Pretend I'd never fallen for his lies. But I knew all too well that erasing bad memories was impossible. The only thing you could do was try to heal. And make new memories to fill up the hollow spaces that the emotional wounds left behind.

Chloe meowed near my pillow. "Coco," I rasped. I'd missed

her. Felt good to have another friend back. After bumping her furry head against mine, she jumped down to explore the room, probably eager for some breakfast.

Blinking the last traces of sleep away, I had a sudden longing to tell Jessa everything that had happened. The awful parts, because best friends always listened when you needed to share things like that. But even more, the wonderful parts.

I'm in love with him, Jessa, and he loves me. Callum O'Neal.

Yes, that one.

Can you believe it? I was so wrong about him. He's the most amazing guy in the world, and he loves me back, and I wish you'd had the chance to find someone like him too.

I still hadn't really talked to Callum about the way I'd freaked out on him the other night. Getting upset when he'd taken himself out of the general manager competition. We didn't even know what Grandpa had decided.

But Callum was right. A job title didn't matter. I loved Hearthstone. That was why I'd stayed in that burning building to try to save it, no matter how foolish that was. I wanted to build Hearthstone back stronger than ever after this.

But not without Callum. Never without Callum. As much as my fears still had a voice in my head, I couldn't let them stop me from loving him and accepting his love in return.

My perfect guy had been waiting for me in Silver Ridge all along.

Callum stretched his arms over his head and yawned. "How you feeling?"

"Okay." Then pointed at my head and throat with a wincing expression.

"Still hurting," he said.

"But," I whispered, barely audible, then pumped my eyebrows as I ran my hand to his bare chest. "Good view."

He grinned and flexed his muscles for me, making his pecs dance and me laugh. My subsequent coughing fit interrupted the show. Worth it though.

"Sorry, baby," he murmured, sitting up with me and rubbing my back.

Smoke inhalation was brutal. Not being able to speak easily was so frustrating, and not just because I couldn't have the deeper conversation I needed with Callum. There was a lot I needed to say to my parents too. Even to grandpa.

Yes, I'd managed to convey a lot of it on the notes app, but my thumbs were *tired*.

And aside from unloading all the words in my head, there was also a lot *I* needed to know. Had the police found Ian and arrested him? How about my phone, which he'd stolen? Had they discovered who or what had caused the fire?

This waiting around stuff was b.s. It reminded me of the investigation into Jessa's death, when I'd felt so alone, and the lack of answers just made things worse. Thank goodness for Callum. Instead of feeling isolated and heartbroken, I was loved and supported.

Callum filled my water glass and grabbed my medications for me. "I'll go down and get some breakfast for us. There's still half a fridge of pureed soup down there for you."

I smiled and nodded. After he threw on some sweats and a shirt from his duffel, I got up and went to the bathroom for a shower.

One thing to say for my parents' house. It had excellent water pressure.

When Mom had begged me to come stay with them, I'd almost said no. But I did appreciate her apology. Even if it had taken Ian's complete betrayal to finally open her eyes.

For once, she actually seemed to be on my side.

So I said yes to coming home with them, Jessa, I thought as I lathered body wash. They'd let Callum come, and they'd put up with his family too. Seemed like progress.

Last night, after my nap, I'd gone downstairs for dinner. Watching our families together had been a trip. I hadn't realized

Auntie Rosie and Piper were close, but it made sense. The market was just down the block from Silver Linings.

On the other hand, Mom had stayed suspiciously clear of Grace. Like she was intimidated. *Really*? Eliza Alvarez, President of the Hart County Golf Club? Whether it was something Grace had said, or the simple fact that Callum's sister was dating a billionaire, I couldn't say.

But last night had probably been the best dinner I'd ever spent at my parents' place. Aches and sore throat and all.

This physical pain was making me want to *finally* let go of the mental stuff I was carrying. I was sick and tired of holding grudges and guilt.

Even with Ian, I just wanted to see him face the consequences for his actions and then leave me alone. Get out of my life for good, so I didn't have to waste another spoon of energy on that man.

I wanted all my energy for loving Callum. After all, he was a handful, always finding new ways to surprise me.

Speaking of surprises.

My head was tipped back, water running through my hair, when colder air hit my skin. Then warm hands found my hips. "Want some company?"

I blinked my eyes open to Callum standing naked in front of me. He pulled me close, pressing our bodies flush together and dipping to kiss me gently.

For a while, we let the steam build. It irritated my lungs a little, but I could handle it. Being close with Callum like this, after all that had happened, had to be healthy for me. I was sure of it.

His cock stayed half hard, not thickening more until I reached down to stroke him from base to tip. "Don't get me going. There will be none of that."

My lips curved with an exaggerated pout, which made him laugh.

"Z, I can't imagine you're feeling up for it. You're hurting."

I shrugged, my thumb rubbing over the tip of his cock again. "Show me I'm yours," I whispered.

And it was like my exact thought beamed into his brain, making him understand, because his pupils suddenly dilated, swallowing up the golden flecks in his irises. "You want to watch me?"

A nod.

Callum turned me so my back was to the cool tile of the shower, and I could rest against it. His palm flattened against the tile by my head, while his other hand gripped his shaft and squeezed. "You just watch how hot you make me. I'm gonna come so hard for you."

Another nod from me, more vigorous this time.

Callum's darkened eyes devoured my body as he started to stroke. I loved watching his cock swell and jump in his fist. His soft moans as he teased himself.

After a minute, he added some conditioner and picked up his pace. His gaze was like a physical touch. I felt it as much as the droplets of water that traced my naked curves.

"Fuck," he groaned, just before pulses of his release splashed my stomach, and he bent to rest his forehead against mine. "That's all for you. Do you feel like mine, Sunflower?"

I did. And I loved it.

Callum had set up Chloe's water fountain and food dish on the tile floor of the spacious en suite. He and I had breakfast in bed. I sipped lukewarm butternut-squash soup while Callum ate leftover lasagna from last night. He told me my parents had asked about me downstairs, and he'd told them I was resting.

"Your mom's grumpy about you not coming down this morning, but she can deal with it. Your dad seemed more chipper. One sneeze, but no signs of cat allergy attacks."

Good. I was glad to hear that. As a woman with allergies, I wouldn't have wanted my dad to be uncomfortable. But if he was okay with Chloe's presence, then I was eager to have her with me.

At some point, my mother was probably going to come knocking on the guestroom door. For now, keeping Callum as a buffer between me and my parents was exactly what I needed. I wanted to heal our relationship, but I had a lot more to say to her, and I needed my voice for it.

However, there was something else on my agenda for today besides sexy showers and cuddle time.

I set down the soup bowl and picked up Callum's phone, which was already unlocked for me.

Any updates from police?

"Not yet. If Teller were in town, he'd be able to get us the latest." Callum tapped his chin. "But I have another idea." He took his phone. Pulled up a number. Then said, "Hi, Dixie. How are you?"

He'd called Dixie Haines, one of the town's most reliable gossips. Also a sweet lady with a biting sense of humor, based on the few times I'd met her.

"Is that right? Yeah, I'm here with Zandra. You heard about us already?" He grinned. "Good news travels fast. Yeah, bad news too. That's true. But I'm actually calling to see if—Oh."

Callum hummed a lot and didn't say much while Dixie talked his ear off. I only caught every few words. Then he said, "Dixie, I'm gonna put you on speaker so Zandra can hear what you just told me."

"Hello, Zandra dear." Dixie's cheerful, rapid-fire voice came through the speaker. "Just awful about what occurred at Hearthstone. That fire could've spread all over Main Street, and from what I'm hearing, the fire investigator thinks it was a clear case of arson. But if anyone asks, you didn't get that from me."

My eyes widened, my gaze landing on Callum's.

"Just this morning, I heard from a tenant of mine whose brother works at a gas station between here and Pine Creek. You still with me?"

"Yes, Dixie," Callum said with a smile.

"Well, an expensive sports car pulled into the gas station this morning. Then, just minutes later, who shows up but Colorado State Patrol. The officer charged out and arrested the driver of the sports car."

"Ian," I whispered.

"Seems there was a warrant out for that individual for attempted robbery. I have it on good authority, another source of mine, that the man is now at the Silver Ridge PD station being questioned. Name of Ian Vanderwall."

"Is he a suspect in the arson too?" Callum asked.

"Don't know, but supposedly the PD is also working on locating some other individuals who could have information on the fire. I don't have those names yet, but I can let you know what I find out."

"Thanks, Dixie."

After he ended the call, I typed out a message to Callum.

The security camera footage from Hearthstone. Chief Nichols said the police were going to review it. But do you still have access to it?

"Probably. You and I both had the app for the security system on our phones."

"I want...to see the video...from the fire," I said, fighting the urge to cough.

"You and I were both there. We already know Ian and Tommy were at the scene. Beyond that, don't you think we should leave the visuals to the police?"

I understood what Callum was doing. Trying to protect me from seeing the fire and drowning in that fear all over again. Or maybe *he* didn't want to have to see it.

I can watch it myself. I need to do this.

"We'll watch it together," he said in response to what I'd written. "I just wanted you to be sure." He pulled up the security app and logged on.

I was worried at first that the police might've taken away our access. But the video clips appeared.

"Now I have to look for the time everything started," Callum said. "And check the different camera angles."

The cameras were set up to record when there was motion. During business hours, that would mean a ton of recorded time. But in the middle of the night, it was much easier to narrow down to just what we needed.

I was also thankful Callum had added an additional camera on the parking lot after I'd gotten that creepy note. Now, it was coming in handy.

A dark silhouette drove into the frame. This was from the camera with the best view of the rear parking lot. A sleek sports car pulled into the lot, a clash of light and shadows.

A man got out of the car and strolled toward the brewery. I knew from his bearing that he was Ian.

Then a few minutes later, another person appeared. Stumbling around between the cars.

"Pickering." Callum jabbed a finger at the screen. "That asshole. I *knew* he had something to do with this."

Tommy stumbled across the frame, acting like he was drunk. This wasn't the first time he'd been lurking in the parking lot after closing. But he hadn't been drinking at Hearthstone that night. Everyone knew not to serve him after Callum had banned him.

So, what was he doing there?

A different camera focused on the back door of the building, and we switched to that feed. In the video, we saw Ian forcing the door open. Ian must've gone straight to Manny's office just as I'd walked out. He'd only been to Hearthstone a couple of times in the years we were dating, but it seemed that had been enough to give him the layout. Typical of him, since he had a habit of acting like he owned everything.

We kept watching the video. Yet another figure appeared, someone smaller, dressed in black. The figure slipped through the back door that Ian had left open.

My heart raced. That had to be the person who'd set the fire. They'd come inside the brewery after Ian. But it definitely wasn't Tommy.

"Let's go back to the parking lot," Callum said. "That third person had to come from somewhere. Maybe we can find some video showing their face."

But there was no luck. Just a view of that same small figure slipping out of the brewery and disappearing again into the shadows.

I imagined the minutes passing. The fire must've caught fast in that back storage room with all the paper products stuffing the shelves. The old wood and plaster. Ian and I had been arguing, with no clue that the flames were spreading near the back of the building.

We saw Tommy again in the footage. He'd kept to one side of the parking lot, bending over behind the dumpster. Was he drunk and confused, or had Tommy been *watching* that person who set the brewery on fire? Had he seen the smoke?

Callum put his hand on my back. "We're almost up to the minute that I drive into the parking lot. Right there."

His truck appeared in view just as Ian streaked across the screen.

"Hate watching this." Callum's fingers slid into my hair, massaging my scalp. "When I realized you were inside... Z, that wrecked me. Like I was splitting into pieces."

I turned to kiss him. "I'm okay," I whispered. "I love you."

"I love you too, baby." His nose nudged against mine.

I wanted to keep kissing him. Maybe I'd been wrong to want to see this video. It was making me feel nauseous, remembering the smoke and the heat. And it was awful for Callum too.

But then, from the corner of my eye, I saw a flash of something strange on the video feed.

"Wait." I pointed. "Go back."

"What is *that*? Looks like a reflection in that car window."

I nodded, peering closer. The angles were odd at first, but then the picture solidified in my mind.

Oh, God. I gasped, rearing back.

That was a *face*.

Someone else had been in that parking lot.

And I knew exactly who it was. The years had changed him, but his features still reminded me of my best friend.

That was Leo Mackenzie. Jessa's brother.

THIRTY-SEVEN

Zandra

Leo Mackenzie was in Silver Ridge. He'd been at Hearthstone the night of the fire.

The shock of seeing him faded, but so many questions remained.

It wasn't clear if Leo was the same person who'd sneaked through the back door after Ian. Unless Leo had taken off the dark clothing, then stuck around in the parking lot to watch the flames. Callum told me that sometimes arsonists liked to see their handiwork.

Leo hadn't been small-framed in high school, though. He'd been tall and broad, like Callum. Could that smaller figure in the video really have been him?

Whatever the truth, Callum called Silver Ridge PD to share the fact that we'd seen Leo on the video. Just in case the police had missed it, and it turned out they had.

At least the police had arrested Ian. Thank you, Dixie Haines, for that bit of info.

Then we learned they'd also picked up Tommy Pickering the morning after the fire for drunk and disorderly conduct, and he was being questioned. Now, they were looking for Leo Mackenzie too. They'd already known Leo was wanted for assault and jumping bail over in Fort Collins—the bar fight incident Teller Landry had told Callum about.

But that just meant more waiting for us. More wondering where Leo was and whether he was responsible for the fire. Wondering if Jessa's brother had meant to destroy the brewery.

Or if he'd actually known I was inside.

If he'd wanted to *kill* me.

The gate around my parents' property provided a little more peace of mind, so Callum and I stayed. He helped Gladys cook dinner one night, and the next Callum and I did the cooking because it was Gladys's night off. Mom and Dad didn't even notice the pasta was gluten free. Though there were complaints about lack of cheese until we brought out the parmesan.

While neither of us had been back to Hearthstone, we'd been getting updates from my grandpa. Repairs would start soon. He was paying all the employees for their missed days of work with the brewpub closed.

Two days after I'd left the hospital, Mom knocked on the guestroom door. "Zandra? There's a call for you on the house phone."

Yes, my parents *still* had a landline. And I still didn't have a cell of my own. Ian had apparently tossed my phone out his car window onto the highway, and by the time the police found it, it was crushed. I'd ordered a new one, but it hadn't arrived yet.

"Just a sec, Eliza," Callum called out.

I heard Mom grumbling out there.

It was morning, and Callum and I had been lounging in bed, doing absolutely nothing but kissing and talking. For a girl with an overachieving streak, it was kind of amazing to have zero goals except being with my man.

Over the last couple days, my throat had gotten better, and my headache was nearly gone. I could actually speak without much pain or a coughing fit, though my voice was still hoarse. Callum and I had even been able to make love the night before, his body heavy and solid over mine, seeming to surround me with his woodsy scent and slow, hypnotic caresses. My limbs still felt languid from the afterglow.

"It's Chief Nichols," Mom added.

My adrenaline shot up, and any pleasant thoughts about last night vanished. Callum and I exchanged a look as I kicked off the blankets.

I threw on a robe over the SRFD T-shirt I was wearing. Then answered the door with Callum just behind me. He'd pulled on some sweats. "Chief?" I rasped, holding the cordless phone to my ear. I cleared my throat. "This is Zandra."

"Ms. Alvarez, I'm calling because Leo Mackenzie just turned himself in."

"Leo? You have him in custody?"

Mom's hands flew to her mouth, while Callum's arm went around my waist.

"We do," the chief said. "But Mr. Mackenzie has refused to speak to anyone. He says he'll only talk to *you*."

Callum pulled up in front of the police station, but he didn't switch off the engine. "Z, I don't want you to do this."

After the phone call from Chief Nichols, I'd gotten dressed as quickly as possible. Mom and Dad had already freaked out about the idea of me coming to meet with a man who might have tried to kill me. Who was wanted for arrest on an unrelated assault charge.

Callum had waited until now to voice his objections.

"Leo could easily talk to the police himself. But instead, he's making demands to get you in the room with him. We're just supposed to trust this isn't some sick ploy to hurt you?"

"He turned himself in. Doesn't that suggest some kind of remorse? Or that, at least, there's a lot more going on than we knew? He'll be in cuffs. I'll be fine."

"But who knows what kind of shit he might say to you."

I turned to face Callum fully. "I can take it. And I can dish out plenty too. Maybe he's the one who should be worried."

Callum reached up to cup my face, his thumb brushing across my cheekbone. "There's my fierce girl," he murmured, then leaned forward to press a gentle kiss to my forehead. "Just wish I could be in there with you."

"I know you'll be close. This is just something I have to do."

Beyond that, I didn't really know how to feel. It was possible Leo had blamed me, *hated* me, for Jessa's death this whole time. Maybe he was the person who'd harassed me by leaving those notes, even though he'd never said a word to my face.

It made me sick to think that could be true. But at the same time, not knowing was so much worse. That was exactly why I had to see him and hear what he had to say. So we could finally have this out.

Callum and I went inside the station. After a short wait, Chief Nichols approached. "Zandra, we're ready for you."

I followed her down a hallway to a closed door. She turned to face me before we went in. "I just want to stress again, this is completely voluntary."

"I want to be here," I assured her.

"If Thomas Pickering was more forthcoming about what he saw outside Hearthstone the other night, maybe this wouldn't be necessary. But that man's clammed up too, and I don't know that we could trust what he says anyway. Everybody knows Pickering is a drunk who likes to stir up trouble."

That was my impression of Tommy exactly. "Is he still here at the station?"

"Well, we let him sober up before questioning him, but after that we let him go with no formal charge. Now your former boyfriend, Ian, he's going to be a guest of Hart County for a good while longer."

I'd already heard that. Ian's bail had been set high for being a flight risk, and since he couldn't pay, the police had transferred him to the county jail to await more hearings. I'd probably have to testify about his attempted robbery of Hearthstone at some point, unless he pled guilty, but I was trying to think about Ian as little as possible.

"Now, we'll be recording this," the chief said. "I've given Mr. Mackenzie a Miranda advisement, letting him know anything he says to you could be used against him. I'll also be watching the video feed, and we have an officer right outside. You can stop this at any time."

"Okay." I took a deep breath. "I'm ready."

Chief Nichols opened the door, and I stepped into the interview room.

Leo Mackenzie was sitting at a table with his hands in his lap. His blond hair was longer than he'd kept it in high school, and he had more lines around his eyes, but his features still struck a chord in my heart. So much like Jessa.

"Zandra. You came. Didn't think you would."

I walked closer to the table, but didn't sit down. "Then why did you ask to talk to me?"

"I had to try. I need to explain this to you first, because you're the one who was hurt most by it. I had to tell you to your face that I'm sorry."

"You're *sorry*?" Conflicting emotions flashed through me. Sorrow for the fact that he'd lost his sister. Building anger at his seeming admission that he'd hurt me. "Did you start the fire at Hearthstone?"

"No."

"Tell me the truth, Leo. That's the only way this will work."

"I didn't do it. But I know who did. I'll tell you, but I need you to sit down first. There's a lot I have to explain." He nodded at me. "Your voice. That's from the fire?"

"The smoke." My stomach churned, nausea rising.

A look of despair crossed his face. "This is awful. All of it."

If Leo was faking, he was putting on quite a show.

The chair scraped against the floor as I pulled it out and sat down. "Then go ahead. Explain it to me."

Leo brought up his hands to swipe his fingers through his hair, and the metal cuffs jangled on his wrists. "I guess it starts way back. Even before Jessa died." He was quiet for a moment, like he was gathering his thoughts. "My sister and I...we argued a few days before."

I sat forward, putting my elbows on the table. "I remember. What was that about?"

"Well, I..." He grimaced. "I read her diary."

"You did *what*? You read your big sister's diary?" I huffed. "Not okay."

It was strange how I suddenly felt pulled back to those days. Remembering Jessa. How alive she had been, how vibrant. It almost made me want to laugh, thinking of how animated Jessa would get when talking about her arguments with her brother.

I was so eager for any new trace of her. Maybe that was another reason I'd come here to see her brother.

"I'd seen her texting with someone," Leo went on. "She'd put the name in her phone as '*Him*.' In her diary, she wrote about having a secret. She'd written that she felt bad about this secret, and she didn't know what to do. It had to be about this guy. I couldn't let some creep mess with my sister."

"She didn't tell me his name either. That was her choice."

"But if Jessa was keeping the guy's identity from even you, that seemed like a bad sign. Right?"

I'd had a similar thought back then. If I'd read that stuff in her diary, I would have freaked out too. Why hadn't Jessa told me this secret if it was upsetting her?

Was it *really* about her crush, or about something else?

"A few days before she died, I confronted her about it. Demanded to know who this guy was. And she wouldn't tell me. Yelled at me for invading her privacy and said I was way off base."

I blew out a breath. "Okay, but why are you telling me this *now*? With everything that's going on?"

"Because I believed you after she died. You said there had been someone else there at the creek that night. Who else could it be but the guy she was supposed to meet? *Him*."

Chills raced over my skin. "But who could it have been? The police thought I imagined hearing someone else's voice, but they still checked on where our school's football players were that night. Everyone was at the bonfire."

Leo looked down at his hands. "I know. I was at the bonfire too. Getting drunk off my ass while my sister was... How could anyone be sure we were all there the whole entire time?"

The same thing I'd always wondered.

Yet Leo didn't know who Jessa's crush was, and neither did I. Maybe it was wishful thinking, the idea that somebody else was there that night. *Somebody* was responsible. When it could just as likely have been a terrible, random accident.

It would've been so much easier to have someone to blame. But that didn't make it *true*.

"What does any of this have to do with the fire at Hearthstone?" My voice cracked from using it so much. "Or the fact that someone has been harassing me and did the same to me back in high school. Accusing me of being a murderer. Maybe even the same person who spread the rumors that I pushed Jessa into the creek. I assume you heard the rumors too?"

He glanced down guiltily. "I'm just trying to make you understand. Some people might've thought you were responsible for Jessa's death. But I never did. I knew how much you loved my sister."

I pushed back from the table, standing up and wrapping my arms around myself. "But you didn't say anything when those rumors were going around. When I felt completely alone."

He scrunched up his face. "Because it got complicated. I found out who was harassing you."

I spun on my heel to face him. "You knew about that? The person who broke my car window. Left those sick notes for me. And you *knew*?"

"It's the same person who broke the window at the brewery earlier this summer. Started following you and harassing you again. I tried to stop it. I swear. If I'd known it could lead where it did, to arson and you being in real danger—"

"Who?" I demanded.

He scrubbed his trembling hands over his face.

"It was my mother."

THIRTY-EIGHT

Callum

I PACED AROUND the waiting area at the station, nearly going out of my mind while Zandra was in that room with Leo.

Finally, I heard a door open. Voices. I went to the mouth of the hallway, just barely holding myself back from racing to Zandra as she murmured with Chief Nichols.

"Mr. O'Neal," the front desk officer warned. "You can't go back there."

"Yeah, I know." Even though it seemed ridiculous to be so formal. Give me a break with this *Mr. O'Neal* shit. Like I hadn't known that guy forever and served him at Hearthstone plenty of times.

I'd also been texting with the Lonely Harts club, keeping them updated on the latest. Both Ashford and Grace had offered to come here and wait with me. But Zandra had already instructed her mom not to follow us here, so she probably didn't want other people showing up. This had to be rough for her, and she didn't need an audience.

Right now, I would be here for her. In any way she needed. I had every intention of supporting her through this, even if I hadn't been thrilled about her talking to Leo in the first place.

Should've known I couldn't stop her. My Zandra was brave as hell.

Zandra came down the hall, looking shell-shocked. "I'm ready to go."

I glanced over her head at Chief Nichols, who'd already disappeared into her office. Then another officer walked down the hall and into the chief's office too. Something was definitely up. A palpable new buzz of tension filled the station.

"What happened? What did he say?"

"I'll tell you everything. But not here. I just want to get out of here." She blinked a few times, then looked up at me. "Can we go see the sunflowers?"

I took her hand. "Of course, baby. We'll go straight there."

I drove my truck out to my friend's property. Didn't clear this visit beforehand this time, but I had no doubt it wouldn't be a big deal.

It was the middle of the day, the sun shining brilliantly from a clear blue sky. We sat on the tailgate. It was warm out, but I still got a blanket from my backseat. I wrapped it around the both of us, and we sat on the tailgate as we watched the small sunflowers dance in the breeze.

"It was Jess and Leo's mother," Zandra whispered. "Paula."

For a moment, I couldn't track what she meant. "What do you mean, baby? What did Paula do?"

"She's the one who harassed me. She thought I was responsible for Jessa's death. That I was a...*murderer*." Her voice cracked on the last word.

That made no sense. But I pulled Zandra close and held her while she fought back tears.

"Leo told me his mom got worse and worse after Jessa died. Then Paula must've heard the rumors from somewhere—that *I* was the one who pushed Jessa because we were fighting about a boy."

"But she didn't say anything to you. Why wouldn't she confront you?"

"Because she thought I'd already gotten away with it, maybe? My family owns important businesses around town. She could've thought the police were biased. But maybe there was no rationale to her behavior at all. Leo said his mom was falling apart, not thinking clearly. She still talked about Jessa like she was alive. Paula even did that in front of me a couple times, like at the funeral."

"Leo didn't go to anyone for help for his mom?" I asked.

"He said he thought about it. Until he found out his mom had been following me around and broke my car window. Left those notes for me. He just tried to keep a better eye on her and convince her I wasn't responsible, but he thought if anyone knew, she'd either be committed or arrested. He was just a kid then. Seventeen."

"Yeah, I guess I understand. This is still messed up."

I'd been through issues with my parents too as a kid, and my siblings and I had been afraid to go to the authorities. Especially after our dad left, and we were basically on our own. At seventeen, Leo had just lost his sister. I had to think he would've been scared to lose his mom too.

"But it gets worse," Zandra said. "Because this is where Tommy Pickering comes in."

I sat back and gave her a questioning look. A few strands of dark hair blew into her face, and I brushed them away.

"Tommy was blackmailing them. He'd seen Paula break my window. Leo paid him five hundred dollars to keep him quiet."

I shook my head in disgust. Yet that sounded like Tommy. He'd always been an opportunist.

"After I left town, Paula seemed to get over her fixation and was doing better. Tommy lost interest in blackmailing them, thankfully. Leo stuck around as long as he could, and he said Winnie tried to be there for him even though she had no clue how bad things were. But he felt trapped here. He decided to leave everything behind. Like I had."

"Did he tell you about his arrest for assault?"

She nodded. "Leo said he came back to Silver Ridge over the years to check on Paula, sent her cards and money, but he couldn't bring himself to live here. It was still too painful. Then earlier this summer, he got involved in that bar fight, got arrested. He claimed he ran because he couldn't go to prison and leave his mom all alone."

"Sounds like a convenient excuse for escaping home to mom when he was in trouble."

"Maybe. I don't know. He's been living in an abandoned cabin in the woods since June. Paula was bringing him food. About a month after Leo came home to Silver Ridge, *I* came back to town. And that was a lot for his mom to take in when her well-being was already so fragile."

I thought of how the house had seemed *wrong* when we went there. Like there were things Paula was hiding. She hadn't seemed outright angry or resentful, though. Mostly tired. Seemed like there was still a missing piece to the story.

"You mentioned you felt like someone had been watching you," I said. "We thought it was Tommy, but could that have been Paula?"

"Even Leo isn't sure of everything his mom has been doing. He thinks she threw that brick through the Hearthstone window. Probably left the note on my car too."

"Wow." I shook my head. This whole situation was bizarre. Sometimes it felt like everybody knew everyone's business in Silver Ridge, and then we found out something like this had been going on. Leo Mackenzie hiding out in the woods. Paula targeting Zandra.

Then again, if I was going to hide from the cops, there was plenty of wilderness around here to do it. Incredible that nobody had seen Leo come in or out of town.

Unless...maybe someone *had* seen him.

"Tommy's all wrapped up in this," I said. "He was outside the brewery creeping around the same night you got that note.

Outside our place on another night. What else did he do?" The guy was like a cockroach, always turning up when there was bad shit going down.

"Tommy must've seen Leo at some point, figured out Paula was helping him hide. So Tommy went to Paula. Said she had to pay up or he'd send the cops after Leo. After that, Tommy was following *Paula* around, trying to get proof of Leo's whereabouts."

I cursed as I made the connection. "And that's why Tommy kept turning up around *you*. Because Paula was already watching you, and Tommy knew all along." No wonder he'd been so smug when I questioned him about Z's harasser. He'd admitted seeing Zandra at the Pine Cone motel, but when he realized Paula was sneaking around Z again, Tommy saw a new opportunity.

The past repeating itself.

"After Tommy demanded money again, Paula seemed to have a harder and harder time telling the difference between the present and the past. It was like she thought Jessa's death had just happened. Leo started watching her more, trying to keep her home so she wouldn't do something else that would put her in jail or draw attention to him."

I could already predict where this was going. "She set the fire."

Zandra wiped her eyes. "It's hard to believe. Like some wild plot to a movie."

"Or a true crime show," I muttered. "Truth is stranger than fiction, Z. Some of the stuff out there? It's freaking nuts."

"And I was in the middle of it."

I gave her a couple minutes, then asked, "What really happened the night of the fire?"

"Paula wasn't answering Leo's calls that night, and he got worried something was up. He took the risk of coming into town to look for her. Drove by our place first, since he'd figured out I was living there with you. When there was no sign of Paula, he went to Hearthstone. He swears he would've stopped her if he could. But it was too late. He would've run inside the building to help, but then you got there."

That's convenient, I thought angrily. "But instead of staying at the scene, Leo took off again. And Pickering was there too. Keeping an eye on Paula, gathering up more blackmail material. He could've stopped her, and he didn't, and you could've *died*."

"Tommy was also drunk," she pointed out. "But now that Chief Nichols knows about the blackmail, she promised she'd investigate whether they can charge him with it."

Sounded like not nearly enough punishment to me. But I waited for her to continue.

"Leo turned himself in because he knew things had gone too far, and his mom needs help. But he wanted a chance to explain everything and apologize. He begged me for mercy for his mom. Leo insists his mom didn't really know what she was doing. He wants me to talk to the police and the district attorney and ask for leniency."

"Will you?"

"I already did. Chief Nichols promised they'd be careful bringing Paula in. I don't want anyone else to be hurt. If she needs help, I want her to get it."

My chest tightened with how much I loved this woman. Even after everything she'd been through, she was showing me what forgiveness looked like.

Zandra leaned against me, her voice thick with sadness. "I'm heartbroken for Jessa's family. I wish it could've somehow been different. It was just a terrible situation, and we've all been suffering all these years." She took a shaky breath. "But now I can see the end of it."

I tightened my arms around her.

"I'll always wonder if someone else was there at the creek with Jessa. But I have to let go of that night, and it finally feels like I can."

"I'm proud of you, Z."

We sat in comfortable silence, watching the sunflowers sway. The afternoon sun warmed our faces.

"Callum?" Zandra's voice was soft.

"Yeah?"

"I feel like I haven't apologized enough for the way I acted the other night. When you emailed my grandfather about the general manager job, basically handing it to me, I got scared you'd change your mind and resent me. I was just scared of losing you."

"I get it. I won't go behind your back again though, okay? I understand where you were coming from."

"But afterward I said, *This is why relationships with coworkers are a bad idea*. I didn't mean it. Well, maybe I did, because it's messy and complicated. But I guess I'm a big fan of messy and complicated. Also a *really* big fan of annoyingly charming men who won't leave me alone."

I grinned. "That works out well for us."

"It does."

Then I remembered the other thing we still hadn't discussed. "Uh, so, I called Grayden the other night."

She inhaled sharply, sitting back. "What? *When*?"

"Same night as the fire. I went to see Grace. We talked. Ended up calling Grayden together, and I left him a voicemail. It dropped to low priority with you in the hospital and everything else happening."

"Has he called you back?"

"Not yet. He sent a quick text, saying he'd really like to chat soon once things calm down. I guess Grace let him know I had other things going on. But when he does call, I'd like you to be there with me. If that's cool with you. Moral support, I guess." I felt sheepish saying that. But how many times had Z opened up and been vulnerable with me? I owed it to her to do the same.

"Of course I will." Zandra put both hands on my face, pulling me in for a kiss. "Callum, I love you so much. I couldn't have gone through any of this without you. You've been my anchor through everything. I want to be yours too."

Here in this field of wildflowers, with the worst finally behind us, I could see our future stretching ahead. I assumed Zandra would be general manager of Hearthstone. I'd go back to bar manager. And we'd keep living together. The rest of the details would work themselves out.

From where I was sitting, it looked pretty damn perfect.

THIRTY-NINE
Callum

A WEEK LATER, a line of people trailed all the way down the block from Hearthstone. Locals, tourists, folks who'd made the trek from every corner of Hart County to support the brewery.

Russ tapped at the microphone in his hand, and it squealed with feedback. "Oh, sh—uh, I guess this thing's on."

Zandra laughed, her arms wrapping around me as she rested her head on my shoulder. I put my hand on her lower back. We stood off to one side of the booth we'd set up for the tasting, directly in front of the brewery's entrance. Other Hearthstone employees stood nearby, ready with stacks of plastic glasses.

Behind the table, next to Russ, sat a keg of our latest brew. All we needed was for Russ to get things started.

After a little more hemming and hawing, he said, "We appreciate all of you joining us today. Most of you know we had a fire here not long ago, so the brewpub is closed for repairs." Cheers of support erupted from every direction. "But not all was lost. My latest creation was saved, and I've named it Smokejumper Stout to celebrate. Any donations will help us complete the repairs and get this place open again soon, because I promise, we won't be gone for long. Now let's tap this keg!"

More cheers blended into a roar. "He finished strong," Zandra said, her voice not completely back to normal but nearly there.

"Best way to do it." I kissed the top of her head.

Thanks to Mayor Barker's office, we'd sped through the permit process to be able to close Main Street to traffic today. A couple food trucks had driven out on short notice, and the mayor had even declared today "Hearthstone Brewing Day," which seemed a *bit* excessive.

But hey, why not?

We had plenty to celebrate.

There were lots of smiles and plenty of bills tossed in the donation jar as we poured tasters of Smokejumper. Pretty much everyone we knew was here. My family, the other firefighters from SRFD. Rosie and Jimmy. Dixie Haines was holding court over by the food trucks, where kids and dogs were running around between the picnic tables we'd brought in.

It had been a community effort to make this happen so quickly, but it just spoke to the love everyone had for the watering hole Manny had built. The man himself had been working the crowd, getting those donations. His last hurrah as general manager.

Manny still hadn't made the official announcement that Zandra was GM. He was giving her time to heal. But as far as I could see, it was inevitable.

When Darius and Niko came to the front of the line, I stepped around the side of the table to give them each a back slap. "Thanks for being here today."

"You kidding?" Darius asked. "Wouldn't miss it. Connor said he'd be here too, but hard to track where that man is these days."

"He seemed tense when I saw him at home earlier," Niko added. "Something about the new girlfriend. Maybe he'll bring her, and we can finally meet her."

Darius snorted. "I'm starting to wonder if she even exists."

Zandra was busy chatting with Winnie and the other brewery

employees, so I gave her a quick kiss and said I was going to hang with our roommates for a while.

Grabbing a taster for myself, the guys and I wandered over to an empty space on the sidewalk to watch the festivities.

"So you and Z are out in the open now," Niko said. "Her grandfather knows all about you two?"

"Oh yeah, we're not hiding anything. Manny was surprisingly okay with it. More than her parents, but they've been coming around to the Callum O'Neal fan club."

I took a sip of Smokejumper Stout. Maybe it was just the dark roast on the grains, but I could almost taste a hint of smoke. A reminder that, even when the worst happened, we could fight our way back to something better.

The same night Zandra had been to the police station to talk to Leo, the police had brought Paula Mackenzie into custody. From what we'd heard, a court-ordered psychologist was assessing if Paula was fit to stand trial.

It was a relief to Z, though. Knowing the person responsible for the fire was now in custody, regardless of the final outcome. The authorities were also considering charges against Tommy Pickering for blackmail. We were all for that, but the whole town knew by now about the entire saga and Tommy's involvement. The community had rallied around his wife and kids, supporting them while also condemning what Tommy had done.

People were showing understanding for Leo and Paula too, with Zandra being one of the loudest voices.

That was what I loved about Hart County. The way people came together, just like they were doing for Hearthstone today.

Zandra had been absent for so long, but now, I couldn't imagine her not being a part of this. A part of my life.

Then Connor appeared, jogging over out of breath. "Sorry I'm late."

We all cheered and clapped him on the shoulder, happy to have the gang back together. "Thought you wouldn't make it!"

"Yeah, I'm sorry. I know I've been AWOL lately."

I ran over to grab another taster for Connor, then returned and handed it to him. "You finally going to tell us what's been going on with you?"

"Actually, that's something I need to talk to you guys about." Connor scratched his forehead, taking the beer without drinking it. "I'm moving out."

My first reaction was disappointment, but this was exactly what Darius and I had been talking about. The end of an era.

"You're moving in with this new girl we've never even seen?" Darius asked skeptically.

Connor took out his phone. "You've met her." He showed us a few pictures of the girl. "I wasn't sure where this was going at first."

I remembered that she'd spent the night a few times with Connor, but none of us had any idea it was something serious.

"But after seeing Callum with Zandra, I realized it was worth a try. I mean, if the most commitment-phobic man-slut in Silver Ridge could fall for someone..."

"*Hey*," I protested.

Connor swept his shoulder-length hair back from his face. "I just mean, I realized I wanted to give it a shot. I didn't want you guys giving me shit until I really knew how I felt about her."

"Which is?" Niko prompted.

A grin appeared on Connor's face, like he'd been trying to keep it in and couldn't anymore. "We're moving in together. It's happened really fast, but it feels right."

Darius wrapped his arms around Connor and Niko. "Look at the three of you, growing up. All getting serious. I'll probably be next."

"Not so fast," Niko said. "Actually, I've been thinking about breaking up with mine. I'm not ready for the one. I'm not old like you guys."

The rest of us booed. I scoffed. "Thirties isn't old. Besides, it has nothing to do with age or growing up. It's about finding the right person."

"Amen to that." Connor held up his fist, and I bumped it.

Darius tapped his taster against the cups Connor and I were holding. "Us old guys have come a long way though. From troublemaking football players at Silver Ridge High to upstanding citizens."

"We were always upstanding citizens," Connor said.

Darius and I shared an amused glance. "I dunno. I remember those old bonfire parties," Dare quipped.

The mention of the bonfire parties turned the bubbly feeling in my stomach to something sour.

Because it reminded me of the night Jessa died, and that was the one piece of the story Zandra still didn't have answered. Who was Jessa's secret crush, and was he there that night? The lingering uncertainty didn't sit right with me. I was proud of Z for finding closure after all these years, yet if I could somehow solve that final mystery for her, I'd do it.

I took the last sip of stout and tossed the cup into a nearby bin. "You guys have heard the whole saga about Mrs. Mackenzie and Leo and what happened after Jessa's death by now, right?"

They all nodded seriously. "Sure," Connor said. "Awful that Zandra had to go through all that. Leo too. He was in my year at school. If I could go back in time..."

"Same." I nodded. "Trust me, your brain can get stuck going around in circles thinking like that. But it's hard not to."

After Zandra had told me about Jessa's secret crush on a football player at our school, I'd briefly wondered about Connor and Darius. Neither had been seniors at the same time as us, but they'd been on the team.

But I'd dismissed that possibility weeks ago, pretty much as soon as it had occurred to me. Because I distinctly remembered both of them being at the bonfire party that night. It was the first one of the year, so it had been memorable already, but after we all heard about Jessa dying the next morning, the party got seared into my mind.

But I'd never asked Connor or Darius who they thought Jessa's football crush could've been. Or if there was a possibility that one of the other guys slipped away from the party that night.

"Did any of you ever hear about someone from our team being interested in Jessa?" I asked. Despite the rest of the story of the Mackenzie family spreading through town, this part still wasn't well known. "Zandra thought someone else was there at the creek that night, maybe Jessa's mystery guy, but the police didn't believe it. They basically convinced her she'd imagined it, and she still doesn't really know."

The guys all seemed to think, knitting their brows. Then shook their heads.

"It was a long shot," I admitted. "But if anything occurs to you..."

Just then, all of our phones buzzed. And we knew what that meant.

I ran over to Zandra, who immediately could tell something was up. "I gotta go. We just got called to a fire in the foothills."

Her expression did something complicated, and she pulled me into a hug. I held the side of her neck, feeling the rapid thump of her pulse.

"I'll be fine, baby," I whispered in her ear. "I'll see you later."

She nodded. "Be safe. I love you."

"Love you too."

The brushfire was just off the highway. Probably a damn cigarette somebody threw out a window.

But we got it under control quickly and started mopping up. The late afternoon sun beat down on us as we doused the last of the smoldering patches, turning the air thick and hazy. My gear felt twice as heavy as usual, and sweat poured down my back underneath my turnout coat.

As the sun was going down, I got a spare moment. I sent a quick text to Zandra, letting her know I should be home in another hour or two, hopefully. She didn't respond, but I didn't think much of it. The street festival in front of Hearthstone would be over by now, but I figured she was probably still visiting with friends.

Niko took off his helmet and wiped his face with the back of his sleeve. "Man, we didn't even get to try the food trucks."

"We could grab tacos on the way home," Darius said, coiling up a length of hose. "Your treat, right?"

Niko made a face. "*My* treat? You guys are the ones with the steady day jobs."

I was shaking my head at them as I put my phone away. Then Connor came over, looking pensive. "What's wrong?" I asked. "You upset about the lack of tacos too?"

Connor scratched his jaw, smearing some dirt across his cheek. "Actually, I was thinking about what you said earlier. About any guys from the football team hanging around Jessa. There was this one afternoon way back, when I was skipping class with this girl I was dating, and we passed Jessa whispering with Russ Wheaton behind the bleachers. I'm surprised I even remember it, but I guess seeing him today at the beer tasting made it pop up in my mind."

My stomach dropped. "But Russ wasn't on the team."

"He was, though. For like the first few weeks of school. He'd made varsity the spring before, but he wound up quitting after the first game or two of the season. He was probably just one of the other new kids to you, since he wasn't a senior."

What the fuck. Russ and Jessa? Was that possible?

I searched my memory. I truly didn't recall Russ ever being on the team. And I'd been working with Russ at Hearthstone for years. How had it never come up?

"I don't know if it means anything," Connor said, "but I figured I'd mention it."

"Yeah. Thanks." My own voice sounded distant. I took out my phone again and called Zandra, pacing toward the edge of the road where asphalt met blackened earth.

No answer.

FORTY
Zandra

"WHAT DO YOU THINK, Zandra? Can we call Smokejumper Stout a success?"

I looked over at Russ and grinned. "Definitely. People loved it. Great job with the name too."

"Thanks. Wasn't too on the nose?"

"It was perfect."

Around us, the remnants of the street fair lingered in the golden-hour light. A few families still sat at picnic tables or on curbs, finishing the last bites from the food truck offerings. Neighbors clustered in small groups. Children meandered between the adults, their faces sticky with ice cream and their energy finally starting to flag, while the cleaning crew picked up.

Rosie had already headed home with Jimmy, and Callum's siblings had said their goodbyes not long after he was called away to the fire. The thought of him out there sent a familiar twist through my stomach, but I was learning to live with it. Being with a firefighter meant accepting that danger was part of his duties. I was so proud of him for stepping up the way he did. A lot of my terror during that first call had been tangled up with losing Jessa in high school. But letting go of that old pain had made it easier to face the reality of Callum's volunteering now.

Some things really did turn out okay, and sometimes, a girl like me got her happy ending.

Winnie approached us, her cheeks flushed from the heat and her smile bright. "Did you see all the donations for Hearthstone's repairs? I couldn't believe how generous everyone was."

"It really was amazing," I agreed. Russ nodded along with me, hands dipping into his pockets. "I'm looking forward to working some shifts with you again behind the bar."

"Even when you're the general manager?" Winnie asked with a raised eyebrow.

I huffed a laugh. "I don't have the job just yet."

Winnie grinned knowingly, like she didn't believe me for a second.

Russ wandered off to help the cleaning crew, and Winnie bit her lip, her expression growing more serious. "Everyone's heard about Leo Mackenzie's big confession. How Paula set the fire, and how she'd been harassing you after Jessa died." Her voice dropped. "I was shocked when I heard. I just wanted you to know I had no clue any of that was going on back in high school. Leo never said a word."

"I never thought otherwise," I assured her. "Leo told me you tried to be there for him, but he didn't tell anyone what was happening."

Relief flickered across her face. "I know you have Callum now, but if you ever need to talk about any of that stuff, I'm here."

"Thank you. That means a lot."

After Winnie headed home, I spent the next hour helping return tables and equipment to the brewery. The donation jar felt heavy in my hands as I carried it inside and placed the money in the office safe. The burned section near the back of the building was blocked off with plastic sheeting, but I could smell the smoke.

For a moment, I was right back in that terrifying night. Heat and flames. Smoke choking off my airways.

But then I thought about the donation jar, about the community that had rallied around us today. The money represented

Hart County's unwavering support. Hearthstone would be back in business before we knew it. Better than ever.

And more than anything, the thought of Callum helped me breathe easy again. His bright smile and steady hands. Always there when I needed him.

I was closing up the office when Russ appeared in the doorway. "Hey, you busy?"

"I was just finishing up. Mostly I'm waiting to hear that the fire's contained and Callum and the other guys are safe."

"Of course," he said quickly. "But if you have time, I was hoping you and I could have a chat."

"You and me?" Something in his tone made me look at him more carefully. Russ's hands fidgeted with his keys, and he kept glancing away from me. "Of course. Is something wrong?"

Russ didn't answer me as I locked up Manny's office. We started toward the front door. The rest of the building was quiet. We were the only two people left.

"I heard you and Winnie talking about Leo Mackenzie," Russ finally said.

"Okay." I waited for him to continue, but his nervousness was starting to rub off on me.

"There's something about Jessa you should know. Something about the night she died."

Shock hit me like cold water.

"Russ, you're freaking me out."

"I don't mean to. But I've meant to tell you this for a long time. I just didn't know how." He took a shaky breath, and then the words rushed so fast they slurred together. "I was supposed to meet Jessa by the creek that night."

I'd heard what he said, but it didn't make sense.

"That can't be right. Jessa had a thing for some football player. That's who she was meeting at the creek."

He stuck his hands deep in his pockets, a red flush creeping up from his neck into his face. "I was on the team for a little while at the beginning of that year. Just because my dad wanted me to play. Jessa and me, we were talking. Texting some. I...I liked her."

I found myself glancing around the brewery's front area, taking in the hostess stand and benches as if I could anchor myself to the familiar.

Just minutes ago, Russ had been my goofy friend from work. Hearthstone's brewmaster.

Not Jessa's secret crush.

He was still talking. Rambling on, though nothing he'd said was sinking in. "I was warming the bench, and after Jessa died, I couldn't bring myself to keep going. I quit the team. I felt so guilty. I still do."

"Guilty about *what*?"

He gripped the bridge of his nose, squeezing his eyes shut. "Guilty for not showing up! I was at the bonfire party, and Leo was there. He was half drunk already. Angry and trying to start something with the football players. Nobody could tell what he was going on about, but I figured it might have something to do with his sister. I..."

"You what?"

"I chickened out about going to meet her. I was afraid Leo would find out and get upset that I wanted to date his sister."

"But *why*? Why keep it a secret at all? If you were her crush, why wouldn't Jessa tell me?"

"It was the football thing. It took forever to even get her number because she dismissed me as being a jock, even though I was barely one of them."

Breathe, I told myself. *Think this through.*

Jessa had said she didn't want me to hate the guy for being a football player. But was there something more she'd been hiding? The secret she'd mentioned in her diary. Had that been something darker, like Leo feared?

My hands shook at the thought that Russ might have hurt her.

"Did you do something to her? Something else she would've wanted to keep secret?"

"No. Never."

"And you weren't there at the creek that night? You swear?"

"I wasn't there. That's what I'm trying to tell you, Z. I chickened out, and I didn't show up, and then she was just...gone. I felt horrible."

"But I heard another voice. I thought someone else was there."

He shrugged, confusion clear on his face. "Then it wasn't me. I didn't leave the bonfire party. I'm honestly not trying to upset you, and Callum's probably going to give me hell about it when he hears. But I wanted you to know how sorry I am. About everything."

"Zandra?" Suddenly Winnie was there, glancing between Russ and me with concern. "What's going on? You okay?"

I hadn't even heard her come inside. My nervous system was going haywire. Cold sweat running down my sides, my heart skipping like a stone across a stream.

Russ's expression closed off. "We were just talking."

I took a sharp breath. "I need to go."

He took a step toward me. "Wait, Zandra—"

"Russ." Winnie stepped into his path. "Maybe you can finish whatever this is later? Come on, Z. Let's go."

We walked outside onto Main Street. Night had fallen, and the street was open again to traffic. All the stragglers from the fair had gone. Chilly air nipped at my skin, yet the cold inside me was far more intense. I rubbed the center of my chest, trying to ease the tightness there.

My phone buzzed, and I glanced at it. Callum had just texted that the fire was contained. He'd be home in another hour or two. I exhaled with relief, about to write back when Winnie grabbed my arm.

"What on earth was all that about with Russ?"

"It was about Leo Mackenzie. And Jessa."

"But what did Russ say that got you so upset?"

Everything about those last days before Jessa died seemed different now in hindsight. I'd barely even known Russ in high school.

But how well had I known my own best friend? What other secrets could Jessa have been keeping?

"It's a long story," I said.

"You're welcome to try me. Is your car here? Or do you need a ride home?"

"I rode here with Callum. He took his truck." We were back to living at the house with Darius, Connor, and Niko. It was pretty far to walk, especially when I was feeling like this.

Like a hurricane was inside me.

"I'll take you home," Winnie said soothingly. "You look way too pale."

We walked to her car, which was parked on a side street off Main, and I stuck my phone back in my purse. I'd text Callum back as soon as I was home.

It was getting darker by the minute, all the colors of the downtown commercial district bleeding away into shadow.

"So, what's this long story?" Winnie asked as she started the engine.

I did my best to convey what I remembered, fitting in the parts Leo had shared with me. How Jessa had a crush on a football player but wouldn't tell anyone the guy's identity. How Leo had read Jessa's diary and had a huge fight with her afterward.

"I remember that fight," Winnie said. "Leo told me his sister was keeping something from him, and he thought it was about a guy. He was worried about her."

"Well, Russ just told me tonight that *he* was Jessa's football crush."

Winnie swerved slightly as her hands tightened on the steering wheel. "Russ? For real?"

"That's what he said. He was a football player at the beginning of the year and quit right after Jessa died. He said he's felt guilty about her death for all these years."

"Why would he feel guilty?"

"Because he was supposed to meet her at the creek that night, but he didn't show."

Yet talking about this didn't make me feel better. Only worse.

My whole body was shaking now, confusion and dismay swirling through my insides. All this time, I'd thought if someone else was really there at the creek that night, it had to be Jessa's crush. But Russ had sworn he wasn't there.

Was he lying?

Had the police been right that I'd imagined that other voice?

Too much of that night was flashing through my mind. Garish still images. Jessa sipping the beer I'd brought. How she'd kept checking her phone. The moonlight on the creek, and the slash of red on her forehead.

Bile rose in my throat. Ugh. I was going to be sick. "Winnie, I'm sorry," I choked out. "I need you to pull over."

She pulled us off the street and onto the dirt shoulder. I shoved the door open, leaving my purse in the car. I took a few steps, bending over and coughing, as if everything I'd learned the past few days was too much. Like every part of me wanted to reject it. Just push it far, far away.

So much for letting go of what happened that night. I'd been fooling myself.

My blood rushed in my ears, but I still heard the car door open and close, and then Winnie was beside me. "Probably adrenaline," she said. "This is really messing you up, huh?"

I was heartsick. I wanted Callum. Everything had seemed good the other night when we went to the field of sunflowers. I'd genuinely believed I could move on from the night of Jessa's death, but here it was again, tearing me apart from the inside out.

Because I still didn't know the truth, and I *never would*.

When I stood up, I realized that rushing sound wasn't in my head at all.

It was the creek.

We'd pulled off the road just before the bridge, and the water was right below us at the bottom of a shallow slope. This wasn't the stretch of the creek where Jessa had died. That was miles from here. But in the dark, it looked so much the same.

"I remember that night too," Winnie said softly.

I turned to look at her, but she was mostly in shadow.

"I was with Leo at the bonfire party. For days, he'd been upset about that fight he had with his sister. That big secret she'd been keeping. He was getting drunk and going on and on about it. He barely noticed I was there."

Her voice was a monotone. Like she was in a trance. And I felt the same thing. A strange vibration in the air, that cold seeping into my bones. I looked back at the water, as if the creek was pulling me. Forcing me back to that night. Making me relive all the small details I'd avoided for so long.

"I loved Leo, even if I wasn't always a perfect girlfriend," Winnie went on. "I had no idea everything was about to fall apart."

I nodded absently. So many lives had been affected by that one night. Paula and Leo's family had been shattered. I'd lost my best friend and my sense of safety here in Silver Ridge. Only Callum had given that back to me.

Callum. He'd texted. I needed him. I knew I should go back to the car for my phone, but I couldn't budge from that spot. Couldn't stop staring at the darkly moving water.

"If one small thing had been different," I said, "maybe *everything* would've been different. If we hadn't gone to the creek that night. If I hadn't left her alone. Or if I'd been able to find her phone to call for help."

"If she hadn't dropped it in the water," Winnie muttered.

Those words echoed in my mind. Replayed.

And every time, they sounded stranger.

"How would you know Jessa dropped her phone in the water?"

FORTY-ONE
Callum

THE BRAKES on my truck squealed as I pulled up in front of Hearthstone. I jumped out and ran to the entrance, afraid I'd find it locked, but the door opened under my hand.

I stopped a few steps inside. Russ was sitting on the bench across from the hostess stand, his head buried in his hands. His shoulders were hunched forward, and even in the dim light, I could see his hands shaking.

"Where's Zandra?" I demanded.

"I'm sorry, man." His voice was muffled, and when he looked up, his face was a mess. Red-rimmed eyes, skin blotchy with stress, hair disheveled like he'd been running his fingers through it over and over. "I didn't mean to—"

I grabbed his shirt and hauled him up, slamming him against the wall. "What the hell did you do to her?"

"Just told her the truth. I didn't mean to upset her."

"The truth about what? *Jessa*? Were you there at the creek that night?"

He shook his head frantically, his eyes wide with panic. "No, I already told Zandra that! I didn't know anything about someone else being there. I felt guilty because I didn't show up. And if I'd been there, maybe I could've... I don't even know. But I swear, Callum. I never would've hurt Jessa. Or Zandra."

The desperation in his voice cut through my rage. I slowly let him go and backed away, my heart hammering against my ribs.

"Did Zandra call you?" Russ smoothed down his wrinkled shirt with trembling hands. "Is that how you knew about me and Jessa?"

"It was a guess. Not important right now." My voice came out hoarse and rough. "But I can't find Zandra. She's not answering her phone."

I'd rushed over here thinking she was with Russ, though I wasn't even sure what I'd imagined he could be doing to her. All I knew was that my gut had been screaming that something was seriously wrong.

She hadn't answered my text. Hadn't picked up when I called.

Russ straightened his shirt, still looking shaken. "Have you tried your place? Winnie was giving her a ride home."

My jaw clenched. "I drove to the house first thing from the scene of the fire. Nobody's there. You said Winnie was driving her home?"

"Yeah. Maybe you passed them on the way here. Or they stopped somewhere else."

I had no idea, but that sick feeling in my stomach was only getting stronger. Something wasn't right. After everything we'd been through, she wouldn't just go quiet like this. Wouldn't disappear without a word to me, especially right after learning the truth about Russ and Jessa.

The lingering scent of the fire here just made my dread worse, thinking of how I'd found her nearly unconscious that night. Nearly lost her.

My mind raced through possibilities. A car accident? Had Winnie's car broken down?

"Call Winnie," I said. "I'll call Zandra's parents."

But her mom said they hadn't seen her. I tried Rosie next.

While I was on the line with Rosie, Russ lowered his phone, shaking his head. So Winnie hadn't picked up either.

"What's going on, Callum?" Rosie asked. "What do you mean, you can't find her?"

"Exactly what I said. But I'm looking. Let me know right away if you hear from her." I hung up, not wanting to waste another second.

I had to be out there driving. Searching for her.

But if they'd been in a car accident, we would've heard sirens. Hell, I would've seen them on my drive here unless Winnie and Z had driven somewhere else.

"If Zandra calls or shows up here, tell me," I said to Russ.

"Okay, but—"

"Call the county dispatcher. See if anyone's reported an accident." Another sickening thought occurred to me. "And make sure Ian Vanderwall is still in the county jail."

"Yeah. Yeah, I can do that. Where are you going?"

"To find her." Rushing out to my truck, I gunned the engine. When I called Zandra again, it went straight to voicemail, and the sound of her recorded voice made the vise around my chest ratchet even tighter.

Z, where are you?

FORTY-TWO

Zandra

"How would you know Jessa dropped her phone in the water?" I'd asked.

Winnie's eyes were frozen on the creek. "I don't know. Just... someone must've told me that."

"*I* didn't even know where her phone went. The police never found it."

"I just guessed."

She's lying, I thought, out of nowhere. But the voice in my head hadn't sounded like mine. It had sounded like *Jessa's* voice.

I flashed back to that night yet again, and this time, the truth *finally* slotted into place.

The voices I'd heard. A sound Jessa had made, difficult to make out over the noise of the creek that night. But now I heard it again. *Echoes*. Twisting into something new and terrible.

That night sixteen years ago, Jessa had said the name, *Winnie*.

"Were you there that night? At the creek?"

Winnie didn't say a word. Maybe she was trying to decide whether to deny it or make some excuse. Another lie. Part of me wanted her to tell me something, *anything*, to explain away what I'd just remembered. To make it not true.

But it *was* the truth. Neither of us could make it go away. Not now.

"Jessa said your name," I accused. "You *were there*. I know you were."

Her chin dipped, like she was looking at the ground. "Then why'd you ask?"

"Because I'm trying to understand this! How were you there? *Why*?"

Her mouth opened. Shut. Opened again. Her blond hair blew around her face in a sudden gust of chilly wind.

"Just tell me," I demanded.

"Fine! I was there, okay? I was there, but I didn't mean for any of it to happen."

Shock had me stuck in place, standing on the slope above the creek. Winnie was a few feet away. The night seemed so dark, as if the moon and stars couldn't reach us here. I could only make out bits and pieces of her features. Not her eyes.

But she seemed to be fixed by the same spell I was under. Like our memories of that night had woven around us, a web that neither of us could escape.

When I next spoke, the words came out low and dangerous. "*Tell me*, Winnie."

This time, she gave me what I wanted.

"I knew Jessa's secret. The one she'd written about in her diary. But it wasn't about a boy. Russ or whoever she was crushing on. It was...it was about *me*."

"About *you*?"

Winnie put her hands over her face, muffling the sound of her confession. "I cheated on Leo. There was a guy at another school. I met him over the summer. It didn't mean anything, but Jessa found out. She said she was going to tell Leo if I didn't confess."

Jessa, why didn't you tell me? I asked silently.

Because she knew how pissed off I would've been? I wouldn't have told Leo without Jessa's permission, but maybe she wasn't sure she could trust me.

Or maybe it wasn't a lack of trust. Jessa was the most loyal kind of friend, a loyal sister, and she wouldn't have wanted to tell anyone before her brother knew. No wonder she wrote in her diary about feeling conflicted. She must've felt awful holding that secret from Leo.

If she'd just told him the truth when he confronted her...

But she'd been trying to give Winnie a chance to make things right.

"You left the bonfire party?" I asked, my voice trembling.

"Leo was drunk. He didn't notice I was there, so he wouldn't notice I was gone. Nobody else was paying me any attention either. I just wanted to talk to Jessa. Make her see my side."

"How did you know we were at the creek?"

Winnie sniffled. "Leo had taken me to that spot before, said it was Jessa's favorite place. That night, he said he was glad his sister was at the creek instead of the football party. He wanted her to stay away from the players. She was his big sister and he wanted to protect her, so of course he was going to believe her over me. I had to convince her not to tell him what I did. It was going to ruin everything!"

The bitter taste of bile was rising in my throat again. "What did you do?"

"I heard the two of you talking when I first arrived," she said, stuttering over the words. "So I hid, not sure what I should do. Then you walked off into the woods. I figured that was my chance. I offered to help get Leo off her back about her football player, if she would keep the secret about me. An even trade."

"And she said no." I could imagine what my best friend would've said.

"Jessa wouldn't even listen to me. Told me right away to leave, that she didn't want *you* to know she'd ever kept my secret at all." Every moment, Winnie's voice got thicker with emotion. "She was standing right at the edge of the bank. Waving her arms around with her phone in her hand. The phone dropped in the water, and she started to lose her balance, and I...I pushed her."

A tear broke free and careened down my cheek. "*No*," I whispered.

"I just couldn't let her tell Leo. I *couldn't*."

The rest played out in my mind. Jessa falling. The gash on her head. I could imagine Winnie hiding. Watching from the cover of the trees as I held my best friend in my arms.

In the days afterward, Winnie had hugged me. Stood there with me and Leo at the funeral. And this summer, she'd pretended to be my friend. When I'd told her how torn up I *still* felt about Jessa's death, Winnie had listened with sympathy in her eyes.

The bubbly former cheerleader, who no one would ever have suspected.

"Did you start the rumors at school that I pushed Jessa?" I asked, already knowing what the answer had to be.

"Not like you got in trouble anyway. Nobody really believed you were responsible."

"Jessa's mother believed it," I seethed.

"I wasn't having a great time either, okay? Every night for months, I couldn't sleep, thinking you or the police or Leo would figure it out. What else was I supposed to do?"

"Tell the truth. That *you* killed her."

"I didn't mean to!"

"Little late for that excuse, don't you think?"

"I lost Leo anyway. Nothing's gone right for me since high school, unlike you. You've got a rich family, a guy like Callum. Isn't that enough?" She wiped her face. "Are you going to tell people? Ruin everything for me all over again?"

"Ruin it for *you*? Jessa's family deserves to know what really happened. *I* deserved it. Paula tried to burn Hearthstone with me in it because of your lies!"

I should've seen Winnie's next move coming.

But I didn't.

She lunged. Shoved me hard. I barely grabbed hold of her. We slammed to the ground, rolling down the slope. Sharp rocks gouged my skin. The wind knocked out of my lungs as her elbow caught me in the chest.

Then the world turned frigid as ice-cold water swallowed me up. I struggled to find the surface, feeling the tug of the current, but hands closed on my throat.

Winnie was holding me under the water.

FORTY-THREE
Callum

I WANTED to speed down the road. Let this primal sense of fear drive me. Zandra was in danger, and my heart knew it.

But I forced myself to drive slowly instead, scanning the dark landscape for any sign of Winnie's car.

My body was on overdrive, though. Desperate for any hint of what had happened. Anything that would lead me to Zandra.

I was almost to the bridge over the creek when I saw it. A glint of reflectors as my headlights hit them. A car was pulled over to the side of the road, far enough onto the dirt shoulder that I hadn't seen it before.

I pulled in behind it, and it took me only a moment to identify the make and model. That was Winnie's car.

Leaving my truck still running and the headlights on, I leaped out and ran to the front of the car. Nobody was inside. No sign of damage. Below me, the rushing of the creek created a constant low hum of noise.

Then a scream rose to cut through the sound of the water. My gaze caught on movement below.

Someone was down there in the creek.

My boots slipped and skidded on damp grass as I hurried down the slope. The moonlit scene solidified, though I still didn't understand what I was seeing. It looked like Winnie was down there in the water, struggling with something. Some*one.*

Terror seized me as I realized Zandra was down there too, and an even deeper sense of horror swept over me. Winnie was holding her under the surface while Zandra's arms flailed, her face briefly appearing before it went under again.

Icy water soaked my boots and jeans as I splashed into the current. "Winnie," I shouted. "Stop!" She didn't even turn as I barreled toward her, about to knock her aside.

But before I could, Zandra's gasping form surged out of the water again and shoved Winnie back. She was completely drenched. The moonlight made her bared teeth look stark white. Winnie stumbled a few steps, falling waist-deep into the rushing creek. As she struggled to stand, Zandra grabbed for her. Her fist pulled back, the scene so vivid as I watched, it could've been in slow motion.

Zandra's fist connected with Winnie's cheek. The blond woman spun and toppled. Her head bounced against an exposed rock. She slumped there, lower half in the water and the rest of her limp against the rocks.

I scooped Zandra's shaking form into my arms and carried her to the bank. "C-C-Callum?" Her teeth were chattering.

"It's me. I've got you."

We reached the grass, and I sat down with her, holding her in my lap. Her arms squeezed around my shoulders, and she put her head against my neck. Her whole body was quaking, and she was breathing so hard I worried she would hyperventilate. I had to warm her up. My hands rubbed at her wet skin. Pushed her hair back from her face.

"I need to go get a blanket for you. I've still got the one in my truck."

"No." She clung to me. "*Winnie.*"

I couldn't begin to fathom what had occurred between Winnie and Zandra to lead to what I saw in the creek, but right now, explanations didn't matter. "You can tell me everything later."

"*No.*" She managed to sit up. "Help her. Can't let her die. P-please."

I stared into Zandra's dark eyes for another split second. Then I nodded. "You have to wait here."

My brain got firing enough to make me pull my phone from my pocket. Lucky it hadn't gotten wet, but I'd hardly been thinking about that.

I handed the phone to her. "Call 9-1-1 if you can. If not, don't worry. I'm going to get her."

My instincts screamed at me to stay with Zandra and make sure she was okay, but instead I found myself wading back into the water, fighting the pull of the current to get to Winnie. She was exactly where she'd fallen a couple of minutes ago. Rolling her over, I got a grip on her and picked her up. She was out cold, and a gash of red crossed the bridge of her nose, dripping blood over her damp face.

Once I had her on the bank, I laid Winnie out and checked her vitals. "She's breathing."

Zandra crawled over to us. "Police coming. Winnie—"

"She'll live." That was all the effort I could spend on her at the moment.

I had to get my girl dry and warm and back in my arms, where she belonged.

Zandra was still trembling as I carried her up the slope to the truck. In the backseat, I grabbed the blanket and started rubbing it over her, trying to dry her the best I could. The water had been icy, but we were still far from winter. I wasn't too worried about her core temperature. About everything else though? Fuck yes, I was worried.

Especially when tears streaked down Zandra's face like a dam had just broken.

"She pushed Jessa. She was there. Winnie killed her."

"Winnie killed Jessa?"

Zandra nodded, those tears continuing to fall. I wrapped her in my embrace. The high-pitched wail of sirens was getting closer.

"I...figured it out. She attacked me. Tried to..."

So Zandra had somehow discovered the truth. And Winnie had tried to kill her for it. I kissed her damp hair above the cocoon of the blanket. "But you wanted me to make sure she was out of the water."

"Couldn't let her die. Not like this."

Some might've called it poetic justice if Winnie had died in the same way Jessa had all those years ago. Though I still couldn't make any sense of why Winnie had done what she did.

But what I *could* understand was my Sunflower. My grumpy, scowly Zandra couldn't bear to see anyone else, even her worst enemy, die like her best friend had.

"More hot cocoa?" I lifted the thermos.

"How about more rum?"

I grinned. "Happy to oblige." Zandra held out her mug, and I poured more liquor into it, then did the same to mine.

It had been a long-ass twenty-four hours, but we were finally relaxing, just us. Even had a small fire going in a portable gas fire pit that Connor had picked up from somewhere and stuck in our backyard.

No field of sunflowers this time, because being home was what Zandra needed. And it certainly suited me just fine.

After the police had rolled up last night, Winnie and Zandra had both been taken to the hospital. Thankfully, Zandra was completely fine. No more than a few scratches. Last I heard, Winnie was being treated for a concussion and had been placed under arrest. At the very least, for the assault on Zandra.

We'd barely slept last night, between interviews with the

police, then sitting up with our friends and family, who rallied around us just like the night of the fire.

We'd ended up over at Ashford and Emma's place, drinking coffee and just being together. Zandra's parents had not appreciated the change of venue, since we'd gathered at their place last time. But they were just going to have to get used to it. The Alvarezes and the O'Neals were going to be one big, happy family if I had anything to say about it.

If Zandra had wanted to go back to her parents' house again, I would've been on board, of course. But things had been getting a little suffocating there.

She and I had wound up falling asleep in Ashford's guestroom, sleeping half the day, then waking up to chocolate chip pancakes, Maisie's giggling, and Stella's antics. I'd been so fucking relieved to see Zandra smile while she played a silly board game with my niece.

And now, we were finally back home. Darius and Connor had been seeing to Chloe, who'd raced over to rub against Zandra's legs the moment we got back. We had both cleaned up, changed into our comfiest clothes—Zandra in my SRFD sweatshirt—and then came out here to the patio.

The smooth flames of the fire shimmered, and for a little while, Zandra and I were quiet, just sipping spiked cocoa and cuddling beneath the wool blanket. We'd pulled two lawn chairs right up against one another.

"Oh, hey," I said softly. "I didn't have the chance to tell you yet. Connor got himself a new girlfriend, apparently, and he's moving out."

Z turned her pretty face toward me, though her head was still resting on the spot where my shoulder met my bicep. "How do you feel about that?"

I rubbed strands of her silky hair between my fingers. "Pretty good. If he's happy, I'm happy. There was a time when I didn't want anything about my life to change, but I'm embracing it now.

He didn't have to be all mysterious about it, though. Keeping her a secret, like he was afraid we'd scare her off."

"I guess sometimes it's hard to trust even the people we're closest to." Zandra's dark eyes got a faraway look. And I knew she was thinking about Jessa and her secrets.

I'd heard all of it by now. How Jessa had been keeping the secret about Winnie cheating on Leo. How Winnie had sneaked away from the bonfire party and gone to the creek to confront her boyfriend's older sister. She'd confessed to pushing Jessa, then hiding and watching as Jessa died in Zandra's arms.

I'd kept things from my family too. Keeping a secret could feel like holding a live grenade with the pin pulled. Like if you made a false move and let it go, it would destroy *everything*.

Yet in reality, the opposite was true.

"You know you can talk to me, right?" I asked. "You can tell me anything, and I have no intention of keeping anything from you. Not anymore."

"I know." But a shudder ran through her. I held her closer beneath the blanket. Even with all the police interviews and updating our loved ones, Z and I hadn't had the chance until now to talk openly about last night. Not just the bare facts, but the ugly details of how it all felt. The stuff that could keep a person up at night.

The flames guttered and swayed.

"Speaking of secrets," I said, "Russ was keeping a doozy, right? After Connor reminded me that Russ was on the football team the beginning of that year, and that he'd been hanging around Jessa, I got nervous. Then after I couldn't find you and you wouldn't answer your phone, I convinced myself he'd done something to hurt you."

"I was shocked when he told me about him and Jessa. Hard to believe he was keeping that secret for all these years. I just..." She gripped my T-shirt right above my heart. "I don't think I'll ever be okay with the fact that Jessa kept those secrets from me. Makes me feel like I wasn't a good enough friend, even though I know she had other reasons. But now that I really know the whole truth, it's strange. I've never felt closer to her."

Zandra sat up a bit, reaching for something under the blanket. She pulled out her small diary from high school, the one she'd found in that box at her parents' house. She must've taken it the last time we were there. Stowed it at some point tonight in her sweatshirt pocket.

"I've been thinking all day about closure. When you suggested sitting out here with a fire going, my first thought was this diary. How it would feel to throw it in the flames and let it burn. As a symbol of letting go of it all, you know?"

I watched Zandra's face. She caressed the cover of her diary with her fingertips.

"But I can't. I think there's no moving on, at least not the way I thought before, as if I could suddenly wake up one morning and not miss Jessa anymore. I'll always miss her. But now that I know everything, and I've remembered *every* awful thing about the night she died, I can finally hold the rest of my memories of her close too." A tear slipped free, and I brushed it away. "I think she would be happy for me, because I really am happy now, Callum. I'm *so* happy to be in love with you."

Fuck. I didn't cry easily. I wasn't counting those commercials with adorable animals, because those didn't count.

But right now, I was on the edge. My nose burned.

Then my damn phone rang.

"Shit, sorry." I fumbled for it. "Thought it was on silent."

I caught sight of the caller ID and hesitated.

"Callum, it's your brother." She nudged my hand. "You should talk to him. Answer it."

"You sure?"

"*Talk* to him."

No time like the present, right?

I held the phone to my ear. "Grayden?"

"Hey. Is this a bad time?"

"It's fine." No denying this was weird, though. I was actually talking to my brother for the first time in forever. "I'm here with Zandra. My girlfriend."

"Yeah, Grace told me about her."

"Can I put you on speaker? Introduce you?"

"Absolutely."

I pressed the button, then said, "Grayden, this is Zandra. Z, my oldest brother."

A long, slow exhale left my chest. As if I'd been holding it in for *way* too long.

Zandra sat closer. "Hi, Grayden. It's great to meet you."

"Likewise. I heard about the fire. Are you doing better?"

The three of us talked for a little while. It sounded like Grace had been filling him in on what was going on in our lives, but she hadn't told him about the events of last night. And that was fine by me. Zandra didn't bring it up either. That was too much of a painful saga for her to tell it all over again right now.

As we spoke, I put my arm around Zandra again, pulling her up against me. It meant everything that she was here. Sharing this moment with me. In a way, I was sharing a key piece of myself with Grayden too. Zandra was the most important thing in my life right now, and I hoped my brother understood that. Not just that she was my priority, but that this was my way of inviting him in, too.

"What about you?" I asked. "Are you seeing anyone out there in Seattle?"

My big brother's low, gravelly laugh was the same as I remembered. "Nah, not me. But I'm good. I've got my own business here. It's a freelance thing, but...yeah. I'm a tattoo artist."

"That's not what I expected. I thought you hated art class."

He laughed again, brighter this time. "It seems it was the class part I hated. When it's my own art, it's different. Figured that out after... Well, after."

I gripped the skin between my eyes. That word said a lot. *After.* The part we were all still struggling to figure out.

I almost brought up his last visit to Silver Ridge. The things I said and my regrets about that. But Grayden headed off that subject, as if he could sense I'd been about to get heavy.

"It's getting late there," he said. "I'll let you go. I just wanted to say I love you, Cal. I'm different now, okay? I need you to know that."

"Same here," I choked out. "A lot's changed. But, uh...I love you too."

I hadn't even known I would say that until I did. But I'd spoken from the heart.

After we said goodbye and I lowered my phone, Zandra cupped my cheek. "What do you need?"

"I think I need to take you to bed."

"Snuggle sex?"

"Hell, yeah." Couldn't imagine anything better.

I switched off the fire, and we carried the mugs and blanket inside. Stripped off our clothes the moment we were back in my bedroom. Kissing her gave me breath, soothed the ragged edges of my soul. I lifted her up and carried her to the bed with our tongues still tangled together.

For a while, I lay back with Zandra on top of me, her hair a dark curtain closing us off from the world. Then I rolled her to the side and rubbed my erection against her butt cheek. "You ready for me?"

"Show me who I belong to," she murmured, and gasped as I entered her.

She was spooned in front of me, my cock deep inside her and my arms holding her tight. So peaceful and perfect and right, even as my heart raced with anticipation for what was next.

After all the false starts and stops we'd had, this truly felt like our beginning.

FORTY-FOUR

Zandra

It was a crisp, early-autumn day when I stepped into the Silver Ridge Cemetery.

Not many of the aspens had changed yet, so their leaves were still vivid green, quaking with the breeze. It wasn't hard to find Jessa's headstone. Even though I hadn't been here in over a decade and a half, I still remembered.

When I reached her grave, I sat on the grass in front of it and placed a bouquet of daisies at the base of the stone.

"Hey, Jess. Sorry it took me so long to get here."

Over a week had passed since that night at the creek with Winnie. Since I'd finally learned the truth. Callum hadn't left my side for more than a few minutes. We'd stayed home mostly, in his bedroom. I still technically had the room next door, but at least half my stuff had migrated to Callum's by now.

I smiled as I pulled my braid over my shoulder, wrapping the end of it around my hand. "Callum and I are so in love it's disgusting. My teenage self would be gagging at us. He's been giving me some more cooking lessons. We made gluten-free chocolate chip cookies the other day, and you wouldn't believe the mess we made."

Of course, I had a lot more to fill her in on. Most of it less pleasant. I stretched my legs out on the grass. "Ian's still in the county jail, but I heard through Dixie Haines that he's probably going to accept a plea deal for a lesser charge than attempted robbery and false imprisonment. Saves me from having to testify. He'll probably serve a few months in jail, and then I hope he heads back to Chicago and forgets he knows me."

My nose scrunched up as I thought of Tommy Pickering. "Dixie also told us Tommy's going to be charged for blackmailing Paula about Leo. It's been too long to charge him for the blackmail in high school, but at least it's something. My real question is, how does Dixie find out these things?"

I pulled at a loose thread on my jeans as I next told Jessa about Leo and her mom. I was pretty confident Paula wouldn't be charged criminally for the fire at Hearthstone. For now, she was in a hospital still being assessed. My heart ached when I thought of everything Jessa's family had gone through because of Winnie.

"Your brother is probably going to serve time for that bar fight and skipping bail. When I talked to him a few days ago, he was completely stunned by what Winnie confessed. Probably even more than I was. But at least he knows the truth now. He's going to share it with your mom, if he feels like she's ready to hear it. She's getting help now."

I rested a hand on the smooth stone, right below Jessa's name. I'd wondered if Paula and Leo would find more solace if Winnie were charged for Jessa's death. But that sounded unlikely, given that it had been so many years and would be so hard to prove she'd meant to kill Jessa.

Winnie would be serving prison time for my attempted murder, though, if a jury found her guilty. The district attorney was not going to be making any deals.

"And then there's Russ. He came by yesterday. First time I've seen him since he told me he was your crush. He really cared about you, and he's been holding that in for all this time. Along with his guilt. I told him you wouldn't want him to feel that way.

For what it's worth, I think you guys would've been sweet together."

There was one more thing I had to say. Though it made a lump gather in my throat.

"I reread my diary. It reminded me of so many great times we had together. I love you so much, Jessa, and I promise, I will never forget you. Friends forever."

I'd dried my last tears by the time I made it to the cemetery gate. Callum was waiting for me there, holding a single small sunflower. He'd offered to come visit Jessa's headstone with me, but this time, I had needed to do it by myself.

Without a word, he pulled me into a hug, tucking the sunflower behind my ear. We stayed just like that for a full minute.

Then he pulled back, and he started walking me toward his truck. "I hate to rush you, but if I don't, we'll be late. I know you hate that."

"Two or three minutes at the most. I'm sure Grandpa will survive."

"But will *we*?" Callum muttered.

When we arrived at Hearthstone, Grandpa was waiting by the hostess stand, leaning on his walker. "About damn time! You two might think you have all the time in the world, but I don't. Could've had a heart attack and been resuscitated in the time I've been waiting for you."

"Papi," Rosie scolded. "That's not true."

"Sorry, Manny," Callum said cheerfully, not sounding remotely sorry.

"Well, come on, sit down. Let's get this done." Grandpa led the way into the dining room and sat at one of the long tables. Callum and I took chairs across from him. From deeper in the building, construction noise buzzed in the background.

"I'll just be over here," Rosie sing-songed. "Waiting to be your ride home, Pop."

"This is a business meeting, daughter of mine. I'll ask you not to interrupt."

"Fine, I'll go sit quietly at the bar." Rosie snickered and gave me a look. I smiled back.

Grandpa cleared his throat, and I snapped to attention.

"This meeting was delayed for unfortunate reasons that we all know. But Zandra, you've assured me you feel up to it."

"I do. I'm eager to hear your decision." Then I reached for Callum's hand under the table. "*We're* eager to hear it," I corrected.

"Yep," Callum said. "Hit us with it, boss."

I'd already told Grandpa I wanted him to consider Callum for the general manager job, regardless of anything Callum had said. And I'd also shared that with my boyfriend too, because I hadn't been trying to go behind his back.

Whatever happened, whichever of us Grandpa chose as general manager, I would be fine with it.

But still, I sucked in a breath and held it as Grandpa glanced between us, his face unreadable.

"You must've figured it out by now, haven't you? My decision?"

"*No,*" I sputtered. "I have no idea what you're going to say."

Callum shrugged. "Me neither."

"Even *I've* guessed it," Rosie said, drifting over from the bar area.

"Want to fill us in?" I asked tightly.

Grandpa huffed. "I mean, come on. I'm choosing both of you! You'll be co-general managers."

My head turned to the side, meeting Callum's shocked gaze beside me, along with his toothy grin.

"Even before I knew you were dating, I was going to choose both of you. *Also* before your email bowing out of the running, Callum, which I had decided to ignore. That made a lot more sense after I learned how you feel about Zandra, by the way. But the two of you have worked well together almost since the beginning. Everyone at Hearthstone said you had things running better than ever. After I got over being offended at that, I realized what it meant."

"Which is?" Callum asked.

Grandpa shifted on the wooden chair. "At the risk of sounding sentimental... I realized you two remind me of Julia and I."

"My grandmother," I whispered to Callum.

"Zandra, your nana and I ran Hearthstone together for many years. We were an ideal team. I think you and Callum could be the same. That comparison fit all the more after you revealed your relationship." His expression darkened. "Just don't screw it up. Either my brewpub *or* your relationship. Hurt my granddaughter, Callum, and losing your job will be the least of your worries. Don't make me regret this."

Callum leaned over to kiss my cheek, then looked back at my grandfather. "I'm going to take good care of Zandra, sir. *And* Hearthstone. We both will."

While Grandpa went to harass the construction workers about the repairs, Callum slipped behind the bar. "Can I get you ladies a drink? I think we need to celebrate."

The bottles were underneath a sheet of plastic, but Callum reached beneath to grab one. He selected a few shot glasses from a low shelf and poured us each a shot of whiskey. The bar top was dusty under our elbows, but none of us cared. I coughed as the whiskey went down. My throat was much better now after the smoke from the fire, but not a hundred percent.

Rosie, on the other hand? She tipped back her shot like it was water and tapped the rim for another. Callum poured it, then aimed a glance my way.

I knew exactly what he was thinking.

Reaching into my purse, I pulled out a small gift box and set it on the bar. "We bought something for you, Auntie."

She downed her second shot and set the glass down with a thump. "For me? How sweet of you, Baby-Z! Whatever for?"

"For letting me stay with you. And generally being amazing."

"I picked it out," Callum added, bouncing on his toes. "Can't wait for you to open it."

Rosie opened the lid of the box. I'd expected a laugh or a shout or something, but instead her eyes glistened as she lifted the ceramic figurine from the styrofoam cushion.

"It's *perfect*! How on earth did you know?"

Callum smirked. "Lucky guess."

We'd found it at a gift shop a couple days ago, when we'd ventured beyond Callum's bedroom and into the world. I'd needed my pistachio latte fix from Silver Linings. The gift shop had been just down the block, and Callum had pulled me in after spotting a bunch of tchotchkes with sunflowers on them.

Then, we'd seen the gnomes.

Rosie held up her new figurine. Two gnomes in pointy hats, one with bright red curls, the other with a grizzled black beard. They were holding hands. It was downright eerie how much they looked like Rosie and Jimmy.

"This is just the sweetest." She wiped her eyes. I squeezed her arm.

"You and Jimmy have been great to me. Callum and I are getting our own place at some point, and when we do, you're welcome any time. Also, Chloe would love to see her favorite auntie and uncle."

"Oh, Baby-Z." She threw her arms around me. "And you don't even know the big news yet!"

"What news?" I asked.

"We're getting married! I asked Jimmy just last night, and he said yes."

"Rosie, congratulations!"

Callum whooped and grabbed the whiskey bottle. "This calls for another round."

"What's all the racket?" Grandpa was making his way toward us. "What're you doing drinking my booze?"

"We're celebrating," Rosie said defiantly. "Callum, pour my father a shot too. He needs one."

Grandpa grumbled. "Celebrating what? It'll be another month before Hearthstone can open again. We've got a lot of work ahead of us. Especially my new co-general managers."

"We're celebrating because *love wins*!" Rosie shouted.

After that, it was only natural for us to call Jimmy and the rest of our friends and family to come to Hearthstone for an impromptu engagement party. We dusted off more of the tables, Grandpa begrudgingly let us break out more of the alcohol, and Rosie dashed over to the market for some pre-made party trays.

I wound up behind the bar with Callum, pouring shots one handed so I could keep my arm around him.

"So, co-general managers," he said in my ear. "We'll be spending a lot of time together."

"True."

"I can think of a few ways to make that time more enjoyable. A benefits arrangement, if you will."

"Callum O'Neal, are you propositioning me? Your coworker?"

"Good thing you love me."

"I do. I love you, co-general manager."

Because *love wins.*

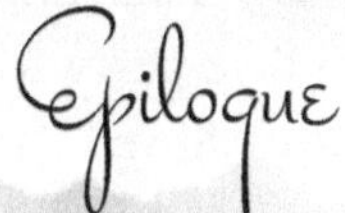

Epilogue

Callum, Thanksgiving

I gazed at the tiny, squirming bundle in my arms. "Look at her, Z. Have you ever seen anything so adorable?" I glanced up to find Zandra eyeing me sardonically. Chloe was giving the same narrowed look, tail twitching.

"Same answer as the first hundred times you asked since we got her. No, I have not."

"Then why do you seem grumpy? What happened to your heart-eyes for our new fur baby?"

Zandra lifted the wooden spoon from the batter she'd been stirring. "I love and adore everything about our kitten. And about you, Callum, except for how you wanted to make gluten-free, dairy-free pumpkin pies from scratch, and now you're making me do all the work. I'm going to mess this up."

I walked over to her to kiss her temple. "First of all, no, you won't. You're a great cook now. Second, Daisy was sad without me holding her. It's like she knows we'll be away from her this afternoon. Could you say no to these eyes?"

I held up our kitten, and Zandra's expression melted. "Fine, keep cuddling until I get these in the oven. But then it's my turn with her."

"Deal." With my finger, I rubbed Daisy's furry little head as she tried to climb up my arm.

A lot had changed for Zandra and me in the last couple of months. My roommate era had officially come to an end, complete with a huge goodbye party for me, Connor, Niko and Darius. We'd invited most of Silver Ridge to the event. There'd been lawn games and other family-friendly activities in the afternoon, followed by drinking and reminiscing late into the night. There'd definitely been some off-key singing. Zandra had joined in with me. I'd never seen my girl that tipsy, and I had to say, it was hilarious.

Our new place was close enough to Hearthstone to walk. Which we did, each and every morning on our way into work. Sharing the general manager job with Zandra was, well, pretty much like that trial period. Manny had combined general manager duties with bar manager, and Zandra and I had our hands in pretty much everything at Hearthstone.

Now that Manny had *finally* retired from management, limiting his role to ownership, we only heard from him about once a week when he came in for lunch and a surprise inspection. I loved those visits, because we could usually sneak in a game of backgammon.

And thanks to Zandra conspiring with Chef Alice, Hearthstone now had chicken nuggets on the menu. Manny had no idea they were gluten free.

Once Zandra had the pumpkin pies in the oven, I handed over Daisy. The newest addition to our family had arrived in October. We'd heard from Dixie Haines about a litter of month-old kittens in someone's barn, and I'd surprised Z with a trip out to see them. We instantly fell in love with this little black-and-white, short-furred beauty.

I mean, when it's love, what else can you do? You just have to go with it.

Chloe was less thrilled about her new sister. Where Chloe was a prickly diva, Daisy was a bundle of energy and snuggles. We'd been keeping them separate most of the time to give Chloe her space. I'd never had cats before, so I didn't know if that would change, but I sensed Chloe was warming up to Daisy. Some things were inevitable.

After I cleaned up the kitchen and we checked on the pies, I sat on the couch with Zandra and Daisy. Chloe leaped up on the cushion on my other side.

"Callum?" Zandra said softly.

"Mmhmm?"

"I think this is what perfect looks like."

I glanced around our tiny, eclectic living room. We'd picked out the furniture together, mostly from resale shops around Hart County. The mantle above the fireplace held my football-player gnome and a collection of framed photos of family and friends. There was one of Zandra and Jessa in a prominent spot, and another of me and Z at the fall festival with me in full turnout gear.

Now *that* had been a good day.

But there was room for more, too. More memories and more people in our lives.

"You're right, baby. This is exactly what perfect looks like. I'm thankful."

"Me too. So thankful for you." She groaned. "Except, less thankful for having to attend two Thanksgiving dinners today. Think my mom will notice if we skip?"

I shot her a grin. "If we don't show up, your mom will call search and rescue."

"Ugh. Truth."

❀

Connor showed up about an hour later. He was our cat sitter for the next few hours. "Where's Daisy?" he asked, instead of actually saying hello.

"Napping."

He pouted. "Can I wake her up so she'll play?"

"You can play with Chloe."

Connor winced. "Sure, if I want to get shredded like a horror movie."

We heard Zandra giggling from the kitchen. She must've heard every word. "We saved you a pumpkin cinnamon roll, Connor!" she called out.

"I would've done it for kitten time alone," he replied, "but I appreciate that."

Connor was going to cat-sit while we were at the Alvarez Thanksgiving. His girlfriend planned to swing by to help him—and for kitten time, naturally—before Darius and the woman *he* was dating took over kitty watch for the rest of the afternoon. No idea what I would've done without those guys.

As we drove to Zandra's parents' place, my truck was filled with the scent of pumpkin spice and pastry crust. A light snow had fallen, draping the evergreens along the road with a soft layer of white. I pulled up next to Jimmy's battered old Chevy, with its *many* Grateful Dead bumper stickers, and then grabbed one of the pies from the backseat.

But before we went inside, I stopped Zandra and pulled her in. "You're gorgeous today, Sunflower." Her hair was down, and she'd worn a cozy red sweater dress that I couldn't wait to slide off of her later.

"So are you." Her pink lips twisted. "Just wish you'd worn your ball cap."

"Your mom would hate that."

The twist of her mouth grew more devious. "I know."

But maybe we were both wrong. Because Eliza answered the door with a careful smile and not a single criticism. Just thanked us for the pie and waved us to join them in the kitchen, where Rosie and Jimmy were stirring up jalapeño cornbread and Manny was wiping the table with Javi at backgammon. "Callum!" Manny said. "Get over here so I can beat you next."

Zandra helped her mom for a while in the kitchen. Later, when I went to offer my cooking services, I found my girlfriend sporting a sunny expression. "Having a good time?" I asked under my breath.

"With the help of wine, yes." Zandra pecked my lips. "I actually am."

Her mom waved at me from across the kitchen. "Callum, take the tamales to the table. They're in the top oven. Then tell Javi it's time for him to carve the turkey."

"Yes, Eliza. I'm on it."

"Thank you, dear."

My jaw dropped, and I turned my astonished expression on Zandra. "*Dear*?" I whispered. "Your mom loves me."

"Don't get carried away."

"Too late." Before I went to grab the glass dish of tamales, I wrapped an arm around Zandra and tipped her back for a thorough kiss. Rosie hooted and cheered, while Eliza sighed and tried to ignore us.

When I put Zandra upright again, she was laughing, and I hoped somebody was snapping a picture. Because this was one for the mantle.

Thanksgiving number two was at Dane and Grace's house. We were the last to arrive, and I held the second pumpkin pie over my head to keep it safe as we navigated through Stella and the kids running underfoot.

"Uncle Callum!" Maisie and Ollie both shouted. Ollie trailed after me. "Cal, can we play football?"

"Later, bud. After dinner." As soon as we got inside, I announced, "We're here. Party can officially begin."

"Thank goodness," Ashford deadpanned. "Zandra, please tell me he ate enough at your parents' house that he's too full for stuffing."

My girlfriend shook her head. "I can't help you there. He's already had a slice of pie *and* a piece of tres leches cake, and he still claims to be hungry."

I patted my stomach as I set the dessert we brought on the kitchen counter. "As soon as I heard about two Thanksgivings, I started training for this."

While Emma roped Zandra into finishing up the table decorations, I went to give Grace a hug. She was making pan gravy just the way our mom used to do it.

I stuck my pinky into the pan and tasted it. "Needs more fresh pepper."

She swatted my arm. "Go find somebody else to bother."

Grinning, I scooted out of the kitchen. We'd had a nice time with Zandra's family, especially listening to Rosie and Jimmy bicker over wedding plans. But this would be the capstone of the day for me. Being with my siblings, blood or otherwise. Teller and Ayla weren't here, but I had no doubt they'd call in at some point for a video call. So we could all be together. Noise and laughter and chaos. Every bit of it.

Together. That word meant something very different this holiday than last year. And not just because of my incredible girlfriend who I loved more than anything.

There was someone else I had to wish a Happy Thanksgiving.

Finding a quiet corner, I took out my phone and sent off a text to Grayden. We'd talked a few times here and there since that first conversation. About simple stuff, not the past or anything heavy. Grayden had mentioned a couple times in passing that he hoped to see us again soon, but he, Grace and I hadn't made any plans yet. Because there was one O'Neal sibling who still refused to speak to him.

I'd finally told Ashford about Grayden coming home to Silver Ridge years ago, and how I'd turned him away. But that hadn't made any difference. Ashford had actually *thanked* me. Because he still didn't think our big brother had a place in our lives. Especially in Maisie's life.

It sucked. But on a day like today, I just wanted to make sure Grayden knew I was thinking of him.

He didn't write back a quick response to my text, not that I expected one. Grayden had said something about Thanksgiving plans with friends. So I hoped he was enjoying a good meal too.

"There you are." Zandra had just turned the corner. "We're about to eat. Food's on the table."

I squeezed her hips through that sexy sweater dress, dipping to kiss her neck. "Damn. No time to sneak off for a quickie in the bathroom?"

"How can you even think of sex after all the food we've eaten? And we're about to eat more."

"Always hungry for you, baby."

Zandra snorted. "Come on. We can burn off the calories later. Assuming we're not in a food coma."

We sat around the table. Passing dishes and filling our plates and carrying on different conversations. Piper was sitting across from us, and I passed her the green beans.

"You good, Piper?" We hadn't had a chance to catch up today, and she seemed distracted. Barely smiling at all, which wasn't like her. "Everything okay?"

She glanced over at Ollie sitting with Maisie at the other end of the table. "Just some stuff with Danny," she replied under her breath.

Her ex-husband. Ollie's dad. An asshole if there ever was one.

Zandra touched my wrist, probably seeing the way I'd just frowned.

Then the doorbell rang. I lifted my chin and said to my sister, "Expecting anyone else?"

Grace shrugged, hands full as she ladled gravy to Maisie's plate. "Can you get it, Cal? You're the closest."

My lips brushed against Zandra's temple as I set my napkin down and jumped up. Covered the few strides to take me to the front door.

But when I opened it and saw who stood outside, my whole body jolted with shock.

He looked older. More than just the years could account for. His hair was longer, and his beard was thicker. But I would know my big brother anywhere.

"Grayden?"

Don't miss Piper and Grayden's story in HOMEWARD COLORADO, a small-town, single mom romance!

A Note from Hannah

Did you enjoy Callum's story? When I introduced him as Ashford's younger brother in book 1, I had the feeling Callum would need someone very special to make him a one-woman guy. Who better than a woman who actually hated him? There was no way he could back down from that challenge. But more importantly, Zandra completes him. I love the way they take care of each other.

Now, we're down to one more O'Neal sibling! The prodigal brother has returned. And surprise (though you may have seen this coming)—Grayden's going to end up with Piper! But what kind of drama will they go through to reach their happy ending? What will her brother Teller think about the return of his former best friend?

I promise, there's a lot more in store for the final book of this series! Expect spice and suspense, as always.

Many thanks as always to my ARC readers, and to my fans who keep reading and enjoying my stories. It means so much to me to be able to share them with you.

Until next time—

Hannah

More from Hannah Shield

Hart County

Starcrossed Colorado (Ashford & Emma)

Moonlit Colorado (Dane & Grace)

Stormswept Colorado (Teller & Ayla)

Sunkissed Colorado (Callum & Zandra)

Homeward Colorado (Grayden & Piper)

Last Refuge Protectors

Hard Knock Hero (Aiden & Jessi)

Bent Winged Angel (Trace & Scarlett)

Home Town Knight (Owen & Genevieve)

Second Chance Savior (River & Charlotte)

Iron Willed Warrior (Cole & Brynn)

One Last Shot (Dean & Keira)

West Oaks Heroes

The Six Night Truce (Janie & Sean)

The Five Minute Mistake (Madison & Nash)

The Four Day Fakeout (Jake & Harper)

The Three Week Deal (Matteo & Angela)

The Two Last Moments (Danny & Lark)

The One for Forever (Rex & Quinn)

Bennett Security

Hands Off (Aurora & Devon)

Head First (Lana & Max)

Hard Wired (Sylvie & Dominic)

Hold Tight (Faith & Tanner)

Hung Up (Danica & Noah)

Have Mercy (Ruby & Chase)

About the Author

Hannah Shield writes spicy, suspenseful romance with pulse-pounding action, fun & flirty banter, and tons of heart. She lives in the Colorado mountains with her family.

Visit her website at www.hannahshield.com, where you can join her newsletter to receive bonus content and hear about new releases.

www.ingramcontent.com/pod-product-compliance
Lightning Source LLC
LaVergne TN
LVHW041059080826
845145LV00007B/1631

* 9 7 8 1 9 5 7 9 8 2 4 3 4 *